THE OTHER SIDE OF THE WALL

ANDREA MARA

POOLBEG
CRIMSON

This novel is entirely a work of fiction. The names, characters and incidents portrayed in it are the work of the author's imagination. Any resemblance to actual persons, living or dead, events or localities is entirely coincidental.

Published 2017
by Crimson
an imprint of Poolbeg Press Ltd.
123 Grange Hill, Baldoyle,
Dublin 13, Ireland
Email: poolbeg@poolbeg.com

1

A catalogue record for this book is available from the British Library.

ISBN 978-1-78199-8328

Printed and bound by
CPI Group (UK) Ltd, Croydon, CR0 4YY

www.poolbeg.com

About the Author

Andrea Mara lives in Dublin with her husband Damien, and children Elissa, Nia, and Matthew. She's a freelance features writer for newspapers and magazines, and blogger at *OfficeMum.ie*. *The Other Side of the Wall* is her first novel.

For Damien, Elissa, Nia and Matthew

Chapter 1

Sylvia - Friday, July 29th 2016

The dog barks, waking Sylvia with a jolt. The bright red digits on the clock radio tell her it's 4.02am. Oh God, she's been in the chair for over an hour. The baby stirs in her arms but he's asleep – now to get him back in the cot. Her eyes start to close again before she can begin the manoeuvre – tried and failed on so many other nights like this one. Maybe she'll sit and rock just a little longer. But the dog barks again and this time Zack starts to whimper. Bloody dog. Pulling herself out of the chair, still shushing Zack, Sylvia pushes the curtain aside and looks down into the garden. It takes a moment for her vision to clear and another before she spots the dog – Bailey is barking at the wall they share with Number 26. Jet-black against the night-time garden, it's hard to make him out. What the hell is wrong with him? Her eyes roam to the garden next door. Untamed bushes fight for space with tangled weeds and uncut grass. Poor Mrs Osborne couldn't look after it before she died, and the new owners have done nothing with it yet. Her eyes move to the fishpond glinting in the moonlight, and stop there. She presses her nose to the glass to see better – is there something in the pond? Everything is blurry still – she screws up her eyes, then opens them wide. Her vision clears and she can make out the shape. Little arms and little legs and floating hair. A child. It looks like a small child, lying face down in the water.

"Jesus. Tom, wake up! I think there's something wrong next door!" Still staring out the window, she shifts Zack from one shoulder to the other. There's no response from Tom. She rushes to the bed. "*Did you hear me? I think there's a child in the pond!*" she hisses. Tom stirs but sleeps on. "Here, take the baby!" Putting Zack down beside her husband, she goes back to the window.

A cloud is covering the moon now, but she can still just about make out the shape. Jesus! She needs to go down there. Tom has his arm over Zack but he's still asleep.

She goes back and bends over him. "*Tom!* Did you hear me? You need to mind Zack – don't let him roll – okay?"

Tom mutters something, and pulls Zack closer.

She races downstairs and goes first to Megan's room. Her daughter is asleep, her hair fanned out on the pillow. In the hall she grabs her keys and rushes outside, closing the door behind her. In bare feet and pyjamas, she runs into her neighbours' driveway. No car – must be in the garage. At their front door she hesitates for just a second before pressing the doorbell. There's no sound from inside. She presses it again, and waits. The bell is loud and shrill in the otherwise silent cul-de-sac. Surely they'll hear it – all the other neighbours must hear it too. But still nothing. She tries a third time, and a fourth, but there's no sound behind the heavy front door. Stepping back, she looks up. The curtains are closed and there's no light in either of the front bedrooms. Unsure now, Sylvia stands barefoot in the driveway, wondering if she imagined the whole thing. She's still bleary-eyed and her head is woozy from lack of sleep – it could have been a trick of the light or nothing at all. But she can't just go back inside without being sure. Her eye travels to the corrugated garage door, and beyond it to the side passage. Mrs Osborne never used to lock the gate – maybe the new neighbours have left it open too. Treading carefully through the dead potted plants and planks of wood that litter the ground, she makes her way along the side passage towards the gate, unlatches it and gives it a push. It swings open, banging against the wall of the house. The noise makes her cringe instinctively, but only for a moment.

The dew-covered grass is cold on her feet – she hardly registers it as she makes her way to the end of the garden – stomach tight, adrenaline pushing her on through the darkness. At the fishpond, she stands on the edge, her feet cold on scrubby soil. Her stomach flips as her eyes search the glittery water. But there's nothing there. No child. No ripples. Nothing. Could the child have gone under? Feeling sick, she bends down and puts her hand into the water. It's cold as she reaches further in and feels around. There's nothing there. She pulls out her hand and, mesmerised by the empty water, stands at the side, staring but not seeing. It's like an old mirror, spotted with algae, holding nothing more sinister than the moon.

Bailey barks from his side of the wall, rousing her from her daze. Oh God, what is she doing in her neighbour's garden in the middle of the night?

She walks back up the garden, her eyes searching shadowy bushes, no longer sure what she's looking for. Bailey barks again and she shushes him, but there's no other sound. At the house, French doors just like hers look out onto the garden, only here the paint is peeling and the glass is still single-glazed. Peering through the panes, there's only inky blackness inside. She raises her hand to knock but drops it again. This is silly.

She closes her eyes to remember and the image seems clearer now: the little arms and legs, the hair floating out just beneath the surface. Her memory is embellishing a picture that wasn't very clear to begin with. The only certainty is that there's nothing here now. Still, heavy air, and nothing. She stands for another minute, just listening, then turns and leaves.

Inside her own house, she goes back to Megan's room and this time goes over to the bed to kiss her cheek and pull the duvet back up over her. Are the patio doors in the room locked? She checks. Of course they're locked, they always are, and the key is up high where Megan can't reach. Breathing a little more evenly, Sylvia goes upstairs, wondering if having Megan sleep on her own downstairs is such a good idea.

Tom is sitting on the side of the bed, rocking the baby. He motions to her to stay quiet as he attempts the cot transfer – success this time. Well versed in night-time practices, they both walk noiselessly to the landing before speaking. In a whisper, she tells him what she saw.

"You imagined you saw something in the pond next door and you rang their doorbell at four o'clock in the morning?" Tom asks, rubbing his eyes.

"I know. It seemed so clear at the time though – I thought I could see arms and legs. It was horrific," Sylvia whispers, shaking her head. "Thank God there was nothing there – I don't know what I would have done if . . . well, you know, if there was a child there and she wasn't breathing. I was thinking of that little girl who's missing – the one they mentioned on the radio."

"Sure. I know," Tom says, yawning. "But look, it's dark out there and you were half-asleep – it was just a shadow. Lucky the neighbours didn't wake up – they'd be wondering what kind of lunatics they're living beside. Come on, let's get some sleep."

She follows him into the room and climbs into bed, hugging herself for warmth – her feet still wet from the dew next door.

The blaring noise of the radio wakes Sylvia with a jolt. How can it be morning already? It feels like she's been asleep for five minutes. Memories of the ghost-child in the pond break through the fog of sleep and her stomach tightens. She stretches, feeling for the volume button, just as the seven o'clock news headlines come on the radio.

"*Gardaí are still searching for two-year-old Edie Keogh, missing from her home in Dún Laoghaire. The child was last seen when her mother checked on her at midnight on Tuesday night, but she wasn't in her bed on Wednesday morning. The front door was open, and one suggestion is that the child let herself out and got lost. Edie has light-brown shoulder-length hair and was wearing dark-blue pyjamas – members of the public are asked to contact Dún Laoghaire Garda station with any information.*"

God love that poor mother, Sylvia thinks, shuddering as last night's apparition materialises in her mind. The news story must have pushed her imagination into overdrive. She switches off the radio. Beside her, Tom groans and rolls out of bed. In his cot, Zack starts to stir, and she can hear Megan's feet pattering across the floor downstairs, on her way to check if it's morning.

In less than thirty minutes, Sylvia is running through the rain to her car, fumbling for her keys and wondering why she didn't think to take them out inside the house. Tom is standing in the doorway with Zack in his arms. He's already in his suit and looking at his watch – rain means traffic and traffic means their childminder may be late arriving. As she reverses out of the driveway, she glances up at the house next door, and takes a sharp breath. The front-bedroom curtains are open now. Someone is definitely there. Where were they last night? Did they just ignore her knocking? Anyway, time to focus on real life, and what's ahead at work today. And Justin. She grips the steering wheel a little tighter.

One long hour of rain-soaked traffic later, Sylvia reaches the IFSC and pulls into the Stanbridge Brown car park to find her space occupied by another car – for the third time in two weeks. It's a new security guard, and he's not impressed when she asks for a visitor spot, even when she points out that her own spot has been taken. That space isn't hers though, he tells her – it's a shared space and she has no entitlement to it. She groans inwardly and explains that it *is* hers, but she's only just back from maternity leave and the records haven't been updated. He raises one sceptical eyebrow and consults his screen. No, he says, the computer has it down as a shared space, and there's no way the system is wrong. She'll have to get her manager to sort it out but in the meantime, since she's stuck, she can use the visitor spot.

Shaking her head, Sylvia parks and takes the lift up to the third floor. In reception she smiles a lukewarm greeting at Breeda.

"Sylvia, that missing child on the news – she's from out near you, isn't she?" asks the receptionist, looking up from her screen.

"Yes, somehow it makes it even worse knowing she's local to us – not that it should make a difference of course, but still . . . Anyway, I'd better head in – is the boardroom booked for my meeting with Justin?"

"Yes, all booked." Breeda leans towards Sylvia and lowers her voice. "But what do you think is the story with that little girl? Awful thing. When you think about the kind of people who are out there . . ."

Sylvia glances at her watch. "I know . . . but maybe she's just lost – hopefully they'll find her any day now." She picks up a newspaper from the stack in front of Breeda. "I'd better run if I'm going to get anything done before the meeting – thanks for organising the room – chat to you later!"

In her office, the leather chair is cold to touch, despite the mild temperature outdoors, and she's glad of the cool air conditioning after the muggy journey in. At least they didn't take her chair while she was gone. Her PC flickers slowly to life and she scans her emails, leafing through the newspaper at the same time. The front page shows a photo of the missing child – a smiling face with still babyish dimpled cheeks and big blue eyes, framed by long lashes and light-brown hair. The Keoghs live less than a mile away from Sylvia, and Edie is not much smaller than Megan.

Sylvia shivers. Taking out her phone, her fingers hover over the screen for a moment, then she types a message to her childminder.

Hi Jane, Megan was a bit off form last night – can you keep a close eye on her today? See you this evening. Thanks, Sylvia.

She shakes herself and pulls out her notes for the meeting – this has to go the way she's planned, or things will only get worse.

The phone rings: Breeda calling to let her know that Justin is waiting in the boardroom. Sylvia takes a deep breath and picks up her notes.

The cool air in the boardroom hits her as soon as she pushes the heavy door open, and she shivers in her sleeveless grey dress. Justin is at the head of the table, intentional no doubt, and doesn't look up when she comes in. He's in a suit, and looks perfectly unperturbed by the icy air conditioning. The door starts to close on Sylvia as she's still struggling through with an armful of folders and notes, and she puts her shoulder to it to keep it open. Damn door-closer thing is too tight again, she thinks, just before the folders and notes slip from her arms and slide like a paper waterfall to the floor. Shit. Suddenly she wants to cry. Down on her knees now, she starts to pick them up, keeping her head lowered until she's sure tears aren't coming. Justin still doesn't look up.

Red-faced and flustered, she carries her haphazard bundle of notes to the table and drops them there, then clears her throat.

Finally, Justin raises his head.

"Oh hi, Sylvia, I didn't see you come in."

That's definitely a hint of a smirk.

"Hi, Justin." She manages a smile. "How are you?"

"Grand." He removes his glasses and his watery blue eyes appraise her.

She sits down, and clears her throat again.

"So, first of all, thanks again for looking after the team in my absence, and of course I'll include it in your performance review at year end."

Justin winces at that and Sylvia smiles inside. He doesn't like being reminded who's boss.

"Right, I wanted to have this meeting to go over some of the stuff from when I was on maternity leave. Obviously, the Zodiac 4 project started and, although I've been reading up on it since I got back, I'm not up to speed yet. And . . ." she pauses and shuffles her papers, then continues, "as you know, I'm working on the audit prep – I'm just having some trouble finding all the daily reports from when I was out, and making sense of the figures. Maybe we can go through them this morning?"

Justin looks at her for a moment. Then he puts on his glasses and looks at his watch. "I've a lot on this morning, Sylvia. I'm not sure how much time I can give this. Do you have specific questions about Zodiac?"

Is this guy for real? She's never in her entire life spoken to Craig or any of her bosses like that. Deep breath.

"Um, yes, I've quite a few questions. I thought we could go through it section by section – a bit like when I went through Charisma 6 with you back when you moved over to our team." *My* team. Why couldn't she just say "my team"?

"Point taken, Sylvia, but things weren't as busy back then. I've brought in a lot of new business over the last few months, so I'm up to my eyes. It's not like it was when you were running things."

When you *were* running things? She's still running things – what planet is he on? A cold suspicion creeps in. Could it be there's a change she doesn't know about – maybe he's staying on as Operations Manager and they haven't told her? No, that was ridiculous – of course they'd tell her. And it would probably be illegal. No, he was probably just finding it hard to accept reporting to her again, and being a dick about it.

"I completely understand, but I can't move forward until I've been brought up to speed on the project. I will of course speak to the Business Analysts and the IT guys, but from an Operations perspective, I need a handover from you." There, that's what she meant to say all along.

"Fine." He sighs unnecessarily loudly and takes off his glasses again. "What do you need to know?"

She picks up a pen and opens her notebook. "Everything, Justin. Just start at the start – what does the new system do?"

Justin sighs again.

Way to make her feel welcome back, Sylvia thinks, and part of her is wondering why she bothers at all.

Chapter 2

Sylvia – Thursday, August 4th

A buzzing sound from under her pillow pierces through the thick fog of sleep. Then comes the slow realisation that it's her phone, announcing excitedly that it's morning. There's really nothing to be excited about. Zack was up for two hours during the night, though now he's sleeping beautifully between his parents. And Megan, who usually sleeps through all of Zack's crying, was also up twice for no apparent reason.

She slides her phone out from under the pillow and makes two failed attempts to snooze the alarm before the buzzing finally stops – just as the radio comes on. Through half-closed eyes, she sees a flicker on her phone. A text. A message that early in the morning is never good news. It's from Jane – she's been sick during the night and won't be able to turn up for work. Great. That means emailing Craig to say she'll need to work from home. God, this will look crap so soon after coming back and she'll be playing right into Justin's hands. Could Tom do it instead? He'd been up late working on a presentation for the head of marketing and he's nervous about it. He's been managing the online sales team for only a few months and is still trying to find his feet. No, she'll have to bite the bullet and send the email. And then actually get some work done to show she's not just switching off. While minding Zack and doing preschool runs, and all on four hours' sleep.

She wants to cry. Tea is a better option than tears, so she nudges Tom with her foot and whispers, "Jane can't make it. I feel like I've been run over. Please save me with tea."

Tom, who is much better at mornings than Sylvia and knows when hot drinks are more important than verbal responses, heads downstairs to put the kettle on.

One Montessori drop later, she's typing a sheepish email to Craig on her BlackBerry, and trying to connect to the office network on her laptop. It's not working. Of course it's not. Picking up her BlackBerry, she emails IT, then goes into the sitting room to check on Zack. He's on his back, snoring gently in his pram, arms splayed above his head. She bends to risk a small kiss on his forehead, then goes into Megan's room to gather up her dirty clothes. With no network connection and no baby to entertain, she may as well put on a wash. The muslin curtains are still drawn – she pulls them back and unlocks the patio doors, pushing them open to let the sunlight in. This is her favourite room in the house – the bedroom she would have loved as a child, instead of the small upstairs room she shared with her sister. Not that there was anything wrong with it at the time – it was Ireland in the 1980s and all of her friends were sharing equally tiny bedrooms with equally annoying sisters. But decorating this room for Megan – the white-painted dresser, the canopy bed, the teepee strung with fairy lights – scratched an itch she'd had since she was eight years old. Of course, Megan never notices at all – her bedroom is just the place where she sleeps and plays with her toys.

Upstairs, Sylvia goes to her own more mundane bedroom

to gather laundry and wonders again if she should repaint the one red wall. It's been red since they moved in – a deep brick red she'd never have chosen, yet somehow it works. Walking over to the bed to straighten her pillow, she reaches out to wipe a smudge off the wall. Just as she touches it, there's a noise from the other side.

There it is again – a muffled sound, coming from next door.

Sobbing? Is it sobbing?

She holds her breath and stays perfectly still. It's the sound of crying. And it's a man. There's a man crying in the bedroom next door.

"Oh, you're home! Here, take this guy," Sylvia says, passing Zack to her husband as he walks through the door. "Listen, something weird happened today."

"What, you went a whole day without Megan having a tantrum?"

"No. I wish. She was okay earlier but she got really cross at teatime and ended up hitting me again. I know it's a phase but, Jesus, I wish it would pass. Anyway, that's not it. The weird thing, I mean. It's that I heard crying through the wall of our bedroom."

"What's weird about that?" Tom asks, bouncing Zack up in the air. Megan comes running to hug his leg.

"Like, I don't mean a baby or a child – it was a man. Have you met the couple next door at all yet?"

Tom shakes his head, still bouncing Zack. "Nope, haven't even seen them really – didn't you meet the wife one time?"

"I saw her in the driveway when I came home from work one evening but we didn't meet or anything – I just said hi and that was it. I don't even know their names."

"Well, I guess it's a bit weird if a man was crying, but who knows what goes on behind closed doors – it could be anything. What's for dinner?"

Sylvia gives him a look. "Yeah, you do know I've been minding a baby and working all day, right? It's freezer surprise or takeaway – you choose. Listen, I need a bit of headspace –" She sits down to put on her trainers. "I need air. I'm going to take Bailey for a walk – can you get the kids ready for bed?"

Outside, the sky is cobalt blue and the evening air is unnaturally warm, even for August. Across the way in Number 34, Georgia is getting out of her car, looking ludicrously immaculate for someone who's just arrived home from a full day's work. Sylvia glances down at her scuffed-but-not-in-a-cool-way trainers and her ancient leggings and wishes she'd put on something with the smallest hint of style, even if it's just to throw a ragged tennis ball for an enthusiastic Labrador.

"How're you doing, Sylvia – how are the little ones?" Georgia asks, walking towards her.

How is her hair so perfect on such a humid evening? Sylvia smooths down her own disobedient brown curls.

"Good, thanks, hanging in there – you know the way."

"Ah, they're gorgeous at that age – I bet Megan just adores her little brother, does she?"

And there it is – the first thing everyone says when you have a second baby. And who can blame them? It's just small talk, they don't mean any harm.

"Well, she's getting there. I wouldn't go as far as saying they've bonded or anything." She laughs.

"Oh my God, listen, I totally get it. Obviously not me personally since I only have the one, but my brother and his wife have the exact same thing with their little guy now that the new one has come along. It's hard work! My sister-in-law was saying my nephew is unbelievably clingy."

"Yes! That's it – Megan is glued to me, and gets cross if I have to give attention to Zack – which of course I do. It's so hard when everyone else is talking about how much their older kids *love* their new siblings. You end up wondering what's wrong with your child."

Georgia nods. "My sister-in-law said the same – people were asking her if Sebastian is jealous, which just sounds so mean, doesn't it? Like, he's only two."

Oh, I could just hug you right now, Sylvia thinks, and she can feel herself starting to well up. "That's it exactly! I know Megan's not jealous, she's just adjusting. But it's so hard in the meantime. She's hitting me and biting in Montessori as well now – it's been really tough."

Georgia frowns. "Oh really? God, that's bad all right. No, my sister-in-law doesn't have that problem. Actually, I can't imagine Sebastian biting anyone – he's a gorgeous little kid."

Sylvia doesn't want to hug her any more. "Yeah, they're all different, I guess . . . anyway, Bailey's getting impatient, I'd better get on. See you later, Georgia."

"See you, Sylvia, and chin up – do something nice for yourself," Georgia says as she turns to go into her house. "Maybe treat yourself to a spa day."

Sylvia walks on with Bailey.

God, she must look a state. A spa day, no less – if only she had the time for a spa day! Though she probably wouldn't know what to do in a spa – all that walking around in robes was a bit odd. Anyway, no fear of it happening any time soon.

Bailey races ahead down to the green in a jet-black blur as she lifts her hand to wave at a car rolling past, and then another. It's all on autopilot, she's not even sure who she's waving at. A car driving faster than the others roars up the road and right past her before her hand is even halfway up to wave. She watches, shielding her eyes from the sun, to see where the car is going. It turns into the house next door. The crying man maybe? Sylvia keeps watching as he gets out of the car, carrying two shopping bags. It's hard to see in the evening sunlight, but he looks like any other suburban man coming home to his suburban wife and kids.

She reaches the green. "You know what, Bailey?" she says, throwing the tennis ball. "It's time we introduced ourselves to the people next door."

Making her way back up the cul de sac, with Bailey running ahead, she's questioning the plan already. It's not weird to just call in, is it? No, it's not. In fact, maybe she should have done it sooner, to be polite. And it's not because of the thing with the pond and the crying through the wall, she decides – it's just being neighbourly. She walks past her own driveway and rings the bell of Number 26.

Just like the last time, nothing happens. Bailey runs around her feet, darting up to the door and back, but there's no movement inside the house. Did the bell even ring? She didn't hear anything . . . and it had sounded so loud when she had rung it on Friday . . . maybe she should try again. Though it would look bad if it really did ring the first time. But then she hears footsteps and for no reason she can pinpoint, her pulse quickens. Why is she suddenly apprehensive? Bailey is barking now at the as-yet-unopened door.

Suddenly Sylvia wants to walk away. This wasn't a good idea. But it's too late – someone is opening the door. It's pulled wide, and Sylvia looks up into a broad, smiling face.

"Hello?" says the man. He's tall, in his early forties, and looks resolutely normal.

"Hi, how are you – I'm Sylvia, I live next door. I just wanted to say hello and introduce myself. Because we didn't already. Me and Tom, I mean, my husband." Her words are tumbling over one another.

"Oh hey, I'm Sam, nice to meet you. We moved in just before the summer but we haven't been here much – Kate, my wife, is in her mum's place in Galway with the kids. And I'm down there at weekends when I'm not stuck trying to fix this place." He gestures behind him.

Sylvia nods. Mrs Osborne probably hadn't done anything in the house since she moved in thirty years earlier.

"Now, my boys would *love* to meet this guy," Sam says, bending down to ruffle Bailey's ear.

"Oh yes, when they're back bring them around to meet him – how old are your boys?"

"I've two – Seth and Jamie – they're seven and five. I don't think they'll be back till school starts but I'll bring them around then."

"Mine are a bit younger – Megan is three and Zack is just seven months. I'm sorry we haven't been over sooner to say hi. We were away for a few weeks on holidays, and then – well, you know, work, the usual. We're only here at weekends really and, even then, we go down to my mother-in-law a good bit. She's in Enniskerry." Oh my God, why is she still talking?

Sam is smiling politely but he probably didn't need to know her life story.

"Don't worry! It's lovely to meet you now, Sylvia."

The conversation seems to be coming to a natural end. Sylvia opens her mouth to tell him about the shape in the pond, but no words come out. It sounds so ridiculous in the bright evening light. Instead, she tells Sam it was nice to meet him, and calls Bailey to come home with her.

"Is everything okay? Were you about to say something else?" Sam asks.

"Actually, yes – this is going to sound very weird though . . ." It's now or never. The words, when they come, trip awkwardly out of Sylvia's mouth. "It's just that I thought I saw something in your pond at about four in the morning last week – I mean that fishpond out the back. I'm sure it was nothing, but it looked like a child lying face down in the water . . ." Oh Jesus, how daft it sounded now!

But Sam is still looking at her, waiting for more.

"It was the middle of the night, so it was probably just a shadow. And you said your kids are away – so don't mind me! Small baby, you know how it is. I'm *very* tired!" She smiles and shrugs, wishing she'd said nothing.

Sam looks at her blankly. "I'd have noticed if there was anything there . . ."

"Absolutely. Don't mind me. It was nice to meet you, Sam."

She calls Bailey and half-runs down the driveway, wondering what possessed her to say anything. And now that she's met him, it's clear there's nothing odd at all about the man next door.

Back inside her own house, she kicks off her trainers and fills Bailey's water bowl. The theme tune to *Peppa Pig* is coming from the sitting room – she can see Tom's long legs stretched out, and Megan sitting cross-legged at his feet. Zack must be in his arms.

"What did you get from the freezer – is it defrosted?" she calls in to Tom, looking at the empty microwave and the clear counters.

"Oh sorry, I didn't get it yet – I'll do it now," he says, starting to get up from the couch. "What will I get?"

"It's fine, leave it. We'll just get a takeaway when the kids are in bed, or do some cheese on toast."

Sylvia starts making Megan's lunch for Montessori, checking work email at the same time.

"So I went in to say hi to our new neighbour," she says, talking over the voice of Mummy Pig.

This time Tom does get up. "What's the story – what's he like?" he asks, coming into the kitchen with Zack on his shoulder.

"Zack's not asleep, is he?"

"No, he's awake," says Tom, craning his neck to make sure it's true. "So go on, what's the gossip? Is he the crying man you heard?"

"Well, I could hardly ask him that! His name is Sam, and his wife is called Kate. They have two kids, older than our guys, and they've been away most of the summer so far."

"And were there tears running down his face or does he seem normal?"

"Very funny. Yeah, he seems nice actually – he was lovely with Bailey."

"Could it have been the radio you heard through the wall? They have it on quite loud a lot of the time. Or the TV?"

"I didn't think of that – I guess actually it could have been their TV. That still doesn't explain what I saw in the pond though." Sylvia's not sure why, but she doesn't tell Tom that she brought up the pond with their new neighbour. She can tell him another time.

Tom gives her a look. "What you *thought* you saw. I think it's pretty safe to say you imagined it. When I'm up at night I'm practically hallucinating with tiredness."

When you're up at night once in a blue moon, Sylvia thinks. She cuts the crusts off Megan's sandwiches and puts them in the lunchbox.

"Yeah, it probably was just in my head," she says, "but so weird – I really believed it at the time. What I wouldn't give for a full night's sleep now, especially with everything that's going on at work."

Tom winces. "Still bad? What was the reaction to not going in today?"

"Craig didn't reply for ages so I was left hanging and then, when he did, he said he'd have to get Justin to cover my work. Which means I'll go in tomorrow to find nothing done again.

But he got to make his point and that's what he wanted. Much as I desperately need Jane to be back tomorrow, there's part of me that's dreading going in – it's just so toxic. I could do with another day away from them all." She takes Zack from Tom. He's looking sleepy – time to get him down before it's too late. "And another day at home with this little munchkin."

"Do you mean you'd give up if you could?" Tom looks slightly panicked.

"Oh, I don't know. If you'd asked me that a year ago, I'd have said no way, but it's just miserable since I went back. They really don't want me there, and they make it so obvious all the time." She shifts Zack to her other shoulder. "Like, they're still leaving me out of meetings, and when I spoke to my biggest client yesterday, she didn't even know I was back."

Tom puts his arm around her shoulders and gives her a squeeze. "I know it's hard but you'll get there. And we can't afford for you to give up. Look at it this way – if they're paying you to go in and do no work, how bad is that? Lots of people would kill for it!"

"Ugh, it's awful though. Time goes so slowly and I just feel useless. It's tough enough going back after maternity without feeling like you're surplus to requirements. Anyway, if I did quit – we'd get by. We'd have to cut back a bit, but we'd be okay, wouldn't we?"

Tom looks even more panicked. "I wouldn't like to try it, so don't do anything to lose your job just yet – deal?"

"Tom, we'd be fine, but don't worry, I'm not going to make any drastic decisions." She touches his arm. "Right, let's get these guys sorted. Is *Peppa* over – can you get Megan?"

Upstairs, before pulling the curtains, she stops to look out at the evening sky, still bright blue after the long hot day. Her eyes are drawn to the garden next door. The pond looks black despite the sun, the water still. Her eyes move to a mound of earth beside the pond – like a small flowerbed but without flowers. That wasn't there before, was it? Maybe Sam is trying to do something with the garden. Zack starts to whimper in her arms and she pulls her gaze away from next door.

Lying in bed later that night, listening to the soft breathing of her baby son, the images play on her mind – the imagined child in the pond, side by side with the flowerbed at its edge, and when she falls asleep she dreams of missing children.

Chapter 3

Sylvia - Friday, August 5th

Be careful what you wish for, thinks Sylvia, reading Jane's apologetic early-morning message. Feck. Work will have a field day with this. She groans and buries her head in the pillow, then nudges Tom.

"Jane's still sick. I'll stay home again. I may as well be hung for a sheep as a lamb."

"Okay, grand – at least it's Friday," Tom says, getting up to go downstairs.

"You'd think he'd at least have offered to stay home instead," Sylvia whispers to Zack, watching his small chest rise and fall in sleep. "Maybe he's writing me off too." She starts to get out of bed, then stops. A tiny act of rebellion is taking shape – she'll keep Megan at home from Montessori as well. There's no point in getting everyone up and out for the sake of three hours of childcare, and how much work will she get done in that time anyway? Feck it! Decision made – they're all staying in bed.

Three hours later, she's calling her decision-making ability into question when Megan throws a toy car at her head while she's trying to change a wriggling Zack on the sitting-room floor. Sylvia gets down to her level to calmly explain why it's not all right to throw toys at people, and Megan launches herself onto the floor, sobbing like her heart is breaking. Zack joins in for good measure, and Sylvia thinks she might cry too. Work is definitely easier than this. And actually, she should be doing some work – it seems like a very good time to put on the TV and break out snacks. And no guilt, because it's work. Well, not too much guilt. She'll bring them out for air in the afternoon to make up for it.

When they finally get out of the house, it's already three o'clock, and cranky levels are at fever pitch. But the fresh air works its magic and, by the time they get down to the green, Megan is chasing Bailey and laughing like a child from a TV ad for washing powder or baby food. The sun is blazing down, lighting everything in green and gold – doing its best to convince her that life is always like this. Could she do this every day? Both kids are in league with the sun now – smiling and giggling and lulling her into a false sense of stay-at-home motherhood.

Laying out the rug she's brought, she gives crackers to Megan and banana to Zack. Bailey is busy running from one end of the green to the other. Now if she just had a coffee for herself, all would be well in the world. The tantrum-filled morning is almost forgotten. Stretching out, she closes her eyes, just for a minute.

A voice breaks the spell. "Hi there!"

She jumps – was she asleep? In a panic, she looks for Zack and Megan. They're still on the rug, eating crackers and banana. Jesus, had she really fallen asleep? Surely not for more than two or three seconds? But oh God, that unknowing moment – she wouldn't close her eyes again. Still disoriented, she looks up, squinting in the sunlight, and it takes another moment to work out that the owner of the voice is her new neighbour.

"Enjoying the sun?" Sam asks, smiling down.

He's hovering right over her now, his shadow covering her body. Rolling onto her side, she pulls herself up to standing. They're just inches apart, and Sam doesn't move. Sylvia picks up Zack, and in the same movement takes two steps back.

"Yeah, the childminder is sick so I'm on the mitch from work with these two – don't tell anyone I was out sunbathing instead of working from home!" She feels her cheeks go red. "Are you off work too?"

"I'm actually off for a few weeks to fix up the house," Sam says, picking up Bailey's tennis ball from the rug and throwing it for the dog. "There's a lot to do, and it's handy while Kate and the boys are away."

"Oh, I can only imagine. Poor Mrs Osborne, who lived there before you – she wasn't up to doing much with the house, and her kids were horrible, never visited, never helped out. Awful."

"That's actually how I ended up buying the house – I'm best friends with Mrs Osborne's son."

Shit! When would she learn to think first, speak later. "I'm so sorry, I didn't mean to say they were awful, I shouldn't judge – who knows what goes on behind the scenes?"

Sam looks pissed off. Then suddenly he bursts out laughing. "I'm kidding. I didn't know them at all – it was all done through solicitors. Sorry, bad joke. But your face!"

"Ha, you had me worried for a minute," Sylvia says. "Well, I'd better start gathering things up here to head home . . ."

"Yeah, I'll head on and get back to the house repairs. Enjoy the sun. See you soon, Sylvia." He pats her on the shoulder as he goes past.

Sylvia watches him walk away, her face still red. He must think she's an awful eejit. Then again, is it slightly odd to joke with someone you barely know? Megan is tugging at her sleeve. "Mummy, can we make daisy chains? I want to make a pretty necklace for you!" She's taking the angelic TV-commercial-kid thing to a whole new level.

Home is trumping work again.

Walking into her own driveway, many daisy chains later, she glances over at Sam's house. Will he paint the front of the house, she wonders – if he does, they'll have to too, to match up. Or what if he changes the windows, like Number 14 did – going for something completely different to their semi-detached neighbours' and everyone else on the road? God, it was easier when Mrs Osborne was there – quiet, unobtrusive Mrs Osborne, who needed nothing more than some groceries dropped in and a chat over a cup of tea.

The swishing of a broom from the house on the other side pulls her from her thoughts. Rosemary is sweeping again, though there couldn't possibly be anything left to clean in that driveway. Sylvia keeps walking, hoping she won't be in the mood for a chat, but it's too late. Out of the corner of her eye, she sees the white-haired head bobbing up.

"Oh, I haven't seen you in ages, Sylvia! How are you and how are these two? Isn't it well for you to have the day off on this lovely sunny afternoon? Offices today are great places – back when my Bob was alive, he worked all the hours God sent him. Never saw the kids!" She steps towards them, taking off her little silver-rimmed glasses and shaking her head at Megan and Zack. "But sure that's the way it was and it was grand."

"Well, it's not time off really – my childminder is sick so I had to work from home," Sylvia says.

Rosemary nods, eying the daisy chain around Sylvia's neck and the picnic rug tucked under the buggy.

"What I mean is, I'm keeping an eye on email and minding the kids." She takes out her BlackBerry and waves it at Rosemary. What is she doing, explaining herself like this?

"Of course. Sure it's probably all different these days. I'm sure your boss doesn't mind at all."

"Oh yes, he's great about it, totally understands. So, I met the new neighbour from the other side – Sam is his name," Sylvia says, moving away from the subject of her fictional benevolent boss.

"Oh, Sam! Oh, sure I know Sam, lovely man," Rosemary says, leaning her sweeping brush against the wall and folding her arms.

"Ah okay, I only met him yesterday. He seems quite nice, doesn't he?"

"A very nice man. You know, Sylvia, there's lots around here wouldn't pass the time of day with an old woman like me, but this fella Sam always stops to chat."

Sylvia thinks this does a disservice to all the neighbours who are regularly caught for chats with Rosemary and too polite to move on, but she just nods. "And did you meet the wife – Kate, I think?"

"No, I didn't meet her," Rosemary says. "She was already gone down to Galway or somewhere, he said. Isn't it great today the way people can just go off on holidays for two months? Back when our kids were small, we were lucky to get a week in a caravan in Courtown."

"Well, I think he said they're staying with the wife's mother, and it's mostly so he can fix up the house – so it's not really a holiday," Sylvia says, pushing the buggy forward and back on autopilot.

Rosemary purses her lips. She's not for turning. "Well, it's certainly not a holiday for poor Sam, stuck doing all the work while they're away at the beach. I'd say there's a fair amount to do there – Mrs Osborne wasn't one for keeping her house in good shape."

"In fairness, she wasn't well for her last few years, and her kids didn't help at all – there probably wasn't much she could do." Where is all this defensiveness coming from? She really needs to say goodbye to Rosemary and get the kids in.

But Rosemary is settling in for a chat. "Anyway, your man Sam's great. He's so busy with his own house, but still offered to take a look at my burglar alarm when it kept going off all the time at the weekend. He fixed it too. Not a bother. Would have cost me eighty euro if I got someone in to do it. And no rushing off either – sat down for a cup of tea and a chat for ages after. You just don't get that any more, you know, Sylvia."

"Ah, that's lovely, he sounds great. It's hard, isn't it, when we're all so busy all the time? Speaking of which, I'd better get these two in. Megan, love, say goodbye to Rosemary."

Rosemary goes back to her sweeping, and Sylvia steps into the cool darkness of her hallway, turning to pull the buggy in behind her.

Sunlight spreads across the walnut floor, down as far as the open kitchen door. Bailey rushes past, straight to his water bowl, while Megan trails behind, inspecting the flowers at the front door.

"Mummy, the pink ones are dying a bit – will I pick them?"

"No, honey, just come on in now and shut the door behind you," she tells her daughter and the sunlight is snapped away to the sound of the heavy front door closing.

Chapter 4

Sylvia - Saturday, August 6th

In a fraction of a second, the scream pulls her from sleep to breathless panic and before she registers time or place she's out of bed and running downstairs to Megan's bedroom. Bursting through the door she runs to her daughter's bedside, pulling her into a hug. Megan collapses against her mother, shaking but no longer screaming, and they rock together.

Moments later, Tom's tall shape appears in the doorway, the hallway light creating a halo effect around his head.

"What was it – a nightmare? Is she okay?" he asks.

Sylvia keeps rocking and purses her lips in a silent shush. Tom slips into the room and hunkers down beside the bed. Teary blue eyes stare back at him, under wet brown curls plastered against a pale forehead. He takes Megan's hand but she pulls it back and retreats into Sylvia's arms.

"What is it, love, did you have a bad dream?" Sylvia asks, smoothing back Megan's damp hair.

"There was a monster in my room," comes the small voice.

"It was just a dream, love – there are no monsters in real life."

"No, Mummy, he was here in my room – right here!" she says, pointing to the middle of her bedroom. "He was huge and black and scary, and he smelled like Daddy does when he goes to watch football matches with his friends."

Sylvia pulls her daughter into a tighter hug. "Love, I know dreams can seem very real, but I promise you there's no monster. Tell you what, why don't you come upstairs with me and sleep in our bed? And Daddy will check the room from top to bottom. Does that sound okay?"

"Yes, I'll sleep with you and Daddy, like Zack does – except I'll be in the big bed and he'll stay in the cot – isn't that right?" When she climbs down from the bed, her bare feet slip a little on the wooden floor. "Mummy, the floor is wet. I think it was the monster."

Sylvia switches on the fairy lights that twist around the canopy above the bed, and puts her hand on the floor. Megan's right – it's wet. "Did you spill your water, love?"

"No, Mummy, I didn't have any water – you forgot to bring it."

Again she's right, there's no beaker of water on the night-stand.

"All right, pet, you head up the stairs. Do you want Teddy?" Sylvia picks up the brown bear and passes it to her daughter. "Tom, will you grab some kitchen roll for that water? And check the back door is locked, will you?"

"You're not starting to believe in monsters too, are you?" Tom asks.

She can't see his face but she can hear the smile.

"Nope, but the water thing is weird, isn't it?" she replies, checking the patio doors in Megan's room. They're locked.

"It could be anything – it might have been there all day," Tom says.

"No, I'm sure there was nothing wet on the floor when I

did her story earlier. Just check the door anyway, okay?"

He heads for the kitchen.

The patio doors don't budge when Sylvia checks them a second time – they're definitely locked, and the key is where it always is, on a hook behind the curtain. Outside, trees shake in the breeze, black against the navy moonlit sky, and the garden path that leads to Bailey's kennel is indistinguishable from the grass that surrounds it. Beyond the kennel, there's nothing to see at all – the end of the garden is swallowed by darkness. And, suddenly, her craving for the whimsical childhood bedroom she never had is utterly foolish – Megan should be sleeping upstairs near her parents. What if there was a break-in and Megan was downstairs on her own? And the patio doors were hardly secure – one simple lock, and otherwise glass. She shivers.

Kitchen towel in hand, Tom comes back into the room and wipes the floor.

"Did you check the back door?"

"Yeah – actually it wasn't locked – I've locked it now."

"Are you serious? Oh my God, maybe someone was in here?"

"No, no way – it was just a bad dream. Why would someone come into our house, and how would anyone know the back door was open?"

"Well, it's not the first time it's been left unlocked at night either . . ."

"Okay, point taken, but you could lock up sometimes too, you know."

"Sorry, I'm not blaming you," Sylvia says, giving him a quick hug. "We should just both be more careful. This has really freaked me out tonight. I think we should move Megan upstairs."

"She's up there now, isn't she – in our bed?"

"No, I mean permanently. When you think about it, it's madness having a child sleep downstairs on her own. She should be near us."

Tom is rolling his eyes.

"Yes, I know it was my idea to do up this room for her, but now the whole thing is giving me the creeps. Especially with that story on the news about the missing child – she's only a year younger than Megan and her hair is so similar – every time I see a picture in the paper it freaks me out. And then there was the thing with the pond."

"Sylvia, I totally get it that the missing-child story is on your mind, but the thing with the pond was all in your head. And I suspect there might be a bit of exaggeration going on with Megan tonight – she seemed fairly delighted about getting to sleep in our bed. This could just be a jealousy thing, because Zack's in our room."

This time Sylvia does the eyerolling. Megan might be a handful since Zack was born, but she had been genuinely upset tonight.

"Anyway, where would Megan go if we moved her upstairs?" Tom asks.

"Well, she could take the guest room – it's not like we have visitors. And we can turn this room into a home office for all these unexpected work-from-home days!" She knows she's making light of it to talk him round and she knows he knows that.

"That's a bit of an overreaction to a bad dream, isn't it?"

She tries again. "I know, but it's not just about tonight – it makes more sense overall. Most people have their kids upstairs. This was all just a notion I took, and in hindsight it was a mistake. Come on, let's try to get some sleep – we can talk about it tomorrow."

Upstairs, Megan is already asleep in the middle of their

bed, curled around her teddy, but Zack is stirring in his cot. Great, this is the last thing they need now.

"I'll go down and sleep in Megan's bed," whispers Tom. "More room for you here then."

"There's loads of space, just stay here," yawns Sylvia.

"No, we'll all sleep better if I go – and then I can deal with any monsters who come back," he says, kissing her on the top of her head before he pulls the door softly behind him.

Zack starts to cry and Sylvia picks him up as the first shards of morning light slip through the window.

Chapter 5

Sylvia – Tuesday, August 9th

The grey early-morning light makes a feeble attempt to brighten the kitchen but fails. Yawning, Sylvia switches on the coffee machine, and reaches up to get a capsule from the cupboard. But there's only empty space where the coffee jar usually sits. She feels her way along the shelf, squinting in the half-light. It's definitely not there. Her eyes scan the countertop – maybe she took it out yesterday and forgot to put it back. No. She tries the other cupboards, then the fridge. It would hardly be in the fridge but then again, autopilot can be glitchy, especially early in the morning and late at night. But the jar of coffee capsules is nowhere. And now she really, really wants coffee.

She sits at the breakfast bar for a moment, trying to straighten out her thoughts. Maybe she'll message Tom in London. Then again, it couldn't have been him – he was gone before she was even up yesterday morning, and she's definitely seen it since then. Hasn't she? Though there's no harm in messaging – he'll be up anyway. She pads back upstairs to get her phone, but no, Tom hasn't seen the coffee. Fine, tea will do for now.

Megan is still fast asleep when Sylvia goes in to whisper that it's morning time. She stretches and opens her eyes, and says she had no bad dreams and there were no monsters in her room. She's been saying this every morning since she moved into the guest room and Sylvia can't decide if it's a good thing or a bad thing. Hopefully the memory of the monster will fade, and she'll stop bringing it up. For now, Sylvia tells her it's time to get up and get ready for Montessori.

Back in her own room, the radio buzzes on before she has time to shush its blare, but Zack sleeps on regardless. The missing child is the top story. She's been gone for nearly two full weeks now, and it's the top story every hour. And Sylvia wells up every single time she hears it. God, the thought of losing a child! For a second, she resists the urge to go back in to hug Megan, then gives in. What is it they always say? The days are long but the years are short.

It's later than usual when Jane arrives and she's full of apologies. Sylvia tells her not to worry, it's no problem at all, then races out to the car to head for the city centre, an uncomfortable knot forming in her stomach at every red light. As long as she makes it in before Craig, it'll be okay. Her start-early-finish-early deal won't last if he thinks she's abusing it.

His car isn't in the car park when she arrives and inside the lift she feels the knot uncurl when she presses the button for the third floor.

As the doors close, a hand is shoved in to keep them open.

Justin. Wonderful.

"Starting late today?" he asks, assessing her over the top of his glasses.

"No, no, my childminder just got caught in traffic. Typical – always happens when Tom's away. Normally I'm in really early. Of course nobody ever notices that." She gives a little laugh.

He nods, then without replying takes out his phone.

Sylvia takes a discreet glance at the screen. He's looking at stock prices. Oh, for God's sake! As if he needs to know about stock prices to work in a back-office operations team in Fund Services. No doubt he'll reel off some fascinating market updates to impress Craig at the management meeting. And why is he still at that meeting now that she's back? She needs to bring it up with him. The familiar knot returns. She'll bring it up soon.

The lift doors open on the third floor and Justin walks out ahead of her.

"Justin?"

He turns back.

"We need to catch up again about the audit prep – I still can't find those daily reports for January to March. They're not saved in the folder. Would you know where they are?"

An impatient frown crosses his face. "They're there – you're probably looking in the wrong place. I'll have a look later if there's time."

He marches off through reception, leaving the door to swing shut behind him. Another lovely day at the office, and she hasn't even had a coffee yet.

Thank you, Jane, Sylvia mouths to herself when she spots the chicken broccoli bake in the fridge. There's far too much for just the kids and herself but it'll do for tomorrow too. Standing at the kitchen window waiting for the oven to heat, she cradles her tea in her hands and stares out at the garden. Everything is grey this evening – even the grass looks drab and dull in the meagre light that's made its way through the rainclouds.

Her eyes drift to the garden wall as her mind drifts to what she saw that night. What she *thought* she saw that night. It wasn't a child. Of course it wasn't. But as time passes, the image in her memory shifts shape and gains clarity – the blurred edges are sharper now, nudging at her night-time thoughts.

A loud crash shatters the silence. Startled, she drops her tea onto the floor.

"*Megan!*" she shouts, and runs through to the sitting room, but Megan is still engrossed in *Paw Patrol*, and Zack is sitting on the rug.

Back in the kitchen, she stands in the middle of the floor, but there's nothing to see. Could it have come from outside? Bailey jumps up from his spot on the patio as soon as her hand touches the back door. As he rushes inside, she goes out to look around the garden, but there's nothing out of place. The air is heavy and quiet – she's sure now the noise came from indoors.

Upstairs, everything is just as she left it this morning – pyjamas stuffed under pillows, hastily made beds, the shoes she changed at the last minute. Standing at the window, her eyes are drawn again like magnets to the garden next door. The bushes and the pond look darker and greyer this evening, but there's nothing and nobody there.

Back downstairs, she checks the bathroom and Megan's old bedroom, then goes into the kitchen. Could she have imagined it?

Then there's a pop, much smaller this time, but very real. It's coming from the oven. Slowly she opens it and finds it covered in glass – and something else. She grabs a tea towel and uses it to pick up one of the objects – a melted coffee capsule. How on earth did they get in there? First things first: she switches off the oven, then tries to sweep out some of the glass with the tea-towel but burns her hand. She cries out, and at the same time Megan comes running in and yanks her shirt, trying to pull her into the sitting room to change the TV channel.

"*Megan, will you let go!*" Sylvia shouts, much louder than she intends, and Megan starts to cry. "Oh, for goodness' sake!" she mutters under her breath, and out loud says, "Megan, I'm sorry, I didn't mean to shout. I've burnt my hand – let me put some cold water on it and I'll be in to you."

This causes Megan to cry harder. Sylvia runs to the sink to cool her throbbing hand, cursing her own stupidity, then she turns back to scoop Megan up and calm her down.

Eventually peace descends and she edges her way back out to the kitchen to assess the situation with the oven. Who put the jar in there – could Jane have done it? Or could she have done it herself, drunk on exhaustion?

All the capsules are for the bin but, as she's taking the chicken broccoli out of the fridge, she spots an unopened bottle of white wine. On a day that hasn't gone terribly well, she'll take her blessings where she finds them.

Chapter 6

Sylvia – Wednesday, August 10th

Her phone is ringing and she's rummaging in her handbag but she can't find it. Jane is still in the doorway, waving with Zack and Megan, and Sylvia knows she's supposed to wave back – all the parenting gurus would say wave back – but she's got car keys in her mouth, a coffee on the roof of the car, and she really needs to find her phone. It stops ringing just as she pulls it out. Craig. Damn, why is he ringing so early?

As she pulls out on the road, Noel from across the road signals at her to stop. Oh Lord, what now? She rolls down the window.

"Sylvia, I haven't seen you in a while – how was the holiday?"

"Good, thanks – we're back a few weeks now. I'm just on my way in to work . . . "

"So, I see your new neighbours moved in."

"Yes, they seem very nice – though I've only met Sam. The wife is away."

"I'd keep an eye on him if I were you. Bit of a player, I'd say."

"A player? What do you mean?" Sylvia asks, risking a discreet look at the clock on the dashboard.

"Ah, just a few little things. I see he has a young lady visiting regularly, and she leaves early the next morning. I never met the wife but I did see her once or twice when I was looking out the window – blonde hair and tall, like a model. This one I've seen going in and out is small and dark. Like a dancer – like one of those women who dance around poles." Noel says all of this with a perfectly straight face.

Sylvia desperately wants to laugh. "Could it be his sister or something?"

"Not the way they were necking at the front door yesterday morning, no."

Necking! She really is going to laugh now. "God, well, that's interesting. I'd better get on though. Tell Georgia I said hi."

Sylvia drives off, wondering exactly how much time Noel spends looking out his window. Funny about Sam next door though. Could he really be having an affair? And the poor wife, oblivious to all of it. Isn't that what they say – the wife is always the last to know? Could that happen to her – would she know if Tom was cheating? He's away a lot with work . . . But then again, when he's home, he's really home – no late nights in the office or mysterious hotel receipts. And realistically, where would either of them find the time or the energy for an affair?

At the office, before she has time to hang up her coat, Breeda announces Craig wants to see her. *Crap*. Dropping her handbag at her desk, she makes her way to his office. At the door, she pauses, then knocks and walks inside.

The view is the first thing that strikes her every time she's in there – two walls made almost entirely of glass give a panoramic sweep from the Custom House right down the Liffey.

Her boss prefers the minimalist approach – the enormous fake-mahogany desk holds nothing more than a laptop, a pen, and a notebook. He's busy writing when she comes in, and doesn't look up.

Sylvia hesitates, then closes the door behind her. Her palm is sweaty. She wipes it on the side of her skirt and stands there, unsure what to do next. Why is he still writing – surely he heard her come in? She clears her throat and finally gets his attention.

"Sylvia – take a seat."

She does, flashing a small smile.

"We need to talk about the audit. Mervin Kinsella were in touch to say they don't have your reports yet. I was very clear to everyone about the importance of getting stuff over to them on time. The last thing we need is to be on the backfoot at this stage. So, what's the hold-up?"

"Sorry about that – it's just we seem to be missing the reports from January to March. I'm not sure –"

"Missing? What do you mean 'missing'?"

"Just that they're not saved on the shared drive. Justin thought they might be in the wrong folder but he and I searched yesterday afternoon and couldn't find them. I've been gathering and sending everything else and we're on top of that – it's just those months that are missing. I'm working on it."

"Sylvia, this is serious. It's part of our obligation to keep daily reports. It's a huge breach if we don't have them. Did you ask the rest of the team?"

"Yes, they say they saved them as normal and they can't understand it. They're suggesting someone deleted them in error, and I've a case opened with IT to investigate. They might have the back-up tapes. But you know how it is – we're just one request in a long line."

"Sylvia, you need to expedite this. Don't take any bull from IT – get them to prioritise this today. We can't tell Mervin Kinsella we've lost those files – we'll look like amateurs at best, or worse they'll think we're trying to hide something. Get on it, Sylvia."

This is evidently her cue to leave and she does, her cheeks burning as she pulls the door shut behind her.

Justin is at the other end of the open-plan office, hovering over Carla's desk. Sylvia raises her hand and calls his name, but there's no reaction. She's about to try again, then thinks better of it and crosses the floor to him instead.

"Justin, do you have a minute?"

Frowning, he looks up. "I'm just in the middle of something here."

"That's fine – when you're done, could you come in to my office?"

He looks like he's about to say no, but can't think of a good reason. It must grate to be summoned to what was his office for seven months. Now, if he could just put as much effort into finding those missing reports as he does into helping the lovely Carla with God knows what every morning, Sylvia would be a much happier person.

It's over an hour later when Justin finally sticks his head into her office. "Did you want something earlier, Sylvia?"

"Yes, it's about those missing reports. I've been on to IT and they're going to bump the request up the list. They should be able to trace if they were moved or deleted, and they might have a back-up."

Justin straightens up and puts his hands in his pockets. "I doubt they can help – I lost some files last year and they said there was nothing they could do. If they're deleted, they're gone." He shrugs.

"Do you mean the client contact list you lost last year?"

"Yeah – there was no way to retrieve it – I had to get the team to put a new one together."

"Justin, IT were just fobbing you off. They do that all the time. If it's not a big deal for us to recreate something, they push back. The only reason they're making the effort now is because this is from Craig."

Justin's mouth opens then closes again.

For the first time since her return to work, he has no putdown. If the situation wasn't so serious, she'd be celebrating.

"Once IT let us know they've got the files, I need you to sit with me to go through them – hopefully there are no holes and it won't take long."

Justin nods and leaves, just as Sylvia's phone rings. IT have the missing reports already. It's time to roll up her sleeves.

"It just doesn't make sense – there's a two-million-euro hole in the account for four weeks, then suddenly it's filled and I can't see how. Was nobody on your back about the missing money during those four weeks?"

Justin is sitting beside her at the desk, staring down at the page.

"I'm trying to remember now," he says. "There was a lot going on at the time."

"But two million? There's no way that could have gone unnoticed for four weeks. Didn't you have to send out the reports every day?"

"Yeah . . . I think maybe that one got categorised as a long-term receivable for a while, so it wasn't on the version of the report that we were sending out to clients and management."

"The *version* of the report?"

"We don't send the full report any more – it's too detailed. They don't read it anyway, and it takes ages to talk through everything. So we just send out a summary of the short-term items."

"But, Justin, this is huge – did Craig okay it?"

"*I* made the decision." There's a hint of the familiar belligerence.

"Right." Sylvia says nothing for a moment. "So, how did the two-million shortfall get resolved in the end? Was it just in the wrong account and then moved back?"

"Maybe. I can't remember now."

"Justin, this is really serious – we need to get to the bottom of it before we go to audit. I'm going in to Craig now to let him know there's a reporting discrepancy, and then I have meetings for the rest of the afternoon – can you take the reports and find out?"

Nodding, he picks up his notes and leaves her office without looking back.

The knife slices through the apple over and over, making a noise that even Tom can hear at the other end of the phone.

"And you won't believe this – he was gone by the time I got back from my meetings," Sylvia says, balancing her mobile between her shoulder and her ear. "Biggest issue we've had in years, and he doesn't stay to fix it."

"Jesus, that's pretty bad. There's a guy in our place like that too. Wants to be the boss but doesn't want to put in the work. There's probably someone like that in every office."

"I know, and if it's just that I'm not too worried. But what if he's covering something up? It might not be laziness this time – it might be fear of being found out."

"What – you think it's not just a reporting error – he's actually run off with two million and he's still showing up at work every day?"

Sylvia smiles into the phone. "No. He'd be long gone if he had that kind of money – living in a harem somewhere or eloping with the lovely Carla to a Bahamian beach. But I've been thinking about it all evening – what if he paid out the two million in error and then covered it up? He can't bear to admit when he makes a mistake – it's just the kind of thing he'd do."

"Ah, there's no way – surely there are reports and checks in place to stop something like that happening?"

"Well, yes, there are – but those are the reports that are missing."

"Look, there's not much you can do tonight so don't be stressing about it – grab Justin first thing tomorrow morning and lock him in an office till he figures it out – that's what I'd do. How are the kids?"

"Kids are good, fast asleep. I'm going up myself now – too tired for TV and Zack will be up in the night no doubt."

"Give them a kiss from me, and I'll see you all tomorrow night."

Sylvia disconnects the call, lets Bailey out, and makes her way softly upstairs into Megan's room. A chink of light filters through a gap in the curtains and falls on her face.

Reaching up to pull the curtain fully closed, Sylvia stops when a movement outside catches her attention. Someone is standing in front of Sam's house, staring up at the top windows. Her stomach muscles tighten. Trying to see better, she edges closer to the window but the movement draws his attention. Her retreat is just a second too late – he's seen her. The man stares for a minute, then turns and walks into the driveway of the house across the road. Is it Noel? He turns one last time to look up at something – at her or at next door, she can't tell – and she sees his face lit by the street light. It's Noel. She lets out a breath. What is he doing, staring up at Sam's house? Knowing Noel, it could be anything. Perhaps he's looking for the pole-dancer.

Closing the curtains to shut out dark shadows and hazy streetlights, Sylvia goes to her own room and climbs wearily into bed, praying that tonight she will sleep.

Chapter 7

Sylvia – Thursday, August 11th

Sylvia's awake, but doesn't know why. Her ears are pounding. The room is pitch black apart from the numbers on the clock. 3.34am. Zack is fast asleep in the cot beside her. What woke her? Megan maybe, with another bad dream? As she's getting out of bed, the dog barks suddenly, making her jump. So that's what it was.

Shivering a little, she goes to the window and pulls back the curtain. Bailey is yapping at the wall again. She looks over at the garden next door but this time there's nothing to see. Nothing in the pond, and nothing moving in the garden except shadows of overgrown bushes in the night-time breeze. It was probably a rabbit or a squirrel. Daft dog. But no harm to check on Megan anyway. She closes the curtains tightly, and makes her way through the darkness towards the bedroom door. As she touches the handle, there's a sudden crash downstairs – like glass breaking, dropped from a height. She jumps, the pounding in her ears louder than ever. Oh God, why isn't Tom here? Pulling the door open she runs into her daughter's room, offering silent thanks that they'd moved her upstairs, and carries her back into her own room. Megan doesn't stir when Sylvia puts her into the double bed and brings the duvet up to her chin.

She stands, steadying her breathing, listening. The darkness feels oppressive and loud, but there's no further noise from downstairs. Was it inside or outside the house? Taking a deep breath, she moves to the window to look outside again. Just below, there's what looks like a terracotta planter in pieces all over the patio, and Bailey is nowhere to be seen now. That bloody dog. She climbs in beside Megan, and waits for sleep, but all her senses are heightened. Each time she starts to dip down into the blissful cotton wool of drifting thoughts, a creak in the floorboards or a gurgle in the pipes brings her back up.

Just after five o'clock, she gives in and goes downstairs.

Head pounding and eyes burning, she heads straight for the coffee machine, before turning to switch on the light. Something dark catches her eye on the far side of the kitchen. Her pulse quickens as she walks around the breakfast bar to look. There are clumps of soil on the floor, just inside the back door. Sylvia stares, trying to work out how they got there. Is Bailey inside after all – did she dream that he was barking in the garden last night? Softly she calls him but there are no running paws in response. Her breathing is slow as she stands staring at the floor. She puts her hand on the back-door handle. Did she lock it last night? The key is where she left it, on the hook inside the door, but did she turn it before she took it out? She pulls down the handle. The door doesn't move. It's locked. She closes her eyes and lets out a long breath. But then, if nobody was in here, where did the clumps of soil come from? Surely she couldn't have missed them when she was closing up last night?

Unlocking the back door now, she steps out into the garden. Shards of terracotta cover the patio like orange confetti. She'll have to pick them up before the dog walks all over them. He's still asleep in his kennel – normally the sound of any human movement brings him running, but even Bailey knows better than to get up at five o'clock in the morning.

Back inside, she sweeps up the mess. It looks like it came from inside the planter, but that doesn't make any sense. Her hand shakes as she tips the dustpan contents into the bin, and clumps of soil spill onto the floor.

She puts her hands on the breakfast bar to steady them, and takes some deep breaths. Time for coffee – everything will be clearer after coffee.

Swallowing the first earthy sip of espresso, she tries to push the broken planter out of her mind and focus on work instead. She'll have to tackle Justin this morning. Either he finds how the two-million error was covered or they go to Craig about it together. Her stomach lurches. What was it they said at the training course – "Clarity is power" and then something about getting what you need if you're clear and up front. It sounded so simple on the day, but in real life hoping people will just *know* seems infinitely preferable. Like the raise. She should have asked for it, instead of assuming her hard work would be noticed and rewarded. And if she doesn't find the bloody missing money, there'll be no raise this year either. She looks at the clumps of soil by the bin and drains her coffee. It's too early to get the kids up, but suddenly she doesn't want to be down here any more.

As she's leaving the kitchen, her eye turns to the dresser. There's something out of place – one of the framed photos is lying face down on the dresser shelf. Slowly, she picks it up, and her whole body goes cold when she sees the black cross through Megan's smiling face. The other photo is face down too and she already knows what she'll find. She picks it up. Zack's face is crossed out as well – deliberate, unemotional black lines block his smile. Her skin is tingling now and the pounding in her ears is back. Who could have drawn the lines? Was someone in the house during the night? No, the back door was locked – there's surely no way anyone was in the house. But then what?

She sits down on a kitchen chair, still holding the photos. Could Megan have done it? But how could she reach the shelf? There's no other explanation – she must have done it. Maybe she climbed up on a chair when Jane wasn't looking. It makes no sense, but the alternative makes even less sense.

Upstairs, Zack starts to cry. Sylvia puts the photos back on the dresser, face down, and goes up to him. Megan is awake now too – they're all up far too early, and everyone will be cranky tonight, but right now she's glad to have company. Sylvia suggests pancakes, earning a cheer from Megan, and they go together to get her dressing gown from her room.

Outside, Sylvia hears a car door and peeps out. It's Sam, reversing out of his driveway. He looks up and waves, and she jumps back out of sight.

"Mummy, why did you jump? Did you get a fright? Is it the monster?"

"No, sweetheart, it was just cold at the window – come on, let's get those pancakes on!"

Even with Megan playing and Zack babbling, the kitchen feels eerily quiet this morning. The radio might help. Except it doesn't, because the news is on, and they're playing a recording of Edie Keogh's mother making a plea for help. Glancing at Megan, Sylvia lowers the volume a little and stands closer to the radio. Imagine getting up one morning and finding an empty bed where your child should be. She reaches for a tissue to blow her nose. God love that poor woman.

Megan comes over and tugs at her sleeve. "Why is it taking so long – I'm so *huuuunnnngry*!"

And just like that, it's back to the everyday world of making pancakes, and complaints about pancakes, and wishing she'd never promised pancakes.

It's only quarter to nine, but she can feel a mid-morning slump coming on already. Fifteen minutes until Justin will be in. Actually, she should leave him a voicemail now to say she wants to see him first thing. No more procrastinating. As she reaches to pick up the phone, it starts to ring. Craig's extension flashes up. Her hand hovers for a moment before she answers.

"Sylvia, great, you're in. Bit of bad news – Justin was in touch to say he'll be out for the next few weeks. He has something called laby . . . what is it he said? Labyrinthitis, I think. Causes severe vertigo apparently. Never heard of it myself – had to google it. His doctor told him he could be out for six weeks. Bad timing with the audit, I know. If you need some help from another team, just shout."

He hangs up before she has a chance to do anything other than mumble thanks for the offer of help. She sits with the phone still to her ear, oblivious to the dial tone. Eventually, when she's no longer in danger of slamming it down, she puts the receiver carefully back in the cradle, and pulls up the reports on her screen. Outside on the floor, she can hear someone laughing.

Sylvia gets up and closes the door.

Chapter 8

The Woman - October 2005

The woman leans against the door to the kitchen and pauses. She can hear faint noises inside – he's home. Maybe he's in a good mood – things had been going well at work this week. She pushes open the door and walks in. He's sitting at the kitchen table, scrolling through his BlackBerry with one hand and cradling a whiskey with the other. He looks up at her, then back to his BlackBerry. A world away from the greetings she was used to when they first met. Dramatic, sweeping-off-feet type greetings that left her head spinning and her stomach fluttering.

The woman sits down noisily on the chair opposite him. He looks up.

"What?" he says.

"Nothing really. Well, it would be nice if you said hello when I walk in."

"Hello," he grunts, then he's back to his phone.

She can see little beads of sweat on his forehead. She sighs and he looks up again.

"What is wrong with you?"

"I just wish it could be like it was when we first met – you

used to smile and laugh and be glad to see me."

"Oh for God's sake, don't be ridiculous!"

"Well, I called in to my brother on the way home this evening, and Olivia arrived in while I was there, and the first thing Ben did was come over to kiss her, and it made me realise you don't really do that any more. It made me a bit sad, that's all . . . Ben just got a promotion at work actually, and they're going out on Friday to celebrate. They've invited us along – will we go?"

"Ben got a promotion, and you want me to go out and celebrate? What, so I can be made to feel even worse about how things are going at work?"

"No! That's not what I mean. I'm just . . . well, we don't seem to spend as much time together any more, and I thought a night out would do us good. And it would be nice to go out with Olivia and Ben – we haven't done that in ages."

"All you ever do is compare me to people you think are better than me," he says, standing up from his chair.

She looks up at him. Where is this coming from?

He walks around the table, and bends his face low, to her eye-level. "Don't you ever come into this house again," he snarls, "telling me about your brother and Olivia and how great they are!"

She stares. She's seen him angry, but never like this. "I just wanted to tell you that I wish we were the way we used to be – it wasn't meant to be about Ben's promotion."

The slap catches her by surprise. A hard slap, that knocks her sideways. She tumbles onto the floor, and lies there, too shocked to speak. She puts her hand to her stinging cheek.

He stands over her. "Is it clear now?" he says, reaching out a hand to help her up. Not sure what else to do, she takes his outstretched hand, and allows him to pull her to standing.

"Would you like a cup of tea?" he asks.

Still dazed, the woman nods, and watches as he switches on the kettle, then carefully and methodically washes his hands.

Chapter 9

Sam - Thursday, March 3rd 2016

The fluorescent light above his head hums like an indignant bluebottle. He never hears it during the day, but at night when they're all gone home it's the only sound. Scroll, scroll, *click*. This one looks interesting – a semi-detached house in Dún Laoghaire, needs some upgrading inside, an executor sale. He clicks on "save" and then hesitates. If he sends it to Kate now, she'll know he's looking at houses, and not working on the board report he'd mentioned in his text. He can hear her voice now. "*Why didn't you just come home to help with bedtime – you could look at houses after the boys are down?*" He'll show it to her later. The PC clock shows 7.42pm. She'd be doing stories with the boys. A twinge of guilt hits, but only for a moment. It's probably better for all of them if he focuses on finding a new home and getting them out of the house in Booterstown. It's all very well being just a few miles from Dublin city centre, but not in a too-small house with a too-small garden. Anyway, it's not like they go out in the city centre any more – so going further out into suburbia wouldn't be the hardship it once was.

Of course, growing up, the house had never seemed small. Every corner was a hideout and every step a spot for stories. The wooden floors rang with his running in the house that was his playground: his and only his. In the mornings his mum got him ready for school while his dad went off to work in the newspaper. In the afternoons, he did his sums and spellings at the old oak kitchen table, while his mum made him toasted cheese sandwiches and hot chocolate with the powdery stuff he still loves today. The long oriental runner in the hall softened the sound of his steps as he ran for the stairs, homework done, ready to read – touching the books on his bookshelf, letting his fingers decide which one to take, then sprawling on the elephant-print beanbag, getting lost in the worlds of the *Famous Five* and the *Hardy Boys* and the *Five Find-Outers and Dog*.

At six o'clock precisely, the key would turn in the red front door, and Dad would be home. Filling them in on the news stories of the day, packing his pipe as he spoke. Mum always had dinner ready – lamb chops or pork chops or sometimes roast chicken – and sometimes apple tart and custard for after. Looking back it was a childhood straight out of the books he loved to read.

But the childhood playground seems so much smaller now. Moving back in after his mother's death, he watched and waited to see his sons feel what he felt, but somehow it was gone. Seth and Jamie's toys sprawled all over the kitchen and bedroom, taking up corners that had once been hideouts. The old oak table was too big, Kate said, they'd have to find something in Ikea. And the oriental runner, faded from years of light and use, was destined for the skip.

Sweeping aside the fog of nostalgia, even Sam could accept that the boys needed a house where they could go outside to play – a house on a busy main road was just too dangerous.

And Kate, since she'd given up work, seemed more restless than ever – struggling against the walls of her self-imposed prison.

His mother would be looking down on him, shaking her head as he browsed house listings. Dún Laoghaire's too far out, she'd say – sure, who do you know out there? But who do they know in Booterstown? Everyone's scattered all over the county now, in starter homes they bought but couldn't sell. And she wouldn't mind really – it was his to live in or sell on, she'd said, so there was no reason to feel guilty. Well, almost no reason. But he doesn't want to think about his father tonight.

The news is just coming to an end as he walks into the sitting room. Kate doesn't look up at first, though she knows well he's there. Cold-shoulder time. He apologises for being late and she looks up to raise one impeccable eyebrow. His dinner is in the microwave, she tells him, and he continues on through the double French doors his mother had loved so much when they were first put in – now the paint is chipped and one of the handles hangs loose and useless. It's cold – the house is too hard to heat in winter, and in spring they stop trying, pretending it's warmer outside than it is.

Dinner is a plate of congealed beef casserole – he puts it in the microwave and presses buttons on autopilot while checking his phone. The kitchen table is covered in paperwork – Kate's been doing a clear-out. Well, half a clear-out. The bit where you take everything out of the box, but not the bit where you file the contents or bin them. There are credit-card bills going back ten years, utility bills, pension statements – all loose on the table, with an empty box on the floor.

He sticks his head into the sitting room. "Can I bin those papers?"

She looks up from her phone. "No, there's stuff in there we need to keep."

"Well, will I put them back in the box?"

"Just leave them. I'll sort them tomorrow. It's not like there's anywhere to store them." She sighs. A Kate-sigh that means the house is too small and she hates it.

"How were the boys?" he asks, with one eye on the microwave to catch it before it pings.

"Fine. Asking why you weren't here again."

"I had to work on that board report – I'll be home earlier tomorrow."

"Sure."

The microwave pings – an unnecessarily loud beep that keeps going even after the door is opened.

"I hate that noise," Kate says, under her breath.

Sam pushes some paper aside to make space and sits down to eat.

He remembers something. "Oh, listen, I was up town at lunchtime and got new PlayStation games for the boys – they were reduced. Will I put them at the end of their beds?"

Kate walks into the kitchen. "I keep telling you – you can't just buy them games out of the blue like that – it's spoiling them. It's not like it's anyone's birthday."

"Ah come on, it's just two games and they were next to nothing."

"Sam, it's not about how much they were – the boys don't understand prices. But you can't give them games because you feel guilty for working late every night. It sends all the wrong messages. Just be here at bedtime instead."

Sam puts down his fork and looks up at her. "That's not fair. I'm working late because it's my job – that's how we get money."

Kate shakes her head. "You can tell yourself that all you

want, but you've been working later and later since I gave up work – you know you have, this isn't the first time I've said it. And when you *are* here, your head is stuck in your phone. You may as well not be here at all."

"Well, I don't exactly get a great welcome even when I am here. I may as well be at work. You hardly say a word to me when I come in. Same every night."

"Oh Sam, it's all about you, isn't it?" She shakes her head again, and walks back into the sitting room, closing the door behind her.

In the quiet kitchen, at the big oak table of his childhood, Sam sits on his own eating lukewarm beef casserole. He pulls out his phone to look at the Dún Laoghaire house again. Everything will be fine once they move.

Chapter 10

Sam – Monday, April 11th

It's only when the cushion fort collapses for the fourth time that Sam gives up and sits down on the (cushionless) couch. The boys try to pull him up again but he's wrecked – he needs five minutes. They're jumping up and down on front of him now and saying something about hot chocolate but he's taken out his phone and he's zoning them out. Just five minutes and he'll be fine. Five quiet minutes in the company of his phone. Ideally tea too, but that would mean getting up. He really should train Seth to make tea.

The boys admit defeat and go back to rebuilding their fort.

"Oh, thank God," Sam says under his breath, sinking down further into the seat.

His phone rings – it's Kate reminding him to put on the pork.

"The oven's just preheating," he lies. "How was the training course?"

She says it was great, and good to get back into the world of work even for just one day, and that she's at Pearse Street station now waiting for a DART.

He hangs up, and another five minutes go by before he can peel himself off the couch to preheat the oven. As soon as he's up, the boys try to drag him to the fort again. "Wait till the pork is on," he tells them, then hides in the kitchen with a cup of tea. Ten short minutes later, they pull him back to the game.

"Right," he says, "I'm the monster and this is my den – *go!*"

Squealing, they get up and run, and he chases them around every room of the house, until the three of them collapse panting and laughing on the beanbag in the boys' room.

"Okay, I've got to check some work messages now and I'd better take a look at the dinner."

He gets up and heads downstairs.

When Kate arrives in, he's engrossed in his Twitter feed in the kitchen and doesn't notice until her keys clatter on the counter. She gives him a peck on the cheek and asks where the boys are. Sam shoves his phone in his pocket and says the boys are upstairs – but she doesn't hear him – she's gone through to the sitting room.

A moment later she's back, and she's frowning.

A Kate-frown that means she's about to ask some pointed questions.

"What's the story with the sitting room – I just found half a banana squashed on the couch and I can see paint on the wall – did you let them paint in there? And why are all the cushions on the floor?"

"Oh, we were just playing cushion-forts. I didn't spot the banana or the paint – I'll clean it up now – you sit down."

"Is their bedroom as bad?"

Sam doesn't answer.

"And what's the story with the washing – please say that's not the same wash I asked you to hang out?" she asks, pointing at the machine.

"Sorry, I totally forgot," he says. "I'll do it now."

"And the dinner?"

"Yes! The dinner is on – actually it should be just done now," he says, opening the oven.

"But where are the potatoes and vegetables?"

She has her hands on her hips now. This is not good.

"Um. Was I supposed to do potatoes?"

"Sam, have you ever heard of anyone having 'pork steak and nothing' for dinner?"

"No, but you didn't tell me to do potatoes." Wrong thing to say.

"Oh God, can I not go out for one day and trust you to keep the place tidy and make the dinner?" She sighs. "Have the boys done their homework?"

This time he knows better than to answer directly. "You sit down, I'll make you a cup of tea, and I'll sort everything. Don't worry."

She goes upstairs to change, muttering under her breath. Minutes later he follows her up with a cup of tea and an apology.

She relents. "Look, I know it's hard to get everything done when you're minding the kids, but that's what I do every day. Imagine if I just played cushion-forts with them and never cooked dinner or checked their homework?"

He hangs his head. You don't argue with Kate when you're in the wrong.

"And I get it that living here you can't help trying to recreate your childhood, but I am not Claire and you are not John, and it's the 21st century now. Men can cook dinners too."

"In my defence, they did have great fun – it was good to have a bit of time with them."

"Okay, but next time just do the basics around the house too – please?"

He nods.

"And I'm sorry for bringing up your dad. That wasn't fair."

"Don't worry," he says, and gives her a kiss.

At dinner, the boys land him in it when Kate asks how the day went.

"Did you have lots of fun playing with Dad?"

"Yeah," Jamie says, "but he was on his phone a lot too."

"Hey! That's not fair. I played with you guys for hours! I was only on my phone at the end when I was shattered tired."

Seth gives him a bit of leeway. "Well, you did play forts with us, and chasing, but you were on your phone while we were painting."

"For two minutes – guys, come on!" Sam rolls his eyes at Kate, but she's not looking over.

As if jumping on the bandwagon, his phone rings loudly in his back pocket. He pulls it out to a chorus of "*No electronics at the table!*" from the boys and a look from Kate. He rejects the call and puts the phone in his pocket.

"Who was it?" Seth asks.

"Nobody."

Kate gives him a funny look. Wrong answer – he should have said it was work.

He gets up to refill his glass of water and, with his back to the table, sends a quick text.

Call you later x

When he sits back down, Kate is watching him. He's going to have to get a lot better at this.

Chapter 11

Sam – Saturday, June 18th

"*Oh my God, look at the big green!*" Jamie shouts, bouncing up and down in the back seat.

"Don't say 'oh my God'," Kate says as she always does, but Sam can hear the smile in her voice.

Seth is quieter, still unsure about the big move. But having his own bedroom will swing it – no more putting up with Jamie's toys all over the floor, and no more hyperactive bedtime games when he's trying to read his book.

As they turn into the cul-de-sac, Jamie tries to sound out the name on the signpost. "*Will-Ow-Valley* – is that what it's called, Mum? I thought you said we were moving to Dún Laoghaire?"

"Yes, Dún Laoghaire is the town, and Willow Valley is the estate, but it's Will-Oh, not Will-Ow – does that make sense?"

"Will-Oh Valley," Jamie repeats, trying it out for size as they pull into the driveway of Number 26.

Kate starts to unbuckle her seatbelt, then stops. "Actually, you'd better park somewhere else – the removal van will need to park in the driveway – well, if it fits."

"Ah, we can move when they arrive – will we just go in and show the boys first?"

"But it's easier if we move now, then we don't have to worry about it."

"Fine."

Sam reverses out. There's no space on their side of the small cul-de-sac, so he parks outside the house across the road.

"God, I'd forgotten how small the road is – what do people do when they have visitors?" Kate says. "But, Sam, we can't park here – this is someone else's house."

"Kate, what do you want me to do? You just asked me to move."

"Yes, but not so close to someone else's driveway! The back of the car is practically on it!"

"I'm not blocking it – they'd be able to get out if they need to. And once our moving van arrives, I'll park across our driveway instead. Come on, let's just go inside."

Kate shakes her head but gets out of the car and all four make their way into their new home. The boys run for the stairs to see their rooms – even Seth is excited. Sam can feel it too – the now familiar house is different when he sees it through his children's first-time eyes. The brown-and-beige stairs carpet will have to go, but Seth and Jamie are shouting about how soft it is compared to the wooden floors they're used to. The gold-textured wallpaper with paisley print will eventually go too, but Seth says it's beautiful, running his hand along the wall as he climbs the stairs.

Kate and Sam follow them up, watching for reactions as they open the first door.

"Mum, it's an orange bath!"

The boys are inside the main bathroom, incredulous at the peach-coloured suite. Kate is laughing now.

Sam smiles. "It's technically called 'peach', and it was very fashionable back when me and your mum were small kids. Not so much now, but we'll get a new bathroom eventually."

"Why would we need a new one?" Jamie is confused. "This is the most beautiful bathroom I've ever seen!" He's running his hand across the furry toilet-seat cover – also peach.

Kate winces and pulls his hand away.

"Come on, let's go see your rooms," she says, discreetly pulling off the toilet-seat cover when their backs are turned.

Jamie runs into the next room and immediately collapses in a dramatic faint on the floor, his current favourite way of expressing delight.

"Oh my God – sorry – I mean oh my gosh – my room is huge! And it has red flowers on the wall – I love it!"

"That's Mum and Dad's room, Jamie – yours is the next one down, just past the hot press," Sam clarifies, steering him back out.

If Jamie is a little less blown away by his slightly smaller room at the front of the house, he doesn't show it. Standing in the middle of the floor, he turns, arms aloft, mouth open, taking it all in – the blue-rose wallpaper, peeling in places, the matching blue carpet, and the long navy curtains.

"I love it, but there's no bed – do people sleep on the floor in new houses?" he asks, lying down to try it out.

"Your bed is on the way – remember the removal van?" Sam says, sitting down beside him. "So you'll have the same bed you slept in last night, just in a different room. Come on, let's see Seth's."

Kate and Seth have gone into the second front bedroom. Bigger than Jamie's, the theme is similar but this time in matching greens. Cabbage roses on a sage background cover the walls, and the carpet is a seaweed-green colour Sam hasn't seen on any floor in twenty years. But Seth is smiling. It's much bigger than his old bedroom in Booterstown and, best of all, it's for him and him alone. Hoisting himself up onto the windowsill, he looks out and tells his brother he can see the green. Just in time, Kate spots him trying to open the window and runs forward to grab him.

"Seth! You know better than to open an upstairs window!" She tries it herself but it's locked.

"Don't worry – all the upstairs windows are locked, and I have the keys downstairs – they're safe," Sam says.

"Sorry, Mum," Seth says. "Anyway, when will my books be here, and my bed?"

Kate turns to Sam. "Actually, the van should be here by now – do you want give them a call?"

Sam nods and goes downstairs to get his phone, leaving Kate to show the spare bedroom to the boys. Outside, there's no sign of the van, but there's a man standing behind Sam's car, taking a photo of his registration plate.

"Everything okay there?" Sam asks, approaching the man, who straightens up and lowers the phone.

"Is this your car?"

"Eh, yeah – we're just moving in. Is something wrong?"

"You're parked outside my house, blocking my driveway – I was about to call the local Garda station to have it moved."

Seriously? Sam laughs. "Sorry, I'll move it now."

"I'm not sure what's so funny. You can't just block my driveway like that."

"But it's not blocking it, it's just beside it," Sam says, eying up the position of the car in relation to the entrance to the house. Two people can play the pedantic game. "But I'll move it now – it was just until the removal van arrived."

"Removal van? You can't drive a big truck up this little road! It'll have to park down at the green."

This time Sam bursts out laughing.

His new neighbour frowns and pushes up his glasses. "I really don't see what's so funny. We're having a birthday party for my daughter, and people need to be able to drive up the road to drop their children off. They won't fit if there's a huge lorry here."

"It's not huge, and it'll probably fit in our driveway anyway," Sam says, trying to work out if it would. "But can't your guests park down at the green? Like, there's no way the moving people are going to carry a bed and a couch all the way up the road, but surely your guests can walk up?"

The man shakes his head and throws up his hands. "This is very inconvenient. It's not how things work around here. You can't just park where you want and have trucks taking up the whole road. It's not on." He folds his arms, and fixes red-rimmed eyes on Sam.

This isn't going to be resolved by standing here talking about it, Sam thinks, so he takes out his keys.

"I'm going to move the car now, and when the van arrives we'll move the furniture as quickly as we can, so we don't inconvenience your guests."

He should say something like thanks for the warm welcome, but then he'll just feel bad so instead he gets into the car and closes the door and misses whatever his neighbour says next.

What a start to settling in – Kate will not be impressed.

He moves the car back across his own drive, and when he gets out his neighbour has gone inside. Other than a slight rustle of leaves there's no sound anywhere on the street. There's no sound indoors either when he goes through the open front door of Number 26. He checks upstairs but they're not there. Then he sees them through the window – at the bottom of the overgrown garden.

He follows them outside, stopping to inspect the twisting, winding shrubs and bushes that cover nearly every inch of the garden. How much work will it take to clean this up? And which ones are weeds? Underfoot, he spots what looks like a path of stepping stones, leading down to a garden shed. The bolt is rusted over and it takes an effort to get it open – the door creaks as he pulls it towards him. Inside it's dark and dusty and there's no light switch. An old-style push lawnmower stands against the back wall, and a metal toolbox sits on the ground beside it. There's a pitchfork, and a shovel, and a rake like the one his dad used to have for gathering leaves in the garden in Booterstown. The memory brings a tinge of sadness and he pushes it away. Up high, there's a shelf with some battered cans of paint, all in various shades of white. Where did the previous owner use those, he wonders – apart from the reassuringly bland spare room, the house is a 1980s rainbow. The shed floor is dusty, and the small window is covered in cobwebs, but it's a good size and he'll be able to fit all four bikes in there once he cleans it up. Blinking in the sun as he walks back out, he pulls the door shut and locks it again, then goes to join Kate and the boys at the bottom of the garden.

The three of them are standing with their backs to him but Jamie hears him coming. "Dad, look at this – there's a pond! Can you believe it! Me and Seth are going to swim in it later."

"No, you're not," says Kate. "Jamie, you wouldn't actually swim in that, would you? Look at all the algae!"

"What's algae?"

"That green stuff on top of the water," she says, turning to Sam. "We'll need to clean the pond. Or maybe drain it and fill it in with concrete?"

Jamie wraps his arms around her waist. "No, Mum! We love the pond – please don't!"

"We'll see. Either way, you're not swimming in it. Gross."

Seth throws a stone into the pond. Delighted with the new activity, Jamie picks up a handful of stones and throws them in too.

"We won't need to fill it in at all," Kate says to Sam. "They'll do it for us if we're lucky. Any sign of the removal van?"

"I rang them and they're about ten minutes away now – traffic apparently. I met a really snippy neighbour though. The guy whose house we parked outside. Not impressed. He was actually going to call the Guards about it."

Kate rolls her eyes. "Seriously? I did tell you not to park there though."

"Ah come on, I wasn't even blocking his driveway. And then he started going on about the removal van and saying they need to park down at the green. Can you imagine me and the moving guys carrying our furniture up the road, piece by piece?" Kate smiles at that. She's the old Kate when she smiles – the silver-blonde with the glint in her eye who caught his attention twenty years earlier. Glimpses of that Kate keep him going when they're drowning in the mediocrity of credit-card bills and school lunches and will we have spaghetti bolognese for tea. No doubt it's the same for her. Can she still see the person he was then? The idealist who was going to change the world, before he settled for the healthy pay packet? But then that same pay packet bought them this place, and allowed her to give up work – ideals don't pay the bills.

One unexpected splash later and the smile is gone, and both of them are reaching to pull Jamie out of the pond. It's shallow, and when he manages to stand up the water only goes to his knees, but he's soaked. He bursts into tears as Kate pulls him out, hugging his wet body to her.

"We need to get rid of it," she mutters to Sam as she walks

back towards the house, Jamie still crying in her arms.

"It was his own fault, Dad, don't worry," says Seth, who is still throwing stones into the pond.

Sam nods, watching the ripples expand out with each splash. So much for day one.

Chapter 12

Sunday – June 19th 2016

He paces up and down the living room, wondering what possessed him to stay here. He should have run – he absolutely should have run. Anywhere. The airport, the ferry – anywhere. That's it – he's going. In his bedroom, he starts throwing clothes into a bag. He doesn't need much – his mother will send him a credit card and he'll buy more. He stuffs his phone in his pocket and picks up his keys from the coffee table, and just then the doorbell rings. He drops the keys on the floor and his heart feels like it's going to jump right out of his chest, and he knows then he should have run – he absolutely should have run.

He doesn't move. The doorbell rings again. Still he stands, promising himself that if he can have just one more chance, he'll go and never come back. But today is not the day for chances.

The doorbell rings a third time, and then the banging starts. And the voice. Low and calm and resigned.

"Open the door, Austin, or I will break it down. I promise you, it will be worse if I have to break it down."

He moves to the door.

"I will literally cut out your tongue and staple it to your mother's kitchen table if you do not open this door."

He takes three steps forward and reaches for the handle, while voices in his head scream at him to push past and run. But there's no pushing past. They're both inside the apartment now, and the door is shut.

"Nice pad you've got here – I like the views," he says, looking down at the rooftops and the river below. "Very swish. I suppose this is how stockbrokers live. Costs a fair bit, I'd say?"

"Yeah, that's why I didn't have the cash for you – my rent was due, plus two of my customers didn't pay me last week. But I'll have it all for you by Tuesday." Austin does everything to keep his voice steady, but it quivers on the last words and he knows he sounds like he's about to cry.

"See, that's the problem – you need to get the cash up front. No money, no coke. Which is what I should have done with you – but I thought we were working together. I thought I could trust you."

"You can trust me! Two days – that's all I need."

"But you were supposed to contact me to meet on Friday, and you didn't. Do you think it's nice to do that? To leave me for two days? I think it's a bit rude, to be honest."

"I know, I'm sorry. I wanted to get the problem sorted before I had to tell you. I thought maybe you'd forgotten . . . "

"Forgotten?"

"Forgotten that we were to meet two days ago . . . " Austin trails off.

"What do you think I am? Some kind of imbecile who just forgets he's owed forty grand? Is that what you mean?"

"No! No way. I knew you didn't forget the money. I just thought you forgot to meet up . . . "

"But I didn't. You were supposed to contact me. And you didn't. Because you hoped I'd just write it off. And you'd get to keep the cash."

"That's not how it was at all – I just –"

"I can't have that, you know. I can't have people like you running around thinking you've got one up on me." He picks up a cream silk cushion from the couch. "Not good for business. You know?"

When he sees the gun, his knees give way. He begs but no-one is listening. He hears the click and feels the softness of the cushion against the side of his head. He screams but it's inside his mind. There's no time for a sound to come out before his lifeless body hits the floor, his blood seeping slowly into the deep-pile carpet.

Chapter 13

Kate – Friday, June 24th

Oh God, would it never end? Kate's really not sure she can get through the final week of school runs. All that driving and waiting and waving. And the small talk. Dear Jesus, the small talk! The weather. The teacher. The "Do you think they're getting enough Irish homework?" conversation, on repeat. The stuff she thought she was missing when she couldn't have it. And now – overdose. All for the sake of picking up two little boys who mostly couldn't care less that she was there every day, instead of the bus they used to take to crèche. Okay, that's not really true. But sometimes, when they're really tired and grumpy, she wonders if maybe they did like it better when they were heading off with their friends.

And then there's the hour in between. Why on earth couldn't the school have Junior Infants finish at the same time as First Class? Or at least provide some kind of supervised homework club. Sitting in the car with hyper Jamie every day isn't good for her sanity, and it's probably not great for his either. And with just one week to go, all attempts at story-time or chat-time are done – he's getting the iPad and there's no way she's feeling guilty about it, even if his teacher walks past the car and waves in.

Weaving in and out of Rock Road lunchtime traffic, she switches on the radio. Nothing but foaming-at-the-mouth texters at this time of day. One person calls for the death penalty for whoever killed that stockbroker last week, and the next person says he got what he deserves if he was taking drugs. The host keeps going on about him being a politician's son, as if that somehow makes a difference either way. She switches off.

On autopilot, she signals left at the turn for the school. A DART speeds by and she feels a pang for her commute, and regret that she didn't appreciate it at the time. Snaking up the narrow road, dipping in and out behind parked cars to let other drivers by, she finds a spot and pulls in. Ten minutes to spare – excellent.

She sits back in the seat and opens Facebook. But before she has a chance to scroll through more than half a dozen pictures, a knock on the window startles her. Looking up, she sees Ruth's eager smile beaming in. Great. Now she can't even have those ten minutes on Facebook.

She rolls down the window, and attempts a friendly smile.

"Are you walking down?" Ruth asks. "So warm today, isn't it? I hardly know what to wear these mornings – the temperature keeps changing. I had a jumper on yesterday, and I'm in a T-shirt today." She holds out her arms so that Kate can see she is in fact wearing a T-shirt. "But thank God it's Friday!"

Thank God indeed, thinks Kate, opening the door and pocketing her phone – nothing like spending ten extra minutes with Ruth.

"So how is your new house going, Kate? You just moved in, did you?"

"Yep, this day last week – so far, so good."

"Ah brilliant, you must be delighted. Your old house was so small, wasn't it? I'd say the boys are only thrilled."

"Well, it wasn't that small – but yes, they're happy to have their own bedrooms."

"Sorry, I didn't mean it was small, I just meant your new house must be so much bigger – we must call out to see you there sometime!"

"Sure, absolutely," says Kate, making a note to put Ruth's kid at the bottom of the playdate list.

"Have you met your neighbours – are they nice?"

"We haven't really met anyone yet," Kate replies, deciding the snotty man with the parking hang-up from across the road doesn't count. "I get the impression most people on the road work during the day, so there's nobody around. I spotted one old lady who lives two doors up from us, but haven't met her yet. And we haven't seen our next-door neighbours either – maybe they're away or something."

"Ooh, took their kids out of school, did they? I totally get why people do it, but it's just not fair on the teachers."

"Well, I don't know if they have kids or not and I don't know for sure if they're away – I just mean I haven't seen them yet. Though in fairness, there's not a whole lot going on at school at this time of year anyway – fair play to them if they did, I reckon."

"Hmm, but if everyone did it, where would we be?"

Not walking down the road having this monstrously boring conversation with you anyway, Kate thinks, but says nothing.

"Are you going away anywhere this summer, Kate, or maybe not with the move?"

"My mum has a B&B in Salthill so we'll head there as soon as the boys finish up. Sam's going to come down at weekends, or at least some weekends – there's a huge amount of work to do on the house too."

"Oh Galway – that'll be so lovely for you, Kate. Just perfect. And even if the weather's not great, sure it's not costing you anything if it's your mum's house. Lovely."

They walk in silence for a few moments, then Ruth starts up again.

"We're off to France. Driving over. We do it every year. I know flying is quicker, but if we have the car we can drive around, see the little villages and the countryside – *really* show the country to the kids. Otherwise, sure, they could be anywhere. It's not a holiday if you're not learning something new, is it?"

"Absolutely, Ruth, absolutely. We'll be down in Galway learning about candy-floss and ice cream and the odd Supermac, I'd say. We'll come back in September fluent in arcade games."

"You will, of course," says Ruth, though she seems unsure how to take it.

Feeling guilty, Kate pulls it back.

"I'm kidding – there's loads to do down there – and I know what you mean – it's great to have a look around when you visit somewhere new. You guys will have a ball in France."

Turning into the school grounds, they wander towards the usual spot, where a group of Junior Infants' mums are already gathered, plus Joe, the token stay-at-home dad. Kate is taking out her phone, wondering if she can get away with checking some messages, when blissfully it rings.

"Kate? Hello?"

It's her mother.

"Hi, Mum, how are you?" Kate says, signalling to Ruth that she needs to take the call.

"I'm good, love – how are you and the boys? Are you all set for next week?"

"Absolutely – they finish on Tuesday and we're coming down to you on Wednesday. I cannot *wait.*"

"Oh, is everything okay? Is the new house okay?"

"It's fine – lots of work needed, but plenty of space. It's not that I'm dying to get out of there, I'm just fed up with the school runs, and fed up having no-one to talk to during the day when Sam's at work."

"Don't you meet other mums at the school?"

"Yes, but one or two of them are just painful," says Kate, walking further away from Ruth. "And the rest all know each other for ages whereas I'm kind of a lurker. I hate the school run."

"It can't be that bad – you just don't know the other parents yet."

Kate moves across the yard, making sure she's out of earshot. "I've been doing this since January and there's literally one mum I've become friends with, and she's only here Mondays and Tuesdays. She works the rest of the week. I think I should have done that – gone part-time instead of giving up."

"Well, would you think about going back – try to get something part-time?"

"I might. Or I might try working for myself from home. We have a spare room in the new house, and I was looking at it this morning – it would make a great home office. I need to have a think about it. But yes, I'm going to lose my mind if this is all I do every day."

"Kate, dare I say it – you're never happy – you spent the last two years wishing you could be there to collect the boys."

"I know, Mum, but maybe there's something in between. I need to use my brain again."

"Ah, I know, I get it. I never saw myself being a stay-at-home mum either – well, you know what happened there."

Kate nods into the phone.

"What about the golf – doesn't that keep you busy?"

"Yes, but like, not every day. I think I need something a bit more challenging on the mental side, you know?" Kate says, glancing up at the school doors. No sign of Jamie yet.

"I know, love. And what about Miller – has he called to see the new house?"

"Yes. Twice already and we're only there a week. I think I need to set some ground rules there."

"Be nice, Kate. You know he means well. And he just wants to be able to spend more time with you and the kids now you're living so close."

"Ha! He barely acknowledges the kids. Which is fine with me, to be honest, but it's just awkward. Anyway, Jamie's class just came out – gotta go! I'll phone you over the weekend."

"Make sure you do."

"Bye, Mum, bye."

Jamie sees her and runs into her arms. Holding him in a tight hug, she kisses the top of his head and inhales his small-boy smell. He steps back and smiles up at her, proudly showing a "*Good Work*" sticker on his school jumper.

"I missed you today, Mum," he says, hugging her again.

I missed you too, she thinks, as she hugs him back. They're not so bad really, these kids of hers.

Chapter 14

Kate- Monday, June 27th

Someone is waving frantically at Kate as she pulls into her driveway – a small figure with flying arms and flyaway white hair, gesturing at her from two doors up. What now? All she wants to do is go into the house to have the coffee she would have had earlier if the household hadn't descended into the usual Monday-morning chaos of unmade lunches and lost shoes.

"*Hellooo!*" says the lady, beckoning her over.

Letting out one last sigh while still out of earshot, Kate plasters on a neighbourly smile and walks around to Number 24.

"Come in, come in," says the lady, walking into her house and beckoning for Kate to follow.

Inside the front door, she has a package, which she hands to Kate with great ceremony.

"For you. It was delivered about half an hour ago but you weren't there. And next door are at work. So I took it in and minded it for you." She somehow make Kate's absence sound like a failing.

"I was taking my kids to school – thank you for accepting it," Kate says, stepping backwards towards the front door again.

"I'm Rosemary. Come on in for a cup of tea!"

"Oh, you're so kind to offer, but I really have to go – we have so much to do in the house – we've only just moved in. Sorry, I'm Kate, by the way." She's unsure whether or not she should shake hands.

Rosemary has no interest in such formalities and, taking the package back from Kate, she places it on the mahogany table in the hall, and ushers her into the kitchen.

"Come on, you can spare five minutes – everyone needs a cup of tea."

If Kate thought her new kitchen was old-fashioned, Rosemary's is like stepping back to the 1940s. Green-painted cupboards surround an old porcelain sink, complete with the orange stains of time. A round table sits in the middle of the room, covered with a lace tablecloth and topped with a small bowl of artificial posies.

Rosemary gestures to Kate to sit down and puts a kettle on the range – a range!

"Your kitchen is lovely," Kate says, still not sure what to make of the time-warp.

"Oh, I know it's old-fashioned, but I like it this way. It was always good enough for my Bob when he was alive, and I'm not about to change it now. I'd say you've a good bit of work to do on poor Mrs Osborne's house though, God rest her soul." Rosemary crosses herself.

"We do, but we'll get there. Don't worry about tea for me," Kate says, waving away the cup that's coming her way. "I'll just have a glass of water if that's okay."

"No tea? I could make you coffee – I have a jar of coffee in the back here somewhere." She begins to rummage through a cupboard. "I remember we had it for Bob's wake, and I'm sure we didn't use it all."

"Honestly, I'm fine, I don't need coffee either. Water is great. Really."

Rosemary frowns, obviously perplexed at Kate's lack of interest in tea, and fills a glass of water from the tap. She places it on the table.

"Biscuit?" she asks, opening a tin of USA and offering it to Kate.

"No, thank you, I still need to get breakfast – I probably shouldn't have biscuits before breakfast."

Rosemary looks at her watch, perhaps trying to work out why anyone wouldn't have had breakfast by quarter past nine on a Monday morning, but she says nothing and puts the lid back on the biscuit tin.

"So have you met anyone else yet?" she asks, pulling on a small pair of silver-rimmed glasses, inspecting her new neighbour.

"No, not really – you're the first!" Kate says brightly, trying to make up for not being a tea-drinker. "Well, actually, my husband did meet the man from across the road – Number 34. He got quite cross with Sam for parking outside his house."

Rosemary takes the bait. "Ah, you met Noel." Her eyes light up behind the glasses. "Yes, Noel is very protective of his house, his garden, his child, and his precious wife. Georgia is her name, but you probably won't have seen her because she's always at work. All day. I don't know when she sees the child at all. I know it's the fashion these days but, between you and me, I don't think it's right for mothers to be out at work all the time."

Kate smiles a beatific smile. "I used to work full-time, and I'm thinking of going back actually. I think it's good for kids to see that both parents can earn a living."

"Well, of course," says Rosemary, "but you probably weren't working the whole time, I bet. That child never sees her mother. She's off in her childminder's house after school every day, and only gets home when Georgia picks her up at six or seven o'clock. And she has no brothers or sisters – it must be lonely. How many do you have?"

"Brothers and sisters?" Kate asks.

"No, children – how many children?"

"Oh sorry, I've two boys. Seth and Jamie. How old is the little girl across the road?"

"Annabel? She's ten. Noel was well into his forties when he met Georgia – she's a lot younger. He's no looker, Noel, but he has a fair bit of money. And Georgia's no fool. She knew just how to play it. Now she has it all – nice house, nice car, a child, a husband who'd do anything for her, and she can swan around all day doing her job in digital marketing – whatever that is when it's at home."

"Oh, I'm a digital marketer too – that's funny."

Rosemary gives her a quizzical look. "So it's a real job? When Georgia said it, I kind of thought she was making it up. Like maybe she worked on reception somewhere but wanted to make herself sound important."

Kate smiles. "Yes, it's a real job. It's just marketing really, but online – on the internet – instead of the old-school way."

"Well, I don't know much about the internet really. Don't have it here in the house and never will – no need for it if you ask me. And what does your husband do, Kate?"

"He's a trader." Seeing confusion on Rosemary's face, Kate elaborates. "He buys and sells stocks and shares. So basically he spends all day watching the stock market, and trying to buy low and sell high, to make money for his clients. He's very good at it."

"Oh, like that poor fella who was killed – Maureen Granger's son. I voted for her once, you know. Awful thing. About her son, I mean, not her." She pauses to think about it for a moment. "So your husband does that job too – is that why you stopped working? Because he has a good job and you don't need to work now?"

Ouch. "My job was also very good, but I found it hard to keep up the hours and be there for the kids," Kate explains, taking a sip of tepid tap water. "Sam can't leave the office during the day, so it always fell on me to run to the school or crèche if one of them was sick. Eventually it all just got too stressful and I decided to take a break and be with the kids."

"It's lovely being with them, isn't it? I was always at home with ours. You never get those days back."

"Oh, I know, and on that note, I'd better go and get something done in the house before it's time to pick them up." She gets up, rinses out her glass and puts it on the draining board. "Thanks for inviting me in and for taking the package – it was nice to meet you, Rosemary."

"Not at all, any time. And sure I'll see you again. I think we're the only two here in the mornings. So we'll do tea again. Or water."

Rosemary walks Kate to the door and hands her the package.

"Oh, I forgot to say – there was a man calling at your door while you were out too. Tall, skinny fella with longish hair and glasses. Looked a bit like a scrawny owl. Or do I mean tawny owl?"

Miller. Great. Saturday's hints had obviously fallen on deaf ears. "Thanks, Rosemary, that was probably my brother Miller. He must have forgotten that I'd be on the school run. Anyway, I'll run, thanks again."

"Miller, that's a funny name. Is that his first name?"

"Yes, my mum was reading *Death of a Salesman* when she was pregnant. I'll see you soon – bye now."

Kate is almost running by the time she gets to her own house, and she goes straight to the coffee machine once she's inside. Maybe it's time to find a job.

"Brilliant. That's just brilliant."

Kate puts her phone down on the table, a little more forcibly than is good for the glass screen or the listening ears. Too late, she sees the boys exchange a look.

"What's wrong?" asks Seth – always the leader of this small band of brothers and poser of tricky inquiries.

Kate turns to look at two small faces: both dark-haired replicas of their dad, with soft, open brown eyes and a scattering of freckles barely discernible to anyone but her. Seth is taller than Jamie, but there the physical differences end. Sometimes it feels as though she's living in a house with three different-sized clones of one person.

"Nothing, sweetheart, just a message from Dad to say that he'll be late home. Again."

Both sets of eyes narrow simultaneously beneath anxious frowns.

"It's fine!" she says. "Sure we'll have tea together the three of us, and then it's bedtime already – we can do an extra chapter of your book tonight."

Shit, she really needs to watch her words. And really, it's not Sam's fault he's working late. Long hours go with the territory – they'd known that when he took the job. It just feels like it's all shifting in opposite directions – she has less to get her out of the house than ever before, meanwhile Sam is coming home later and later. Of course that's easy for him – the pressure is off. No more school drop-off in the morning, no more debating who should pick up when someone is sick.

But maybe Sam's enjoying it a little too much. Or maybe she's enjoying it a little too little.

Sam, as usual, is clueless.

It had flared up again on Friday night, when he called to say he was going for drinks with a client.

"But I have dinner ready – I told the boys we were all eating together tonight – why didn't you tell me?" Kate had said.

"I didn't know about it till just now. Sorry – it's a big client, I can't say no. Sure keep dinner for me – I'll have it when I get home. It won't go to waste – you know me after a few beers."

"That's not really the point. I've been here with the kids all afternoon and I'm wrecked – I was looking forward to you coming home and helping out. Now I have to do bedtime on my own again. Believe me, it is *not* about dinner."

"Kate, you know I'd come home if I could, but with this new client I have to be able to put in the social hours as well as the work hours. And it all pays off – you know it does. You didn't mind using last year's bonus for the ski trip – you can't have it every way, you know!"

It took everything in her power not to throw the phone across the room at that.

"It was your ski trip too – don't try to put this on me. What is this, 1952?"

But she knew, even as she hung up the call, that he didn't get it at all. The same argument had been bubbling just below the surface for months, bursting through occasionally, and never fully resolved.

And now Sam is working late again. Just brilliant.

Chapter 15

Kate – Wednesday, June 29th

The ladder wobbles when Kate rests her foot on the first metal rung. She puts more force on it. It doesn't inspire confidence, but Sam was up and down to the attic over and over at the weekend and it held, so it's probably fine. Probably. Taking a deep breath, she starts to climb, then hoists herself up into the dark hole in the ceiling. Must and dust invade her nose immediately. She coughs and tries not to breathe too deeply as she crawls in a little further, feeling around for the light. Sam had said it was on a beam just to the right of the opening. There it is. She blinks as light fills the attic. Now where would he have put the suitcases? Her eyes travel the breadth of the space, trying to make out objects in dark corners. Baby furniture they should have passed on long ago, Christmas decorations, winter clothes – and suitcases. She crawls towards the biggest one and lugs it back over to the opening, then awkwardly down the ladder. They could probably do with the smaller case too, but maybe Sam can get it later – one trip up the shaky ladder is enough for now.

Back in her bedroom, something feels different –

everything has gone quiet. The boys had been running around the back garden, yelling and laughing, before she went up into the attic. What are they up to now? She walks to the window and looks out, her eyes going immediately to the pond. But there's nobody there. They must have gone back into the house. She heads downstairs, calling their names.

"We're in the kitchen, Mum, making tea for Miller!" comes Seth's voice.

In the kitchen, her brother is sitting at the table, staring into space. Despite the June sun, a beanie covers his unkempt hair and his washed-out grey T-shirt does nothing to hide the thinness of his frame. His bony fingers are cupped around a mug of something.

"Miller. I didn't know you were calling today? And boys, you can't make tea – please tell me you didn't touch the kettle?"

"No, we didn't go near the kettle, Mum. We put the teabag in the cup and filled it with water from the tap. That's okay, isn't it?"

Kate looks at the brownish water in Miller's cup and wonders if he's tasted it. Or if he'd notice either way.

"Okay, well done for not touching the kettle – but who answered the door? That's another thing you know well you're not to do."

"But we looked out the sitting-room window and saw it was Uncle Miller, so it was safe. Wasn't it, Mum?"

In theory, she thinks, but out loud she just tells the boys to go back out and play, then sits down opposite her brother.

"Is everything all right?" she asks.

He turns his gaze to her. "Yes, all fine."

"We're really busy here getting ready for the Galway trip – I didn't realise you were calling. You should have phoned." Seeing confusion and a hint of hurt cross his face, she starts to feel guilty. "I just mean we might not have been here – it's a good idea to phone before you come over."

"It's not far. I don't mind if you're not here sometimes. It's much better than when you lived in Booterstown."

Kate sighs and gets up to boil the kettle. "I'll make you a proper cup of tea, but I have to pack then, okay?"

No reply, but a hint of a nod.

"So, how's your flatmate doing – Brax, is that his name?" What kind of name is Brax anyway? Millennials and their hipster names.

"He's fine, I guess. I don't really see him. He doesn't like me."

"I'm sure he does like you – he's probably just busy with his job. What does he do again?"

"He's a bike courier. I think he gets annoyed that I'm in the house all day. That's why it's good to come here."

Kate squeezes her eyes shut and takes a deep breath. "Well, you pay the rent, you're entitled to be there, so don't mind him. Though would it be a good time to try looking for work again? That would get you out of the house."

"I *have* tried. Nobody will hire me. And anyway I'm still working on my novel."

Oh Jesus, the famous novel. Kate fills two cups with boiling water. The novel that's been underway for ten years now, while their mother and Social Welfare pay his rent between them.

She is putting a cup of tea down in front of him as a key turns in the front door.

Sam is home on time for once.

"Hey – oh hi, Miller," he says, dropping his keys on the counter. "I didn't know you were calling in?"

"He's just dropped in to say bye to me and the boys before we head tomorrow, because he won't see us for the rest of the summer," Kate says, shooting Sam a look.

"Well, I could still call over to see Sam, I guess," Miller says, looking at his brother-in-law expectantly.

"Ah – I'll be working a lot while they're away – I won't be here much at all, buddy."

"I could come at the weekends?"

"I'll be going down to Galway a good bit at the weekends, and I have some business trips too. At the weekend."

Kate raises her eyebrows at Sam and he gives a tiny shrug. In fairness, Miller is the last person to wonder why business trips would take place on the weekend.

"Okay," Miller says, standing up and draining his tea. "I'll be around in the morning so."

"Oh, Miller, come on – you heard what I said!" Kate says, louder than she plans.

Miller turns to look at her, his grey eyes filled with all too familiar confusion.

"I'm sorry," she says. "I just mean we're going early in the morning so there's no point in calling around. And, look, after the summer when we're back, we can talk about a regular time for visits. You can't keep just showing up unannounced."

Miller stares at her, then walks out without a word, pulling the front door softly behind him. A slammed door would have helped with the inevitable guilt. Damn him anyway.

"Kate, that was a bit much, wasn't it? I don't love when he calls around either, but there's probably a better way to tell him, right?"

"Sam, you don't get it. You really don't."

"What? What do I not get?"

"Unless you grew up in my house, you can't get it."

"But that all happened such a long time ago – maybe it's time to get past it?"

She shakes her head. "No. Not possible. He never got past it, so the rest of us can't either. Look, he's fine, but I don't want him around all the time, and I don't like him around the boys when I'm not there. You know they let him in without asking me?"

"Well, he's their uncle – they don't know any better. Do you want me to talk to them?"

She shakes her head again and scrapes her hair back into a tiny ponytail, tying it with a bobbin.

"I'll do it – on the way down to Galway tomorrow. Can you keep an eye on them – I'm going for a run."

As her feet hit the pavement and the breeze hits her hair, it's working its magic already – me-time that lasts longer than the usual flick through Facebook while the boys watch TV. She glances at her neighbours' houses as she runs past. There's a car next door now – they're not away after all. And Rosemary is in her driveway, watering plants – she waves at Kate as she runs by. Someone drives past her – a woman in a silver car, with a child in the back. The car turns into Number 34 – it must be Georgia and her daughter. Kate runs on, down past the green, out to the main road, and down towards Dún Laoghaire. Irritations slip away with each footfall as the evening sun warms her face. Miller and Sam and home and school – it's all gone – there's only air and sky and ground and sea. And everything is good again.

On her way back into Willow Valley forty minutes later, she slows to a walk. The woman in Number 34 is carrying a bag in from the car and stops when she sees her. Reluctantly, Kate takes out her ear-buds.

"Hi – you must be the new person in Number 26? I saw you coming out of your house for your run. I'm Georgia."

"Yes, we just moved the weekend before last. I'm Kate, nice to meet you."

"So, how are you and your family settling in – is it two little boys you have?" Georgia asks, looking Kate up and down.

"Yes – Seth and Jamie. I think my husband met your husband the day we moved in." Kate waits to see what kind of reaction this brings, but Georgia doesn't seem fazed.

"Oh yes, the parking thing. Don't mind Noel, he gets very het up about things sometimes. I'm very nice and normal, I promise. So what do you do?"

"I'm in digital marketing. Well, I'm taking time out with the kids at the moment."

Georgia tilts her head to one side. "Aw, fair play to you. I couldn't do it, but you're absolutely right – they're only small for such a short time. I just couldn't deal with the drudgery side of it – the housework and all that." She looks at her nails. "And I'm terrible at crafts and baking. But I'm in awe of you mums who stay at home and do all that – seriously, fair play."

Kate digs her nails into the palm of her hand. You mums? Seriously, fuck right off!

"I'm no good at baking or crafting either," she says, making a huge effort to sound civil. "I'm not very good at being at home at all sometimes. But hey, I muddle through like everyone else, dreaming of that glass of wine after they go to bed."

Georgia smiles. "Now *that* I can relate to. You know who'd swap places with you though – your next-door neighbour in Number 25 – Sylvia. Now she'd love to be at home, I'd say. She *always* looks stressed and she never stops worrying about the kids. Have you met her?"

"No, not yet."

"Oh, you've probably seen her – small, brown curly hair, always looks rushed? Sometimes wears glasses? I mean she's lovely and everything, just a little neurotic, I think. And always a bit breathless, if you know what I mean?"

Kate doesn't really, but she's itching to get inside and under the shower. "Yes, I know . . . Listen, I should head on in, but nice to meet you." She gives a little wave and starts walking backwards towards her house.

"You too! Oh – watch out for Rosemary as well. Have you met her? She has a tendency to ambush people and drag them in for tea."

"Yes, I've met her and, yes, I've been ambushed."

"Ah, then I'm too late. But you know what, she's not a bad old thing – I think she's just lonely."

Kate nods and waves again, and this time she makes it home and through her front door, and even all the way up the stairs and into the peach-coloured shower before anyone else interrupts her.

Chapter 16

Sam – Friday, July 1st

He raises his glass. The first swallow makes him feel much better than it should, and the second one is even better. He takes a third, and puts the glass back down on the bar. His phone beeps – a text from Michael to say he's running ten minutes late. But Sam's not in any rush. No bedtime to worry about, and no texts home. Nobody to answer to for the whole weekend. He grins to himself, and unfolds the paper. It's a very long time since he's had a night like this.

Michael rushes in fifteen minutes later. "Sorry, man, I got a taxi from the flat and then the traffic was a nightmare – I should have walked and I'd have been here quicker."

"No worries – I'm happy out here with my paper and my beer. What'll you have?"

"No, I'll get this – same again?" Michael orders, taking the bar stool beside Sam. "So how're things – how's the new house looking?"

"Grand. Loads to do – more than I thought really. And, you know me, I'm not the best with DIY."

"Well, look, if you need a hand, I can come out to you – no bother."

"Ah, I'd hate to ask, but maybe for some of the electrics. I remember you did a great job on your mam's place the year before she . . . passed away." Shit, he didn't mean to bring up Bella.

Michael doesn't seem perturbed. "Listen, it's much easier if I give you a hand with it – Kate won't be pleased if you electrocute yourself trying to show you can do it, will she?"

"No, and actually they're away now for the summer so if you wanted to come out some night during the week we could try to get a few things done? Have a few beers after?"

"I've a few jobs on this week but what about next weekend?"

The barman puts a fresh pint in front of Sam and he takes a sip. "I'm meant to be going down to them in Galway but let me chat to Kate – it might make more sense if I stay up here. I'll give you a shout during the week about it. And thanks for the offer – I owe you."

"Don't worry. You've done enough for me over the years. It's the least I can do. So apart from all the work, how's it going?"

"Yeah, good. The main thing is the boys get to play outside the front now without worrying about traffic, and there's more space for all of us."

"The leafy suburbs, eh? You'll be having drinks on the lawn and barbecues with the neighbours in no time."

"We haven't met anyone yet at all actually. Early days though. Loads of time."

"The closest I ever got to a barbecue with the neighbours is that time the little shit two doors down set fire to his mam's couch," says Michael, grinning.

Sam snorts into his beer, trying not to laugh mid-swallow. "Jesus, Michael, I'd say you see it all in those flats. Did you ever think of moving?"

"Nah, I couldn't part with it now after all these years. And my mam'd be looking down in horror if I did. Remember her chasing us with the wooden spoon that time we stole penny sweets from the shop on the corner? She'd get me from the grave – you know she would. No better woman."

Sam remembers the wooden-spoon incident – he hasn't thought about it in years. Claire had had to go into hospital for something – he was only six or seven at the time. Funny, they'd never said what it was. He'd gone to stay with Bella and Michael for a few nights, sleeping on their battered old couch. He remembers a musty smell now, and an orange cushion for a pillow. And sweet wrappers down the back of the couch. They'd had fish and chips for tea, and Coke to drink – he'd never tasted Coke before and the bubbles had gone up his nose. He remembers Bella laughing as she wiped his face, then giving them 20p each to go to the shop for sweets. "For afters," she'd said, hooshing them out the door and warning them to be back in ten minutes. How they'd decided to fill their pockets with stolen Wham Bars and Cola Bottles, Sam wasn't sure, but they'd come home delighted with themselves. And then he'd wrecked it all by taking his stash out to count the sweets. Bella had gone mad with the two of them – shouting till she was red in the face. He'd nearly collapsed when she took out the wooden spoon – his mum never did things like that. Bella didn't do anything more than wave it but it was enough. Sam never got on the wrong side of her again.

"True – she certainly kept the pair of us on the straight and narrow," he said. "Do you remember the old biddy who lived on the ground floor – the one who hated us sitting on that wall outside her flat? Remember that time she said she'd call the police on us? For sitting on a wall. It's funny when you think back – it was so innocent. Kids today don't bother sitting on walls any more – they're all on their iPads and phones, getting in trouble for Snapchatting and cyberbullying. To be honest, I'd much rather have Seth and Jamie hanging around on a green than locked in their rooms doing God knows what online. Simpler times, the 80s, weren't they?"

"Jesus, your lads don't have phones yet, do they?"

"Ha – no, I just mean when they're older."

"All ahead of you so, Sam. Sometimes I'm glad I've no kids – I wouldn't know where to start."

"Still time! You never know, you might meet a nice young one who's only dying for kids – happens all the time. A guy in my work is in his fifties and just announced he's marrying a twenty-eight-year-old! From Thailand. But I suppose that's different."

Michael looks at him across the top of his pint. "How do you know I haven't met someone already?"

Sam puts down his drink. Now this is a first. "Go on – tell me – who is she?"

"Ah, early days, I'll fill you in when I know it's going somewhere."

Sam's phone beeps and he checks the message. Nina – she wants him to call in. He keeps looking at the screen, trying to work out what to say to Michael. It's going to look rude no matter what he says. But he can't say no to her either. He types a quick reply then looks up at Michael. "Listen, something just came up at work – I'm really sorry, but I'll have to head in there to sort it out . . . "

"You're grand, don't worry. As long as you leave me your paper. And, sure look, I'll be out to you next weekend to have a look at this fancy new house of yours, as long as Kate's okay with you staying up in Dublin."

"Cheers, man," Sam says, putting his phone in his pocket and sliding the paper across the bar.

"Hope it doesn't take you too long."

"What?"

"The work problem."

"Oh yeah, me too. Right, I'll give you a bell during the week."

Sam walks out into the bright evening light, and turns towards the river, texting to say he's on his way.

His phone pings again but this time it's Kate.

Just a reminder – new fridge being delivered in morning between nine and eleven. Boys asking to Skype – is now good?

He punches letters in quickly as he crosses the bridge, pushing guilty thoughts out of his head.

Still at work – bit of a problem this evening. Will Skype in morning when waiting for fridge. Give them hugs from me.

He makes his way across the road and up to her apartment block, ringing the familiar bell, and wondering not for the first time how exactly he got himself into this.

Chapter 17

Sam – Friday, October 5th 1990

Sam races down the stairs and makes it halfway through the front door before his mother calls him back.

"Sam, where are you going?"

"Just out."

"Where to?"

"Molly's outside."

Claire rolls her eyes.

"Mum! Don't be like that."

"I'm joking. It's fine, go on. Be home by six for dinner. Remember we're going to the play at the Olympia tonight – if you can tear yourself away from Molly, of course. Young love, eh?"

"That's just gross," Sam says, pulling the front door shut behind him.

Molly is sitting on the low wall at the end of the front garden, her back to the house. Sam stops for a moment to look at her, wondering again what she sees in a guy like him. She raises a hand to her mouth. Is she smoking? Jesus, she is, and right outside his house.

"Molly, my mum is there – put out the smoke, quick!" Sam hisses, running towards the wall.

"Sure," she says, dropping it on the ground and twisting it underfoot.

"Aren't you worried you'll be seen smoking in your uniform?"

"Nah, the nuns aren't usually out wandering around Booterstown on a Friday afternoon. Come on, head up to the Bowler?"

Sam looks at his watch. "I've got to be back by six – I don't know if there's time."

Molly stands up and links her arm through his. "There's loads of time. Come on, Sam, live a little! You never know which day is going to be your last."

They turn up the avenue, kicking leaves as they walk, free from heavy schoolbags and grown-up eyes.

In the distance, two figures walk towards them, slowing as they approach. Sam recognises the uniforms – they're from St Michan's. When they reach Sam and Molly, they stop.

"All right, man, any chance of two naggins of vodka, twelve Dutch Gold and four packs of Silk Cut before tomorrow night?" says the taller of the two. "I have the cash here like."

Molly looks at Sam, eyebrows raised.

"Eh, I'm not sure what you mean?" Sam says. "I don't have any drink or cigarettes!"

The smaller boy gives his friend a subtle dig in the ribs. "Ah gotcha, yeah, we'll catch you later so. No worries. My mistake," he says, giving Sam a huge wink.

The boys walk on down the avenue, muttering to one another, and Sam and Molly link arms again and keep going towards the Bowling Alley.

"What was that about?" Molly asks. "Have you become some kind of dealer in booze?"

"I have no idea. I guess they thought I was someone else. Jeez, I'd be lucky to get served myself – remember that time we tried to get a flagon of cider from O'Donovan's and they just laughed at me?"

"I do indeed, Sam, I do indeed. It's lucky I'm not with you for your drink-buying skills. Speaking of which, Albie's having a party tomorrow night at ours – Mum's going out – want to come? I mean, it'll probably just be a load of sixth years getting stoned and trying to pretend the Leaving's not happening but it could be a bit of craic. Albie seems to have got his hands on a ton of drink somewhere."

I'll bet he has, Sam thinks. "Is Albie at home at the moment?"

"No, I think he's in the Bowler actually – why?"

"I just need to check something with him – I'll catch him there."

"Anyway, what about the party?"

"That sounds cool, but I'll have to check with my mum."

This time it's Molly's turn to roll her eyes.

"Sam, you're fifteen – surely your mum won't mind you going to a party on a Saturday night? And you're in Transition Year, for God's sake! It's not like you need to study!"

"Yeah, course she'll be fine – I just mean I need to check in with her."

Molly squeezes his arm. "I know, and I shouldn't be slagging you. I wish I got on even half as well with my mum as you do with yours." She goes quiet after she says this, and looks at the ground.

Sam elbows her gently. "Hey, your mum is nice. Don't be silly."

When she looks up at him again, her eyes are suspiciously wet. He's never seen Molly upset – not even when her grandmother died last summer.

"What is it – is something wrong with your mum?"

"No," she says. "Unless you count her state of mind."

"What do you mean?"

Molly sighs and says nothing for a minute. Then she looks up at him again and takes a deep breath. "My mum is moving to Philadelphia, and apparently that means me and Albie are moving to Philadelphia. In the States. That Philadelphia."

Sam shakes his head. This doesn't make any sense. "Why?"

"She says there's nothing for her here, with my dad gone and my grandmother dead. Her sister is in Philadelphia, and she can get Mum work. So it's all sorted – all neat and nice. No need to worry about uprooting your fifteen-year-old daughter from school and friends and . . . well, from you." She blinks, and two tears roll down her cheek.

Sam pulls her into a hug, because she looks like she needs a hug, and because he doesn't know what to say, and because he's fairly sure he doesn't want her to see that he's about to cry too.

Sam turns the key in the front door at six on the dot, and walks through to the welcome warmth of the kitchen. Beef casserole smells fill the air, and the table is set for three. His mum is in her favourite chair, engrossed in a book – a cup of tea on the small table beside her looks untouched. She hasn't heard him come in.

Sam walks over and kisses the top of her head, then puts on the kettle. "I'll make you a fresh cup, Mum – is Dad home?"

"Any minute now. How's Molly?"

"She's . . . she's fine. Is it okay if I go to a party in her house tomorrow night?"

"Well, will her mother be there?"

"Yes – it's just a small party with a few friends – I won't be late home."

"All right then, you can go. You need to get changed before the play."

Sam looks down at his jeans and hoodie. "Do I?"

His mum nods as they hear the front door open and shut.

John brings the outside in with him – smells of autumn leaves and cold and pipe smoke and even newspaper ink, though that might be Sam's imagination. He puts his briefcase down and kisses Claire's cheek, then pats Sam's shoulder.

"Sam, have you seen the key to the shed?" he asks, taking off his coat and sitting down at the table.

Shit, this isn't good. "No – why? Is it missing?"

"Yes. Your mother doesn't have it and it's not on the hook – I think you were the last person to use it?"

"I . . . don't think I had it recently, Dad." Sam can feel his face going red and turns towards the counter to pour water into cups. "Do you need something from the shed?"

"Well, nothing urgently this minute but there's a lot of stuff I need on and off all the time – a locked shed without a key is pointless. If it doesn't turn up, I'll need to break open the door and put on a new lock. Are you sure you don't know?"

Sam busies himself with a teabag.

"I'm sure, Dad, but I'll keep an eye out for it." Still facing the counter, he discreetly checks his pocket. It's still there. But he'll have to do something.

"I'm just going up to change, Mum!" Sam calls, running upstairs.

He puts the key in his bedside locker, then goes back out and into his parents' bedroom. He tiptoes across the carpet. It doesn't matter how carefully he sits on the bed, there's always a loud creak, and tonight it's louder than ever. They have the TV on downstairs though, so it's probably okay. He picks up the phone on his mother's bedside locker. The dial tone sounds excruciatingly loud. He looks over at the door – oh, for God's sake, he hasn't closed it. Sneaking back across the floor, wincing when the old boards squeak, he carefully shuts the door, then retraces his steps.

He dials the familiar number, wondering what he'll do if she answers instead of him. But it's okay, he gets lucky.

"You need to move the stuff," he whispers, skipping the small talk. "I know it's bad timing but my dad's noticed the key is missing, and he said he'll break the lock if he can't find it. I don't know if he suspects something or not, but I can't take a chance on it. We're going to a play tonight – we'll be gone from seven till about eleven – you need to do it then. I know it's short notice but we can't risk waiting any longer."

Sam carefully puts the phone back in the cradle and sneaks back out.

Downstairs, his mum is elbow deep in sudsy water.

"Where's Dad?" he asks.

Claire points to the study.

"He needed to make a quick phone-call – work."

Shit. He hadn't heard any click on the line but then he might have missed it. Could his dad have heard? What if he asks for the key now? Sam starts to feel a little bit sick. His mum passes him a tea towel and he picks up a plate as his dad comes out of the study. He looks in at them and Sam tries to read his face but there's nothing.

John says something about recording a documentary on RTÉ 2. Anything to avoid the dishes, Claire says.

The sick feeling ebbs away as Sam watches his dad go into the sitting room. He's never going to put himself in this position again. All going well, it will be over for good by tonight.

The curtain falls to enthusiastic applause and people begin making their way to the bar, trying to look like they're not rushing, but of course they are. A fifteen-minute interval isn't a long time to queue for, pay for, and drink a pint.

John pulls out his wallet and asks Claire what she'd like. She shakes her head – she doesn't want anything for now. It's warm in the theatre, but she's shivering and pulling her winter coat tightly around her. Her eyes are glassy and her cheeks are flushed. He asks if she wants to go home – at first she shakes her head but then she nods. They get to their feet, then he takes her gently by the elbow and helps her past the row of people beside them, signalling for Sam to follow.

Outside in the crisp night air, Claire's high colour subsides but she's still shivering. She tries to talk them into going back in – she'll wait in the lobby with a glass of water – but John insists they're going home.

Sam trails behind as his parents walk towards the car park, chewing on a thumbnail. He looks at his watch for the third time. The hands haven't moved. It's still only five to nine. And there's no way to make a phone call to warn him they're coming home early. *Shit.* He drags his feet, wondering how long it will take to get back to Booterstown at this time of night. There won't be any traffic. Feck it anyway, it was a stupid idea in the first place. *Stupid, stupid, stupid.*

His dad tells him to hurry – they need to get his mum to the car.

Sam speeds up – he'll have to take his chances.

At home, Sam makes as much noise as possible closing the car door and chatting loudly to his parents in the driveway. If he's out at the shed, he'll know to stay out of sight. Hopefully.

Inside, he goes straight to the kitchen to get a glass of water for his mum. He looks out to the garden – there's no light on in the shed and no sound. He must have been and gone. Sam's hand is still shaking as he fills the glass. That was too close.

His mum goes straight upstairs to sleep. Sam stretches and

yawns and tells his dad he's going to do the same. The phone is sitting quietly in its cradle on the hall table but he can't risk a call now.

Upstairs, he pulls out a Stephen King, but tiredness takes over, and a few pages in he's asleep.

Someone has pulled the duvet over him but he's still in his jeans when he wakes. It's bright outside – what time is it? He squints at his watch – just after ten. Jesus. Swinging his legs over the side of the bed, he pulls open the drawer of his bedside locker and takes out the key. Is it too soon to pretend to find it for his dad? He should make the call first, just to be sure. Hopefully his mum and dad are still asleep.

Creeping downstairs, he lifts the receiver and dials the familiar number.

"Did everything go okay last night – we got home early and I was worried?"

Everything went fine, he's told, the stuff was moved.

He hangs up, and makes his way into the kitchen, the stone floor cold under his stocking feet.

He's pouring Rice Krispies into a bowl when he hears a movement behind him. Startled, he turns around.

John is sitting in an armchair, staring into space.

"Dad?" The word catches in his throat and he tries again. "Dad, hey – I didn't know you were up."

John's gaze turns on his son. There are dark circles under his eyes, and his face is pale under his Saturday-morning stubble. He's dressed already, in the same clothes as yesterday.

"I couldn't sleep."

Something cold flutters in Sam's stomach.

"Maybe you're coming down with the same thing Mum has. I'll make you a cup of tea."

Maybe now is not the time to find the key after all.

Chapter 18

Kate - Saturday, July 2nd 2016

White-tipped waves splash against their small legs and they squeal again – it never gets old. Running backwards, they wait and watch, then step slowly forward again, until they're up to their knees. And along come the waves, and again they're surprised. Jamie's shorts are too long but each time Kate rolls them up they fall down, and now they're soaking. But today it doesn't matter. Kate leans her head back to face the sun – feeling her skin greedily gobbling up the unfamiliar Vitamin D. A breeze lifts the corner of the rug, then it flops back down. She brushes the sand off and turns her face to the sky again. Then two small wet bodies hurl themselves at her, cold from the water and feet covered in sand. They're delighted with their attack, and she lies back on the rug, feigning shock. It's only the sixth time they've done it this morning. They could do with more sun-cream, she thinks, inspecting their shoulders. Factor 50 is probably overkill for an Irish summer, and the boys have Sam's sallow skin, but still. After rubbing cream into their sandy shoulders, she plasters it on her own arms and legs too – even if the boys can withstand it, her own whiter-than-white skin can't. She puts on a wide-brimmed hat and pulls out her book.

"Mum, will you come into the sea with us?"

"I will later – I just want to read my book for a bit. You guys run down again. Nana will be here soon and we can have the picnic then. Go on – I'll call you."

Once they're back down at the waves, they'll forget about wanting her there too. Hopefully.

When her mother flops down beside her a few minutes later, she has two bottles of water and ice-pops for everyone. The boys must smell them – they race back and throw themselves on the rug, staring at the ice-pops like two hungry puppies.

"Go on, eat them before they melt – but you have to have a healthy snack after, okay?"

The boys run off again, and Kate gives her mum a look.

"What?" says Laura, as she stretches out her legs, and slips off her flip-flops. Her skin is not quite as fair as Kate's, but still burns easily. She reaches for the sun-cream and starts to rub it in, then pauses and looks at her daughter. "Sure they're only small."

"The ice-pops or the kids?"

"Well, both. And they're on holidays. It won't kill them."

"I don't remember you being so generous with treats when we were kids," Kate says, picking up her book.

"It's different being a grandparent – you'll see. Any word from Sam – are you going to Skype him later?"

"I think so – he was working late last night but should be fine today. I hope he remembered the fridge and didn't go out somewhere. He's scatty sometimes."

"Ah sure, isn't that part of what you love about him? Life would be boring if we were all perfect."

Kate gives her mum a sideways look but she's got her eyes

closed and her head back. It stirs a memory – a family holiday in Kerry or maybe West Cork when they were tiny. Lying on a golden beach, her mum's profile the same as it is now, but with black hair instead of the gunmetal grey she has today. Her dad sitting beside her mum, his shoes and socks off and his trouser legs rolled up. Miller sitting in the sand, digging. And Kate running up and back to the waves, like Seth and Jamie are doing today. So similar but so utterly different too. That was before Whitecross Hill. When everything was still good. Or mostly good.

Shaking her head to dislodge the memories, she goes back to her book, but Laura's in the mood for a chat.

"Sorry I took so long getting down – Mrs O'Shea was a divil at breakfast time. She wanted runny poached eggs and then claimed the ones I served her weren't runny enough. As if I have the time to be poaching perfect eggs. At least that other couple are going on Wednesday, so I'll have a bit more time for you and the boys."

"No new bookings from Wednesday on?"

"No, nothing till the weekend."

"Mum, I know I sound like a broken record but if you ever need our rooms back let me know – we can easily go to Dublin on and off over the summer. I don't want to take up space that you could be letting to paying guests."

"Not at all, love. Sure what would be the point in having the place at all if I couldn't have my grandkids to stay? I love having them here. And they're all I've got – it's not like Miller's going to give me grandkids, is he? God forbid."

Kate sits up straight. This isn't like her mother. Sweep It Under The Table is her usual approach, if not outright Pretend It Never Happened. Kate moves her hand across the rug so it covers her mother's and gives it a squeeze.

They sit there, two faces to the sun, thinking different

thoughts about the same person, watching two small boys running in the spray.

Back at the house, Mrs O'Shea is sitting in the conservatory, knitting something long and shapeless in a muddy green colour. The clatter of the boys' feet on the kitchen tiles prompts a frown and a pointed look at Kate, then she goes back to her knitting. Silly woman. The kids are just being kids. Still, she puts her finger to her lips and urges them up the stairs, telling them they can Skype Sam from her bedroom once they've washed the sand off their feet.

She starts the call while they're still in the bathroom and Sam picks up straight away. His face fills the screen but the familiar smile is missing.

"Is everything okay?" she asks.

"Yeah, fine, but where were you? I thought we were going to do this in the morning while I was waiting for the fridge to be delivered?"

"Sorry, we were at the beach, then we went for lunch in Salthill and a walk along the promenade. It's a beautiful day here – is it nice there?"

"I don't know. I've been indoors all day."

"Sam, don't be like that," she says, glancing over at the bathroom door. "In fairness, we wanted to talk to you last night but you couldn't do it then. We can't make all our plans around you – that's not fair on the boys."

"Yeah, but I couldn't do it last night – with work."

"Well, couldn't you have done it from the office? It's important for the boys to feel they can speak to you when they want."

"No, I couldn't talk from work – it was an emergency. Anyway, it doesn't matter – how is everything?"

"Good – they had a great day on the beach. If the weather

keeps up, it'll be the holiday of a lifetime. Fingers crossed it'll keep up for next weekend anyway, and you'll see for yourself."

"Yeah, about that – Michael has offered to give me a hand with the electrics in the house, but he's only free at the weekend. So I might stay up here and get that done with him?"

Oh, for fuck's sake! "Seriously, Sam? You're joking, right?"

"What? The house needs to be done. This is the only way to do it. You know what I'm like with DIY – I need to take help when it's offered."

"Yes, but you won't have seen the kids in weeks – they need their dad. And lovely and all as it is here, I could do with a break too."

"But you have your mum there."

"Yes, and she's running a B&B. I could do with some help, even if it's just at the weekend. It's full-on with the boys – you know that." Pity she's just told him about the lovely day on the beach. It sounded too easy.

"I'll be down the following week, Kate – it's not that far away. And it's not like I'll be enjoying myself here – I'll be working on the house."

"Fine. Just don't skip another weekend or they'll be getting worried. Actually, one more thing . . ." She looks up to see if the bathroom door is closed before continuing. "Can you pick up Seth's birthday present and bring it down when you're coming? It's ordered and everything – you just have to collect it."

"Grand – just email me the reference number. Are the boys there?"

Seth and Jamie bound into the room, ecstatic to see their dad's face on the laptop. Kate slips into the background, picking up sandy shorts and bits of shells from the bedroom floor, while they chat.

The boys won't like it, but perhaps the longer gap would do Sam and herself some good.

Chapter 19

Kate – June, 1984

They were fighting again. They're trying to hide it now with plastered-on smiles and breezy voices but Kate knows the signs. Her mum's eyes are bright with tears and her dad's cheeks are red. He's playing with his toast, twisting it round and round on the plate. She has pushed hers away untouched. It was never like this in Dublin. Bloody Carnross. And bloody Granddad for dying. That was a bad thing to think but, really, that's how it all started. If it wasn't for him dying, they'd never have had to move here to take over the practice.

Her mum clears her throat and stands up to kiss her good morning, but says nothing. Kate reaches her arms around her mum's neck and pulls her into a quick hug.

More tears now, which her mum tries to hide by making toast. Like there's not enough uneaten toast on the table already.

Miller wanders into the kitchen, oblivious to everything as usual. Oh, to be eight with not a care in the world! Though that's not fair – he has enough going on at school.

He sits up at the table and starts eating his porridge without a word to anyone.

No doubt there are normal families up and down the country right now, chatting over breakfast and being nice to each other. Not here though. Not any more. Now it's just quiet and horrible.

Her dad scrapes back his chair – it makes a loud noise on the old tiles and she jumps. He straightens his tie and nods to her, then walks out the door to work. Who does that? Who nods to their ten-year-old? What would be wrong with a kiss or a hug or even saying goodbye? And nothing to her mum or Miller. But some of the tension leaves the room with her dad, and she can hear her mum let out a long breath behind her.

Kate sits down to eat as her mum puts her lunch box in her schoolbag. Bloody school. Bloody tiny school with its freezing classrooms and bitchy girls. They aren't all bitchy – Clara is nice. But the rest of them – bitches.

She hears the sound of letters hitting the mat at the front door and runs out – maybe there's a letter from Dublin. But there isn't. Just boring brown envelopes for her dad. Throwing them on the hall table, she picks up her schoolbag and goes in to say goodbye to her mum and Miller. Her mum wants her to wait – she's going to walk Miller down in a few minutes. It would be good for him to have his big sister walk him into school, she says. Kate's about to argue but something in her mum's face stops her. It's not like she has any street cred to ruin anyway. They already think she's a loser. She picks up her schoolbag and taps her foot impatiently. Eventually, all three are outside and her mum is locking the door.

"Ah, sure now, you don't need to do that – this isn't Dublin," says a voice. Mrs Daly from next door.

Her mum smiles tightly and locks the door anyway.

Mrs Daly shakes her head, disappointed with the untrusting townies.

They set off in silence for the short walk to the school.

Bloody Carnross.

Chapter 20

Kate – Friday, July 15th 2016

The doorbell rings. He's here. Finally.

Seth and Jamie bounce off the couch, *Scooby Doo* utterly forgotten. They race out to the hallway to open the door, and Kate follows, smiling, caught up in their excitement. Sam's tall frame fills the doorway and he stoops, arms out, to gather both boys in.

Laura comes downstairs and ushers them all into the kitchen, then sets about making tea.

Sam turns to Kate and grins.

"Nice to be home – kind of home," he says, kissing her on the cheek.

"Good to see you," she whispers, and she means it more than she'd thought she would.

Laura pours tea and asks Sam if he's eaten – he says he has – and the boys start to search his bag for presents.

"Seth, Jamie, stop!" Kate tells them. "You know that's rude – Dad didn't have time to get presents. Now, I let you stay up till Dad arrived as long as you promised to go straight up then, so scoot and brush your teeth – Dad will be up to do stories tonight." And Kate will have a very large glass of wine, she thinks, and a very long lie-in tomorrow morning.

As soon as Sam heads upstairs with the boys, Kate goes into the living room and flops full-length on the couch. It is blissfully quiet and she almost dozes off.

Eventually Laura joins her, bearing a bottle of wine and three glasses.

"You read my mind," Kate says and gratefully accepts a glass.

"So, what have you got planned for tomorrow?" Laura asks, sitting down. "Will the four of you head into Galway maybe and get lunch?"

"Eh, no, I'll head in on my own. It's definitely me-time. I need shops and coffee and nobody needing me. Sam can do stuff with the boys – they'll be delighted."

"Aha! And does Sam know this?"

"Not yet, but he can't complain, can he?" Kate says, taking a welcome sip.

"I suppose not. And sure you can do something tomorrow afternoon. What time will he be heading back on Sunday?"

"Don't know, Mum. I haven't really thought past tomorrow's escape, to be honest. I'm mostly thinking about Brown Thomas and shoes and cappuccinos at this point."

"Well, just be sure to let your husband know when he comes back down – he may not realise you have this escape plan."

Laura picks up the remote control to put on the *Nine O'Clock News*. There's a flicker of light at the centre of the screen of the tiny, box-shaped TV, and slowly, slowly, the picture emerges. The headlines have already started by the time sound joins picture.

" *. . . and the Central Bank says it will take the matter under advisement.*

In other news, Gardaí investigating the fatal shooting at an apartment complex in Dublin 2 on June 19th last are renewing their appeal for witnesses, specifically anyone who saw a tall, dark-haired man in the vicinity, or a bike courier, at about ten o'clock in the morning. The shooting is believed to be drug-related, although the victim, Austin Granger, son of Independent TD Maureen Granger, worked as a stockbroker, and was not known to Gardaí."

The door opens and Sam looks in. "Hey – does anyone need anything before I come in? Boys are down now."

"We're fine, come on in and sit down – you must be tired after the drive," Laura says. "Glass of wine?"

"Yes, please, that'd be great." Sam stands at the door looking unsure, then comes in and sits on the old red-velvet wing-tipped chair near the TV.

Kate smiles to herself. At home they sprawl on the same couch, but visiting the in-laws is still visiting the in-laws. Well, just one in-law really. A sudden pang hits her, as it occurs to her that her father has never met Sam. Where has that come from? He's never met the boys either, and she's thought about that on and off since they were born, but it hasn't struck her before that he's never met Sam. Well, it's his own fault. *Asshole.* Looking over at her mother, she wonders if there has been any contact over the years – even through lawyers. Her mum never mentions him, and she never asks.

"How's everything going with the house, Sam?" Laura asks as she hands him a glass of wine.

"Not bad, though there's still loads to do. My cousin's been giving me a dig-out with it, thank God."

"Any more run-ins with your man across the road?" Kate asks.

"No, haven't seen him since. What an idiot! You have to wonder what he has going on in his life that he was ready to call the Guards over a parking problem."

"And has Miller left you in peace?" Kate asks, glancing at her mum.

Sam shifts in the seat. "Actually, he did call in one evening. I meant to tell you. I thought he'd forgotten you were here, but he said he knew that, and was calling to see me."

"Oh God, will he ever get the message?"

"Kate," Laura says, "that's not fair."

"Mum, come on! What is he doing calling in annoying Sam when we're not even there?" She turns back to Sam. "What did he even talk about?"

"Well, nothing, to be honest. I made tea and we sat at the kitchen table, and he said nothing. I asked him about his flat and his flatmate and his, um, novel, but he didn't really reply."

"And did he stay long?"

"Around forty-five minutes."

"Oh Sam, that's ridiculous – it's okay to tell him you have things to do or to not answer the door when he calls."

"Ah no, I'd feel bad doing that – it's no hassle," Sam says.

Laura turns to Kate, frowning. "Come on, that's really not nice. Your brother needs family support, and you're all he's got in Dublin."

"Fine, Mum, but it's not fair for Sam to have to deal with him when I'm not there."

"Well, what if I invite him to stay down here for a few weeks, while you're here?"

"*No!*" Kate sits up straight. "Mum, don't. Leave him where he is. I don't want him around the boys too much."

Laura's cheeks go red and when she answers her voice is low and tight. "Kate. I won't have you saying things like that. He's my son, and he's your brother. He's had his problems, but he deserves our love and support – that's what families do."

"Fine, Mum, but just don't go out of your way to invite

him down, okay?" Kate turns to Sam. "Anyway, Sam, were the boys happy enough going to sleep?"

Sam's engrossed in a message on his phone, and doesn't hear her.

"Sam? Did the boys settle down all right?"

"Sorry." He puts down his phone and takes a sip of wine. "All good. I read them a couple of stories and then they were out like lights."

"That was close earlier – when they were searching your bag – did you get to hide it away?"

"Hide what away?"

"Seth's present."

"Oh shit!"

"*Sam!* Please say you didn't forget to pick it up?"

"I did pick it up, I just forgot to pack it – it's still at home. But sure I'll be down for his birthday anyway – I'll bring it then."

"I know, but I wanted to wrap it up with the other bits I've picked up – that was the only thing I asked you to bring. How could you forget?"

"Oh, come on, it's not a big deal, Kate. I've a lot going on – it just slipped my mind."

"Your own son's birthday slipped your mind?"

Laura excuses herself, saying something about setting the table for breakfast.

"That's not fair – you know what I mean," Sam says. "I came straight from work, so I packed in a hurry this morning – I just didn't think to pack the Scalextric. Sorry. But look, I'm after driving all the way down here and now you're giving out to me – can we not do this?"

Kate stares straight ahead as she picks up her wine again.

"What, so you're going to ignore me now?" Sam asks.

"What do you want me to say? That you deserve a medal

for coming to see your wife and kids a whole week later than planned?"

"Jesus, Kate, I wish I hadn't bothered at all. I'm going to bed." Sam downs his wine in two gulps and walks out of the room.

He leaves the door open. So much more annoying than a satisfying slam, Kate thinks, as she gets up to close it.

Laura comes back in, wiping her hands in a tea towel.

"Were you a bit hard on him there, love?"

"Mum, he's just not even meeting me halfway any more when it comes to the kids. I have to do everything – order everything, organise everything – if it wasn't for me, nothing would happen at all. I'm just fed up. He thinks because he has a job and I don't, that lets him off the hook."

"Then talk to him. Don't sulk – talk."

"I'm not sulking, but I'm not in the mood for talking either. Let's just put something on TV."

Upstairs, they can hear Sam moving around, then silence. He's really gone to bed. This isn't the visit Kate had imagined. Tomorrow will be better.

Chapter 21

Kate – Saturday, July 16th

Snoring. She'd forgotten all about Sam's snoring in just two short weeks, and somehow it's even louder in her mother's house. She pushes him over onto his side and tries to go back to sleep but it's no use. Early-morning sun is creeping in under the slatted blinds, and suddenly the appeal of a quiet run on the beach is far greater than any futile attempt at sleep. She puts on her running gear and, leaving a note for Sam, creeps out of the house.

The run is everything she's missed for the last two weeks: the early sun on her face, the salty air, and the empty beach stretching out for miles. When it's enough, she slows to a walk, and heads towards Jan's Café at the edge of the village. There are no other customers at this early hour, and she takes her cappuccino outside to sit in the small outdoor terrace. Instinctively she reaches for her phone, but decides to leave it face down on the table. Ten minutes with sun and coffee and nothing else would be better than anything else she could do right now. She closes her eyes.

A chair dragging against the paving stones startles her, and she opens her eyes again. An elderly woman makes a slow but steady descent onto a chair at a nearby table, and nods at Kate. A man – presumably the woman's son – joins her, carrying a tray with tea and scones. They begin a conversation about the weather and move on to a rundown of what a seemingly huge number of children are doing now – possibly the man's family. He pauses and seems to be about to say something, but doesn't. The woman carries on asking about the children. It sounds as though she's mixing up their names – even Kate can remember that Isaac is twelve and Amy is ten – it's not the other way around. If he's impatient, the man hides it well.

Jan comes to ask if Kate would like another coffee, but she decides against it. Five more minutes, then she'll head for home.

The man and his mother are still chatting – she's just visiting for the weekend and will go home tomorrow morning. Kate can see the son is holding a brochure under the table – she can't make out what's on it, but he seems unsure about showing it to his mother. What could it be, Kate wonders. A holiday he's planned? But why the hesitation? More like a care home, she speculates. Now the woman is talking quite loudly about her cat and how much she misses him this weekend – she says she should never have left the cat with her neighbour and won't do it again. The man nods, and quietly crumples the brochure into his pocket.

With her peace well and truly broken, Kate takes out her phone and clicks into Facebook. But scrolling through pictures of everyone she knows on beaches all around the world having the best time ever, does not, it turns out, make her feel amazing, so she closes Facebook and tries Twitter.

Something makes her look up, and she finds the elderly lady staring at her. She stares back for a beat, then turns to her phone again.

"I know you," says the lady.

Oh great. A little old lady striking up a random conversation – she's really not in the humour for this. The son will surely jump in to stop her – Kate keeps looking at her phone.

"Excuse me, but aren't you Kate Jordan? Laura Jordan's daughter?"

Her stomach does a somersault. Nobody has called her Kate Jordan for thirty years. She looks up, smiles, and shakes her head.

"You are – it *is* you! Look, Bernard, don't you remember Kate who lived next door? You were only about ten years old at the time, Kate, but I remember you – you look exactly like your mother did then. Is she still alive?"

Oh dear God. Mrs Daly from next door in Carnross. Kate feels suddenly sick. Bernard, who Kate remembers as a troublemaking little brat, is smiling over at her now too. Her throat feels blocked – they're waiting for her to answer but no words are coming out. She stares helplessly at Mrs Daly.

"Have you been back at all, Kate – to Carnross? Do you see your father much?"

"I have to go," she manages finally, pushing out her chair, and knocking the cappuccino cup onto the ground.

She tries to pick up the pieces, and Bernard comes over to help. Jan comes out with a dustpan and brush and tells all of them she'll take care of it. Grateful for the distraction, Kate picks up her phone and turns to leave.

"We didn't all blame your family, you know, Kate," says Mrs Daly softly.

Kate stops for a moment and then keeps going, back towards the beach and the B&B, wishing she'd stayed in bed.

Back at the B&B, everyone is up and sitting around the kitchen table eating breakfast. Conversations are flying over and back between the boys and Sam and Laura, and nobody notices that Kate is quieter than usual. She could tell her mum later about Mrs Daly. Or maybe not at all.

The boys want to know what the plan is, and Sam suggests a family day at the beach.

Kate ignores the pointed look from her mother. "Actually, I was going to head into town myself – I've a few things to get. I thought you could take the boys out?" She focusses intently on buttering her toast.

Sam doesn't answer, and she glances up at him. He's annoyed.

She puts down her knife and sighs. "Sam, I've had them for two weeks – I just need a morning to myself. We can meet later and do something, right?"

"Fine. I thought we'd do something as a family. But no worries – you do your thing and we'll do ours. Won't we, boys?"

She's not taking the bait. She's got her morning to herself and that's all that matters. She quickly finishes her breakfast. "Boys, give me a kiss in case you're gone when I get out of the shower," she says, grabbing Seth and Jamie for quick hugs before heading up the stairs.

In her bedroom, Sam's phone is buzzing in the middle of the bed. She reaches over to pick it up but it's stopped. "**Missed call, N**" pops up on screen. Who is N – why just an initial? She brings the phone back downstairs and hands it to Sam, telling him she didn't catch it in time. He looks at the screen.

"Work," he says, pocketing the phone. "So annoying on a Saturday. Well, they can wait. I'm on my holidays, right, boys?" He picks Jamie up and tickles him.

Kate goes back upstairs. She smiles. It's only for a few hours, but she's free.

Her phone beeps – Sam wants to know where she is. They're back at the B&B already. Crap. She checks the time – how is it quarter past two? It feels like she's only been here five minutes. Putting down her shopping bags, she replies to say she'll be home by three. No response. He's annoyed. She probably shouldn't have got her nails done – that took up too much time. Then again, they're very pretty, she thinks, admiring them in the light. Right, two more shops, then back to the car. Well, maybe one more takeaway coffee too, and she'd take a cake home to the rest of them – that would clear the air.

In the end, it's almost four o'clock when she pulls into the driveway. She leaves the bags in the boot for now and lets herself in. The boys are playing with a Frisbee in the garden, and Sam is leaning against the counter in the kitchen, looking at his phone.

"What took you?" he asks, looking up.

"Sorry, traffic was horrendous on the way back out of town."

"But even at that I thought you'd be home much sooner – what about the plan to do something?"

"Well, why don't we all go out for dinner? The boys would love it, and we could treat Mum if she doesn't need to be here for guests tonight."

"You know what, Kate, I'm not in the mood to play happy families tonight. Your mum said she has a stew on – that'll do. And anyway, I've to head back early in the morning. Pity we've hardly had two minutes together since I got here."

He puts his phone in his pocket and walks upstairs, leaving Kate speechless in the kitchen. This isn't the Sam she knows. *Fuck*. She pushed it too far. But he's overreacting too. And what's with heading back early in the morning? Sure he was hardly here at all. What was the point in even coming? She turns to follow him upstairs, ready to tell him exactly that, but thinks better of it and stays put.

Laura comes in from the garden with a basket of washing. She gives Kate a look but says nothing.

"Mum, remember Mrs Daly who used to live next door to us?"

Laura stops and puts the basket down on the floor. "Yes – why?"

"What was she like?"

"Oh, she was as nosy! Always asking questions when she'd see me. 'How's your husband, Mrs Jordan – he must be doing well for himself now he's taken over the practice?' – that kind of thing. Forever looking at the car, or asking me where my coat was from. And once she said she's seen Father Burke come out of Richard's office and then she stopped and waited as if I was going to fill her in on the parish legal affairs! Not that I'd know anyway – your dad was nothing if not ethical when it came to work."

"Pity that didn't carry through to the rest of his life," Kate mutters.

Laura purses her lips but says nothing.

Kate hadn't really expected an answer – her father falls into the Do Not Discuss category of family conversations.

"Why are you asking about Mrs Daly?"

"No reason, she just popped into my head. I saw someone earlier who reminded me of her, that's all."

Mrs Daly would be gone back to Carnross in the morning and Bernard would hardly recognise her mum, nor she him.

"I wonder if she's still alive – she wasn't the worst, you know. Nosy and desperately competitive, but she was kind too. She was very good to me at the end, at a time when everyone else was crossing the road to avoid me." Another topic normally in the Do Not Discuss box.

Kate can't decide if this is a healthy twist in the emotional valve, or old ground best left untouched.

"Anyway, washing won't fold itself – will you give me a hand?" Laura says, making the decision for her.

Kate nods and picks up a sheet, pushing Mrs Daly and Carnross out of her mind.

Chapter 22

Kate – June, 1984

Hugging her knees to her chest, Kate continues to ignore her mother's silent appeal to get up and join the other girls. She's not moving from this bench. How can her mother not see they don't want her there anyway? Her mother digs her gently in the ribs and mouths "Go on!" then turns back to the woman on her other side – a mum from Miller's class. They're talking about a picnic now, about getting the whole class together for a day out. Oh my God, please get me out of this dump, Kate thinks, stretching out her legs. A picnic with a class of eight-year-olds! There is literally nothing she'd rather do less. She looks up from under her fringe at the girls across at the railings. They catch her looking, and now they're giggling. As soon as she's sixteen, she's out of this dump and back to her real friends in Dublin. Only six years to go.

Her mum elbows her again, and she gets off the bench, but only to stand to the side, out of her reach.

She looks over at Miller – he's sitting on top of the slide, not doing anything. There's a queue of kids behind him, and they're starting to get cross.

Kate walks over. "Come on, Miller, down the slide – there's people waiting behind! Good boy – let's go!"

Still he doesn't move.

"It's very high – you don't have to slide down if you don't want to – you can go back down the ladder. We can ask the others to let you past. Is that what you want to do?"

Miller nods at her and turns to make his way back down the ladder. The kids behind him are not impressed. An older boy says something about the "dumb new kid" and everyone laughs. Kate's face burns. She reaches up for her brother and helps him down, and they walk together to their mother who is still discussing the picnic – they'll have it on the last day of school before summer break. How completely mortifying. As if she and Miller want to hang out with these horrible local brats – how can her mum not see?

Walking home, she tries to talk her mother out of it, but she is determined.

"It's a good way for Miller to get to know the kids in his class – you know how hard he's finding it to settle in."

"Yes, I do, Mum – because they're rotten. Spending even more time with them isn't going to make things better."

"Oh Kate, it will – it's always hard when you move somewhere new but we have to try. It's hard for me, too, remember – I had to leave my job and all my friends to come here." She gives Kate's arm a light squeeze. "Come on – do it for Miller. Once the other boys get to know him, they'll see he's just like everyone else and they'll start to talk to him and play with him at school too."

Kate kicks a stone into the gutter. "He's not really just like everyone else though, is he?"

"Of course he is. It just takes time. And you'll make friends too."

"I have no interest in making friends – I'll be moving back

to Dublin in a few years to my actual friends."

Her mum sighs and puts her arm around her. Kate shrugs it off and immediately wishes she hadn't. Their footsteps are the only sound on the cracked pavement, and their long shadows cut three silent figures making their way to the very last cottage on Main Street, Carnross.

Chapter 23

Kate – Friday, July 22nd 2016

Kate is kneeling on the wing-tipped chair, cleaning her mother's best lamp – the ornate brass one she'd taken with her all those years ago when they left the cottage in Carnross. A monstrosity really by modern lighting standards, but a reasonable fit for the sitting room in the B&B. Mrs O'Shea certainly seems fond of it – she's hovering by the wing-tipped chair, waiting for Kate to finish so she can sit down with her knitting. Kate keeps polishing. Maybe Mrs O'Shea will go to her bedroom for a lie-down if she takes long enough. The only downside of a B&B is the guests really – it would be lovely to be here all summer if only there were no guests. Kate keeps polishing and Mrs O'Shea keeps hovering. Neither speak. And in fairness, the lamp does need a good clean – it looks like it hasn't been touched in a while. The unofficial standoff comes to an end when Mrs O'Shea turns on her heel and walks out – unwilling, it would appear, to trade down for a spot on the couch.

Kate waits till she hears her door close upstairs, then sets aside her cloth and flops down on the coveted chair. Her phone rings just then, as though it had been waiting for her to take a break. Or waiting to intrude on her break. It's Sam. And he's not coming down this evening.

"You can't be serious!" She uncrosses her legs and sits up straight in the chair. How is she going to explain this one to the boys?

As if reading her mind, Jamie waves in at her from the back garden.

"Sorry, there's nothing I can do. I'll be here in the office till ten o'clock tonight trying to fix this, and there's no point in driving all the way down tomorrow for just the night."

"Sam, you know what, I don't want to hear it. I don't know what's going on with you but you'd better fix it or the boys are going to start thinking we've split up."

"Don't say that."

"I'm serious. This is a joke. We may as well be separated when you look at how the last few months have been."

"Kate, it's not months – you've only been down there since the end of June."

"I'm not just talking about the summer – this has been going on for much longer than that, and you know it. The late nights at work, avoiding the kids' bedtime, working at weekends – it's like you're just not bothered any more."

Seth looks in the window at her and smiles, then runs back to his game.

She lowers her voice. "It makes me feel sick. I always thought this was the kind of thing that happened to other people, not to us."

"Kate, nothing is happening to us – it's just a busy time. I'll come down next weekend, I promise."

"Don't bother. Seriously, don't put yourself out. We're fine. I'll see you when we're back in Dublin." She disconnects the call, and flings the phone across the room onto the couch.

Fuck him! Fuck him anyway!

Running her hands through her hair, she sits in her mother's sitting room, with no idea what to do next. The overloud sound of pots and pans comes from the kitchen – Laura pretending she didn't hear. This is what it was like back then during the fights, only their roles are reversed.

Dust mites dance in the sunlight over the table, and through the window beyond she can see Seth and Jamie still kicking a football. It's all so idyllic, until you scratch the surface. What does her mother always say? *There isn't a person you wouldn't love if you could read their story.*

She walks to the window to look out at the boys, then sits down again, head in hands. Laura comes into the room.

"Are you okay, love?" she asks.

There's nothing to say. Kate shakes her head.

"Sam not coming down?"

She shakes her head again.

Her mother comes and gives her shoulder a squeeze. "It's hard for him, trying to manage everything – fixing up the house, a busy job – don't be too tough on him."

Kate looks up. "It's not just that, Mum. He's been gone for a long time now. When he's here, he's not really here. He's pretending. I can't describe it properly, but it's just not the Sam I used to know."

"Kate, you've got to meet him halfway though."

"What do you mean? I'm doing everything I can!"

"I don't want you to get defensive, but in all the years you and Sam have been together, you're the leader and he's the follower. You're the boss, he's the guy putting his coat over the puddle. You shred him to pieces and he comes back for more. I'm just trying to say you don't always make it easy for him."

Kate swivels around in the chair. "I shred him to pieces?"

"I don't mean it in a bad way. But when you tell him what's

what or put him in his place, he's takes it – he's like a loyal puppy. I don't mean he's a pushover but maybe with you, just a little bit, he is . . . Come on love, I'm not telling you anything you don't know. You're together twenty years!"

"I don't think I put him in his place . . . I suppose I'm a bit bossier than he is, but he's never minded."

"I know that. But I'm saying that the dynamic you've developed between you – which has been perfectly fine all these years – may not work so well when you're trying to bridge a gap or fix something that's not working. Does that make sense?"

Kate's shoulders start to shake, and she bursts into tears – big, ugly tears, the kind she hasn't cried since she was a teenager, heartsick over Henry Byrne from the year above.

Laura bends to her level and pulls her into an awkward sideways hug.

"Remember when we first met?" Kate sobs. "You were horrified that I'd – as you said – 'picked up one of the customers and at his own aunt's funeral' – do you remember?"

Laura smiles. "I probably made it sound a bit worse than it was. In fairness, it's not the loveliest 'how we met' story I've ever heard."

Kate can feel a watery smile breaking through too. "Like, it's not as though I picked him up at the graveside. And in fairness, he picked me up – I was the innocent waitress."

"You had your eye on Michael at the time if I remember – am I right?"

"*Ha* – a little. But Michael wasn't interested in me. And I went for the coat-over-puddle guy. And now . . . now I just don't know."

A ball hits the window, breaking the conversation.

"I'll go," says Laura. "You sit here and I'll bring you in a cup of tea."

"Thanks, Mum, but I think I'm going straight to wine tonight – I'll sit here for a minute if that's okay, then I'll deal with the boys. And Mum?"

Laura turns back from the kitchen.

"Thank you."

"Boys . . ." She plucks at something pink and sticky dried into her jeans. Strawberry yogurt maybe. "There's something I have to tell you . . . Dad can't make it down this weekend."

She waits for the tears but none come. Two relatively disinterested faces look up from their books.

"Was he meant to come down tonight?" Seth asks, cocking his head to one side.

"Well, he tries to come down at the weekends when he can – but he had to work tonight."

"Okay," Seth says, then looks down at his book again.

"Jamie, would you like me to read for you?" Kate asks.

"Two stories, Mum – fair? Cos Dad's not here?" he says, milking her concern but showing none of his own.

"Fair, Jamie." She starts to read.

It's not the best wine she's had all summer but it'll do. It's one of those supermarket special offers – not the proper offers where the good wine is a bit cheaper than usual, but the ones where they sell off cheap wine for next to nothing and hope nobody notices the taste. And in a way, it's an appropriate wine for the night that's in it.

Mrs O'Shea is the only guest and she's safely tucked up in her room with her knitting, so Laura and Kate have the remote control to themselves. Most guests don't come near the sitting room at night, but Mrs O'Shea can go either way. And she doesn't like anything violent or dark on TV, or any swearing, or anything that's not a documentary.

"Did I mention . . ." Laura says carefully, in a way that suggests she most certainly didn't mention, "that Miller is calling tomorrow?"

Miller. That's all Kate needs on top of no Sam. She rolls her eyes.

"Kate, come on, he's your brother. Please."

"I know, Mum, but it's hard work when he's here. He doesn't say a word. He just hovers. The boys still never know what to make of him." She looks down, not meeting Laura's eye.

"Well, what if he took them out somewhere and gave you a bit of time off? I'm stuck here with that new family arriving, but Miller could take them to the beach and you could go into town?"

Kate sits forward, rubbing her middle fingers up and down her forehead for what feels like a long time.

"Kate? Do you want to do that?"

Without looking up, and almost under her breath, Kate answers, "No."

"Well, I think it would be nice – it might be good for Miller."

"Maybe it would be, but no." Still she doesn't look at her mother. "Mum, I don't want him on his own with the kids."

"That's not fair." Laura's voice is quiet now too. "What happened wasn't his fault, and he was only a child for God's sake."

Kate looks out between her fingers at the small TV, the dusty, colourful books behind it, and the antique fireplace that gives the whole room its personality. She counts the candles on the mantelpiece. Seven. There are seven candles. What's that Danish thing about being cosy and lighting candles – *hygge*?

"Kate."

"I know that, Mum. And I'm not talking about what

happened – or at least not just that. I mean what it did to him – the person he is today. He's my brother and I love him, but I am not sending him off with the boys. Miller's your son and you are looking out for him – I get that – but Seth and Jamie are mine, and I'm looking out for them – above all else."

Laura is twisting a button on her cardigan around and around.

Kate turns her head to watch. It's going to pop off if she keeps turning. Her mother's unmanicured nails are short – no way to grow them when you wash dishes all day, she always says. She stops twisting and lets the button go.

"His life has been ruined by something over which he had almost no control – he was eight. He was only eight."

Kate put her hand on Laura's. "I know, Mum," she says softly. "But people come through great tragedies – look at Sam and what happened to him. People come through. Somehow, Miller got left behind, and there's nothing we can do to change that now." She swirls her wine in the glass and takes another sip. "I'll always be there for him, but it doesn't mean I'm going to pretend none of it happened."

Chapter 24

Kate – Tuesday, July 26th

Fragments of a fight about Rice Krispies drift from the kitchen to the hall but Kate can't really hear them – she can only see the letter, stark white against the red carpet. It seemed to make a noise when she dropped it, though of course that's not possible – it's only paper, no matter what's written on it. The torn envelope is still on the table. Her name and address have been typed – it looks like a business letter, except for the stamp. Pull yourself together, she thinks, as she stoops to pick up the letter. She closes her eyes for a moment then forces herself to read again.

Dear Kate,

I don't know you very well, and I hope you'll forgive this intrusion, but I thought you should know what's been going on while you've been away. I'm sorry to say your husband has a woman staying in the house – I see her coming in with him late at night, and leaving early in the morning. And although you may imagine there's a good explanation and nothing untoward is happening, I'm afraid I've seen them arm in arm and kissing. I don't do this to upset you, but I don't think it's fair that you're being left in the dark. You should know what kind of man your husband is.

Yours,

A Wellwisher

She sinks to the floor, trying to make sense of it. Sam wouldn't cheat. He just wouldn't. Though he did once. But that was back before they were married, and long before they had kids. He wouldn't risk everything for a midlife fling – would he? And in their house?

Laura's voice floats out from the kitchen – she's telling the boys to go upstairs to brush their teeth.

Kate pulls herself up off the floor and runs to the guest bathroom under the stairs before anyone comes out to the hall. Closing the toilet seat, she sits down, trying to straighten her thoughts. Her breath is too fast. Laura is calling her, but she can't come out yet. She needs to think. She reads the letter a third time – it still says the same thing. *Fucking hell.*

She splashes water on her face, hesitating before drying it with the guest hand-towel, then puts on a smile and goes into the kitchen to tell her mother she's just had a call from a friend in Dublin and needs to drive there this morning. The friend's husband has left her, she whispers to Laura, out of earshot of the boys. Laura casts a sceptical eye on her daughter but tells her to go – the boys will be fine. Ten minutes later, with nothing but her handbag, Kate is on the road.

When she pulls into Willow Valley two and half hours later, her fingers are stiff from gripping the steering wheel and her eyes feel like they're filled with sand. She cuts the engine, then sits in the car without moving. Her stomach feels sicker than ever, and lack of food isn't helping. What is she expecting to find anyway? Her eye is drawn to a small movement in the house across the way. There's someone in the sitting room looking out at her, trying to hide behind the curtain. Wonderful, an audience now. Maybe the author of the letter? Irritated, she gets out of the car, and marches up to her front door.

Inside, the hallway is cool and silent. And there's nobody there. What had she expected – to find them at it on the floor? Sam would be at work for a start. This is so silly. She walks through to the kitchen, familiar and alien all at once. The brand-new table, the cracked lino, the ancient pine cupboard doors they'd eventually have to replace. A cereal bowl sits on the draining board, with the remains of what looks like dried-in Weetabix inside. The kettle is still slightly warm from Sam's morning tea. On autopilot, she hits the button. There's post on the counter – unopened, addressed to her. Bank statements and her Visa bill. She opens the fridge – not as empty as she'd expected. Cheese, ham, milk and beer. Normal. Just like everything else. What was she thinking, driving the breadth of the country on foot of an anonymous letter, like some deranged, scorned wife from a made-for-TV film? Laura would have a good laugh at this later.

The kettle trundles to a stop. She warms a cup and switches on the coffee machine, running some water through it first to clean it – Sam only drinks tea, despite her many failed attempts to convert him. She reaches for the coffee but it's empty. Now she desperately wants a coffee. Wasn't it at least half full when she was leaving? She makes tea instead and, taking a roll of black sacks from the cupboard, she carries her cup upstairs to gather some clothes for the next few weeks.

The house feels strange – so very quiet. She switches on the radio in her room, and a song she's never heard blares out.

Quickly she turns it off again. What is he doing with the volume so high? Opening her wardrobe, she begins pulling out coloured T-shirts and fresh pairs of jeans and a dress for going out even though she has nowhere to go. She reaches under her bed to pull out a box of beach towels and swimsuits – they need some extra towels – and knocks something over. A shoe. A high-heeled silver peep-toe court shoe, the kind she wouldn't wear in a million years.

Oh Sam. She puts it down and stands up, looking around the room for other unfamiliar objects. There's nothing in plain sight. Her eye falls on her bedside locker – the top drawer is ajar, just the tiniest bit, but she never leaves it open. She pulls it out. Inside, there are some bangles, a pair of earrings and a magazine screaming headlines about soap stars she's never heard of. That sick feeling is trickling back. A little unsteady on her feet, she backs away from the locker, and goes into the ensuite bathroom. In the mirror on the medicine cabinet, her cheeks look paler than ever and her hair is all over the place. For a second she pauses, then bracing herself she opens the cabinet. A bottle of MAC foundation, a tube of BB cream, and six or seven eye-shadow palettes, none of which are hers. And a little flat packet of some kind of medicine. She picks it up and turns it over. Yasmin. She's not on the pill any more, though she used Yasmin for a long time before they had kids. Frozen to the spot, she turns the packet over and over in her hand. Three pills gone, eighteen still there. *Oh Sam.*

Back in the bedroom, she lifts the lid of her laundry basket – underwear that isn't hers sits on top of a pile of towels that are. So she's not only leaving her belongings all over Kate's house, she's using her best towels too. Her eyes are drawn back to the bed – in spite of all the evidence to the contrary, she still can't picture Sam sleeping with someone else. The pillows sit side by side, just as they always do, lined up in marital harmony. Sam's is usually higher than hers until she fixes it, because he doesn't fold his pyjamas – he just stuffs them underneath in a ball. But today there's perfect symmetry. She pulls them back. Under her pillow there's a thin black negligée, the kind only women who don't have the battle scars of childbirth wear. And underneath his, there's nothing.

She steps back until her shoulders touch the wardrobe, then slides down to sit on the floor. *Jesus Christ. Sam.* In twenty years, other than that one horrible time – when he promised he'd never do it again – she'd never suspected he'd stray. Not for a minute. They weren't perfect – far from it – and the last year has been tough. But surely it was nothing more than the typical domestic struggle that parents of small kids go through? And of course there wasn't as much time for dinner and dates and sex and meaningful conversations. But that was normal. Or had seemed normal until he started working late and stopped coming to see them at the weekends. And now this. *Jesus Christ. Well, fuck him and fuck her!* She gets up off the floor and pulls a black sack from the roll. Then, without touching anything, she tips the laundry basket contents into it. The jewellery, the make-up and the pill packet follow, then the negligée, and as an afterthought the pillow goes in too. It's not the most sophisticated response but it'll do.

She gathers her own clothes and some from the boys' rooms into another bag and puts them in the car, then returns to the kitchen to write a note to her husband. Leaving it under the empty coffee jar, she pulls the door closed behind her.

Chapter 25

Kate – Tuesday, July 26th

The key turns easily in the lock but it takes every ounce of energy to put on a smile and walk back into the B&B. The kitchen door is open, and from the doorstep she can see the boys scooping food into their mouths, their faces low over the bowls. Instinctively, she wants to tell them to sit up straight but for now she just stands and watches. Laura comes into view and taps Seth on the shoulder, telling him to slow down. Glancing up, she sees Kate and waves.

Kate lifts her hand automatically, then drops it to her side again.

Laura walks towards her, wiping her hands in a cloth. Her brow creases as she comes closer.

Kate runs her hand through her hair – she must look a state.

"Are you all right, love? Is your friend all right?" Laura takes her by the arm and leads her into the hall.

Kate nods.

"I thought I saw the car around five o'clock but it must have been someone else."

"No, that was me – I got here then I decided to go to the beach for a walk on my own. Sorry, Mum – I left you with the boys all day."

"Don't worry, they're grand. I'll tell you what – sit here for a minute," she points to the bottom step of the stairs, "and I'll put a DVD on for the boys. We can have a glass of wine in the kitchen and chat."

Laura presses her down onto the step and goes in to give the boys the good news. Cheering, without noticing Kate, they race to the couch in the sitting room to watch who knows what from her mother's ancient DVD collection.

Kate pulls herself up off the step.

In the kitchen, Laura is struggling with the corkscrew – Kate takes it from her and pops the cork. She pours, watching the deep-red liquid fill the glass. The only other sound is the ticking of the clock on the wall. Without looking at her, she hands Laura the glass and pours her own.

"So?"

"It's not a friend."

"Is it Sam?"

Kate nods and takes a deep drink from her glass. Shifting on the chair, she pulls the crumpled letter from her jeans pocket and slides it across the table to her mother.

Laura reads it, her face falling.

"Oh Kate! And is it true? Are you sure it's not just a mistake? Sam would have to be mad to do something like this. It has to be a mistake. Who sent it?"

"I don't know. I wonder if it was that old lady Rosemary I was telling you about – she's a bit of a gossip. Though how she got the address here is beyond me."

"And did you go there today – is that where you were?"

Kate nods again. "Yeah. I went home. And let's just say neither Sam nor his girlfriend were expecting a visitor – her stuff is everywhere. Ugly hooker shoes and cheap tacky underwear. In my laundry basket. I wanted to puke."

"Her stuff is in your house? My God, he must have lost the plot – surely he'd realise there's a huge chance of being caught? Did you see him – Sam?"

"No, he was at work. I left him a note. I told him not to contact me." She checks her phone, then switches it off. "I'm so angry and so pissed off and so surprised too – I just never pictured Sam as a cheater."

Laura nods.

"Fine, I know he cheated before but that was different. We weren't together that long, and it was a stupid fling with an ex. That's very different to a middle-aged married dad of two sleeping with someone in his own house. In *my* house." She groans, and pours more wine. "Fucking whore!"

"Kate –"

"Sorry, Mum."

"No, I was going to say talk to me any time, vent, swear, do whatever you need to do. And stay here as long as you like. You and the boys are always welcome. I know what it's like, I've been there."

"Oh Mum, what you went through – it was so unbelievably awful, and what Dad did was unforgivable. And you came through it like a hero – like a pro. I don't think I've ever said how much I admired you. I know I was horrible at the time but, Jesus, with every bone of my body I knew you were incredible." She puts her hand over Laura's. "What Sam has done is so horrendously clichéd in comparison – we are nothing more than a suburban cliché. Another statistic, and another dumb wife who didn't see what was going on under her own roof."

Laura shakes her head but doesn't reply. They sit drinking wine, listening to the ticking of the clock and the sound of two small boys laughing at the TV.

The phone lights up with notifications when she switches it back on. Four text messages, all from Sam.

Please talk to me, Kate – I'm so sorry. I need to speak to you to sort this out – please.

Please text me at least – we have to sort this out.

Kate, I'm so sorry, I really fucked up here. I'm an idiot – it was all a stupid mistake.

I feel like we've been growing apart, and I was lonely. And flattered by the attention. I know, it sounds so weak when I put it like that. And it is. Men are stupid, I'm stupid.

Oh God, how had she ended up with this loser? She stabs her reply into the phone and hits send before she changes her mind.

Goodbye, Sam.

She switches off the phone.

Chapter 26

October 22nd 1990

The whine of the car alarm starts up just as the Nine O'Clock News *headlines begin. John groans and pulls himself up out of the couch.*

"That's the third time this week – I'll have to bring it in to be serviced," he mutters, walking out to the cold hallway, as Claire pushes the sitting-room door closed after him to keep the heat in.

The noise of the alarm is deafening when he opens the front door, a rude interruption on the quiet October evening. The neighbours would be cursing him. He clicks the button and the noise abruptly stops, although it's still ringing in his ears.

Then he hears it – a faint rustling. Where is it coming from? There it is again – louder now, and then a thwack, like something hitting the ground. A fox maybe, eying up the bin? He picks up what Claire calls the "rubbish rock" and puts it on the lid of the bin – that might keep them out. He hears the rustling again, and another thwack. It's coming from the bushes across the road. That couldn't be a fox – what is it?

One of Sam's friends messing? Or was someone trying to take the car after all? He walks slowly out onto the road to take a closer look. Now there's no sound, just an eerie silence. He moves closer to the bushes and kicks one with his foot. Nothing. He steps back onto the road, scratching his head.

A car engine is purring softly somewhere behind. He turns and squints into the darkness. The engine revs suddenly. Someone's in a hurry. He can't make out whose car it is – the new guy from the corner house? He's forgotten to turn on his lights. John raises his hand, pointing at the front headlights. So easy to forget in a lit-up area – he did the same one night last week. He keeps waving and pointing. The car is coming down the road towards him now, gathering speed. It's coming right at him – can't the driver see him? He tries to jump out of the way but it's too late. Now there's only screaming pain and he's lying on the cold, black road.

The car reverses. It's almost out of sight. Why is the driver not helping him? John tries to shout but he can't. Then he hears the car again. It's coming towards him, faster and faster. Understanding now, he tries to crawl to the side but he can't move. He claws at the road, scrabbling for a grip, anything to pull his body out of the way, watching in horror as the car comes straight for him.

And then everything goes black.

Mourners spill out onto the street because, in spite of the vastness of the church, there isn't enough room.

In the front pew, Sam grips his mother's hand.

Claire looks nothing like herself – she's aged a decade in three days. Her eyes are wide and vacant, staring into the nothingness in front of her – ceremony and Valium each playing a part to get her through.

The coffin they spent so much time choosing looks just like every other coffin now. Except there's a photo of his dad on top. It's one from the office – the black-and-white shot they use for his byline in the paper. It was the only photo they could find of him on his own. John's eyes look out over the top of his glasses, surveying the congregation with just a hint of a smile behind his pipe. He had insisted on having the pipe in the photo – to show the real him, he said, to contrast with the formality of the shirt and tie. And now, he has no say in any of it. Inside a wooden box, about to be put in the ground.

Sam's shoulders shake. Claire continues to stare straight ahead and doesn't notice, but Bella is on his other side, and gently touches his arm. He can't look at the photo any more. He follows Claire's lead and, side by side, they stare straight ahead, now a family of two.

He hears movement to his left and turns to see Michael slipping into the pew beside Bella.

"Did you let the hotel know about the changed time?" Bella whispers.

Michael nods. "It's all sorted – they were great."

Sam closes his eyes, giving silent thanks that these two are here – not to God, because what kind of God would let his dad die such a horrible death – but maybe to the Universe. The two of them had been there late Monday night, when the ambulance and the Guards had left, and the house was horribly quiet. Between them they made dozens of cups of tea, and held Claire's hand as she sat staring and not speaking. Bella had phoned the funeral home on Tuesday morning, and Michael had called to pass on the news to John's boss. They spoke to the priest about what kind of ceremony they wanted, when Claire was unable to get out of bed on Wednesday morning. They took turns to leave at times, but they always came back. They greeted well-meaning visitors and passed on their condolences when Claire was too ill to see anyone. They accepted casseroles and cards and flowers and wreaths. They waited for the forensic team to finish examining the blood on the road outside the house, and made sure that it was cleaned up afterwards before Claire or Sam could step outside and see the dark red patch. Bella chose hymns, and found a suit for the burial.

The burial. It still sounds all wrong to Sam. His dad, who had been trying to grab the remote control from him just minutes before, lying in a crumpled, broken heap in the middle of the road.

On a Monday night. Just a normal Monday night. Nothing would ever be the same again.

Chapter 27

Kate – Tuesday, August 2nd 2016

The heart in her cappuccino disintegrates at the turn of her spoon – what was with all these shapes in coffees today anyway? She turns her phone over and over idly in her hand, wondering if she should have brought her book. Maybe that's a sign she's coming to terms with the affair – ready to stop wallowing? Or perhaps she just needs distracting from herself – she's boring herself to tears now with the whole thing. She pulls her hoodie around her as the breeze picks up. Her receipt flutters to the ground and she reaches down to grab it – she can almost see the stain from where her coffee fell when Mrs Daly ambushed her. Was that only two weeks ago? It seems a world away now.

Her phone screen lights up with a text: Sam's usual apology. There's more today though – he wants to come down for Seth's birthday. As if. Maybe her silence is giving the wrong message – does he think she's going to forgive him?

Sam, I've told you not to contact me. And no, of course you can't come down for Seth's birthday. I don't want to see you.

His reply is immediate. Have you told the boys?

No, not yet. What could I possibly say to them? I'll tell them you had to work. They'll be fine – they haven't been asking for you.

She hesitates with her finger on the send button, then deletes the last part before sending.

What about Seth's present? It's still here.

So send it in the post.

It's too big to post. I could get Miller to take it – he was saying he might go down again in the next few weeks?

No! Please don't encourage him. The last visit was painful.

Ugh, this is starting to sound like a normal conversation.

Michael is another option. He said he'd do it if you didn't want me to go down.

So does Michael know about your cheating?

That's more like it.

I told him at the weekend. He gave me a bollicking.

I always liked Michael. Fair play. Fine, if he wants to bring it down, tell him to come Saturday.

Will do. And I'm sorry.

Too late for that. Bye.

Her phone beeps again – Jesus, he's not getting the message at all. But this time it's Miller.

Hi Kate, how are you? I'm thinking of coming down to Galway again soon. I hope Sam isn't lonely without you all. I called again twice recently but he didn't answer. Isn't that strange?

Oh for Jesus' sake, would he ever take a hint? Although Sam seems to have lost his "Ah Kate, don't be so mean to Miller" attitude, now that he's the one dealing with it on his own.

Miller, it doesn't make any sense for you to call when we're not there – Sam is at work. And maybe you'd be better

focusing on getting a job than coming down to Galway again – you were only here just two weeks ago.

She hits send and waits for the reply, but there's none. Feck, that was probably a bit harsh. Bloody Miller.

The door swings open and Jan comes outside to gather empty cups from another table. The wind knocks a chair on its side and she picks it up, nodding towards Kate, and looks up at the grey sky.

"That's the end of the summer, I'd say," she says.

It is indeed, thinks Kate, it most certainly is.

Chapter 28

Kate – June 1984

It's definitely going to rain. And, of course, the one day her mum trusts them to walk home without her, Miller doesn't show up. Kate folds her arms and frowns, looking around the increasingly empty schoolyard. Miller's not at the door, even though she told him three times this morning he was to wait for her. And the last few kids from his class are gone now too. It starts to rain, and she pulls up the hood of her ugly green rain-jacket. Maybe he's still in the classroom. She picks up her bag, cursing him under her breath.

But only the teacher is still in the room, and she says Miller left ten minutes ago with all the other kids. She goes back to her marking.

"Thanks for nothing," Kate mutters, as she goes outside.

Would he have gone on without her? She walks out the school gate and looks down the road towards the village. There's a cluster of boys outside the sweet shop and they look about his age, but the rain is heavier now and distorting her vision – she can't make out if Miller is among them. She starts walking. It *is* Miller, and there's a group of boys in a circle around him, throwing something. She picks up her pace. Miller is running from one boy to the next as they throw whatever it is. It's a shoe. They're throwing his shoe. She starts to run. He has one shoe on, but his other foot is bare, splashing down in rapidly forming puddles every time he runs. The boys are laughing as Miller tries desperately to catch his remaining shoe, but he can't. Not when it's five against one. Kate races up to the group, and just as one boy raises the shoe above his head to throw it, she grabs it. He turns around and laughs when he sees her.

"*How dare you!*" she roars at him. "*Do you think that's funny?*"

"Chill! It's just a joke."

"Where are his socks?"

The boy shrugs.

She turns to Miller. "Where are your socks?"

"Back at the school," he says, his head down.

"You took his shoes and socks at the school? He ran down here barefoot? In the rain?"

The first boy answers. "Well, he got one shoe back at the school. So not totally barefoot. And anyway, he's too dim to notice. Retard."

He whispers the last word, but Kate hears it. She thumps him hard, catching him on the shoulder and knocking him back. He trips over a schoolbag and lands on the ground, red-faced and surprised. The other boys snigger and start to slink away, leaving just Miller and Kate, his shoe in her hand.

"Come on," she says, putting her arm around him. "Put this on, and I'll help you find your socks."

"I just want to go home now," he says. "Can we leave the socks?"

"I wish we could leave the village too," Kate says, as she helps him tie his lace.

At dinner, glancing over at Miller, she tells her parents what happened. He pays no attention, methodically eating his lamb chop and mashed potato. When she tells them Miller had to walk from the school to the village with only one shoe on, Laura claps her hand over her mouth and looks like she's going to cry. She gets up and walks around the table to hug Miller. He keeps eating.

"Oh love, I'm so sorry this happened to you. I should have gone down to collect you. This is all my fault. I'll be there every day from now on."

Great, thinks Kate. Because being the only kid in her class still collected from school won't *at all* make life harder for her.

But her dad has other ideas. He puts down his knife and fork before speaking, like it's some kind of big pronouncement – like he's the boss of the house. As if. She rolls her eyes but makes sure he doesn't see.

"No," he says, folding his arms. "Laura, you're not to collect him. He needs to learn to stand up for himself. Miller, how do you feel about the fact that your sister had to help you today – that you had to be rescued by a girl? It's supposed to be the other way around. So the next time someone tries to take your shoe, you punch him and walk away."

Laura stands up straight. "Richard, that's not the right message to be giving him. He should tell a teacher or find Kate – you can't be telling him to hit other children."

"That's what we were taught as kids and it didn't do us any harm. I'd never have let anyone bully me like that – he needs to stand up for himself or it'll still be happening in thirty years' time." He turns to his son. "Miller, leave the table now and go upstairs to think about what happened today. I'll be up in a while to speak to you, and I want to know that you've listened and understood what I'm saying."

Kate's sure Miller isn't paying any attention at all, but then he pushes back his chair and walks out of the room. They wait silently, listening to his slow footsteps on the stairs, and the sound of his bedroom door closing.

Laura sits back down and looks at her husband. "That's not fair – he's only eight, and he needs our sympathy after what happened today. Sending him to his room will feel like a punishment."

"It *is* a punishment. He should never have let them take his shoes. It's our job as parents to teach him lessons like this." Richard picks up his knife and fork again and cuts off a piece of lamb.

Kate watches him, her stomach churning in time with his chewing. She's conscious that her mum is close to tears again, but she doesn't look at her. What a dick, she thinks. Even kids know that's not a good lesson. And not for the first time, she wishes it could be just the three of them – Laura, Miller and Kate.

Chapter 29

Kate – Saturday, August 6th 2016

Kate stands in the doorway with her arms folded, watching as Michael gets out of the car, with the present tucked under his arm. Where exactly is bloody Scalextric going to fit in her mother's B&B? At least it's wrapped – that's a first for Sam. Michael looks unsure about how to greet her and, inexplicably, that makes her happy. He opts for a quick smile and a shrug in the end, and asks if he should bring in the present or leave it in the car.

"Sure, bring it in, he's out in the garden," she says, and turns to walk back inside. Michael follows.

"Do they know it's me that's coming and not Sam?" he says to Kate's retreating back.

"Yeah. It's fine."

Outside, Seth and Jamie squeal when they see Michael, and race to hug him before grabbing the present and ripping off the paper.

"I love it!" Seth says, putting down the box to hug Michael again.

"Well, it's not from me – I have something else for you in the car. This one is from your mam and dad."

"Is Dad here?" Seth asks, his big brown eyes wide with anticipation.

Kate starts to plan her answer but Michael gets there first, hunkering down to talk to Seth at eye level.

"He had to work – he has a huge amount of work at the moment, and his boss said he had to stay in the office all weekend. He really wanted to come down, and he really misses you two, but he couldn't."

Two chins meet two chests.

Dammit anyway. Sam and his bloody mess. Kate puts her arms around the boys. "We'll have great fun with this," she says. "I don't even know how Scalextric works – will you show me?"

"I don't know either, Mum," Seth says, his head still down. "Dad was going to show me . . . "

Michael takes Seth's hand. "You know, I've a pretty good idea how this works. Will I give it a try?"

Seth nods, and Kate mouths a "Thank you" to Michael.

The track takes up half the patio outside the kitchen window, and Michael really does seem to know what he's doing. The boys are hanging on every word while he lays it out and talks them through each step.

Kate watches from inside as she searches for birthday candles. The cake – a rainbow cake, because rainbow is Seth's favourite colour – is still in the box from Jan's, and there are buns and jellies somewhere in the cupboard too. Would it be enough? Well, apart from the obvious gaping hole left by the absent father. What's he doing right now, she wonders, instead of celebrating his son's birthday? She pulls out her phone and her finger hovers over the **Find My Device** app. It doesn't help her *at all* to know where he is. And if he's somewhere other than home or the supermarket, what's she going to do about it anyway? If anything it's going to annoy her. But she already knows she's going to look. The map takes a few seconds to show up, but when it does, the pin is neatly tucked into 26 Willow Valley. He's at home. And now she just feels sad.

McDonagh's smells of turf and sawdust and spilled Guinness when she pushes open the heavy door. Every person in the bar turns to look at them as they walk in, and she wonders what possessed her to say yes. It had been Laura's idea – she'd mind the boys, she'd said, and Kate could get out for lunch. It would do her good, Laura insisted, to have adult company other than her own mother. Kate would have preferred to stay in the garden with the boys and let Michael go back to Dublin, but then of course Michael hung back, waiting for her to answer, and she couldn't say no.

They take a small table beside the fireplace and Michael goes to the bar to get menus. "I'll just have the soup," Kate calls after him. "Don't worry about a menu for me." The locals aren't paying attention any more. They probably look like a couple. There's a newspaper on the table and she picks it up – the front page shows a picture of that little girl who's gone missing. That poor mother. Where's the dad in all this? Curious, she turns to the inside pages, but then Michael comes back from the bar. He has a coffee for himself and puts a glass of red wine in front of her.

"It's a bit early for wine, isn't it?" she says, but takes a sip.

"Ah, I reckon you've been cooped up at home for long enough – you could do with something stronger than coffee," he says, sitting down opposite her.

Kate nods and takes another sip. "So, let's skip the small talk. Just tell me – is it serious?"

"God no, Kate. Just one of those things – he's an awful eejit. You know how it is."

"Well, no, I don't know. Tell me – what exactly do you

mean by 'one of those things'?"

Michael picks up his coffee and pauses before answering. "First of all, tell me, how much do you want to know? Think about it, Kate, you might not feel any better for knowing the details. There's a lot to be said for just leaving it . . ."

Kate shakes her head. "I can't leave it. I'm so pissed off with him, and it's been driving me mad since I found out. If I'm going to move on – in whatever direction that might be – I need to know the details."

Michael nods. "Okay. There's not much to tell really – it's a girl he works with. They were put on a project, and they were spending a lot of time together, and it just sort of happened. Well, that's what he told me anyway."

Kate feels queasy. Michael was right, it's horrible hearing the details. But she can't stop now. "What does she look like?"

"Does it matter?"

"Absolutely it matters. She has stayed in my house. I've seen her gross underwear. At the very least, I deserve to know the details."

"She's young. Long hair – look, I'm not good at this. She just looks like every other girl to me."

Kate puts her head in her hands. "God, I can't believe I'm sitting here having this conversation. Like, Sam! Sam who has always been the good guy, whiter than white, never hurts a fly. How did we end up here?"

Michael shakes his head. "I honestly don't know, Kate. It's not like him at all. I was shocked when he told me."

Kate sits up straighter. "Hang on a sec – did you know about her before I did?"

"Jesus, no. I'd have made him stop if I did, or made him tell you, or I'd have told you myself. Kate, I swear, I wouldn't have let it go on. But no, he only told me after you left the note."

The barman drops two soups to them and Kate butters some soda bread – the wine is already going to her head.

"Shit, I wonder do the people in his work know? I didn't even think of that till now – imagine them all feeling sorry for me. Or thinking 'lucky Sam'. Jesus!" She looks at Michael, waiting for an answer.

"I've no idea, to be honest – he hasn't said they do, so I'm guessing not. I'm sure it wouldn't look good to his boss. I don't think anyone knows – well, other than your brother – I take it you told him?"

Kate puts down her spoon. "Miller? No, I haven't said a word to him – what makes you think I did?"

Michael looks confused. "He's been calling in to the house a good bit even though you're not there. Sam mentioned it – he reckoned Miller wanted to have it out with him about the whole thing. Sam just doesn't answer the door now. Are you sure he doesn't know?"

"Definitely. Unless my mum told him . . . I'll text him to stop calling either way." She picks up her phone. "Jesus, I only said it to him in a text a few days ago," she mutters as she types. Then she laughs. "Actually, maybe I shouldn't tell him to stop. It serves Sam right to have to put up with Miller bugging him."

Michael laughs then too and for a minute it feels like old times, except of course it's not – they're here talking about her cheating dick of a husband. She takes a deep breath before asking her next question and when she does speak her voice is uncharacteristically small.

"Is he still seeing her?"

Michael looks down at his soup without answering, and it tells her everything.

"Jesus! Really? He swore blind to me in his texts that it was all a big mistake and it was over. Are you serious? The fucker is still seeing her?"

Two men at the bar turn to look at her and she scowls at them.

Michael looks like he's choosing his words. "He told me he's finished it, and if he's said the same to you, then he must have."

"But?"

"Oh Kate, I really don't want to be in the middle of this."

"Michael, just tell me."

He throws up his hands. "That's all I know. He says he's done with her."

"Look me in the eye this time and tell me again."

"Kate, you need to sort this out with him yourself."

"That's fine, but if he's apologising and begging me to meet, and yet he's still seeing her, that's kind of a difficult basis on which to sort it out – wouldn't you say?"

Michael chews his lip but says nothing.

"I mean, you just swore to me that if you'd known, you'd have done something about it. This is your chance to do something about it – is he still seeing her?"

The nod is barely perceptible.

Kate can feel the familiar knot in her stomach forming, but she pushes for more. "Tell me."

"He told me he'd broken up with her, but I saw them. We had made a plan that I'd call out on Thursday night to rewire the light in the main bathroom. Then Sam phoned at lunchtime to say he had to work late, so I should leave it till another time. I had nothing on that evening, so I decided to head out and do it – it's not like I need him there to help – he'd only stand there telling me to be careful and panicking about being electrocuted – remember that time in your old house?"

Kate nods but she's in no mood for banter

Michael continues. "So I didn't bother phoning him at work or anything – I have a key because I've been in and out working on bits and pieces all summer. And when I turned into your road, I saw him ahead of me, walking into your house."

"And?"

"Well, there was a girl with him, and it was her."

Kate puts her wine down. Her hand is shaking – she keeps it wrapped around the glass. "He swore to me . . . the fucking liar." She thinks for a minute. "Are you sure it was her though? Could it not just have been someone calling at the door?"

"I'm sure. I met her once – at a night out with Sam's office."

"Were they seeing each other when you met her?"

"No! No – that was ages ago. Like, back in February or March."

But how long had it been going on? Maybe it had already started back then. He was working late in the office since the beginning of the year – maybe even earlier than that, but it's all a bit of a blur now, with her leaving work and the house move. Jesus. This is like being in the middle of a soap opera.

She drains her wine and signals to the barman for the bill. A cheap, nasty, tacky soap opera, with no happy ending for any of them.

Chapter 30

The Woman – Christmas Day 2005

The woman sits at the table, silently picking at her ham. He sits across from her, slowly, methodically eating his dinner, but never taking his eyes off his wife.

"Are you going to sulk all day?" he says eventually.

"I'm not sulking," she replies, not looking up.

"Well, then, would you eat properly and get that puss off your face – it's Christmas Day, for God's sake!"

"Not that you'd know it," she answers, under her breath.

"What did you say?"

"Nothing."

"Is this not good enough for you – is that what it is?" he asks, putting down his knife and fork.

She swallows. "It just doesn't feel like Christmas. The house is cold, there's nobody calling, it's like every other day. There's nothing to show that it's special."

The plate catches her on the side of the head. Stunned, she reels backwards, and topples onto the floor. She reaches up to touch the place where it made contact, staring wide-eyed at her husband. Gravy trickles down her neck and down her back. Tears sting the back of her eyes.

He's standing over her, fists clenched. "Now look what you've done, you stupid bitch – clean yourself up!" he hisses.

She can't move. He looks as though he's going to say something else, but he turns and walks out of the room without another word.

She sits, still unable to move, gravy and stuffing all over her dress and all over the floor. She puts her hand to her head again to check if it's cut – it's throbbing but not bleeding. She shakes the food off her skirt, and wipes away the tears. She should never have criticised him. She would try harder. She wouldn't give him reason to do it again.

The woman sits back on her chair in the silent, empty kitchen, wondering not for the first time that day how she had ended up in this place.

Chapter 31

Sylvia – Monday, August 15th 2016

Is it worse to be awake before everyone else and unable to go back to sleep, or to be in a deep sleep and woken by a crying baby? Sylvia can't decide. And of course, it's always one or the other. She's read about people who wake to the contented babbling of a child in a cot, but she's not convinced – it's never happened with Megan or Zack. This morning everyone else is asleep – it's just her and the bedroom ceiling and the missing two million swirling around and around in her brain. Maybe she should just get up and log in to her laptop.

Sliding her phone out from under her pillow, she clicks into the texts she's sent Justin. Five now, all unanswered. And three calls. Also unanswered. And now there's a meeting with Craig this morning to give him an update, only she has no update. It's pretty clear now that the money was paid out, and somehow the hole was filled, but she can't see where the cover came from. Craig will lose it when he finds out it's not just a reporting discrepancy. And it's going to sound so weak and so unprofessional, but she'll have to remind him that it was on Justin's watch. She turns on her side and closes her eyes, but account balances and audit requests flood her brain. It's no good. She gets up, grabs a sweatshirt, and slips out the bedroom door.

At the top of the stairs, she stops for a moment. What's that sound? Something hissing. Or flowing. Water? Skin tingling, she starts down the stairs, listening as the noise gets louder. Then she works it out – it's just a tap – someone has left a tap running. Megan no doubt – she's constantly leaving on the water in the downstairs loo. Sylvia sticks her head in the guest-bathroom door but, even before she looks, her ears tell her that's not where the sound is coming from. It surely can't be the kitchen – neither she nor Tom would ever leave a tap on at night. But when she walks in, that's exactly what's making the noise – cold water is flowing down into the kitchen sink and there's a half-full glass of water on the counter beside it. There's no way they went to bed without noticing – it doesn't make any sense. She stares at the running water, trying to work it out, but nothing fits. Anxious again, she turns off the tap and turns on the light, and then she sees them. Sitting around the table, like tiny ghouls, all eyes on her. She screams, then clamps her hand over her mouth. Jesus! Who put them there? Reaching out, she picks the first one up. Her hand is shaking, and she wants to laugh but she can't. Mildred. The rag doll Megan got for her first birthday. And on the chair beside her, the huge Our Generation doll she'd got for Christmas last year. A stuffed Rapunzel doll sits on the next seat over. All eight chairs have dolls on them, each staring at her with plastic eyes that follow her around the room. The mass-produced immobile faces that look so innocent when Megan plays house and school now look like they're sneering at her.

One by one, the dolls make a satisfying thunk when she throws them into the toybox in the corner, building a jumbled pile of plastic legs and arms and synthetic hair. Then she takes one of the chairs herself to wait for the pounding in her ears to subside. How did they get there – Tom's idea of a joke maybe? They weren't there when they locked up last night so it can't have been Megan. Or were they – surely she'd have noticed? There's a sound on the stairs. Her throat tightens and she stands up from her seat, staring at the kitchen door. Someone steps off the bottom stair, and she hears soft footsteps on the hall floor. The kitchen door opens and Tom peers in, blinking in the light.

Sylvia slumps back down onto the chair. Tom wants to know if she's okay – he thought he heard someone throwing something? Yes, she says, and tells him about the dolls.

"What do you mean?" Tom asks, trying to hide a yawn.

"There were dolls sitting on each of the chairs when I came down – did you put them there? I'm sure it was meant to be funny but it freaked me out."

Tom shakes his head. "Could it have been Megan? That sounds like one of her games. And where are they now?"

She points at the toy-box. "I put them back. I should have waited to show you."

Tom walks over and hugs her into his chest. "Come on, let's go back to bed. And when Megan wakes up and wants to know where her dolls are, you can explain that you undid all her work – rather you than me."

She pulls out of the hug. "But Tom, she couldn't have done it – sure we'd have seen them last night when we were going to bed?"

He shrugs. "I wouldn't notice either way. Come on, alarm's not going off for another hour – I need sleep."

"The tap was running too – did you leave the tap on?"

Tom looks at her without answering at first. "Come on, love, you're shattered. Let's go back to bed. And look, at the weekend, you have a lie-in both mornings – I'll take the kids off some place." He takes her by the hand and switches off the light. "I think all the stress at work is really getting to you."

She follows him back up to bed. Within minutes he's snoring again, and Sylvia's back to staring at the ceiling, but the missing two million and the audit reports have been replaced by the smiling faces of plastic dolls.

The meeting with Craig is at half eight, and there's no time to try Justin's mobile again before she goes in.

Craig gets straight to the point – Sylvia needs to finalise her reports and get them to the auditors by close of business Wednesday. Of course, she says, wondering why her mouth is making promises her brain can't keep. He dismisses her with a nod and turns back to his screen. She takes a deep breath: it's now or never. The one thing she's been told on every management course she's ever been on is that you don't blame other people. You don't blame your team or your predecessor, or even your deputy who loses two million and goes on sick leave.

"Craig, there's something you should know. I've been going over the reports at home all weekend and . . . remember the problem with the two million that seemed to be incorrect on the reports? Well, it looks like a payment for two million euro was actually sent out in error. At the start of the year. When I was on maternity leave." She squirms as she says that last part.

Craig looks up from the screen, his mouth open. Nothing comes out at first. When he does speak, his voice is an octave higher than usual. "Two million paid out? But it would have shown up everywhere – that can't be right?"

"It is, I'm afraid. It looks like it was covered from some long-term cash that doesn't appear on the daily risk management reports. So it wasn't spotted. Then the reports were deleted. It was only when the auditors needed them that this all came to light. And I still can't see exactly which money was used, but I'm fairly sure the original payment was a mistake, and we're short two million. I think it went to DBK, and I'm chasing it."

Craig stands up and runs his hand through what's left of his hair. "Jesus, Sylvia, how could you let something like this slip through? Have you completely lost your ability to manage the team?"

His words hit like a slap and she can feel her cheeks turn red.

"I'll call Risk," he continues, "and you'd better get out there and get the money back, and find out what funds were used to cover it. Jesus Christ, this is serious. What's going on in your team – how could you let this happen?"

She finds her voice. "But I wasn't here – I was on maternity leave." Shit, it sounds so weak and defensive. "Justin was managing the team."

Craig puts his hands on the desk, and leans forward. "Sylvia. You're here now, and you're the manager, so you need to fix it. Please don't spend time telling me whose fault it was — it would be far better spent finding the money. *Now go!*" He shouts the last bit.

In fifteen years working, she's never been shouted at. She turns and walks out of his office, cheeks blazing. With blurred eyes, she walks quickly to the bathroom and locks herself inside a cubicle. Tears come but they're shortlived – she's too angry to cry now.

Georgia's silver Mercedes purrs into the cul-de-sac just ahead of Sylvia's more prosaic seven-seater, making almost no sound as it glides to a stop.

Sylvia waves when she gets out of her car and crosses the road to catch Georgia before she goes into her house.

"Hi, Sylvia, how are things? I'm just dropping off some bits I picked up after work before I get Annabel from the childminder," Georgia says.

The "bits" are in the shape of two big Brown Thomas bags, and the smell of salon shampoo is wafting its way on the evening air to Sylvia – Georgia must have found time to get her hair done too. If only Sylvia could have a job that ended so early in the day, but still paid enough for clothes shopping and hairdressing! Though she'd probably feel guilty and just go straight home to the kids.

"Sure, I won't keep you. I just wanted to ask if you know anything about the new people next door to us?"

"Oh, you mean about the woman who's been in and out – God, don't mind that – has Noel been talking to you?"

"Well, yes, but that wasn't it . . ."

"Listen, each to their own. If your man next door to you wants to have a shag on the side, that's his business."

"Well no, I wanted to ask if you *know* Sam, and what he's like."

"Why, Sylvia, are you thinking of taking a lover yourself? Joke! Seriously, I'm just kidding. But no, to answer your question, I don't really know him at all. Why do you ask?"

"Just that we've had a few odd things happen in the house in the middle of the night and it's all since the new people moved in."

Georgia puts her bags down, and leans against the car, folding her arms. "Really? What kind of things?"

"Oh, just noises. Things being moved around. And I thought I saw something in their garden – in their pond."

"Interesting!" Georgia flashes a big white smile. "Things that go bump in the night! Maybe you could turn ghost-hunter and go on one of those TV shows – you know, the ones that have those special cameras in the dark. We could all do it – it'd be gas!" She touches Sylvia's shoulder with one perfectly manicured finger.

Oh God, she must sound like an idiot. "Well, it was a child I thought I saw in the pond. A dead child." Instantly she regrets it.

"What do you mean? Do you think it was that missing little one – Edie – is that her name? The one on the news?"

Why oh why did she say it? "Oh no, I don't think it was really a child – it just looked that way. When I went in to check, there was nothing there. It might have been a trick of the light."

Georgia is looking at her as though she's completely insane. Understandably.

"Okay . . . well, it's been lovely catching up, Sylvia, but I'd better get on with it – Annabel goes mad if I'm late picking her up – as if she doesn't see enough of me already!"

"Okay . . . bye, Georgia!"

Sylvia turns and walks towards her own house. Why didn't she keep her mouth shut! Georgia would probably tell Noel, and then who knows who he'd tell – he might even say it to Sam. What was she thinking? And all over a few dolls and some photos and a shadow on the water in the middle of the night. This thing with work is turning her into a crazy person. Deep breaths. She puts the key in the lock and braces herself for the chaos of the "real job", as her mother calls it.

But no running feet come to greet her. The house is completely silent. It's quarter past six – they should definitely be here.

"Jane?" she calls out, but there's no reply.

The kitchen is empty and silent. Maybe they're out the back – it's still quite warm. But even as she opens the back door, it's clear they're not there. Bailey rouses himself from the last sunny spot on the grass and comes to lick her hand. Nothing else stirs. Running upstairs, she calls again, but there's no answer. Was Jane's car in its usual spot at the end of the cul-de-sac? She goes outside to check. It's not there. Standing in the front garden, she scans the road. This has never happened before. Jane knows she's home by six at the very latest every day.

Back inside the kitchen, with fumbling fingers she tries calling. It's ringing. But then there's another, louder noise. Jane's phone is ringing from somewhere inside the house.

Following the sound of the phone, she finds it under the hall table. Just one missed call – hers. Panic starts to creep in. Where are they and why doesn't Jane have her phone with her? She calls Tom – he's still at work and hasn't heard from Jane. Who else to call? Does she know anyone in Jane's family? Her mother lives in Ballinteer, but that's as far as her information goes. And Jane's phone is locked. It sits in her hand, sleek and flat and useless, mocking her.

Back outside, she paces up and down the road, willing the little red Micra to come around the corner.

Rosemary appears at her front door, and Sylvia walks over to ask her if she's seen Jane.

"I saw her going out earlier with the children – she stopped to give a lift to Sam, then they headed off – why, is something wrong?" Rosemary asks, with a hint of breathless anticipation.

The first prickles of hysteria are setting in. Her brain is telling her to do something – anything – but her body is frozen to the spot.

"Sylvia, are you all right? You look pale – come in and sit down."

Sylvia shakes her head and dials a number on her phone.

There's a tremor in her voice as she tries to explain her story to the desk sergeant on the other end of the line. His voice is kind and calm as he asks for the registration of Jane's car. Sylvia has no idea. He asks for a description of Megan and Zack, and she wants to throw up, but she gives it. He asks for Jane's home address – she doesn't know that either, but she can find the CV Jane gave them when they hired her and then phone him back. There's something else, Sylvia tells him. There was a man called Sam in the car with them. She doesn't know his second name but his address is 26 Willow Valley, Dún Laoghaire, and he's their neighbour and there's something strange about him, and now he's with her kids somewhere.

"That's good you mentioned it," the sergeant says, "but no doubt there's nothing to worry about."

What does Sam look like, he asks, just in case he's still with them – though they probably just dropped him off somewhere. Tall with dark hair, she says, in his early forties. He tells her to find the address and call him back. And not to worry.

Rosemary listens to the one side of the conversation with her mouth open and her eyes wide. "Do you think something happened to them? Are you worried about Sam?"

But Sylvia can't answer – she goes inside to look for Jane's address. The laptop won't switch on at first, then it takes ages to load up. Where the hell would Jane's CV be? Maybe in an email. Nothing comes up when she searches under "CV", so she tries "Jane". Dozens of results come back – including every email between Sylvia and Tom where Jane's name was ever mentioned, and all the mails she's sent to the Jane in Finance at work. Her fingers keep typing the wrong letters and her hands are shaking – this is going nowhere.

She needs Tom. He picks up on the first ring, and she asks

him to find Jane's address.

"They're still not home," she tells him, her voice catching in her throat. "I'm sure it's fine but just in case there was an accident, I phoned the Guards. They want Jane's address."

Tom, to his eternal credit, tells her he'll get the address and phone the Guards back with it, then he'll phone hospitals. She's to sit tight in case Jane arrives home or phones.

"Tom," she says, just before he hangs up, "what if it's something to do with that missing child – Edie Keogh?"

"It's not, I promise you that. The latest rumour is that the child's father has her – the parents are split up and they're saying he may have taken the child out of the country. Don't worry. Jane wouldn't let anyone near our two – I bet she's just forgotten the time."

Pacing up and down, she clicks into news on her phone – there's no headline about an accident, but then every accident wouldn't be on the news. The Edie Keogh investigation is still the top story, though there's nothing new to say today, it seems, and nothing about her father.

Then, from outside comes the unmistakable sound of a car pulling into the driveway.

Sylvia runs to open the door, just as the red Micra comes to a stop.

Jane waves, and gets out to open the door for Megan.

"Where were you?" Sylvia is close to tears now, as she takes Zack from Jane's arms.

Jane looks at her blankly. "Sorry, are we really late? I can't find my phone anywhere. I got a flat tyre, so we had to go to a garage. I'd have called you but my phone has disappeared. I'm so sorry, Sylvia – were you worrying?"

"Yes! I called the Guards and everything – I was afraid something had happened. You've never been out when I got home before, and then when I found your phone in the house,

I didn't know where you were."

Jane looks confused. She must think she's a raving lunatic. Or that she sees her as a would-be kidnapper.

"It doesn't matter, you're home now." Sylvia smiles weakly at her. "I have a tendency to overreact where the kids are concerned. Sorry."

Jane frowns. "No, that's fine, but I definitely had my phone with me when we left – I texted my mother just before we drove off – from the car – it couldn't be in the house."

Shifting Zack up onto her shoulder, Sylvia gets the phone from the hall and gives it to Jane. "It was under the hall table. You must have texted your mother earlier and forgotten. Look, it's grand. These things happen. And I totally overreacted. It was just when I couldn't reach you . . . And then Rosemary said you gave Sam next door a lift, and I didn't know what was going on."

Jane's face reddens. "Sam, yes, he was walking down to the shops so I gave him a lift. Is that okay? Sorry, I would never normally give anyone a lift when I have the kids with me, but he's a neighbour, so I thought it would be all right? It won't happen again."

"I . . . yes, I think it's better not to give lifts. And sorry, I must seem like such an eejit calling the Guards – I was just afraid there'd been an accident. Actually I'd better call them back now, and Tom too."

Jane waves her away, apologising again.

Sylvia closes the front door and sits down on the hall floor, pulling Megan into a hug and kissing the top of Zack's head over and over. She rings Tom to tell him they're back.

"I feel so silly now but, Jesus, it made me realise I take them for granted and let little things get on top of me. My God, when I thought they were gone – it's really given me perspective." She traces her finger along Zack's face.

"I know – look, I'll phone the Garda station now, and then I'll head home – I'll see you very soon."

She disconnects the call but stays on the ground, hugging both children. After a minute, Megan wriggles out of her arms and says she's a bit bored and wants to watch TV. Zack is whimpering and rubbing his eyes, and when Sylvia takes too long finding the right cartoon for Megan, he starts to wail. She tries putting him in his chair to watch TV with his sister but he cries harder. So she makes a one-handed start on dinner while balancing Zack on her hip, wondering if this is a world record for abandoning perspective.

Chapter 32

Sylvia – Tuesday, August 16th

As fond as Sylvia is of Bailey, his hints at sleeping indoors go unheeded, as they do every night. Lazy dog, she tells him, rubbing his head and shepherding him out to his kennel. On the way back inside, she hears a car pull up out front – Tom's taxi, earlier than expected. As she turns the key in the back door, she can hear him fumbling with his key in the front door, and he looks surprised when she pulls it open.

"Oh dear, are you a bit tipsy?" she asks, stepping aside to let him in.

"I'm grand," he says, giving her a beery kiss.

"Good, because I need advice."

"Ah, here – it's nearly midnight. Could we do something else instead of advice?" He leans in for another kiss.

"No, thanks, it's advice I need. I'll even make you a cup of tea – come on." She leads him by the hand into the kitchen and puts on the kettle. "So, I contacted DBK – that's who the two million euro was sent to. They have no record of an outstanding payment received – I thought I was going to throw up when they said that. They weren't too interested but

I got an email address for their investigations department and sent over the payment details." She rubs her eyes and her voice gets wearier. "In the meantime, we're still short two million, and Justin is still out sick. I texted him again today, asking him to write something up from home – just whatever he can remember about fudging the reports. Well, I didn't say fudging."

Tom is making every effort to look interested, but his eyelids are drooping.

She shakes his arm. "Tom, this is serious – I'm under huge pressure from all sides to fix this, and everyone seems to have forgotten I wasn't even there when it happened!"

He opens his eyes and straightens up. "Look, they know you didn't make the mistake but you can't expect them to preface every conversation by saying that – they just want to get on with finding it. My place is the same – no-one cares whose fault it is as long as it's not theirs, and as long as it's fixed."

"I know, I know, it's just horrible being at the centre of it. And if Craig put as much effort into actually finding the money as he does into covering his ass, we'd have it by now."

"Well, then you keep doing that – keep trying to trace the money, and you get to be the good guy who fixes Justin's mistake. If anyone can find it you can – that's what you do best."

"Yeah, but I got hauled into Craig's office again and told to stop texting Justin. Apparently he told HR and they say he could have a valid complaint if he decided to make one – because I'm 'impeding his recovery'. It's such bull. I'm fairly certain there's nothing wrong with him at all."

Tom looks at the clock and waves away the tea she's offering. "I know, but there's nothing you can do about that now – just focus on finding the money. Don't waste your energy on Justin. Come on, I need sleep."

Tom's advice rings in Sylvia's ears when she's lying in bed, still wide-awake an hour later, trying very hard not to think about work. The soft stereo snoring from Tom and Zack isn't helping. It's too hot for a start. She throws off the duvet and tries again, scrunching her eyes shut and looking for something calming to think about. But work creeps back in every time. She's never going to sleep tonight.

Zack starts to cry, rousing her from a dream about Bailey and the garden next door. It's 2.23 according to the clock radio. Scooping Zack up, she hugs him to her and he settles back to sleep immediately. Now the hard part – getting him into the cot. Each time she lies him on to the mattress, he stirs again and starts to cry. She grits her teeth and, holding him, slips into the nursing chair, rocking slowly and willing him to sleep. Tom is still snoring quietly, oblivious to all of it. And tomorrow she'll be delirious with exhaustion, facing Craig and the missing money. This really isn't fair.

A noise. Sylvia snaps awake, her head jerking up. What was the noise? She can't remember now. Her neck is stiff and she rubs it, still holding Zack with her other arm. He's in a deep sleep now, and gently she transfers him to the cot. Looking at the clock is counterproductive, but she does it anyway – 4.02 say the bright red digits. Then she hears it – footsteps, and a door opening.

"Tom!" she whispers, shaking him. He opens his eyes. "There's someone downstairs!"

He sits up, listening. They both hear it then. Faint footsteps, and a drawer opening.

"It's next door," he says, lying down again. "Someone in the bedroom next door. It always sounds like it's our house."

Jesus! The exhaustion is really getting to her. She slumps

back against the pillow, and nudges Tom. "What's he doing up and about at 4am?"

"I don't know – what are you doing up and about at 4am?"

"Zack was awake," she hisses at him. "If I had a choice, I'd be asleep."

Tom turns over and mutters goodnight.

Sylvia turns over and dreams of running away.

She's still unconscious with sleep when Tom shakes her to say there's tea on her bedside locker and he's going in to wake Megan. His words are barely audible but he's saying something about cups. It doesn't make any sense and she's too tired to open her eyes. She burrows further under the duvet. Another ten minutes fly by in what feels like thirty seconds, and this time she really does have to get up. Tom is already dressed and looking at his phone when she finally swings her legs over the side of the bed. The tea is lukewarm now.

"Why did you put all the cups out?" Tom asks.

"What cups?"

"On the kitchen table. Every single cup – were you cleaning out cupboards in the middle of the night?"

"No – I don't get what you mean."

"Go down and you'll see. Maybe you were sleepwalking. Or sleep-cleaning."

Down in the kitchen, she sees exactly what he means. Every single cup they own is on the kitchen table. Arranged in a perfect rectangle, all the way around the edges, like a ceramic daisy-chain. The Denby cups they got as a wedding present, the colourful Cath Kidston mugs, the logo-covered freebies they'd picked up over the years, and the little glass coffee cups she'd just bought in Ikea. It would be pretty if it wasn't so bizarre. She picks up one cup and puts it back down, trying to work it out. Maybe it's Tom's idea of a joke? Because she was spooked by the noises from next door?

But upstairs, he insists it wasn't him.

"If it wasn't you, then who was it? Jesus Christ, Tom, does that mean someone really was in the house last night?"

"Arranging our cups for us? A domesticated burglar?"

"Tom, it's not funny."

"You must have done it when you were up last night – do you not remember?"

"I didn't. I know it sounds crazy but I think someone's been in the house. Remember the night Megan said there was a monster in her room? Then those photos were scribbled on, and someone laid out all the dolls on the chairs? And at night, I keep hearing noises. This all started when I saw the child in the water."

"When you *thought* you saw a child in the water. There was nothing there, remember?" He sits down beside her on the bed and takes her hand. "I think this whole thing with work is getting to you. And you're wrecked with the baby up every night. Just wake me when he's up tonight – I know I don't hear him, but I'll get up if you tell me to. And work will be okay – you didn't do anything wrong, and you know DBK have the money. In another few days, it'll be sorted. Trust me?"

Sylvia nods, picking at the grey piping on the edge of the duvet. He's probably right. But with all the stress in the world, she hardly laid out the cups in her sleep? And if it wasn't her – if someone was in the house, why on earth would they be moving things around her kitchen?

Then Zack starts to cry in his cot and her phone beeps with the first emails of the morning and there's no more time to think about any of it. And in some ways she's grateful for the cries and the beeps because the whole day lies ahead and night-time is never so far away as it is first thing each morning.

Chapter 33

Sylvia – Saturday, August 20th

It's alien to be sitting on the step in the midday sun – there's a touch of guilt when the kids come to mind, but it's fleeting. Anyway, after four hours at the laptop, she deserves a break. And it's Saturday – nobody else is even working – certainly not anyone in Stanbridge Brown. Though, to be fair, three of the team had come to her office yesterday to offer to stay late to work on the missing-money investigation. She had told them to head on home, then regretted it when she was still on her laptop at midnight.

Sipping her coffee, she looks around. It's eerily quiet on the road – maybe everyone's at the beach, making the most of the late summer sun. Her phone beeps, breaking the silence – a message from Tom with a photo of Megan on her grandmother's lap. Tom's mother had been thrilled when she heard they were going down for the weekend – she hadn't seen them in months and months, she said, and they'd probably forgotten what she looked like. That wasn't strictly true but it had been a while. Another twinge of guilt. It was a lot easier to visit when she lived in the city centre, no matter how often she claims Enniskerry is only a stone's throw from Dún Laoghaire.

An unfamiliar car pulls up outside the house next door, and a tall woman with short blonde hair gets out. Sam's wife? Sylvia thought her hair was longer, but it might be her. She watches as the woman takes a suitcase from the boot and walks up to the front door. She waves and smiles, and the woman nods over then lets herself into the house. So it must be the wife. Goodness. Suddenly the jokey conversations about affairs and pole-dancers feel less jokey.

Quiet minutes tick by, and the coffee is gone, but Sylvia's not moving. She watches as the blonde woman goes back out to the car carrying a bag and a lamp, then goes inside for a box of what sounds like crockery.

A voice from her left draws her attention away from Number 26. Rosemary has come out to take a look too, it seems.

"Isn't it well for you, getting a bit of sun there," she says, walking over to the dividing wall. "Are the kids watching the telly? They should be out in the sun!"

"Oh hi, Rosemary, no, they're away for the weekend – down with Tom's mother in Enniskerry." Sylvia stands up reluctantly.

Rosemary raises her eyebrows. "Oh, that's *very* nice – lovely little break for you. What will you do with yourself while they're away and their daddy is doing all the work?"

"Well, it's because I'm working – I've a lot to get done over the weekend, so we figured it'd be easier if Tom took them away."

"Why have you to be working on the weekend? That was never the way when my Bob was working – did all the hours God sent during the week, but always took the time to be at home with us at the weekend."

Rosemary's earnest blue eyes show no hint of malice – they never do – but, God, it could be draining.

"Yeah, it's just very busy," Sylvia says, and looks at her watch. "Actually, I'll have to head in now and get back to it."

Rosemary looks like she's searching for more conversation topics but then her phone rings from inside of the house, and she rushes inside.

God love her, she probably doesn't get many callers, Sylvia thinks. Then conscious of eyes on her back, she turns to find the woman next door midway between the house and the car, another box in her arms. The woman nods towards Rosemary's house.

"God forbid you'd spend some time away from your kids, eh? Who died and made her the parent police?"

Sylvia laughs. "Yeah, you wouldn't want to be sensitive. Well, actually, I am pretty sensitive a lot of the time. And prone to giving too much information – as you can see."

"I've only met her once and it was hard going. Is she like that all the time?"

Sylvia walks closer and lowers her voice. "Always. Like, I'm here five years – since before we had kids – and she always finds a way to make a point. Back then it was about us having more than one holiday a year. Then it was about me going back to work after my eldest was born. Now it's about work and the kids and my husband and being a good wife and just generally the horrors of modern life and the utter depravity of the internet."

The woman laughs. "That sounds utterly exhausting – you were much nicer to her than I would have been. I'm Kate, by the way."

"I'm Sylvia. I live here," she says, pointing at her house. "Well, obviously, or it would be weird to be drinking a coffee in the garden. And yeah, I find no matter how annoying

Rosemary is, I haven't the heart to be mean to her. Her husband died about ten years ago and she's lonely."

"Well, hats off to you – I think I'd just avoid her if it was me," Kate says, shifting the weight of the box from one side to the other.

"Yeah, I need to get better at that – my New Year's Resolution every year is to learn to say no – I'm terrible at saying no. If you want something done, ask me, because I'll probably say yes, even if it's something I can't actually do at all, like teach your child Spanish or revive your dead rhododendrons. Not that your rhododendrons are dead or anything . . ." Sylvia looks around the front garden, wondering why she's still babbling. "So I met your husband and he said you were away for the summer – I guess you're back now?"

"Kind of. It's a long story. As you can see, I'm packing more than unpacking."

"Well, if you need a break, mine was just cut short by Rosemary, so I'm making another coffee . . . you're welcome to join me if you like?" As soon as the words are out, Sylvia knows she's going red. This is exactly the kind of thing Rosemary does. Oh dear God, she is the new Rosemary.

But Kate doesn't seem fazed. "You know what, this is the last box, and there's no coffee in my house. I will actually, if you don't mind. Thank you."

The kitchen is bright with midday sun and Kate is impressed, bemoaning the ancient cupboards and lino she has next door. There haven't been any new visitors here for a while and Sylvia has forgotten how good the place looks to fresh eyes. They sit on the high stools at the breakfast bar and drink coffee and eat the scones that Sylvia picked up that morning from the fancy bakery – not the supermarket – and start the ritual of swapping their stories.

Kate says she has two kids, Seth who has just turned eight, and Jamie who is five. They're with her mother today – she has a B&B in Galway. Not in the city – a few miles out, on the coast. Sylvia tells her about Megan and Zack and their trip to Enniskerry, and it feels both freeing and decadent to be drinking coffee with this elegant stranger instead of poring over her laptop.

Kate tells her with a sigh that she used to work in digital marketing and that, although she loves the boys to bits, she really misses work. Sylvia totally gets that, she says – she's back and wishing she wasn't, but doesn't think she could stay at home full-time.

"Stick it out," Kate advises. "If the problems can't be fixed, go somewhere new. But don't give up without being really, really sure."

Sylvia is nodding – it all makes sense. She tells her a bit about Craig and Justin – not the whole story – it's probably a breach of confidentiality if she does – but some of it. Kate rolls her eyes and says she's worked with people like Justin before.

"Why not go to his house and get pictures of him – show he's not really sick?" she says.

This sounds a bit extreme, though a little part of Sylvia starts to think why not? She has his address – how hard could it be? Kate looks like she wouldn't put up with this kind of shit from anyone. Kate would totally catch Justin in the act and tell Craig where to go.

Sylvia makes more coffee as they move on to the "where did you to go school" conversation. It turns out that they were both in UCD at the same time – Kate doing History and English, and Sylvia doing Pure Maths.

"We probably passed in the hallways," says Sylvia.

"Or more likely the bar," says Kate. She was in UCD when she met Sam, she tells her. "Well, not actually *in* UCD, but I was a student there at the time," she clarifies.

"Wow," says Sylvia, "that's a long time. I only met Tom six years ago. Straight from dates to engagement to marriage to baby – no waiting around when you're already in your mid-thirties."

Kate shrugs. "There's a lot to be said for waiting till you're older than twenty."

She looks sad for a minute, Sylvia thinks, wondering about the boxes she'd been carrying to the car.

"Yes, we're splitting up," Kate tells her, reading her mind.

Sylvia is bewildered to find she's close to tears for this relative stranger and her soon-to-be-broken marriage.

"It's such a cliché," Kate continues. "Oldest story in the book. Husband has affair with work colleague. See, it doesn't even make a good headline, it's so bloody boring."

They sit in silence for a minute, Kate staring at her coffee, Sylvia staring at her neighbour, trying to find the right words. None of Sylvia's friends have split up – though it's bound to happen some time in the future.

Kate looks up again. "It's fine," she says. "We'll get through it, like millions of other families." She tells Sylvia that her little boys don't know yet, and she keeps going over and over different versions of the conversation but she can't find the right words. No matter how she puts it, it translates to 'Dad doesn't live with us any more'.

Sylvia feels tears coming again. This woman is going to think she's a lunatic, crying for children she's never met. But it's so sad. What an asshole Sam is. She knew all along he wasn't as nice as he was pretending to be. And it looks like Noel was right after all – well, except about the pole-dancer bit. In spite of herself, she smiles. She thinks about telling Kate, but stops – she may be her new best friend, but she doesn't know her well enough for that bit of gossip just yet.

The phone beeps on the counter, making a rumbling noise that startles both of them. It's Tom again, checking in to see how work is going. The giant clock on the wall says it's almost two. Oh dear. Apologising to Kate as she types, she tells Tom work is fine, and sends kisses to the kids, then puts the phone back down on the counter.

Kate pushes her stool out and stands up. She's a good head taller than Sylvia, even in her impeccably of-the-moment trainers. Stretching, and running her hands through her hair, she thanks Sylvia for the chat and says she should get going. She wants to be back in Galway before the kids go to bed – and out of the house before Sam comes home. He agreed to go into town for a few hours, she explains – to give her space. She stops at the door and turns back to Sylvia.

"Actually," she says, "he's probably with *her*. What a fucker!"

Sylvia nods. "Will we do this again?" she asks. The words are out before she can stop them. It feels like asking someone on a date.

But Kate says yes – she'll be back in Dublin to get schoolbooks and uniforms next week – they'll do coffee then. They swap numbers, and off she goes, like an exotic cloud of pale gold.

And just like that, it's back to spreadsheets and reports and the missing two million.

Chapter 34

September 1987

"It's all back to the books now, isn't it, love – September doesn't be long coming around," says the librarian, smiling up at him, her teeth stained yellow from coffee or cigarettes or both.

"Oh, it is, and it's an exam year for me."

"Goodness, you look very young for exams – well done for getting stuck in so soon. There are desks over there in the corner – that's the quietest part. Easier than studying at home, is it, love?"

He nods. "I've four younger brothers and sisters – there's never a moment's peace in the house. If I'm going to do law, I need to get to study in one way or another. Actually, we're doing a project and I need to look at old newspaper articles. Is there a way to do that here?"

The librarian gets up and moves around the desk, beckoning for him to follow her to the microfiche room. "Do you know what year you want?" she asks.

"I think I'll need to look at the early seventies – I'm not sure of the specific year. It's a project about the courts system."

She shows him how to search, and how to view the microfiche, then leaves him to it, patting him on the arm as she leaves. "It's great to see young people taking an interest in history," she says, closing the door.

He sits down and takes off his jacket. This is going to take hours and hours. But it will be worth it when he sees the look on the lying bitch's face.

Chapter 35

Sylvia – Tuesday, August 23rd

The lift doors close, and the only sound is the serene robotic voice announcing "*Going down.*" Going down indeed – that sums it up, thinks Sylvia. Senior management need a scapegoat, and she fits the bill beautifully.

And of course, not one single person from this morning's meeting is still in the office – once they'd finished firing questions at her, they'd gone for a liquid lunch in Elliot's across the way. Craig's breath smelled of a stomach-turning wine-and-garlic combination when she bumped into him in the kitchen later on – though at least he came back to the office. There was no sign of the others – someone said something about Temple Bar. They were due to fly back to the UK early tomorrow morning, and no doubt keen to make the most of the jaunt. Whereas this morning apparently nothing mattered more than the money and the cover-up. Why didn't they roll up their sleeves and bloody help her then?

The doors glide open and she looks out into pitch darkness. Putting her hands out in front of her, she steps into the basement lobby, wondering why the lights aren't coming on. Don't they operate on a sensor? She's not sure now – she's never seen them off before. Keeping her hands in front of her, she moves towards the exit door, feeling around on the wall for the card-reader. Her hand finds the light switch, but when she presses it nothing happens. She takes out her phone to shine some light on the wall, wishing she'd downloaded that torch app Tom was always going on about. Now she can make out the reader. But when her card slides through, there's no familiar click. She tries again. Still nothing. Oh, for goodness' sake! She pushes the door and it opens. There must be a fuse gone in the basement.

The car park is in darkness too. She feels for the light switches and tries them, but she already knows they're not going to work. *Shit.*

There's a musty smell down here that she's never noticed before, and it's deathly silent at this time of night. With her arms outstretched, she steps forward tentatively. How is she going to find her car? Her phone screen gives a small amount of light but not enough to see anything ahead. Inching forward, then left, she searches for a concrete pillar to get her bearings. Is there a pillar between each parking bay? Or every three maybe? It's hard to remember now. There's the first one. If there's one for every three spaces, then there are only two more to go, and she should be at her car. She starts forward again, then freezes. There's someone else here. She can feel it. Or maybe she heard a breath – she can't tell. She stands paralysed, her skin tingling. Everything seems terribly loud and utterly still all at once. The noise is all in her head – beyond it she can hear nothing. If she can just get to her car, it will be okay, but she's afraid to reach out her hands now, in case she touches something that's not concrete or air.

Then it happens. Something touches her face. She screams and adrenaline kicks in – she runs to where the car might be, praying her instincts are right. Her hands touch a wall, but the car should be beside it. Panicking, breathing fast, she feels her way along the wall, crying now. Putting her hand back behind her, she touches the car door. Where are her keys? She hunkers down and sticks her hands in her bag, pulling out everything that's not a key and throwing it on the ground. She hears footsteps. At the very bottom of the bag, her fingers make contact with her keys. She takes them out but drops them on the ground. Still she can hear footsteps, slow and deliberate. Frantically, on her hands and knees, she feels around the stone ground for her keys. There they are. She pushes the button and the orange lights flash. Pulling open the door she climbs inside and sticks the key in the ignition. Her handbag and phone and wallet are still on the ground but it doesn't matter. Slamming the door, she lurches forward and out of her car space. The headlights aren't on. She doesn't want to see who's there, but she can't make it out of the car park in pitch darkness either. Forcing herself to do it, she clicks on the headlights. They light up the car park in front of her as she swerves towards the exit, and there's nothing there but stone grey walls and empty spots. She lets out a cry of relief.

At the top of the ramp, the barrier is up, and part of her knows that if it wasn't she might have driven through it rather than go back down for her swipe card.

The card is still there the following morning, lying on the ground beside her wallet and her handbag, but her phone is gone. The lights are back working – a blown fuse, says the security guard – it knocked out everything at basement level for the night. From her desk, Sylvia tries to ring her mobile but it just rings out. She tries once more then contacts IT – they say they'll cancel her old phone and organise a new phone by tomorrow. Next stop is an email to Tom to let him know she still has no phone. He thought she imagined it all, of course – too little sleep and too much stress making her hear things that aren't there. The hand that touched her face was probably her own hair, he reckoned, pointing out that it wouldn't be the first time she had taken a strand of hair for a spider.

She couldn't have imagined the footsteps though. There was someone in the car park and now that someone has her phone.

Chapter 36

Sylvia – Saturday, August 27th

The clatter of Saturday morning cups fills the air as Sylvia bounces Zack up and down on her knee, and cuts off little bits of scone for him. It's a brown scone, so probably not too bad for a baby. Probably. She looks again towards the entrance, then at her watch. Maybe Kate won't show. But there she is, pushing open the swinging door, scanning the coffee shop. Sylvia waves but she's too far away in the corner – Kate can't see her. Standing up, she waves again. Kate spots her and makes her way between the tables.

Sylvia immediately regrets her Saturday-morning combo of old jeans and even older trainers. Kate's in a biker jacket and impossibly skinny black jeans, and her I'm-not-wearing-make-up make-up is perfect with her shimmering hair. It looks more silver than blonde today – did she colour it since last week? Sylvia pulls at her own mid-brown curls and wonders if she should try something new. Shifting Zack to her other hip, she leans forward to accept Kate's hug, and they sit.

Kate orders black coffee and relaxes back into the banquette, dropping her shopping bags to the floor. "So how are you? I've just spent all morning queuing for uniforms – how do they need new uniforms every year?" She shakes her head. "All ahead of you, Sylvia. So this must be Zack?" She takes his hand and says hi.

Zack stares at her, and goes back to the scone.

Sylvia says she doesn't know how long Zack will last before tears take hold – he was up again last night and he's wrecked. She doesn't tell Kate that she lay awake long after Zack went back to sleep, trying to ignore the noises – the little creaks and lifts the house makes at night, wondering if she'll come downstairs to find something else has been moved. And she doesn't tell her about the scare in the car park and her stolen phone.

"And how is work?" Kate asks. "How's that asshole boss of yours?"

"Work is horrible, to be honest," Sylvia says. "I'm trying to focus on getting the money back, but they keep calling me into meetings to explain it. And of course everyone has completely forgotten I wasn't there when it happened. The blame game is strong in our place."

Kate picks up her coffee cup and hugs it with both hands. She has beautifully manicured nails, covered in blue-black polish. A diamond the size of a marble sits on her ring-finger. Well, it's not quite a marble, it just looks like that compared to Sylvia's engagement ring.

"So why don't you do what I suggested," Kate says. "Go find Justin and catch him in the act – tell them he's faking, and get some of the negative attention where it should be?"

"Yeah, I don't know . . . I think it would look like I'm trying to deflect – which of course I would be. I'd be in trouble then for doing that instead of focusing on the investigation. Also I'm pretty sure it's completely illegal." She kisses Zack's head and looks back at Kate. "I think I just have to suck it up and hope it's not a lifelong black mark against me."

"Well, what if you catch him out, then tell *him* he has to go back to work and take ownership, and if he doesn't, you'll tell – what about that?"

Sylvia tries to imagine it for a minute. What would Justin think if she showed up outside his house and started taking photos? And of what – him coming out to get milk from the doorstep?

She smiles. "I love it on one level – like the version of me who once wanted to be Nancy Drew – but I'm not sure it would work in real life."

"Why not? You can't just sit back and let this happen. There's no way I would. Do it this afternoon – leave Zack with your husband, go to Justin's road, park across from his house, and see what happens. He lives – what – ten minutes from your house, you said?"

Kate is serious, and Sylvia is in no doubt that she'd do it if it was the other way around. It wouldn't be that hard to just drive past the house and see if the car is there. If it's not, that's telling in itself.

Kate starts again. "Is he married? Does he have kids? Is he on Facebook? Maybe we can see what he's posting. What's his surname?" She pulls out her phone.

Sylvia has never checked if he's on Facebook, but Kate finds him easily.

"Damn. Privacy settings. We can't see anything. Does he have a family?"

"No, he's single. I think he's waiting for a time machine so he can go back to the 1950s and find a proper little wife who'll stay at home, pregnant and barefoot."

Kate laughs at that.

"Well, I don't know," Sylvia says, "that's probably a bit mean. But he's definitely single."

"Right, promise me you'll do it – just drive past?"

Sylvia nods, wondering if people ever say no to Kate. A waiter comes by to take their empty cups and Kate orders another coffee.

Zack is getting fidgety but Sylvia decides to risk one more. "Actually, could you bring that in a takeaway cup?" she calls after the waiter. Just in case.

"So, are you going to move back up now – with the boys starting back to school?" she asks Kate.

"Yes, but not into our own house. My mum still has her house up here – it's in Stillorgan – and her tenants are moving out this week, so we'll move in." She sighs. "It means I definitely have to tell the boys this week. I'm dreading it. And I suppose part of me keeps thinking it's all a bad dream – that Sam will tell me it was a joke. I know," she says, rolling her eyes. "Ridiculous."

Zack starts to cry then – loud wails that fill the entire coffee shop. Sylvia can feel her face grow hot. She offers him a mini rice cake but he bats it away, and does the same to his soother.

Kate waves away her apologies. "I have to go now too – I need to get new schoolbags for the boys. The ones they had last year are fine but they were in the spare room, and Sam had locked it when I was there last week. I couldn't be bothered going back again to get them."

"Well, do you want me to do it? I could call in and get them from him?" Sylvia asks.

"No, don't worry, it's as easy to get new ones. And I need a few bits for myself too – I need to think about going back to work now that I'm a lone parent." She sucks in a breath through her teeth. "That's the first time I've said the words 'lone parent'. God."

Sylvia touches her arm. "If you need anything, I'm here.

Sometimes it's easier to let off steam with a relative stranger – give me a shout any time you want to meet for coffee. Maybe I can leave this little guy at home next time."

Kate touches Zack's nose. "He's been great – I probably bored him to tears. But tell you what, how about next time we go for a glass of wine instead?"

"Perfect," Sylvia says.

They weave their way between the tables to the exit – Kate striding ahead, turning heads, Sylvia slower behind with a crying Zack in her arms – and say their goodbyes.

"Don't forget the Justin plan – I want to know how it goes," Kate calls as she gets into the lift to the carpark.

Sylvia clips the buggy straps into place and waves, nodding politely, wondering if it would be harder to actually do it or to confess to Kate that she hadn't.

Chapter 37

Sylvia – Sunday, August 28th

Lazy man's load – Sylvia can hear her mother's voice in her head. And indeed, a moment later, one of the four shopping bags slips out of her hand and onto the ground, spilling its contents all over the driveway. Putting down the other three, she scrambles to catch rolling apples and peppers, sighing at the two broken eggs.

"Oh-oh! Let me help you," says a voice behind her.

She turns and finds herself looking straight into Sam's eyes.

"That's okay," she tells him, "I can manage."

But he insists, and together they repack the fruit, meat and surviving eggs.

"Will I help you to clean up the egg?" he asks.

"Not at all. You're very good, thanks."

Why is she being nice to him? This is probably what he does – charms people then goes off and cheats on them with work colleagues. He smiles and, in spite of herself, she smiles back. It's obvious now what Kate saw in him, and the girlfriend too. But seriously, what an asshole. Abruptly, she stops smiling.

"Is everything all right?" he asks.

"Yes, absolutely. Just, you know, thinking about . . . well, I suppose I should say, I met Kate and she told me about . . . well, that you guys have separated."

His face clouds over. "Right. I didn't know she was telling people."

"I'm sure she's not telling loads of people – it's just that we met and had coffee and got chatting. Don't worry, I'm just one person. And it's probably easier to let it out with someone you don't know very well." Oh for goodness' sake, now she's feeling guilty.

"Did she tell you why?"

A familiar heat spreads across her face. "Well, yes . . . "

"You know, there are two sides to every story."

Now this she didn't expect. How could there possibly be two sides to an affair with a work colleague – what's he going to say – that he was lonely and it's Kate's fault? Sylvia says nothing, waiting to see what will come next.

"Let's just say there are a lot of things in Kate's background that make her see things in a kind of skewy way. Has she told you much about her brother?"

Sylvia shakes her head.

"Or her dad?"

She shakes her head again.

Sam nods. "Well, maybe some time she will, and you'll understand the bigger picture. She's a tough nut and not the easiest person to get on with – she has ridiculously high expectations after everything that happened when she was a kid."

Sylvia bristles. "Well, I don't know about all that, but it seems fairly black and white to me. No matter what's happened in Kate's past, cheating is cheating." Her cheeks are on fire now, and somehow her hands have found their way to her hips.

She sees what looks like a flash of anger on Sam's face but he hides it quickly with a smile, and holds his hands up in surrender.

"Mea culpa, you're right. Look, are you sure you don't need any more help?"

Her hands drop back to her sides. "I'm good – thanks though." Maybe she should say sorry too. It hangs in the air for a moment, then she turns to go indoors. Kate wouldn't say sorry.

Two hours later, the lamb is almost ready and the conversation is still burning a hole in her conscience. Why did she say anything at all? It's none of her business, and now she's possibly made things worse for Kate. Tom thinks she's overthinking it but Tom always thinks she's overthinking everything. One of her mother's many favourite sayings flashes into her head: "*A problem shared is a problem halved.*" Her mother mostly said it when she wanted Sylvia to tell the truth about whatever boy she was meeting or whether her friends were drinking, but perhaps it would help in this instance. Or maybe just confessing to Kate would take a load off her mind – either way, it would be better than sitting here worrying about it.

Clicking into WhatsApp, she starts typing.

Just to let you know, I bumped into Sam in the driveway and mentioned that we met for coffee, and that I knew you guys were splitting up. That was probably overstepping and I wanted to apologise – it wasn't my place to say anything … hope all OK x

Two blue ticks – Kate's read the message. Then nothing. No reply. No comforting little "**Kate is typing**" notification. Shit. And who could blame her – they hardly know each other and yet Sylvia's gone plodding into her marriage break-up. Kate must think she's a moron. There'll be no more coffee, and no meeting up for a glass of wine – it's actually completely mortifying the more she thinks about it.

Finally, a reply comes through.

God, don't worry. I'm sure he wasn't thrilled but I don't care. At some point all our friends and family are going to know and he'll have to deal with it then. I haven't really been telling people at all. I'm leaving that lovely task to him. So you probably caught him off guard. No harm 😃

Phew. Maybe Tom was right – she probably was overthinking it. There's another message from Kate.

Did you confront that guy from work yet?

She types a reply.

No! Not something I can rush into – I need to have a think about it.

Kate comes back a few minutes later.

Don't spend too long thinking – just do it. You've nothing to lose! Your work sounds shit at the moment, and he's laughing about it all, hiding out in his house. I don't know him obvs but I'm getting cross about it every time I think about him. Do. It. Seriously!

Sylvia types again.

I might drive past his house and take it from there. I know it sounds like a no-brainer but tbh the thought of it makes me feel a bit sick! Anyway, I'll keep you posted. And I promise not to say anything else to your OH about anything – sorry again x

The reply is swift.

Don't worry, honestly. I promise I'm not annoyed. Tell you what, let's do that glass of wine – this Friday if you're free?

A fizz of butterflies pops inside Sylvia's stomach. She's not dumped after all.

Yep, well, I'll check with Tom to make sure he's here, but that sounds good.

Putting down her phone to take the roast out of the oven, she feels lighter already.

Chapter 38

Sylvia – Monday, August 29th

The water hits her back like hot needles and with it the tension starts to ease. The whine of the shower motor sounds louder than usual – if it wakes Zack, she might actually cry. She might cry anyway at the thought of facing into all of it again tomorrow. Getting them ready on her own, waiting for Jane, then rushing late into work, hoping nobody will notice. It's always the same when Tom's away – maybe they should just ask Jane if she could come earlier and avoid all this extra stress. Or maybe she should give it up altogether – it's not like work is bringing any joy to life right now. Imagine if she handed in her notice in the middle of the investigation – *ha!* It would nearly be worth it to see Craig's face. But she won't – she knows she won't leave them in the lurch.

Lathering shampoo into her hair, she closes her eyes and lets the water trickle down her face and neck. For the first time today, there's no rush. She rinses, and then just because it feels good she shampoos her hair a second time. The shower door is steamed up now – the dark square of the bathroom window is only just visible through the fog. Standing perfectly still, she lets the water massage her shoulders, watching it cascade down onto her feet.

There's a noise – is it crying? She turns the nozzle away for a moment to hear better. No, it's just the shower's whine. She closes her eyes to rub exfoliator onto her skin – the expensive one, because it's been one of those days.

Suddenly, everything is dark. Her eyes are closed but it's darker than that – the light has gone out. Disoriented, she tries to rinse her face so she can open her eyes – she half-slips on the shower tray, but catches herself. Is the electricity gone? But the shower motor is still running: it's not the electricity. Maybe the bulb is gone, or maybe Megan is up and has switched off the light. She calls Megan's name softly, then a little louder, but there's no answer. Her eyes are only half open and stinging with exfoliator, and the bathroom is pitch black. She presses the button to stop the shower and slides the glass door open to feel around for her towel.

Outside, the landing light is still on – not a fuse then, just a blown bulb. There are spares downstairs – she may as well change it now. She reaches for the bathroom light switch to turn it off. But it's already in the off position. Her stomach tightens. It can't be off – that makes no sense. She switches it on, and light floods the bathroom. Who turned it off while she was in the shower? She rushes into Megan's room – she's sprawled across the bed, in a deep, soundless sleep. In her own room, Zack is safely in his cot.

Pulling on a dressing gown, she makes herself go downstairs, wishing Tom was there. It's quiet – the kitchen light is on, just as she left it, and there's no movement anywhere. In the sitting room, she pours herself a gin and tonic, and drinks half of it in two swallows. Perched on the edge of the couch, she takes a third swallow and thinks about phoning Tom.

When the footsteps come, the glass slips from her hand. Down the stairs, fast and heavy. Her breathing stops completely as she waits, paralysed, for the sitting-room door to open. She hears a handle turn. But it doesn't move. It's the front door – opened and then closed. She pulls open the sitting-room door and without looking to see what's to her right, she runs back upstairs and in to Zack. He's still asleep, just as he was. Megan too. Breathless, at Megan's window, Sylvia pulls back the curtain. There's a shadow moving down below – a man.

Someone is going into the house next door.

Her fingers fail to hit the right pin code three times in a row. On the fourth try, she unlocks the phone and gets through to Tom. The words come out in a rush and she's crying now. Slow down, he tells her, and she tries again.

"Tom, there was someone in the house. I was in the shower, the kids were asleep, and the light in the bathroom went out. I thought it was the bulb or a fuse but it wasn't – someone actually pressed the light switch off while I was in there." She stops to gulp a breath. "Then when I was down in the sitting room, someone came down the stairs and went out the front door. Tom, I think it was Sam from next door."

Tom is trying to calm her down now, telling her she might have made a mistake and asking if the kids are okay. He's sure there must be a logical explanation, but for the first time she can hear worry.

"Tom, I hate it here – I loved this house for such a long time but I hate it now. I don't feel safe any more. I dread going to bed every night, wondering if something will happen. I don't know how much of it is in my head, but tonight was real. There was someone in our house – upstairs, where our children sleep. If we can't do something about it, then I want to go somewhere else. At least temporarily until we know what's going on. Do you understand?"

Tom does, and tells her to try to get some sleep. They'll talk about it when he's home tomorrow night, but moving isn't really an option.

She shakes her head at the phone, as fresh tears muffle her response.

"What did you say, love, I didn't catch that?" he asks.

"I said I'm not staying here. If we can't figure out what's going on and put a stop to it, we're going. Somewhere. Anywhere."

She hangs up and carries Megan into her room, then locks the door. For the rest of the night, she lies awake, listening to the sounds of her house and the sounds of the house next door.

Chapter 39

1990

Jean Duggan is crying. Big fat tears flow down her red face as she frantically pulls everything out of the cutlery drawer for a third time.

"A whole month's rent, I can't find it anywhere, what am I going to do?"

"Don't worry, Mrs Duggan, between us we'll find it," he reassures her as he goes through the newspapers that are piled up by the side of the couch.

"Just call me Jean – I'm not missus anyone," she replies, standing still at the sink for a moment, before searching the top of the cupboard above it.

One of the children walks out of the bedroom, nappy around his ankles. Paul – or is it Peter? He never knows which is which.

"Paul, why did you do that! Can't you see Mammy is busy and upset. Come here so I can put that back on you."

"I'll search through the kids' toybox, will I, Mrs Duggan – Jean, sorry – it might be there?"

"You're a star, I don't know what I'd do without you. Your

parents must be very proud of you. I hope my boys grow up to be just as kind to their neighbours."

He reddens at the compliment. "Not at all, sure I'm only next door."

"I'm just glad you called when you did – sorry, I didn't even get you the teabags you wanted to borrow," sniffs Jean, still rummaging through papers.

"Teabags are the least of my worries, I can get them in the shop in the morning anyway. Let's focus on finding your rent money."

Peter emerges from the bedroom now too, carrying an open carton of chocolate yogurt, most of which is slowly travelling down the front of his T-shirt, heading towards the floor.

Jean hasn't spotted it, so he scoops up the child and grabs a tea towel, deftly catching the big dollop that was about to land on the carpet.

"Sorry, thanks, you're a lifesaver," says Jean as she grabs the yogurt from Peter and puts it in the bin. "What have I told you about taking food from the fridge without asking?"

Peter grins up at his mother, not at all put out. He walks over to the fridge and takes out another yogurt.

"It's not here, it's not anywhere – I can't understand it. I'm sure I left it in the coffee tin in the high press like I always do, but maybe this time I didn't. I remember the twins were writing on the wall and I ran to stop them, so maybe I put it somewhere else this time . . ."

"What will you do if you can't find it?" he asks hesitantly, not wanting the tears to start again.

"I don't know," she sighs, flopping down on the couch. "I'll have to borrow."

"I don't have much but I can give you twenty pounds – does that help?"

Her eyes fill with fresh tears, and she puts her hand to her chest.

"I don't know what to say. You're so sweet. I can't take your money, but thank you for offering. I think that's the nicest thing anyone has done for me in years."

He nods, looking at his feet. "Who will you borrow from?" he asks.

"I suppose one of those lenders – I know the rates are a scandal but what can I do? If I can't pay the electricity, we'll be cut off, and if I can't pay the rent, we'll be evicted." Her voice wobbles over the last word.

"Take care about dealing with lenders – you know they can cause trouble if you don't pay them back. I mean real trouble," he tells her.

"I know, it's not something I'd normally do but what choice do I have?" She breaks into tears again, head buried in hands, shoulders hunched.

He walks over and pats her on the shoulder, handing her a tissue.

"Sorry, love, what am I like? You go on. You've been so good to me since I moved in – look at the state of me!"

"All right, I'll head on, but only if you're sure you'll be okay and you don't need any more help? Even with minding the boys for a while?"

"No, I'm fine – you go, and thank you."

She closes the door behind him and he goes back next door.

"Did you get the teabags, love?" she asks.

"Sorry, no, Jean was in a state – she's lost her rent money for the whole month. She took it out of the post office earlier, to pay her rent and her bills. She's in bits in there."

His mother nods, but she's distracted.

"I'm just heading out again to see if I can get some teabags for you – the corner shop will still be open," he says.

"Ah no, leave it, love, I'll be grand until tomorrow – and there's something I wanted to chat about."

But he's already pulling on his green bomber jacket. "I'll only be ten minutes. Sure, stick the kettle on – I might even bring you some biscuits." He winks at her as he walks out the door.

Hands deep inside his jacket pockets, hunched over against the evening chill, he walks quickly down Canon Street, turning onto a small side-street as dusk unfolds across the sky. Ahead, he can see two figures, both wearing black hoodies, the orange glow of their cigarettes just visible in their cupped hands. He slows his pace, still walking towards them. They look up and stand up straighter, watching his approach.

"You got something for us?" says the smaller of the two.

"Yeah. A woman near me – Jean Duggan is her name. Number 12. She's desperate. Tell Grogan he could probably charge what he likes with that one," he says.

"I bet you had something to do with that, did ya?" the other one says.

"None of your business. I'm giving you what you want, as agreed – that's all you need to know."

The smaller one takes the two steps towards him and thrusts some notes into his waiting hand.

"And I'll get my cut as usual once it's up and running," he reminds them.

"Yeah, now go before you're seen here."

He walks back up the laneway, pocketing his cash. It's not much, but the real money will come with his cut of the weekly repayments, just like all the others. And anyway, he thinks, pulling a wad of cash from his inside pocket, he has Jean Duggan's rent money too, so that's not bad for a day's work. Whistling quietly in the dark night air, he heads towards the shop to get teabags for his mother.

Chapter 40

Sylvia - Friday, September 2nd 2016

The person looking back at Sylvia from the mirror looks familiar but it's a while since she's seen her. Eyeliner, blusher, heels she hasn't worn in months, and her hair loose around her shoulders. Tom walks in as she's putting on one last coat of mascara, and he almost manages to keep the surprise out of his voice when he tells her she looks nice. He's still confused about why she's going out for drinks with someone she hardly knows. Doesn't she usually do coffee with her mum-friends? It's easier than coffee with Zack in tow, she explains. And she needs a night out – a break from everything. He suggests they have a night out soon – get a baby-sitter – and she nods, but she knows she won't leave the kids with anyone until they sort out the thing with the house.

She hears a car and goes to Megan's room to see if it's the taxi. It's not but, looking down, she sees Noel walking purposefully into Sam's driveway. What could he want with Sam? Curious, she lingers for a moment but then he's at the front door and out of sight. Her taxi pulls up and she runs back to her own room to get her bag. She takes a final look in the mirror at her black strappy top and skinny black jeans – for once she might have got it right.

When Kate walks into the bar in a black strappy top and skinny black jeans, Sylvia realises she got it a little bit too right, but Kate doesn't seem to notice, or is too polite to say. She kisses Sylvia on the cheek and orders a glass of Pinot Grigio. The post-work buzz is loud but side by side at the bar, heads close together, they can just about hear one another. Kate says she's moved into her mother's house in Stillorgan now, and it's not as bad as she thought – plus they're a little bit nearer to the school than they were in Dún Laoghaire. She's told the boys the news, and that wasn't as bad as she expected either – on some level they seem to have been anticipating it. Seth was relieved, she reckons, after hearing nothing for so long. Jamie didn't really get it, but took it in his stride. And she told them it's just how it is now – things might change after Mum and Dad have had a break. She's not sure the last bit is true.

Sylvia swallows a lump in her throat, picturing these kids she's never met hearing this awful news, and imagining the horror of some day having to have that conversation with Megan and Zack. She'd never let it happen. Then of course, that's easy to say – no doubt Kate and Sam never thought it would happen either, back when they first decided to get married.

"Where did you two meet?" she asks.

"Well, when I think about it now, maybe it was an omen. We met when his aunt died. Perhaps not the best start for a relationship? I was working as a waitress in the Meridian Park Hotel, and he and his family had just buried his aunt – they had the funeral reception in the hotel, and that's where we met. My mum thought it was hilarious. I didn't care – I thought he was gorgeous."

"He is very good-looking," Sylvia agrees, floating just a little on her second glass of wine. "And very charming too."

Kate gives her a funny look. "Do you think so?"

"Well, he seems quite charismatic – I can see why you fell for him. I mean, obviously he's also a complete dick for cheating on you. Sorry, I should have said that the other way around. He's an asshole, but a charming one. Right, I'll stop talking now."

"Did he say anything the other day when you told him you knew about the split – anything about us?"

"No, not really."

Kate puts down her glass and looks Sylvia squarely in the eye. "He did, didn't he – just tell me."

"Well, he said something about two sides to every story, as though I was taking your side I guess, and then I got a bit annoyed and said cheating is cheating. Sorry. You must think I'm a lunatic, butting in on your marriage. I'd normally run a mile rather than confront anyone."

"Oh, come on – if you were defending me to my soon-to-be-ex, we should drink to that! I thought you were going to tell me he said something bad about me."

Kate orders more wine and Sylvia promises herself she won't mention anything else from the conversation with Sam. Whatever happened in Kate's past is her business, and surely has nothing to do with the break-up. She's almost certain she's going to keep her promise. As long as she doesn't have too many more drinks – the wine is just starting to warm her nicely from the inside out.

"So I take it you've been together ever since you met at the funeral?"

"Yes, well, we did break up once back when we were first seeing each other – he cheated on me with an ex-girlfriend who was home from the States. See – I'm parroting him –

that's all he kept saying at the time, that she was an ex and that she was home from the States. As if that made it okay." Kate closes her eyes for a moment and, when she speaks again, her voice is so quiet Sylvia can hardly hear. "I guess I should have known. Once a cheat, always a cheat."

Sylvia touches her arm. "Well, that does seem different – I mean you were very young then, weren't you? Lots of people do dumb stuff like that."

"Yeah, and we were only together a few months. I think the reason I was so pissed off was because I'd been there to get him through a rough few months after his aunt died, then Molly swanned back in and he was off with her just like that. Jesus, he was a mess back then. I'm surprised I stuck with him when I think about it."

"Was he really close to his aunt?"

Kate's face changes. "Not so much that he was close, but he was there when she died. She took her own life. That's pretty hard on anyone."

Jesus. Suddenly Sylvia is feeling sorry for Sam again. Who really knows what goes on in people's lives? "God, that's awful. Did she have any history of depression or was it just out of the blue?"

"Ah, looking back they could all see it – that made it worse, because they all blamed themselves then. She'd been deteriorating for months – not leaving the house, talking about hearing voices – that kind of thing. Sam said she was getting more and more paranoid – thinking everyone was out to get her. She kept saying someone was in her house at night. She'd come down in the morning and claim things had been moved around and say someone had come in during the night and done it."

Sylvia grips the stem of her wineglass so tightly she's afraid it's going to snap. Her stomach is in a knot. "And did they?"

"Did they what?"

"I mean, was someone coming into her house at night?"

"Of course not! She'd done it herself and couldn't remember, but it was a tough time for all of them dealing with it."

Sylvia is suddenly nauseous and excuses herself to go to the bathroom. Splashing water on her face sobers her up a little. She grips the sides of the sink, going over what Kate just said. It can't be coincidence, can it? Or maybe Sam's aunt did imagine all of it, and maybe she's suffering from some kind of disorder too? She googles paranoia and loss of memory on her phone, and the first three results are Depression, Schizophrenia and Bipolar Disorder. Jesus, put the phone away she tells herself, and goes back out to Kate.

"Are you all right? You look pale?"

"I'm fine – I just didn't eat before I came out and the wine is going to my head."

Kate grabs a menu off the bar. "I'm famished too – let's eat."

Two burgers with rustic fries later, the conversation turns to Willow Valley – Kate is curious about the street on which she almost lived. It's quiet and nice, Sylvia tells her, and with some notable exceptions, people keep to themselves. Then Kate tells her about a letter she got during the summer – an anonymous letter saying that Sam was cheating. She still doesn't know who it was from, she says. After a moment, Sylvia realises Kate is looking pointedly at her.

"Oh no! It wasn't me – honestly. If anyone on the road would send a letter like that, it would be Rosemary. She knows everyone, and loves a gossip. Or Noel who lives just across from your house – he's always been a bit odd and he seems to have a lot of interest in your husband."

"Oh?"

"I saw him outside your house one night quite late, and I saw him calling in just before I left this evening – no doubt out of pure nosiness. And he did say to me one day that he thought Sam was seeing someone . . ." Damn. Wine-mouth strikes again.

Kate sits up straighter. "Seriously? Did he see her? Did he say anything about her?"

"No, nothing, he was just gossiping. That's what he does. So yes, I guess he could have sent the letter. How would he have your mother's address though?"

"I have no idea. God, it's weird to think of these people I've never met knowing my business. Sam really is such a fuckwit."

Sylvia snorts the wine she's trying to swallow and suddenly they're both laughing, neither of them quite sure what's so funny.

Her phone beeps – Tom asking if she's coming home soon or should he head on up to bed? She checks with Kate – will they have another one? Kate looks at the time – she's paying a baby-sitter by the hour and had better go home actually. But it's been great and they'll do it again, she says.

At the taxi rank outside, Kate asks her about work – did she catch Justin in the act yet? Not yet, she says.

"Bloody hell, Sylvia, don't be a wuss, just do it. Tomorrow, right? I want photographic evidence."

She hugs Sylvia goodbye and jumps in a cab.

And Sylvia nods and waves and this time she knows she'll do it.

Chapter 41

Sylvia – Saturday, September 3rd

"You have arrived at your destination," says Satnav's plummy voice, as Sylvia drives past the narrow townhouse.

Justin's car is in the driveway and she can't decide if she's disappointed or not. There's a perfect parking spot just opposite the house next door to his, removing her remaining excuse to turn for home. She takes a sip of water and wishes for the hundredth time today that she hadn't had that last glass of wine.

Now what? This is silly. Five minutes, and then she's going home. Her phone is on her lap, ready for action, and there's a newspaper on the passenger seat, in case she needs to hide her face. Now all she needs is a Cagney for her Lacey, and she's all set. Seriously, this is ridiculous. Tom would be in fits laughing if he knew what she was doing. A manicure was an easier excuse for heading out – although as she looks at her short, unpretty nails, she wonders if she'll need to go for an actual manicure now to make the story credible.

Five slow minutes tick by, and there's no movement inside or outside the house. All the curtains are open, so he's not in bed, but that doesn't mean much, and he could have a bedroom at the back of the house. A boy is dropping pizza leaflets in letterboxes, and he walks into Justin's driveway too but walks back out without leaving one. Squinting, Sylvia can see the "NO JUNK MAIL" sticker on the letterbox. She'll give it five more minutes, then she's going, and never telling anyone she did this. Except Kate. Kate will get a laugh out of it. Picking up her phone, she takes a photo of the house, then messages it to Kate.

Look what you've done to me – I'm outside Justin's house – I'm like James Bond but lost in a parallel suburban universe.

Kate's reply is immediate.

Ha – I love that you did it. Even if nothing happens, at least you know you can. Take back some of that power. Go, you!

She's about to reply, when the front door opens. It's definitely Justin, and he's definitely not a pyjama-clad bedbound patient. He's in a rugby jersey and shorts, and has a kitbag over his shoulder.

Sylvia crouches down behind the steering wheel, wondering again what possessed her to do this. Scrabbling for her phone, she waits till his back is turned and gets photos of him locking his front door and putting the kitbag in the boot. She ducks down further as he reverses out of the driveway but gets some shots of him driving away, including his registration plate – because that seems like something that might be useful, though she's not sure exactly how.

Sitting up in the seat after he's out of sight, she messages Kate to tell her she did it.

The reply comes instantly:

Result! Now, when are you going to confront him?

That part she hasn't thought about yet.

Chapter 42

Sylvia – Saturday, September 3rd

The sound of the doorbell chime is loud and lonely behind the stained glass, echoing in an empty hall. Nothing stirs inside. The car is here, but maybe he's gone back out for post-match drinks. It's probably a good thing that he's not here – this is a terrible, terrible idea. As Sylvia turns to leave, she feels more than sees the shadow behind the glass, and then the door is open and it's too late to walk away.

"Yes?" he says, not realising at first who it is.

She turns to face him, trying to smile.

"Sylvia! What are you doing here – is everything okay?"

She clears her throat. "Hi, Justin – I just wanted to see how you're doing?"

"Sure, come in," he says, though he doesn't look sure at all. "I'm not bad, but need to stay off my feet. Come on through to the sitting room."

The hall is sparse – beige carpet and no pictures on the walls – like he just moved in and never did anything at all to make it his own. The sitting room is similarly devoid of personality – although what would Justin's personality look like in a room? – maybe the bare-and-beige look says it all.

He lowers himself slowly into a black-leather armchair and gestures for her to take a seat on the couch.

"I'd offer you coffee, but even getting up to answer the door has taken it out of me. Feel free to make one for yourself though?"

She shakes her head, no thanks, and asks how he's feeling, then wishes she hadn't: confronting staff who are faking illness is probably much easier without the small talk.

"I'm all right – it's really knocked it out of me though. I won't be back for another six weeks or so. Taking longer than expected, the doctor said. Probably because I just didn't take it easy at the start – kept going in to work even when I was in bits. You know what I'm like – it's all about work with me. I hate being away from there." His mouth turns down and he shakes his head sadly, to show her just how tough he's finding it.

Sylvia digs her nails into her palm. "So you can't get out of the house at all? How do you even get groceries – gosh, I should have brought some with me."

He waves away the suggestion. "I buy them online, they get delivered. I sleep a lot to be honest, so I'm hardly even aware of what day it is half the time. It's Saturday today, right? Or is it Sunday?"

If he wasn't currently ruining her career, she'd laugh. "It's Saturday, Justin. And you're probably wondering why I'm here. I was chatting to HR, and we were all a bit worried about you. I know you don't have a family, so we agreed I'd call out to check in on you – to see if you need anything."

He smiles – a great big fake smile. "I'm grateful for your concern. And thank HR for me too, but I'll be fine."

He stands up. The visit is over.

"There's just one more thing," she says, feeling a lot like Lieutenant Columbo.

Justin raises a mildly curious eyebrow in answer but she's almost sure she spotted a glimpse of worry.

"I came by earlier to call in – around two o'clock." Ah, there's the worry now. "And when I pulled in across the road, you were getting into your car. In rugby gear. Playing a match, were you?"

Justin's mouth opens and closes again. His pale, pink-rimmed eyes never leave her face. When he speaks, his voice is hard. "I'm entitled to leave the house. Don't you dare spy on me."

"It's not spying, Justin," she says, thinking about the photos on the phone – it probably is spying. "I came out of genuine concern but it seems you're doing a lot better than HR and Craig realised."

"I have a doctor's note. That's all that matters."

"So you don't think you should maybe turn up at work on Monday – so that I don't need to mention any of this to Craig?"

"Who do you think Craig will listen to – me or you? I'll just say you're mistaken."

Oh, she really hoped she wouldn't have to do this. She pulls out the phone and clicks into the photos, then turns the screen to show him. She scrolls through, watching his face growing redder at each one. He stands up and walks over to her. For what feels like the first time, she's aware of how tall he is. She slides back on the couch a little and turns her face up to look at him. He's towering over her and little bits of spit fly out of his mouth and down onto her face when he speaks.

"*How dare you! You came onto my property and took photos of me without my knowledge. How fucking dare you!*"

Before she realises what's happening, he has grabbed the phone out of her hand. His face is just inches from hers now and she wants to wipe away the spittle but she can't. Why didn't she tell Tom where she was going? *Shit*. She tries to think of something to say but she can't.

"Get out," he says, finally standing up straight.

On the doorstep, she finds her voice again and asks for her phone.

He looks down at it but doesn't hand it over. He presses something on screen, and then again.

"Justin, I need my phone. It's a new one from work – they won't be impressed if I tell them I don't have it."

"Have it then – the photos are gone now."

The phone hits her in the chest and she's still recovering from the shock when he slams the door in her face.

Running to her car, she locks the doors from inside before pulling away, wondering again why she ever thought this was a good idea.

Chapter 43

Sylvia – Sunday, September 4th

Is there anything better than waking up without a hangover after struggling through a long day of dehydration and headaches, Sylvia wonders, stretching in the bed. Zack's cot is empty, and TV sounds tell her Tom is downstairs with the kids. Another little snooze won't hurt. Then she remembers the visit to Justin, and all hopes of going back to sleep slip away. She touches the spot on her chest where the phone hit – it's hard to believe it happened. And what next, now that she has nothing to show for the visit?

The jarring sound of the doorbell interrupts her thoughts. Who on earth calls at nine o'clock on a Sunday morning? Tom will answer, but curiosity gets the better of her and she slips out to the landing to take a look down the stairs. Through the glass, she can make out a dark-blue shape in a high-vis jacket – a Guard? Oh shit, did Justin make a complaint? Grabbing her dressing gown, she rushes downstairs, but the Guard is already walking away.

"What was it?" Sylvia asks, as Tom closes the door.

"Apparently Noel has disappeared – or done a runner –

who knows? They're going door to door to ask if anyone has seen him."

"Jesus! That's odd. How long has he been gone?"

"I'm not sure but they were asking if I'd seen him Friday evening or any time since, so I guess that's when he disappeared. He's always been a strange fish though – I wouldn't be surprised if he'd just decided to up and leave. Like that time –"

Sylvia interrupts. "I saw him Friday evening. I need to go and tell them."

Upstairs, she throws on a tracksuit and hoodie, then goes to Megan's room to look out the window. There's a police car outside Georgia and Noel's house, but no sign of the Guard who just called – maybe he's gone inside. Rosemary is in her garden, pretending to weed a flowerbed, but there's nobody else out on the road at all. Slipping on trainers, Sylvia goes outside. She'll wait till they come back out – calling to the house doesn't seem right. God, poor Georgia, and poor Annabel!

"Did you hear the news?" Rosemary says, standing up from her pretend weeding.

"Yeah, just now – Tom said Noel has disappeared and the police are investigating?"

Rosemary takes off her gardening gloves and lays them on the ground. "Apparently so. I heard that he went for a walk on Friday night and never came back. Poor Georgia is beside herself, and I don't want to think what that little child is going through. Of course the police said he might have just decided to get up and go – that's what Georgia told a friend of mine who lives on the next road up."

"And could that be it – or do they think now something happened?"

"Well, according to my friend, Georgia said he was a bit preoccupied with something on Friday night. But who knows.

Georgia's brother's a Guard – that's why they're taking it seriously, I suppose. And I imagine they can't rule anything in or out till they find him or hear from him, or . . ." she lowers her voice, "find a body."

"Oh God – they think he might have . . . ?"

Rosemary nods solemnly. "Lot of pressure on people today. Men are expected to be breadwinners and do childrearing and housework too." She shakes her head. "Wasn't like that in my day."

Oh, here we go, thinks Sylvia.

"Back then, men went to work and women minded the kids – worked well since Our Lord was a boy, so I don't know why they had to go changing everything."

Sylvia grits her teeth then smiles to cover it. "And did anyone say anything to them about seeing Noel in Sam's house on Friday evening?"

Rosemary's eyes widen. "Really? No, I didn't see that. And I usually see everything. So, what are you thinking?"

"Oh, nothing really – I just thought the police should know. So they can put everything together – you know, his final hours. At home, I mean, not final hours on earth . . . "

The door of Number 34 opens and two Gardaí come out – one male, one female. Georgia is just behind them, holding the door. Her beautifully groomed hair is loose and unwashed around her shoulders, and instead of her trademark dress and heels, she's wearing a dressing gown. She closes the door without seeing her watching neighbours.

Sylvia swallows and gets ready to step out of her comfort zone for the second time this weekend. She raises a hand to attract the Guards' attention, and they come over.

"Hi, sorry, it's just I heard you're looking for Noel, and I saw him Friday evening."

There's no response at first – two blank faces look her up

and down – and she wonders if she's picked it up all wrong.

Then the female Garda takes out a notebook and asks for the details.

"I was looking out the front bedroom window at about quarter to eight, and saw Noel walk across to the house next door to us," Sylvia says, pointing behind her at Sam's house. "But when he got to the front door, I couldn't see him any more, so I don't know if the door was answered."

The Guards thank her, still giving nothing away.

"There's one more thing," she says.

The Guards look only mildly interested.

She's going red, but she makes herself speak. "There've been a few odd things going on recently," she tells them. "It's since the man in Number 26 moved in. Noises at night, and I think someone might have broken into my house."

Now they're interested again.

"Have you reported the break-in?" the male Garda asks.

"No," she says, "I couldn't be absolutely certain that someone broke in – it was just that things were moved around at night."

She watches as the interest drains from both faces simultaneously and she can practically hear them writing her off as a demented housewife with nothing better to do than waste police time.

Back inside, Tom asks her what happened, and she fills him in.

"So you stood in our driveway telling the Guards there's something odd going on next door – *pointing* at next door – and you weren't remotely worried that Sam would see you?"

Shit. Was his car there? She runs upstairs and looks out the front window. It is, and the Guards have gone in there now as far as she can see. Neither Cagney nor Lacey would ever have done something so daft. Nor Kate. *Shit.*

Chapter 44

Sylvia – Monday, September 5th

The front door closes softly and Tom is gone again: another Monday morning pre-dawn flight for him and another solo-parenting stint for her. There's a whole hour till the alarm will go off, but she's too high above the sleep-tide now and, no matter how tightly she closes her eyes, there's no going back. Just after six, Sylvia gives up and goes downstairs to make tea. It's quiet – somehow quieter than usual. She shivers. This place is getting to her. As the kettle boils, she walks slowly around the kitchen as she does every morning now, just looking. Nothing seems out of place, though it's becoming difficult to tell any more. The ticking of the clock is the only sound once the kettle stops – why is it so quiet? Then she knows. It's Bailey. He's usually jumping up at the back door as soon as she comes into the kitchen.

Outside, the sky is still dark, and nothing stirs in the garden. The dog isn't in his kennel – has he somehow got out the front? She checks the side gate – it's open. *Damn.* This is all she needs. The last time he ran away it took three days to get him back – and of course this only ever happens when Tom is away. She'll have to wait until Jane arrives, then go out to try to find him. Something sharp digs into her foot as she walks back – another broken plant pot. Where did it come from? There's more of it further down the garden as she walks barefoot through the dewy grass to pick it up.

At the end of the garden, behind the picnic table, there's something dark lying on the ground. Dropping to her knees she touches it, then pulls back her hand, letting out a cry. Bailey. She reaches out her hand again . . . his poor body is already cold to touch. Gulping back a sob, she checks his body and looks around for blood but there's none – just bits of terracotta, like misshapen flowers in the grass.

There's an old blanket on the shelf in the shed and she uses it to cover Bailey's body, then goes inside to ring the vet. It's too early according to the automated voice on the other end of the line. If only Tom was here – dammit anyway, he's always away when things go wrong. She'll have to tell Craig she'll be late in – she can't just leave the poor dog lying there all day. When Jane arrives, Sylvia whispers what's happened, and together they carry Bailey to the boot of the car. Poor old thing – this isn't how it should end for you, she thinks, closing the boot.

Their local vet is not known for either patience or tolerance, and when he finds azalea petals caught in Bailey's teeth, his response is sharp. Doesn't she know that azaleas are poisonous to dogs – what was she doing keeping them in the garden? She doesn't have azaleas, she tells him – she knows they're poisonous.

But her protestations are ignored.

Outside, she calls Tom but he's in a meeting. What is she supposed to do now? The clinic offers a cremation service but that seems too awful when none of the rest of the family even know Bailey is gone. She and the vet carry him back to the car instead.

Jane is out with Zack when she gets home, and lifting the body out of the car on her own is a struggle. The blanket slips off as she's walking towards the side of the house, and when she tries to grab it, she stumbles. She lands hard on her knees and manages to hold on to Bailey, but her tears are thick and fast now. Her knees hurt like she's six again and she wants to get up but it's too hard so she stays kneeling on the driveway, holding the dog and crying.

A shadow falls across the ground and she looks up to see Sam standing over her. He doesn't say anything at first but reaches out to gently take Bailey from her arms. Cradling the body against him with one arm, he holds out a hand to help Sylvia up. Her knees are badly grazed and they sting when she tries to wipe away the little stones that are stuck to her skin.

Sam holds out a tissue and she takes it though she's not sure if it's for her eyes or for her knees.

"Your childminder told me what happened – I'm so sorry," he says, still holding Bailey. "Can I help you? Do you want to bury him in the garden?"

She's busy dabbing at her knee with the tissue and doesn't reply.

"I know it's hard, but you probably need to do something – you can't really just leave him out in the elements. Let me help you – I know what it's like. I buried my dog Max when he died. And nobody understands, do they, because it's a pet and not a human." He smiles at her. "Come on – I know it's an awful situation – Jane told me your husband's away too. You look like you could use some help."

Oh for goodness' sake, what was Jane doing telling him Tom is away? He's still standing in front of her, holding the dog, waiting for an answer.

She nods, and leads the way around to the back.

There's a spot at the end of the garden, under the one and

only apple tree in what Megan calls their "orchard" – Bailey always liked to lie there, so it seems like a good final resting place.

When Sam asks if she has a shovel, she hesitates, her mind in overdrive. Misunderstanding, he says he can go get his if she doesn't. Without a word, she takes the spade from the shed and passes it to him.

Neither of them speak as he digs. The earth is hard, and it takes longer than she expected. On TV, they always seem to dig graves quickly – though it's usually someone digging his own grave with a gun in his back.

Suddenly the silence feels odd and uncomfortable.

"Would you like tea?" she asks.

Sam would, so she goes inside and fills the kettle, then tries phoning Tom again. This time he answers.

"Tom, Bailey's dead. That's why I was calling you."

Silence on the other end tells her she should have broached it more gently. "I'm sorry, I know it's horrible news to hear when you're away."

"What happened?" Tom sounds stunned.

"The vet says it's because he ate an azalea plant. I just don't understand it though. I read up on all the plants that are toxic for dogs and I never have any of them in the garden – no daffodil bulbs, no tulips, no azaleas."

"Maybe you bought one without realising – it's not like either of us are well up on gardens and plants. Oh my God, poor Bailey! Do the kids know?"

"Not yet. Tom, I didn't buy one – I know I didn't – someone must have put it there," she says, holding the phone with her shoulder as she takes out cups and teabags. "There was a shattered plant pot in the garden."

"Oh, come on, Sylvia – someone put a plant in our garden to kill our dog? Why? And how would they know he'd eat it?

Since when does Bailey even eat plants?"

"That's a good point. Maybe it wasn't the plant. Maybe someone injected something and made it look like it was the plant?"

"Sylvia," Tom says, in his calm-down-now voice, "that doesn't make any sense. I know you're upset, but why would someone do that? It's not like he's barking all night and upsetting the neighbours."

She glances towards the back door. "Well, there's one neighbour who might be bothered by him . . ."

"Who?"

"You know who – next door," she answers, pouring boiling water into two cups.

"You think the man next door poisoned our dog by injecting something into him and making it look like he ate a plant? Come on – you see how crazy that sounds, right?"

"I know how it sounds," she whispers, "but I just don't trust him and it's only since he moved in that all these things have been happening. And what about Noel visiting his house just before disappearing?"

Tom sighs. "Sylvia, you don't even know if he actually went into the house . . . Look, I have a meeting now – I have to go. But I'll be home tomorrow night and we'll talk then – okay?"

She says goodbye and puts the phone down on the counter. Turning to the back door, she flinches when she sees Sam standing there, watching her. How long has he been listening? His face is neutral but something in his eyes tells her he heard her conversation.

She summons up a smile and passes over the cup of tea. He accepts it, nodding thanks without taking his eyes off her face, and goes back out to dig.

Suddenly, with every bone in her body, she knows she

doesn't want him here. What was she thinking letting him in? She should have said no when he offered. And she should get an autopsy. Can you even do that for dogs? She googles it quickly on her phone – yes, some clinics do offer autopsies for pets.

Outside, Sam looks surprised to see her running down the garden towards him. He stops digging.

"I'm sorry to have put you to all this trouble," she says. "But Tom wants to say goodbye to the dog, so I said we wouldn't bury him yet."

Sam looks unconvinced and even to her own ears it sounds ridiculous.

"Sure, I can understand that – I was the same when Max died. Well, look, the hole is there now anyway, so you'll be able to use it after your husband says goodbye. When will he be back?" He still has the spade in his hand.

"Tonight." She reddens with the lie. "So, thanks again for your help."

He nods and puts down the spade.

She lets out a quiet breath.

Sam hunkers down and pats Bailey who is lying on the ground under the blanket, and when he looks back up at Sylvia his eyes are sad again.

"I'm so sorry. I know how hard it is. Mind yourself."

As he leaves, she stands for a moment staring after him. Could she have it all wrong?

Inside, her phone is vibrating on the counter – a missed call from Craig. She hits the button to return the call but then changes her mind and disconnects.

Instead, she calls UCD, to find out about booking an autopsy for a dog.

Chapter 45

Sylvia – Wednesday, September 7th

If Tom is surprised to find her drinking a glass of wine on a Wednesday night, he doesn't say so. Two days of holding it together for the kids and answering questions about Dog Heaven earned her a bottle, she reckons, but a glass will do for now – plus some of the Toblerone Tom takes out of the Duty Free bag. He pours himself a glass of wine too, and only when he's taken a few swallows does she tell him about the autopsy. The results will take six to eight weeks, she says, and the people were lovely – they do this all the time apparently. Tom is predictably sceptical and thinks it's misplaced guilt about the azalea plant. He says *he* might have been the one who bought it, which is kind, because they both know he never buys plants.

"Tom," she whispers, when they go upstairs, "I think we need to call in next door to try to make sense of all this. There's definitely something wrong, and I can't keep dealing with this by myself – I need you on board too."

He sits on the bed and pulls her down to sit beside him. "Sylvia, you have to let this go. You're tired, you're stressed with work, you're up at night with the baby. It has nothing to do with the guy next door."

"Well, then explain all of it," she says, rubbing her temples. "The child in the water, the black crosses through the photos, the cups and the dolls on the table, the light going off in the bathroom, and now the dog." She looks up at him. "And even if you think some of those things were my imagination or that I did them myself, none of it explains the fact that someone ran down our stairs and out the front door that night."

"But you know yourself that sometimes noises from next door sound like they're coming from in here – the walls are paper-thin." He raps lightly on the bedroom wall.

Sylvia climbs into bed as Tom begins to undress. "Yes, and I know sometimes I've made that mistake, but this was very loud and very close. It couldn't have been next door. And what about Noel – the police were in talking to Sam about it. That must mean something, right?" She sees him open his mouth and cuts him off. "Yes, yes, I know only because I sent them in there but still. Please, Tom, there's nothing to lose – let's just call in to say hi or to thank him for helping with Bailey the other day. There's something not right with him – you'll see when you meet him."

Tom gets into bed too and his eyes are closing as soon as his head meets the pillow. "Fine, let's do it straight after work tomorrow when Jane is still here – anything for a quiet life."

If only, thinks Sylvia, as she stares at the ceiling. If only.

Sylvia steps back from the sitting-room window. "Tom, he's home – he's just pulled into the driveway. Let's go in now – Jane says she's fine to stay on as long as we need."

Tom puts down his phone. "Grand, but give him a chance to get into his house – he'll think we're hounding him if we go in straight away."

It's a good ten minutes before Sylvia can tear Tom away

from his phone, and in heavy rain they run up Sam's driveway. The tiny shelter above the front door provides no cover at all, and though they huddle as close as they can, both of them are getting wet. The car is still in the driveway, but there's no response when they ring the doorbell.

Tom looks delighted and is turning to leave, but Sylvia pulls him back and presses the bell again. Still no reply.

"If he's there and not answering, that says something in itself," she whispers to Tom. But then they hear footsteps, and the door opens.

Sam looks surprised, then he smiles and it transforms his face.

"Oh hey, is everything okay?"

"Yes, I just wanted to thank you for all your help on Monday with Bailey – this is Tom, my husband, and he wanted to say thanks too."

On cue, Tom nods and says, "Thank you."

"No problem – God, don't stand there in the rain – step in." He pulls the door wide. Tom hesitates, but Sylvia walks in and he follows. The carpet underfoot is wet now from their shoes and Sylvia apologises.

"Don't worry, it's all being pulled up anyway – as you can see, the house is a work in progress. Come in and have a cup of tea, will you?"

Tom starts to say something about letting the childminder go home but Sylvia interrupts and says they'd love tea, following Sam through to the kitchen.

It's like stepping back in time, and Sylvia feels a pang for Mrs Osborne and the quiet life she lived here in her 1970s kitchen. It looks exactly as it always did, but somehow the familiarity isn't comforting.

"So how is the work on the house going?" she asks, looking out the kitchen window at the still overgrown garden.

"Yeah, I know, the kitchen and the back don't look great, do they? I've mostly been focussing on the upstairs so far. Tea or coffee? I'm sorry now, I don't have any biscuits – Kate's always the one who buys the biscuits in case people call – I don't think of it now she's gone."

Tom looks uncomfortable and waves away the apology – he never eats biscuits anyway, he says.

"I met Kate for drinks on Friday actually – she seems to be doing great in spite of everything," Sylvia says, conscious of the horrified look Tom is giving her.

Sam's sheepish smile disappears momentarily, but it's back just as quickly. "Ah, I'm glad she's got someone to talk to. Most of her friends are living in the UK and the States now so it's all email and WhatsApp. Not the same as having someone real to talk to."

"Yes, especially with all she's going through. I mean –"

"So, Sam, I spotted the golf clubs in the hall – do you play?" Tom asks, cutting Sylvia off mid-sentence.

"I do, though those clubs are Kate's – she took up golf a few years ago and of course she's passed me out now – she's way better than me already. I must get back out there actually. Any good courses around this neck of the woods?"

And they're off – talking about golf and then football and then whether or not the Dubs will do it again this year.

Sylvia sips her tea, listening to everything and saying nothing. Tom has forgotten all of his unease and is delighted to have found a fellow Leeds fan – what were the chances? Every now and then, Sam's eyes flick back to Sylvia, watching her watching him.

She gets up to walk over to the back door, looking out into the garden. The pond is just about visible.

"Do you mind if I take a wander outside? It looks like the rain has stopped," she says.

Sam looks at her, searching her face. "Sure – the door's open."

The garden is soggy and the air smells like oncoming autumn. Sodden leaves lie on the ground between the tangled bushes. There's no green space at all until right down at the end, and then there's the pond. The dark brown water sits still now the rain has stopped, and Sylvia hunkers down to take a closer look. A stick on the ground makes a handy probe – she pokes it in to the water. Deep enough for a child to drown.

"We'll have to cover it over of course." His voice behind her makes her jump.

She gets to her feet and drops the stick.

"Even with my kids gone, I'd hate for anyone else to wander in here and fall in. Like your little girl."

She tries to answer but her mouth has gone dry. Swallowing, she tries again. "Covering it over sounds like a good idea," she manages, barely above a whisper. "In the meantime, I'll keep Megan on our side of the wall. Just in case."

He smiles and his voice is light and friendly when he replies, "Just in case."

She turns and heads back up to the house, walking fast now through the water-logged grass.

"Tom, we should go – Jane needs to leave soon."

Tom drains his tea and shakes Sam's hand. "So listen, if I can get an extra ticket for that match I'll give you a shout, yeah? And let me know if you dust off those golf clubs – I could do with a round myself."

Back home, once the kids are in bed, Sylvia rounds on Tom. "You're going golfing with him? And to a match?"

Tom looks confused. "What?"

"We went in to get a better sense of who he is and what's

going on – not to become best friends with him!" It's raining again – she pulls the sitting-room blind halfway down and switches on the table lamp.

"I was just being friendly. In fairness, he just seems like a nice, normal guy who's a bit lost since his wife left him." Tom picks up the remote control and switches on the *Nine O'Clock News*.

The Austin Granger murder is the top story tonight, with Gardaí following a new line of inquiry. And Edie Koegh is still missing.

Sylvia mutes the TV. "She didn't *leave* him – he had an affair and she found out – that's a bit different."

Tom throws his hands up in the air. "Whatever. Look, you need to get past this – he's just a regular guy. He's not breaking into our house at night and putting cups on the table."

"Tom, he just threatened our daughter."

"What?" He sits up straighter.

"Down at the pond. He said I'd want to be careful that she doesn't wander in there. That it's dangerous."

"Do you even hear yourself, Sylvia? How is that a threat?"

"We need to go, Tom, at least for a while. I think we need to consider moving in with my mum."

"You cannot be serious. Look, you just need a break – I know work has been awful. Any sign of the money?"

"Well, there's a chink of light at the end of the tunnel – DBK were in touch today to say they've an unapplied payment that matches it." She holds up crossed fingers. "I'm fairly confident it's our money, so I just need to spur them on to send it back. But, in the meantime, I'm still being pulled into daily meetings to give updates and still nobody remembers I wasn't there when it happened."

"I take it Justin's not back then?"

"No. Actually there's something I didn't tell you. Don't go

mad, but I went to his house last Saturday – when I was getting the manicure? I stopped outside his house, and saw him getting in the car – it looked like he was going to play a rugby match. Anyway . . . okay, look this is going to sound a bit mad, but I took photos of him."

Tom's eyes widen.

"And then I called in to him when he came back, and said I'd show the photos to Craig. He's supposed to be sick in bed – I knew well he wasn't."

"Jesus, Sylvia – could he complain about you to HR?"

"No! He's faking an illness so he can avoid admitting a huge error – he doesn't have a leg to stand on!"

"But he didn't show up at work?"

She slumps down against the back of the couch and closes her eyes. "No. He deleted the photos. It was a complete waste of time. I can't decide what to do. I could tell work about calling to him but, knowing Craig, I'll just end up in trouble again, and without photos I've no proof he's faking."

Then he surprises her. "What if you get him to admit it, or at least not deny it?"

She opens her eyes and sits up. "What do you mean?"

Tom nods. "I mean record him on your phone – there's loads of apps out there you can use. It means you can do it without confronting him in person – you just call him, and the app records the call. Then you email it wherever. Like straight to Craig's inbox."

"Is it legal?"

Tom nod. "Yep, totally legal to record a call if you're party to the call – it's not the same as tapping a call between two other people."

"Wow. Okay then – can you find me a good app?"

Tom takes her phone. "On one condition – let's do this and fix the situation at work before we do anything drastic like moving in with your mum – agreed?"

Raindrops pelt the window outside and she gets up to pull the blind the rest of the way down. "Agreed. But if anything else happens, we're going."

Chapter 46

Sylvia – Friday, September 9th

"Gardaí say they are satisfied that two-year-old Edie Keogh, missing from her Dublin home since July, is not with her father. Earlier reports suggested that the child had been taken out of the country but this has now been ruled out. The search is continuing, and Gardaí wish to speak to a man in his forties who was seen in the area on the night of July 27th."

Sylvia turns down the radio as she pulls into the driveway. God, the thought of what might have happened to that little girl! She needs to check with Jane that she'd never let Megan out of her sight – not even for a second. Though Jane will think she doesn't trust her at all . . . maybe she'll get Tom to say it – he's better at that kind of conversation. A movement catches her eye – someone is ringing the doorbell of Sam's house.

Curious, she gets out of the car and takes her time to check her phone and gather her handbag. The caller is tall, and wearing glasses that look far too big for his thin face. He has his hands in his pockets as he waits. He's in a grey hoodie and black jeans, and doesn't look like a delivery person. Sam's car is there but there's no answer. Sylvia keeps checking her phone, and watches as the man eventually gives up and walks away.

"*That's the brother!*" Rosemary's stage whisper startles her.

"Sorry?"

"The man you were watching – it's the wife's brother. Miller is his name if you don't mind. Something about a salesman who died."

"Oh yes, I wasn't really paying attention, I was looking for my keys. I'm just back from work. I'd better go inside."

Rosemary's face falls. Poor old thing. She can spare two minutes.

"Though I'm a bit early, they won't be expecting me yet – how are you anyway?"

Rosemary beams. "Not bad now, though the arthritis is playing up with all the rain. Did you hear anything new about Noel?"

Sylvia shakes her head. If anyone on the road is likely to know the latest on Noel, it's Rosemary. And indeed, she does have news.

"The Guards were at their house again today," she says, nodding towards the house across the road. "Called in early this morning – two of them. What do you think that means?"

Sylvia looks over. Georgia and Noel's cars are in the driveway, and there's another car parked outside too, but no police. "I guess they were giving her an update on the search?"

"I wonder . . ." Rosemary says, going back to a whisper although there's nobody else around, "do you think he ran off with another woman?"

"Ah listen, I'm not even sure what Georgia sees in him," Sylvia says, also whispering. "I can't see him finding a mistress too!"

Rosemary's eyes light up and a smile twitches at the corners of her mouth. "Oh, we're terrible, we shouldn't be saying that!"

But she's delighted. Sylvia's job is done.

Sylvia looks over again. Maybe she should call in to Georgia to see if she can do anything – or would that be intruding? She looks at her watch – there won't be time this evening anyway – she's meeting Kate at eight, and there's something important she needs to do first.

Tom checks again on the kids and closes the sitting-room door.

Sylvia's stomach is in knots as she picks up Tom's phone and tests the call-recorder app one final time. What if he doesn't answer? What if he guesses what she's doing? What if the recorder doesn't work? But Tom insists it's worth a try.

She dials Justin's number and waits. The little red light on the top left-hand corner of the phone tells her that the recorder has switched on.

After four rings, he answers.

"Justin, it's Sylvia. Look, don't hang up – I just wanted to clear the air after the last time. I hate falling out with people – especially key members of the management team like you."

Thumbs up from Tom, silence from Justin.

"So, how about we forget everything – forget what happened when I called – and get back on track. You come in on Monday and help me with the audit, and the rest is water under the bridge."

More silence.

"Justin?"

"Sylvia, I'm a little surprised to be honest – do HR know you're harassing me like this?"

Oh, for goodness' sake! She closes her eyes and presses the phone against her temple. "No, I thought we could just sort it out between ourselves."

"You seem to be under the illusion that I can just get up and come back to work – I'm *ill* in case you've forgotten, and I have a sick cert to prove it. So no, sorry, you'll have to handle things on your own for another while."

"Please, Justin, you're a lot better at going through the accounts than I am – you were always strong on problem-solving. The team are lost without you, to be honest. And so am I. I'm still finding my feet after being off." She waits.

"Nice try, Sylvia, but no go. I'm not coming back until I'm ready. Actually, I'm feeling a bit stressed now because of this call – I might need to go back to the doctor. I've a feeling she's going to sign me off for even longer."

She can hear the sneer. The smug prick.

When she speaks again, her voice is a taut wire. "Justin, I thought we could sort this out like grown-ups but clearly not. You and I both know you're faking this illness. I saw you going to play rugby less than a week ago. I took photos of you for God's sake!"

"And where are those photos now, Sylvia?"

"You know well where they are – you deleted them just before you threw my phone at me."

"Exactly, you have no photos any more. So fuck off, Sylvia, and don't phone me again."

He hangs up.

No, you fuck off, she thinks, then quickly opens the call-recorder app to see if it worked. She puts it on speaker and Justin's voice fills the kitchen.

Tom is smiling.

"Do you think it's enough?" she asks him.

"Definitely. You mention the rugby and the deleted photos and throwing the phone at you and he doesn't deny any of it – Craig's eyes will be well and truly opened."

"Should I send it to Craig now?"

"Do. Give him the weekend to sit on it, rather than ambushing him on Monday morning and forcing him into a corner."

She hits the share button and types in Craig's email address.

"I think I've earned my night out now," she says, putting down the phone and kissing Tom.

"Oh yeah, I forgot you're out tonight – who are you meeting?"

"Kate."

"Again? You don't even see your real friends that often."

"Well, she is a real friend. I think. And she's trying to adjust to a broken marriage and being a lone parent, and she could do with someone to talk to."

"She could do with someone who'll jump every time she whistles," Tom says, but Sylvia doesn't care – she's running upstairs to get changed, feeling lighter than she has done in weeks.

Chapter 47

Sylvia – Friday, September 9th

Traffic is crawling through the rain-soaked streets like Dublin has decided to dress up as New York for the night. Some football game with loads of American tourists, says the taxi driver. Sylvia doesn't mind. The falling dusk glows above the streetlights, and the Friday night feeling is seeping into the cab – everything has upped its game to match her mood. She should have made the call weeks ago. She smiles.

Kate's already sitting at the bar, scrolling through her phone, and two white wines appear as Sylvia pulls out a stool. As they clink, Kate asks what they should toast.

"Justin," Sylvia says, "and the grave he's just dug for himself!"

Kate wants to hear everything.

Sylvia is only halfway through the story when the wine is gone and they order more. They clink again, and she continues her play-by-play account. Kate claps when she hears about the call recorder, and Sylvia takes out her phone and ear-buds to let Kate hear the confession for herself.

"Oh God, he's so pleased with himself! What a dick!" she says when the call comes to an end.

"Yeah, he's so smug. But not for long, I hope. I doubt Craig can do anything formal with it – like with HR, I mean – it's probably not quite legal to trap someone into admitting they're faking sickness, but at least it takes the focus off me."

Kate nods. "Yeah, they probably can't go down the disciplinary route but perhaps he'll be quietly managed out. I'm pretty sure no matter where you work, it's seen as fairly serious to fake an illness to get six weeks off work, especially if it's to cover up a mistake. Brilliant – well done for doing it!" She raises her glass. "Actually, I have news too. A really odd thing happened today – kind of life-changing really, or it would have been before my husband screwed up our marriage. I was sitting in the car at the school – "

Sylvia's phone vibrates on the bar and she glances down. "Oh sorry, Kate, it's from Craig – I need to see what he says."

She looks up a moment later, beaming.

"Okay, listen to this. He says the recording made for very interesting listening, and he thinks it may need to go to the board because of the seriousness of the audit situation. He says we'll discuss it further on Monday morning, and – wait for this – he says 'Sorry you've been left to deal with all of this due to Justin's incompetency.' *Ha!*"

"I notice he doesn't take responsibility himself though – kind of brushing it under the carpet, no?"

"I'll take it. It's a hell of a lot better than sitting there being blamed for everything."

"You're right. It's a good result. Here's to a long and successful career with Stanbridge Brown." Kate holds up her glass again.

"No chance – I'll stay until the audit is closed, then I'm going."

"Will you take time out with the kids?"

"Maybe for a while. But then I'll find a job I actually like.

Or at the very least, one that doesn't make me miserable every day."

Kate smiles. "Well, fair play to you! We should have ordered champagne."

Sylvia raises her glass but her smile has slipped away.

"Are you okay?" Kate asks.

"Yeah, I just feel a bit bad to be celebrating. This is going to sound silly, but our dog died this week." And just as she knew would happen, her eyes well up. God, she could be such a wuss sometimes.

"Ah, I'm sorry. Did you have him long?"

"Five years – since we got married. I know it's not like a human dying – of course it's not, but he was part of the family. Even if he was really annoying sometimes." She wipes away a tear with the back of her hand, trying not to smudge her mascara. "God, what am I like!"

"I always wanted a dog – we couldn't have one when we were kids because my dad didn't like them. Then, when my parents split, my mum said it was too much work for her on her own. I was absolutely certain I'd get my own dog when I grew up, then I only went and married the one guy in Ireland who is petrified of dogs."

"Oh, I didn't realise – how did he get over it?"

"He didn't – he's still shit-scared of them – he'll literally cross the road if he sees a tiny puppy. I used to think it was cute. Now it's just pathetic."

Sylvia shakes her head. "But Sam's not scared of dogs – he was always great with Bailey whenever we bumped into him."

Kate looks surprised. "Maybe he's managing to hide it better now and I just haven't noticed. I bet if you think back now, you'll realise he kept his distance and scarpered as quickly as he could. What kind of dog was Bailey?"

"A Lab. But no – Sam played with Bailey every time he saw

him – it was one thing I liked about him from the start. He would rub his ears and tickle him and give him loads of attention."

Kate stares at her. "No – you must be mistaken – Sam is honestly petrified of dogs. There's no way he'd rub one."

"No, he did. He was mad about Bailey," says Sylvia and sips her wine. How well does Kate actually know her husband?

Kate is shaking her head. "No chance. He was attacked by a Doberman when he was a kid – he went into the field behind their house, and a Doberman chased him from one end to the other. The dog caught him and bit him in the face. The owner pulled the dog off, but Sam needed stitches – that's where the scar came from. And he's never gone near a dog since – which you can understand. I feel a bit mean now saying he's pathetic."

"What scar?"

"The scar on his cheek! There's no need to be polite – he's well used to it."

"God, I've never noticed it at all."

Kate smiles. "Seriously, it's okay. He's not sensitive."

"I'm not just being nice – I've genuinely never seen a scar."

"The white line that goes from just under his left eye all the way down?" Kate traces a line on her own face.

Sylvia shakes her head.

"Look, I'll show you," Kate says, picking up her phone from the bar. She scrolls for a moment then holds it up to Sylvia. "See – even without zooming in it's obvious. That's from earlier on this summer when he had a bit of a tan, which always makes it stand out more."

Sylvia takes the phone and stares at the picture, then looks up at Kate. "But that's not Sam."

"Of course it's Sam. Jeez, he can't have changed that much

over the summer. Here, I'll get another one." She scrolls again and zooms in on another picture.

Sylvia takes the phone. The man is similar to Sam – tall, tanned, brown eyes, brown hair, but it's not Sam. She shakes her head.

"I don't know what's going on, but that's not Sam."

"Um, in fairness, I think I know my own husband. Maybe there's someone else new in another house in Willow Valley and you're mixing them up?"

"I'm not. Honestly. Sure we've been in his house – your house. We had tea with him. He helped me dig a grave for poor Bailey on Monday, and told me all about burying his dog Max."

Kate stares at her. "Sam never had a dog. Max was Michael's dog. His cousin Michael."

Chapter 48

Sam – Monday, July 11th 2016

Everything hurts. His mouth feels like someone filled it with sand and shook him. He tries opening his eyes but even that makes his stomach lurch. Feeling his way to the bathroom, he gets there just before throwing up. The bathroom tiles are blessedly cool when he slides down onto the floor afterwards, panting and sweating. What time is it? Oh God, work. How is he going to go into work like this? A shower might help. He turns the water down cold and forces himself to stand under the icy needles, imagining the vodka washing out of his pores. And the tequila. What the hell was he thinking? Blurred memories of shot glasses and slices of lemon filter back as he dries himself – and blaring the Stone Roses at full blast. On a Sunday night – Jesus, what would the neighbours say? Kate would kill him if she knew. And all because he tried to give Michael money for the work he'd done over the weekend. He should have known better. If Kate was here, she'd have known it would embarrass Michael, but at the time it seemed like the right thing to do. If you did it for any other customer they'd pay you, he'd said to Michael. And his cousin just shrugged and said family is different. Then he'd taken the money to buy drink and a takeaway for both of them – way, way too much drink. Sam's stomach lurches again.

Downstairs, Michael is already up and dressed and looking far chirpier than Sam feels. He's cooking something on the grill and Sam needs to open a window to avoid throwing up again.

"Morning. Sausages and pudding?" Michael asks.

Sam just shakes his head and pours a drink of water. "What time did we finish up at?"

"Near two, I reckon. You look a bit shook today – are you all right?"

Sam shakes his head again. "I don't know if I can cope with work today. I need to find the paracetamol."

On his way to the bathroom, he peeks into the sitting room to assess the damage. Two empty vodka bottles, an open bottle of tequila, and too many beer cans to count. Remnants of Tikka Masala congeal on plates, and empty cartons sit on the floor. An overflowing ashtray is perched on the windowsill, evidence of the plan to only smoke out the window. Kate would go nuts if she saw this. There's no way he can stomach the clean-up now – literally – it'll have to wait until tonight.

"Don't worry, you head on to work, I'll clear it up," Michael says, coming up behind him.

"Ah no, I can do it later – sure you've been working non-stop all weekend on the house."

"Not at all – it's my fault we overdid it and you're going into work in that state. I'll do it – I've no jobs on this morning."

"Okay, cheers for that. I'll give you a key so you can lock the door after."

Sam finds the spare key and passes it over to his cousin

then leaves for work, wondering how on earth he's going to get through the day.

Turning into the driveway that evening, the only thing on Sam's mind is hitting the couch, and maybe, just maybe, summoning up the energy to make toast for dinner. Michael's car is gone – it'll be just himself and the remote control for the evening.

The first thing to hit him when he walks into the hall is the smell of steak and onions. In the kitchen, Michael is standing over the hob, shaking salt on the pan. He turns when he hears Sam come in.

"Hiya – I thought you could do with something like this after the day you've no doubt just had," he says, nodding at the steak.

"Oh right – I didn't realise you were here – where's your car?"

"I moved it into the garage – it's easier to get equipment in and out of the house that way," Michael says. "Look – I've chips in the oven too – homemade ones now, not chipper chips."

"You're very good but there was no need – I thought you'd be long gone by now."

"Well, I had two jobs to do after I cleaned up here this morning," he says, gesturing towards the sitting room, "but I came back then to take a look at the wiring in the spare room. Pretty bad state overall – there's a lot of work in it still."

Great. And now it's going to be awkward if Michael does the work and won't take money. Maybe he should just pay someone else and be done with it.

"Listen, man, if it's this big a job, I might see about getting someone in. I can't be pulling you away from your other work."

"You're grand, Sam. I don't have much lined up for the next few weeks and I can fit it in around the work here. Listen, I've said it before. It's the least I can do. Your mam was very good to me after my mam died – she might not have approved of my da, but she didn't let it get in the way."

Claire didn't approve of Michael's dad? Sam raises his eyebrows in a bid to hear more but Michael has turned back to the pan. He wanders into the sitting room – it's spotless now, like last night never happened.

"Do you think any of the neighbours heard the music – did you get any dirty looks when you were in and out today?" he calls back to Michael.

"Nah, but I didn't bump into anyone either. You said you thought next door are away – they're the only ones who'd have heard it. Don't be worrying. As long as Kate doesn't suss you, you're grand."

Kate. Was he supposed to Skype the kids tonight? He looks at his watch and picks up the iPad. Michael is singing in the kitchen. Maybe it would be better to do it from upstairs, he thinks, as he heads for his bedroom, followed by the smell of frying onions.

After dinner, Michael suggests they have a few cans but Sam just shakes his head. No more beer on a school night for him. Michael decides to have one anyway, and flops down on the couch, switching on the TV.

Sam hesitates in the doorway, wondering how many beers Michael is going to have. Will he be able to drive back into town? It's probably rude to ask. Feck. Maybe he's waiting to be invited to stay over again tonight.

"Listen, if you're kipping here another night that's cool. I'm sure you're wrecked after all the work today and don't fancy driving back to town?"

Michael looks over at him but doesn't reply.

Shit, maybe it sounds like he's expecting him to stay over and get more work done on the house tomorrow.

"Or I mean I can give you a lift in to town later if you want to have a few beers – you could pick up your car another time? Whatever suits you best . . . " Sam trails off.

Michael is still looking at him with that weird unblinking stare he does sometimes. He takes a swig of beer.

"Yeah, I was thinking it'd be as easy if I stay over again," he says then. "I'll need to be up early to get a start on that spare room if I'm going to get some of it done before a meeting I have at eleven. Bit of a problem to sort out." He turns back to the TV.

Sam sits down too but the smell of the open beer can turns his stomach and he moves further away. There's a programme about cars on TV – possibly the least interesting programme Sam has ever seen. He takes out his phone and scrolls through Facebook instead. Kate has put up pictures of the boys on the beach – they look happy and healthy and brown. Only four more days till he's down there with them, and suddenly he's looking forward to it so much it almost hurts.

Chapter 49

Sam – Tuesday, July 12th

Tonight's offering is another sausage dish of some kind – according to the smell that's filling the entire downstairs when Sam gets in from work. Michael's repertoire appears to be confined to meat that can be cooked in a frying pan. He shouldn't complain – it's better than coming home to nothing at all. Although a quiet evening to himself wouldn't be such a bad thing at this stage.

He sneaks upstairs to change before going in to say hello, and stops to sit on the bed for a few quiet minutes catching up on online news. When he hears footsteps on the stairs he jumps up and puts away the phone, like a guilty spouse caught cheating.

Michael is standing in the doorway.

"Oh, I didn't hear you come in – dinner's just about ready. You still eat bangers and mash, right? Remember my mam used to make it for us all the time?"

Sam nods. "Yeah, sorry, just couldn't wait to get out of the suit. Long old day. I think I'm still feeling the effects of Sunday night."

"Come on, bit of food and you'll be grand. I was going to

get out a DVD for later – anything you fancy?"

Sam blinks. So Michael is staying again. It probably makes sense . . . but still. He stifles a yawn and follows his cousin downstairs for more sausages. He never thought he'd miss Kate's insistence on vegetables with every meal, but suddenly he has a longing for some broccoli.

Watching Michael settle down afterwards with the remote and a beer, Sam braves asking if he's staying over. God, now it feels like an awkward date. Michael nods and keeps flicking through the channels, but then he stops and turns to Sam.

"Actually, I might just stay full-time for a few weeks. It makes more sense, doesn't it? I can get all your rewiring done – it'll save you hundreds of quid, and I don't need to be worrying about buses and getting in and out of town. I'll even cook you dinner every night." He laughs.

Sam's not sure what's funny but he laughs too.

"That's settled then," Michael says. "I'll run into the flat tomorrow and pick up some of my stuff."

He puts on a programme about UK social welfare cheats and settles back to watch – clearly the conversation is over.

Sam stares at the TV but he's not seeing the picture. How did that just happen? Michael's grand craic for a night or two, but a few weeks? Maybe the rewiring wouldn't take as long as he thought, or Michael would get some new paid work that he'd have to say yes to. And surely he'd have to accept payment if he was going to do a few weeks of work on the house – actually, that might be a way out.

"So listen," he says, "if it's a much bigger job than you thought and it's going to take a few weeks, I insist on paying the going rate – I can't let you work for nothing. So either I pay you, or we call it quits now – is that fair?"

"Tell you what, you can pay me in kind. One skill for another – deal?"

Sam has no idea what's coming next, but he nods because he can't think what else to do.

"Computers," Michael continues. "You were always good at them, because of that computer your old pair bought you when we were kids. My mam couldn't afford something like that. And there were no computers in our school – do you remember that time I was over in your house and I didn't know how to use a mouse, and you were laughing at me, asking why I hadn't learned it in school?"

Sam's face grows hot. There's no way he had laughed at him – at least, not in a mean way. Anyway, how was he to know they didn't have computer classes in Michael's school? "I don't really remember that . . . "

Michael shakes his head. "Really? You thought it was hilarious. Like the time you were going on a ski trip, and we were going to a farm in Wicklow – you went on and on about it, like it was the funniest thing ever. But look, no hard feelings – I get it. When you go to a school like Mount Derry, it's like living in a bubble. You've no idea what it's like out in the real world. Not your fault." He reaches across and pats Sam's shoulder. "But anyway, yeah, with the computers – I can do the basics but that's about it – how about if I do your rewiring, and you give me lessons in computers? Maybe on how to invest money too?"

Sam stares at his cousin – this is the last thing he expected to hear. "Well, sure, but the investment side could take years to learn – like I did courses and exams after college and I've been doing them throughout my years at work too, as well as all the day-to-day experience I get at the office. It's probably not something you could learn in a few weeks . . . "

"You mean it's only for college boys, is that right?"

Sam shakes his head. That's not what he'd said at all. Is it? "No, no – I don't mean that. Just that it'd take more than a few weeks."

"Well, let's start with the computer stuff and see how we go – how about that? I'm not as bad as I was – I've figured out how to use a mouse." He laughs again.

Sam gets up to fetch his laptop. This is going to be hell.

Two hours later, he's eating his words – Michael is a fast learner, and it's far more interesting than the TV programme on social welfare cheats. Michael's even put down the beer and moved to the kitchen table to focus on the lesson – the two of them sit together, poring over Sam's screen.

"Actually," Sam says, "I have an old laptop upstairs – I think it's still in pretty good nick. I can set it up for you if you like?"

"Cheers, man, but that's too much – I can't take a computer from you."

Sam brushes off the protests and goes to get it. After a few minutes it's up and running, side by side with Sam's on the kitchen table.

"Thanks for that – I feel like I've been taking handouts from you and your family my whole life, and here we are, still at it."

"Not at all, it's just an old computer – sure we've more than enough devices lying around the house. The kids won't even miss it."

Michael laughs at that but Sam isn't quite sure why.

"Do you remember the time your mam gave me your old bicycle – the red BMX?" Michael says. "She meant well, but it was way too small for me. And my mam wouldn't get rid of it because she didn't want to offend Claire. So it sat in the living room, taking up space and gathering dust for two years. One day I just took it out and sold it and my mam never asked where it was gone. Should have done it two years earlier."

Sam remembers the bike. "Ah, that's a shame, I didn't realise you never used it. So kind of a pain more than a present then . . . My mum meant well though . . . "

Michael claps him on the back. "Course she did. She was always trying to help, even when she got it wrong. She always felt sorry for me about my da, you know?"

"So did I. I remember feeling so sad the first time mum told me about what happened – you were the only person I knew who had lost a parent and it just seemed awful."

"What did she tell you?"

Sam shifts in the chair. "Like, just about what happened – about the car accident."

Michael laughs. "So she never told you the truth?"

Something in the laugh makes Sam think he might not want to know. "That's what she told me."

"Herself and Bella – a pair of them in it. My da didn't die in any car crash. He was in Mountjoy."

Sam swivels around to face his cousin. "Oh Jesus, I never knew that. What was he . . . I mean . . ."

"What was he in for? You're grand, that's all anyone wants to know when someone is inside. He was in for arson, racketeering, and one count of murder."

Sam's stomach does a flip. How had his mother never told him this? He tries to keep his face neutral. "Are you serious? I'm sorry, man – that's nearly worse than – well, I don't know . . . "

"You mean the truth is worse than the lie? More like a rock and a hard place, I'd say. Dead da or convict da – not a great set of options either way, is it? I wonder who gets to decide our lot in life. Like, why does one person get a successful father with plenty of money and a big house and Latin lessons in a posh school, while the other person gets a shitty flat and a da in prison? Strange, isn't it, when you think about it?"

Sam shifts again on the hard kitchen chair. "I guess it's a

testament to you and your mum that you came through it and did so well for yourself." Oh my God, that sounded so patronising.

"Do you think so? An electrician, living in the same shitty flat? While you're out here in the fancy house with the gorgeous wife and the big job? I don't know if things really came that good."

The kitchen is very still. Sam wants to reply but everything that comes to mind sounds trite and he's not sure Michael really wants an answer. An email pops into his inbox, breaking the silence.

"Bloody work emails at this time of night."

"You have work email on your home laptop too?" Michael asks.

Sam turns the screen to show him. "Yes, see here, I have two email accounts open – one is work and one is personal. I have access to my work drives too, so I can catch up at home when I need to. It's a pain in some ways because you're always on, but it means you're not tied to being in the office."

Michael wants to see how it works and Sam shows him. This is a hell of a lot easier than talking about his dad. Jesus, who knew? Well, his mum obviously, and she'd gone to her grave without telling him. And his dad must have known too. He looks at Michael, engrossed in the laptop, and wonders what kinds of conversations went on back then that he knew nothing about. But he's not going to ask him now – that's more than enough family history for tonight.

Chapter 50

Sam – Sunday, July 17th

Seth's voice is still ringing in Sam's ears when he arrives home from Galway on Sunday evening.

"You're the best daddy in the world – there's nobody you love more then me, Mum and Jamie – isn't that right, Dad?"

He had nodded his agreement and hugged Seth and said, "Yes, absolutely – there's nobody else I love more than you three." An uncomfortable image of Nina had flashed up in his mind as he spoke, and again when he hugged Jamie. The goodbye kiss from Kate had been muted. Kate is the only person who can make him feel bad for something she did. Surely disappearing for most of the weekend was worse than forgetting Seth's birthday present? As if he didn't have enough to do between the house and work and now Michael's computer lessons. Though he'd decided against mentioning the new lodger to Kate. Next weekend maybe.

Inside, the lodger is sitting at the kitchen table, busy at his laptop. A smell of stale cooking mixed with cigarette smoke hangs in the air and Sam opens the kitchen window. Tentatively he reminds Michael that he'll need to smoke outdoors – Kate will go mad if she comes home and realises. Michael is apologetic, and says something about not wanting to offend Princess Kate – Sam doesn't hear what exactly because he's already on his way upstairs to wash off the journey.

A text arrives while he's in the bathroom – Nina, suggesting she could meet him at his house, since Kate is away. That's never going to work with Michael there. **No. We'll have to stick to your apartment – my cousin is staying.** They agree that Sam will call to her tomorrow night instead, and he puts the phone down. And really it's easier this way – having her out to the house seems like an even bigger betrayal.

Downstairs, Michael is still at the laptop, opening a can of beer. Sam says no at first when he offers him one, but then changes his mind. Why not, after the weekend he's just had?

Sighing heavily, he pulls up a chair and opens up his own laptop.

"Checking work emails?" Michael asks.

Sam nods.

"You're very quiet – everything okay?" Michael asks.

Sam shrugs. "Ah, just tired. I might get an early night."

"Everything all right in Galway? How're Kate and the kids?"

"They're fine. To be honest, I'd say they're perfectly happy down there, and I just upset the routine."

Michael closes his computer and turns to Sam. "Go on – what happened?"

"Nothing really. Well, Kate went nuts at me because I forgot Seth's present. Like, it was a genuine mistake, and I've just been up to my eyes with work, but she acted like I did it on purpose to annoy her. Then on Saturday she just disappeared for the whole day and left me with the boys. But of course I'm the one in trouble."

Michael goes to the fridge to line up the next two beers, though Sam is only halfway through his first can. "Listen, Kate's tough on you – she always has been. Don't be minding her."

"You think she's tough on me?"

Michael laughs. "Why, do you think she isn't? Jesus, she's always been like that – right back since you two met. I was surprised when you ended up together, to be honest – I didn't see you with a ballbreaker like her."

Sam sits up straighter in the chair. "Really? I always thought we were well matched."

Michael laughs again. "Your mother thought you were well matched because Kate prodded you along when you were sleepwalking your way through college, not because you were any kind of perfect couple. I can't believe this is news to you."

Sam sips his beer. Maybe there's some truth in it.

"You always had your pick of the girls back then," Michael continues. "It's amazing what a posh accent and straight teeth can you get you."

"I don't know – I always thought Kate fancied you. Remember the day we met – I was sure it was you she was interested in."

"I wouldn't have noticed if she was. That day was a blur. Poor Mam."

Shit. What kind of a tool brings up a funeral in casual conversation? "Sorry, Michael – of course, an awful day for you."

Michael fixes his gaze on Sam, searching his face for something. "You know, I never held it against you."

Sam lets go the beer can he's holding. Suddenly it feels very cold. "What do you mean?" But he knows.

"About Mam. About what she did. I know you blamed yourself for not stopping her but she knew exactly what she was doing, and she waited till I was away – that was deliberate. So don't be blaming yourself – because I don't."

Sam swallows thickly and nods.

"And your mam was a big help to me with the funeral, and I know it was heart-breaking for her, burying her sister just a few years after what happened your da. I'll never forget it. I owe you, Sam – you know that? I owe you." Michael turns back to the laptop and opens it again, keying in his password.

Sam finishes his beer and nods. He should say something but he's not sure what. Why is Michael bringing this up now after all these years?

Memories of finding her cold in her bed come flooding back. The tea soaking slowly into the old sheepskin rug on the floor. The grey skin, the empty pill bottles. The dark silence and the horror and then later the guilt. The ambulance, just because it seemed like the right thing to do, even if there was no hope at all in her still chest and unmoving lips. And the call to his own mother. That horrible call. She had phoned Michael for him. He should have done that himself, but his poor mother, sick with grief for her sister, had taken that burden from him. And they'd never talked about it. He'd said all the things people say – they'd done the platitudes, the handshakes, the bowed heads. But they'd never talked about it – about him being there and Michael not, and about finding her that morning. He hadn't even gone to the inquest – Claire had gone with Michael, while he stayed at home pretending it was better for them if they were left to their grief in private. My God, what was he thinking? And why didn't his mother just insist he went? He remembers now Kate had been surprised he wasn't going – he hasn't thought about that in twenty years.

He opens the next beer and clears his throat. "Cheers to Bella – she was an amazing woman." He lifts his can towards

Michael. It's pathetic but it's the best he can come up with right now.

"She surely was, and no doubt was justly rewarded in Heaven. She's up there now with your da, isn't she, Sam?" Michael raises his can too and takes a drink, never looking away from the screen.

Chapter 51

1984

The kitchen door is open but he stops in the hall when he hears his name being mentioned. They're whispering, but arguing, and he can hear most of what they're saying.

"Michael's a bad influence, Claire – I don't want them spending so much time together," John says.

"That's not fair. Just because his father is in jail doesn't make him a bad person. Sure he's never even known his father."

"Claire, if you can't see it, you're just fooling yourself. Sam is enthralled by him – it's not healthy. If Michael says jump, Sam asks how high. I understand you want to look out for him but you can't spend your whole life feeling guilty for making better choices in life than your sister did."

"That's not fair either. She was only sixteen when she met Michael's dad – sure she hadn't a clue what she was doing or what he was like. We don't always make our choices with full knowledge. Have some compassion."

He peers around the door, careful to avoid being seen. They're sitting at the kitchen table drinking tea, Claire in her house-coat to keep her dress clean, and John in his suit, ready for work. He pulls back behind the door.

"How long is he staying though?"

"Just a week or so. Bella's been asked to do a whole load of extra shifts and she doesn't want to turn them down."

"Fine. A week. But if Sam is giving you cheek when Michael's around, you need to nip it in the bud – don't let either of them away with it."

He hears John pick up the newspaper.

"Can we talk about the school suggestion?"

John puts down the newspaper again. "Claire, we can't afford it. We can't pay two sets of fees."

"If we really wanted to, we could. If things had gone as we'd hoped, we'd have two children now and we'd find a way to pay two sets of school fees."

"But that's just it!" John says, throwing his hands up in the air. "We don't have two children. Michael is not our child."

"He's not our own child but he's still family, and there's no way Bella will be able to send him to a private school – not in a million years."

"But he doesn't have to go to private school – what's wrong with his local school?"

They've both forgotten about whispering now.

"Well, if his local school is so great, then why don't we send Sam there?"

He hears John bang his fist on the table. "Claire, you're being ridiculous! I will pay for my son to go to private school. I will not pay for your nephew to go to private school. That's the end of the conversation."

He pushes back his chair, and Michael slips into the sitting room, out of sight.

John picks up his briefcase and coat in the hall and slams out the door.

Michael stays for a while in the sitting room, then goes in to the kitchen to go say good morning to Claire. She's still sitting at the table in her house-coat, chin in hands. She smiles when he comes in.

"Will I make you some more tea, Auntie Claire?"

"I'll make it, love. You're a good kid, Michael, you know that?"

He smiles back and nods and sits down in John's chair to read his newspaper.

Chapter 52

Sam – Saturday, July 23rd 2016

It's the loud female laugh that wakes Sam, pulling him out of a dream about a hunting trip with his boss. It takes a moment to work out where he is – sunlight's flooding in the window and it feels like he's been asleep for days. It's after eleven – he's been in bed for twelve hours straight. When's the last time he did that? Before the boys were born anyway. There's the laugh again – is the TV on downstairs? He walks out onto the landing and leans over the bannister. But it's not the TV – the voices are coming from the spare room – Michael's room. Sam steps backwards and quietly closes his door. Jesus, Kate would have a fit if she knew Michael had someone staying. Actually, she'd have a fit if she knew Michael was staying all this time too. He must think Sam is down in Galway. Awkward. Sam stands with his back to the bedroom door, trying to decide what to do. His decision is made for him when he hears the spare room door open. Michael and his guest walk past and down the stairs. She's still laughing at something Michael is saying, but his voice is too low for Sam to hear. The front door opens and shuts, then he hears footsteps in the hall and the kettle boiling. He thinks for another minute, then walks heavily across to the ensuite and switches on the shower.

Downstairs, Michael is cooking a fry. Again. "I didn't know you were here till I heard the shower upstairs – I've put on a few extra rashers now – will you have some?"

"I'm grand, thanks," Sam says, getting out porridge oats and milk. "I need to keep an eye on this." He pats his stomach.

"Sure I keep forgetting – you were raised on organic everything, weren't you – only the best for Sam Ford."

"Ha – there was nothing organic in Ireland in the eighties – we had meat and spuds for dinner like everyone else."

"We didn't always have meat," Michael says.

Sam tries to look sympathetic, though he doesn't remember there ever being a lack of food in Bella's.

"So, how is it you're not down in Galway?" Michael asks.

"I got caught up at work – big problem with a trade so I had to stay on to try to fix it. I was in the office till ten and then just came straight home to bed. I was out for the count – didn't hear you come in at all." He chances a look at Michael but his face is neutral. "Kate was pissed off. So I'm here for the weekend now – no point in going down today."

"Ah, don't mind her," Michael says, flipping the rashers. "Women are very hard to please."

Sam pauses, then seizes the moment. "Speaking of which, have you met someone yourself?"

Michael is still looking down at the pan but he's grinning. "I'm saying nothing. Time will tell. Listen, if you're not going to Galway, any chance of a lift in to the flat today? I need to pick up a few things and check for post, and my own car is full of gear – I can't even see out the back window."

"Sure. It'll be strange to see it again, it's years since I've been there."

"It is, isn't it? Years and years."

Sam hears a note of something in his voice but can't work out exactly what. Is he annoyed that Sam doesn't visit him there? In fairness, he's never invited him.

He sits down with his porridge and opens his laptop. "Will we say one o'clock so? I want to get out on the bike for half an hour to try to blow away some cobwebs, then I have to go through some more of these emails that came through overnight."

Michael joins him, his plate full of rashers and toast. "One o'clock is grand. It'll be good to get you back to the old place, Sam. It's been too long."

There's no parking on Chiswick Street so Sam turns down a side street and feeds the meter. He's never driven here before – the last time he came he didn't even have a car. But very little else has changed, and it's as busy as it always was on a Saturday afternoon. They pass two elderly women shuffling to the newsagent's on the corner, and a group of boys around thirteen or fourteen sitting on a wall. That used to be us, Michael says to Sam, nudging him and saluting the boys. They nod back at him, going silent as he passes. They turn onto Chiswick Street and walk towards the flats. Two women out having a cigarette say hello to Michael, as does a younger woman holding a toddler by the hand. He seems to know everyone. But then that's how it is when you've lived somewhere all your life, Sam supposes. As they wait for the lift, a youngish guy comes up to Michael and mumbles something to him. "Not now," Michael says, and waves him away. The lift door shudders open and they step in – unexpectedly it smells of stale cooking fat. Sam wrinkles his nose. Michael grins.

On the third floor, they walk along the concrete corridor

until they reach Number 32. Michael slips the key in the lock and Sam is back in time. Nothing has changed. The ratty old couch is still where it always was, the yellow paint is still peeling off the walls. No better, no worse. It's like Michael somehow froze the state of disrepair – for nostalgia's sake perhaps. Or maybe it's just Sam's memory playing tricks on him. The room smells slightly musty but it's a welcome contrast to the lift. The carpet – brown like the couch – is threadbare now in parts, and there are orange marks in the corner. Sam remembers now – they were trying to clean beer out of the carpet and he'd had the idea to use bleach. Bella had gone ballistic – she didn't care about the beer, but she wanted to throttle them over the bleach.

Michael tells him to sit down and he'll make tea. Sam lowers himself carefully into the couch, doubting there are many springs left in it now. His eyes rest on the armchair at the other side of the room – Bella's chair. Would her bedroom be the same? He hasn't seen it since the morning he found her. He shivers, and looks over at Michael. But he's busy with mugs and hot water, not reliving old memories.

The tea is weak and tastes of metal – something to do with the water maybe, or the staining inside the cup. Michael is rummaging through cupboards looking for a packet of Jaffa Cakes but Sam is fine with just the tea, he says, patting his stomach again. Michael sits down and points over at his bedroom – he's moved into his mother's room, he says, because it's bigger. His old room is just for storage now. It's a relief to Sam somehow – knowing the bedroom is no longer as it was that day.

Then Michael suggests they go out for a few beers in his local and stay here tonight. Sam is stuck for words. There's nowhere he'd be less inclined to stay. But Michael is only joking – he wouldn't dream of tearing Sam away from his lovely home, he says.

There's a knock on the door, and Michael gets up to answer, peering out the window first.

"Jean, how's it going?" he says, when he opens the door.

Jean says hello and walks into the flat, looking Sam up and down.

"Sam, this is my neighbour Jean – Jean, Sam is my cousin – you might remember him from years ago? He used to stay here every now and then?"

Jean is shaking her head. Sam is fairly sure he'd remember Jean too – she's unusually tall, with brown hair curling around her shoulders, and large gold hoops dangling from her ears.

"Actually, that was mostly before you moved in, I think," Michael says to Jean. "When was that – 1990?"

"Yes, 1990, long time ago now."

"How're Peter and Paul doing?"

"They're grand. Well, Peter just quit his job – it wasn't what he expected and he didn't like the boss, but sure he'll pick up something else soon enough. He likes variety, that one, though I wish he'd stick at something longer than four weeks. And Paul – well, he's just bought a house out in Malahide and he's been promoted again at work. I still don't know what he does – something to do with marketing – but he's doing great at whatever it is."

Michael beckons her further into the room to sit down, and offers her tea.

"It's gas, isn't it," he says, putting a cup on the small coffee table in front of her, "the way they ended up with such different lives even though they're brothers. It's like us – our mams were brought up together in the same house by the same parents, and then Claire – his mam," he points at Sam, "ends up living in south Dublin in a big house, married to a man with a great job. My mam on the other hand marries a fella daft enough to get himself locked up in Mountjoy and lives hand to mouth in this place – no offence, Jean – for the rest of her days. Funny, isn't it?"

Sam's not sure if it's a question.

Jean is nodding. "It's funny all right. I dunno what it is with my two – to be honest, Peter was always the sharper one, but maybe I spoiled him a bit and let him away with too much. Paul had to work harder – maybe that's why he's doing so well now. And it's gas, cos they look exactly alike – spit of each other. You two are very alike as well, aren't ye?"

"That's what they say, though I'm obviously way more handsome, isn't that right?" Michael says, and she laughs.

Sam laughs too.

"What about us, Sam – what do you think?" Michael says, turning to him.

"Huh?"

"Why did we end up with such different lives – you and me? Maybe I did something wrong in a past life or maybe I was being punished for my da's crimes or maybe it's just the way it is and there's nothing any of us can do about it – what do you think?"

Sam still isn't sure if this is a real question but suddenly the old sunken couch is feeling very claustrophobic. Michael is waiting for him to speak.

"I suppose it's just the way it is – probably a lot to do with who they married, right?"

"So I'm being penalised for my ma's bad choices, is that what you mean?"

"Ah no, it's not like that. You've done great for yourself." Shit, he has no idea what to say without sounding patronising. Michael's doing that weird unblinking thing again, and Jean is just quietly sipping her tea. Sam looks at his watch. "Well, I'd better get back soon to get a bit more work done. Is that okay with you, Michael, if we head on in a few minutes?"

"Grand, I'll get my stuff. Tell you what, will we get Jean to take a picture of us here in the flat for old time's sake? Jean, will you do that?"

He passes her his phone, and hunkers down beside Sam.

It feels silly but there's no way to say no, so Sam just smiles.

"Great stuff, I'll stick that up on Facebook – Jaysus, what would Bella make of Facebook, eh, Sam? Listen, Jean, good to see you – call in any time I'm here, though I'll be gone for the next few weeks. I'm on holliers on the southside for a few weeks – isn't that right, Sam?"

Sam pulls himself out of the couch and picks up his keys. This flat doesn't remind him of Bella any more, and he desperately wants to go home.

Chapter 53

Saturday, September 29th 1990

"Did you get it?" Michael says, flicking his cigarette butt onto the ground.

Sam passes him the key. "My dad will go mad if he ever finds out – I'm not sure this is a good idea."

Michael puts his hand on his arm. "Don't worry. You said it yourself – your da hardly ever uses the shed. And I don't even need it for that long. But Mam's been in and out of my room and I think she suspects something so I need to move it at least for now. Might be all my imagination – when I know it's safe, I can take it back."

"Okay. Where is it?"

"I borrowed a van – it's just there, about three houses down," says Michael, pointing. "Are your old pair out for the day?"

Sam nods.

"Right, let's get moving – I'll pull into the driveway. They're all in plain cardboard boxes so none of your neighbours will cop it's booze and fags inside – it could be anything."

The van fits neatly in the driveway and, with the rear doors open, it's easy to carry packages around the side of the house without being seen. All the boxes are the same size, and heavier than they look. Packed with salt, Michael tells Sam – to keep the bottles from breaking and to make sure the cigarettes don't get damp. Sweat beads gather on Sam's forehead despite the cool September air, and he takes off his bomber jacket. On it continues, as the stack in the van grows smaller and its counterpart in the shed grows higher. There's little else in the shed – a toolbox, a shovel, a pickaxe and a lawnmower, and none of them will be needed again until spring, Sam reckons.

"You better be right about that," Michael warns him.

There are just two boxes left when Michael looks at his watch and says he needs to get the van back. He jumps into the driver's seat, leaving Sam to carry the last two packages into the shed and lock up. Winking at his cousin, he passes him a twenty-pound note. "Buy Molly something nice with that. And don't go near the boxes, sure you won't? I'll sort you out with any drink you need – but the packages have to stay intact or I can't sell them on."

"Jesus no, I wouldn't touch them. Cheers for that," says Sam, stuffing the note in his jeans pocket.

"I need to keep the key too – so I can get in and out. I'll only come when no-one is here though, yeah?"

"Yeah, no worries."

"Shit, do I need to stay here now so you can lock the shed after you?" Michael looks at his watch.

"No, you're grand – there are two keys – I got an extra one cut." Sam holds up the other key.

Michael pauses for a moment then starts the engine. "All right. But don't be going in there, okay? Just leave it locked."

Sam nods and waves him away, then carries the other two packages around to the shed. He pulls the twenty-pound note out again after he locks up – not bad for an hour's work. This could be the start of something really, really good.

Chapter 54

Friday, October 5th 1990

One bloody week. What a fucking waste of time! Michael can't park the van in the driveway this time in case they come home, so it's up the road near the laneway. Carrying the boxes all the way up there is hard work and cursing John as he does each trip isn't making it any easier. So much for Sam's certainty that his da wouldn't need the key.

The stack in the shed is reduced to about half when he hears the car in the driveway, but it's just after nine – they should have been another hour. He switches off the light in the shed and stands in the dark. The kitchen light goes on and he ducks down. Sam is filling a glass of water and looking out, trying to be casual. The light goes off again. They must be sitting down now in the front room – he'd better wait another while though. Lighting a cigarette, he shuffles from one foot to the other to stay warm – it's cold in there when he's not lifting and carrying. Then he hears the back door open, and footsteps.

"Is someone there?"

John.

Michael hunches down beside the packages and waits. The door handle of the shed is moving now, and then the door is pushed open.

John presses the switch and light floods the small space.

"Jesus!" John says, jumping back.

Michael stands up.

"It's only me, Uncle John. It's Michael, sorry I scared you."

"Michael! What are you doing? I saw a match flare from upstairs and thought maybe a tramp had taken up residence. What's going on? What's all this?" He points at the packages.

Michael doesn't answer.

"Michael, what's going on?"

"Nothing. I just called over and no-one was here so I decided to wait in the shed instead of out in the cold. Sorry about the smoking." He stands on the cigarette butt.

"But what are all these boxes?"

"I'm selling schoolbooks. I got them cheap and Sam's giving me a hand to sell them on to kids in his class at school."

"You don't actually expect me to swallow that, do you? Since when are teenagers interested in buying cheap schoolbooks?"

Michael shrugs his shoulders. "Even rich kids like to make a saving every now and then, John." He watches as John's eyes travel across the boxes and then down to the toolbox on the floor.

They both see the box-cutter at the same time, and Michael reaches for it but he's not quick enough – John is nearer. He pulls it out and cuts into the nearest box. Brown powder trickles out onto the floor, picking up momentum as the seconds go by.

"What is this?"

"Salt. Well, cigarettes. The salt protects the cigarettes. I'm sorry about this, Uncle John. I sell them to make a bit of extra cash on the side. I know you're disappointed with me. And it's not Sam's fault – I talked him into letting me store them here. I'm truly sorry."

"That's not salt." John cuts deeper into the box. "And there are no cigarettes inside."

Michael says nothing.

"Is this what I think it is?"

Still Michael doesn't reply.

John steps outside and Michael hears footsteps go up the garden path, then a creaking noise, then a gush.

When John reappears, he has a hose in his hands, and he trains the water on the packages.

"*Don't do it.*" Michael's voice is like steel.

But John ignores him, drenching every single box in water until they're all soaked through. Brown powder becomes brown mud, all over the floor of the shed.

"Now, I'm going inside. You clean up this mess – I don't care how you get rid of it as long as this place is spotless in the morning. And don't come near this house again. I won't say anything to Claire – it would break her heart – but you stay away from here, or I'll tell them all – Claire, Bella, and the Guards. *You're just like your dad!*" He spits the last words. "There's only one place you're going to end up, and I always knew it. Stay way from my family – you are *poison*."

The shed is deathly quiet once John storms back up to the house and slams the back door.

The brown mud underfoot mocks Michael – thousands of pounds literally down the drain. And Michael will have to pay for this, but he won't be the only one.

Chapter 55

Sam – Tuesday, July 26th 2016

Sam is wrecked. Wrecked after a long day at work. Wrecked after another late night with Michael. Probably wrecked from eating crap food too. Turning the key in the lock, he has a sudden longing for a grilled chicken salad and an empty house. Maybe Michael will be gone out – perhaps with the mysterious laughing girlfriend.

But Michael is where he is every evening now, sitting at the kitchen table. He has his laptop open, and closes it when Sam comes in.

"How's it going? Any post today?" Sam asks.

The usual evening greeting – they're like a married couple, though with a lot more beer and junk food.

"No post, but there's a note for you there." Michael nods towards the empty coffee jar sitting on the island.

Sam picks it up the piece of paper and unfolds it.

You utter shit. I can't explain how hurt, how angry, how betrayed I feel right now. If you had to do it, couldn't you have had the decency to keep it out of our house? Moving your slut in is disgusting, beyond anything I'd ever have imagined you doing. Do not under any circumstances try to contact me or the boys. Consider us gone.

Sam looks up at Michael, then down at the letter again. It's Kate's writing, but it must be a prank.

"Where did this come from – did you write it?"

"No, it was here when I got in from town earlier. I guess someone who has a key to the house dropped it in – your neighbour maybe?"

"No, it's not from a neighbour – it's from Kate – well, supposedly. But it must be some kind of piss-take – I don't get it."

"Why, what does it say?"

Sam shows him the note.

Michael whistles and shakes his head. "Jesus, Sam – what did you do?"

"Come on – did you write it?"

"No way – not me. Whose writing is it?"

"It's Kate's – but she can't have written it. She's down in Galway, and even if she was here, what the hell is it about? She thinks I'm having an affair?"

"Seems so. Are you?" Michael asks.

"No! Of course not! Jesus, do I look like the kind of guy who has affairs? This is insane. I'll try calling her. Shit, I don't have my phone – did you see it around today? I couldn't find it when I was leaving this morning."

"No, I didn't see it – I'll keep an eye out though."

"Can I borrow yours?"

"Sure, it's upstairs, I'll grab it now," Michael says, getting up from the chair. "Oh hang on, I'm totally out of call credit. I meant to go to the shop earlier but I forgot."

"Can't you top up online or something?"

Michael just looks at him blankly. All those computer lessons and he can't even top up his phone. Sam sits down, running a hand through his hair.

"I need to speak to her. Where would she even get the notion that I'm having an affair? This is the most ludicrous thing that has ever happened. Someone must have told her something – but why would anyone do that?"

Michael takes a beer from the fridge and passes it to Sam. "I don't know what's going on, but we'll figure it out. Have you been speaking to her recently?"

"Yes, last night. She was totally, totally normal. Well, like she's still annoyed at me for not going down last weekend but there was nothing like this."

"Okay, and how have things been going over the last while?"

"You know yourself – not great over the summer but we're both stressed with the move. It's been a tough few months. She doesn't like being at home, even though she's the one who wanted to do it in the first place." Sam opens the beer and pauses. "I suppose she's been quite distant for a while now . . . and when she does pay attention, she seems annoyed with me. But like, this is a whole other level. An affair! It sounds ridiculous. Like something from TV."

"Well, she obviously thinks you are. Or maybe it's something else."

"What do you mean?" Sam asks, his head in his hands.

"Could it be that she wants a break, and didn't know how to say it? Accusing you of seeing someone else solves that, doesn't it?"

Sam looks up. "Ah listen, I know things haven't been going great, but I can't see Kate making up a story like this – she'd be more upfront."

"Could it be that *she's* met someone – down in Galway? Might be why she's been distant over the last few months?"

Sam shakes his head and tries to order his thoughts. Could

it be about Nina? Kate couldn't possibly know about Nina.

"I'll drive to Galway," he decides, pushing away the untouched beer. "If I leave now, I'll be there just after nine. I'll get her to talk to me face to face."

"That's not a good idea," Michael says. "She's angry, you're upset. Leave it till morning. Driving in this state wouldn't even be safe."

"No, I'll go tonight. I'll never sleep anyway, worrying and wondering."

Michael sighs. "She clearly said she doesn't want you to contact her. I really think you should wait – give it a few days."

"I know you're trying to help, Michael, but this is my marriage, and I need to resolve it my way."

Michael sits across from him, looking, but saying nothing. Sam suddenly has the image of a reptile in his head – bulbous eyes, unblinking. A lizard, or a snake.

"I'm going to grab a few things upstairs," he says, pushing out his chair.

Still Michael says nothing.

Later, when he thinks back, Sam can see the signs of what was to come, but not now. Now he's only thinking of fixing things with Kate. He turns and goes upstairs, leaving Michael at the kitchen table.

In his room, he throws a clean shirt into a holdall in case he stays over – he can leave early in the morning and still make it back to the office on time. His phone isn't on the locker or the dresser, nor in any of the drawers. That doesn't make sense – he definitely had it last night. He hears the back door open downstairs – Michael going for a cigarette. Shit – if Kate was in the house today, she probably smelled the stale smoke. Anyway, that's the least of his worries. What else should he take – maybe Seth's birthday present? Then he hears the soft creak of someone coming up the stairs. What does Michael want now, he wonders, throwing some socks into the holdall – that was a very speedy cigarette. He's conscious of Michael standing in the doorway, but doesn't turn around – there's no time for another debate. Transferring pyjamas and a wash-bag from bed to bag, he ignores him. But eventually, unnerved by the silence, he turns.

Michael is standing in the doorway, watching. And for reasons Sam can't work out, he has a sledgehammer in his hand.

"I think it's time," Michael says.

He walks towards him, and with shocking speed he swings the sledgehammer towards Sam's left knee.

Sam screams in pain and shock as he falls to the floor, clutching his shattered knee. He stares up at his cousin. Michael's mouth is moving, but he can't work out what he's saying. The pain is like nothing he has ever felt or imagined. Then, horrified, he watches as Michael swings the sledgehammer again. This time it comes crashing down on his right knee, as he lies on the floor, unable to move out of the way. The pain is unbearable. Sam screams again. Bright lights dance in front of his eyes, and his own voice sounds distant and alien to him. Somewhere beneath the pain, a question. Why? Then, as he finally loses consciousness, the room goes dark.

Chapter 56

Sam – Wednesday, July 27th

Darkness and pain. Nausea. Background noise. A police siren. Or an ambulance? Is he in hospital? Has he been in an accident? His brain tries to grab tufts of memory as they swirl by, but fails. Another siren, and voices – doctors? He can't tell if his eyes are open or not. Where is Kate? Something stirs in his memory. Michael? Is Michael with him? The doctors are speaking but sound faint in the background. Then louder.

"I'm sorry, we did everything we could, but we weren't able to save him."

But he's not dead – he can hear them!

Sam wills his eyes to open, begging the fog to lift. He hears a low moan – it's coming from him. Surely they can hear that? His eyelids lift briefly then close. He tries again, and again. This time he keeps his eyes open, squinting in the darkness. There's a light up above, in a corner of the room. Voices again. Someone beside him. He tries to turn his head but a surge of nausea stops him. Focus. Focus. The doctors' voices are gone now and he can hear music in their place. His eyes are drawn to the light in the corner. A television. The credits are rolling.

The loud, familiar theme tune of *Casualty*. No doctors, no ambulances, not in real life. Just this room, his own spare room. And Michael.

Sam slips in and out of sleep all morning – or is it unconsciousness, he wonders, during the interim moments of lucidity. He's heard of people's bodies shutting down to deal with pain – maybe that's what's happening. Michael had injected him with something at one point – poison? He'd tried to pull away, but couldn't move. If Michael had wanted to kill him, he'd have smashed his head in with the sledgehammer, but nothing makes sense any more.

The next time he wakes, Michael is not there. He tries to lift his head to look around – it's stiff, and every movement brings fresh waves of nausea. The pain in his knees is red hot but more bearable than before – maybe because of whatever Michael has injected. Somehow he can see his legs – he's wearing shorts now – how can that be? But on closer inspection, they're his work trousers, cut into makeshift shorts. His knees are red and black and purple and swollen – he looks away and focuses on the room around him instead. It's darker than usual – Michael has pulled the old wardrobe across the window. Beyond that, the room looks like it always does – magnolia walls, beige carpet, white bed linen and matching white curtains. The small television on the wall. The little white bedside locker. The only dash of colour is the old-fashioned blue vase in the corner: a wedding present Kate didn't like but couldn't throw out – perfect for a spare room where nobody would ever see it. A nondescript room, typical of guest-bedrooms everywhere. And no evidence that Michael has been staying here at all. He must have moved his stuff out. Is he leaving – maybe he's gone? Small buds of hope begin to filter through Sam's still-foggy mind, and he looks on the bedside locker for his phone. Not there. He reaches carefully into his trouser pockets, slowly, one at a time – no phone there either. Then he remembers it was already missing before any of this happened. The brief flicker of hope is replaced with panic – what if Michael is gone for good and he has no way to call anyone? Has he left him here to die alone? He needs to shout for help. He swallows – his throat and lips are dry, as though he's been out all night drinking. He tries to make a sound, then to form a word.

"Help!" It comes out like a whimper. He tries again. "Help! Help me!" A little louder this time, but still no more than a whisper. There's no hope that anyone will hear. Deep breath. "Help!" he croaks.

Footsteps on the stairs. It's Michael. Of course it's Michael.

"Ah now, Sam, we can't have that. I need you to stay nice and quiet. Understood?" There's a pair of crutches under his arm, and he stands them awkwardly against the far wall.

Sam stares up at him. "*Why?*" is all he can manage.

"Why the crutches? Because you'll need to go to the toilet – I'll lift you a bit but the crutches will help too."

"No, I mean . . ." He sucks in a breath as pain hits again. "I mean why did you do this?"

"Because we have things to do, you and me. I need you here, and I need your wife not to be here. That's it, simple."

"But . . ." Sam struggles to form words, and to find the energy to keep talking. "What things?"

"You'll see. Not yet. Not till you recover enough."

"Recover?" His cousin had beaten him half to death and wanted him to recover?

"Yes. I need your mind. I need your hands. I don't need your legs." He says it as though he's speaking of nothing more important than a shopping list.

"*Why?*" Sam asks again.

"Later. Have some water now. And I'll make you some

toast."

He leaves the room, and Sam lies still, trying to make sense of it. Had Michael taken some kind of turn – a psychotic episode? Would he get back to normal and be horrified? The most frightening element is that Michael doesn't seem any different from how he always is. He speaks and looks exactly like the guy who ordered in Chinese two nights ago, the one who talked football over beers every night for the last two weeks. The same person he'd known since he was a child. The same laid-back voice that fifteen-year-old Sam had listened to talking about stashing drink and cigarettes is now telling him he'll explain later why he crippled him.

The smell of toast makes Sam retch when Michael comes back into the room – he's not ready to eat. He shakes his head when Michael offers it and even that small movement makes him feel horribly sick. Michael sits down on a chair beside the bed and bites into the toast himself. The TV screen is showing the news – Sam squints to try to see the time in the corner of the screen but can't. It's disorienting to have no clock and no phone.

"Do you have my phone?" he asks.

"You don't need a phone," Michael says, still chewing his toast, engrossed in the TV. "Kate doesn't want to talk to you."

"The affair . . ." A picture is forming. "You told her?"

Michael nods, still looking at the screen. "Very easy to make it look like someone is cheating on the missus. Friend of mine, good-looking girl, all fake tan and white teeth. She's been in and out every few days for the last two weeks, getting the neighbours talking while you're at work." He turns to face Sam. "You nearly met her – that Saturday when you were meant to be in Galway – remember?"

Sam nods.

"Then I sent a letter to Kate on Monday morning, letting

her know about your cheating. Yesterday, my friend left some of her stuff around the bedroom – underwear, make-up, her pill. You know – women's stuff. And I kept an eye on Kate's phone through that **Find My Device** app you both have on your phones. I have your phone by the way. I wasn't sure if the letter would get there yesterday or not, and I didn't know if Kate would try to call you, so I took it just to be on the safe side. But anyway, sure enough, the GPS tracker showed her heading for the Dublin road and I knew we were in business. And Kate performed like clockwork, God bless her – hell hath no fury or whatever that saying is. When I got in, the stuff was all in black bags and the room was a state. She must have been livid. I cleaned it up." He explains the last bit as though he'd done Sam a favour.

Jesus Christ. Sam tries to absorb what he's saying, but his mind is still fuzzy from the pain and whatever drug Michael has been injecting. What the fuck possessed him to do all this? And Jesus, no wonder Kate was so upset.

"Please . . . please let me text Kate – just to tell her there's no affair."

Michael smiles. "Now, Sam, I can hardly let you text her, can I? Why would I go to all this trouble to get her out of the house, only to have you tell her the truth and bring her running back? Anyway, don't worry – you *have* been texting her."

Sam's brain is still like cotton wool. What is Michael talking about now?

"Look, I'll show you." Michael pulls Sam's phone out of his pocket and clicks into a text. Sam reaches his hand out to take the phone, but Michael pulls it further away. "No, no touching. I'll read it for you. You said '*I feel like we've been growing apart, and I was lonely. And flattered by the attention. I know, it sounds so weak when I put it like that.*

And it is. Men are stupid, I'm stupid.'" He puts the phone back in his pocket. "You might be surprised to hear this, but she didn't reply, other than to say goodbye to you. You know, Sam, women don't let us away with things like that these days – sleeping around. You should have known better."

A surge of nausea stops Sam as he tries to lash out at Michael – his head comes two or three inches off the pillow then he flops back down.

"So Kate's seen your mistress's things in your room, and someone's written her a letter, and you've been texting her apologising for your affair. I'd say your marriage is over, buddy. But don't worry, I'm here for you." Michael pats Sam's shoulder and covers him with a light duvet..

Sam closes his eyes, blocking it out.

"Listen, I'm heading out for a few hours, so look, I'll sort you out with a bed pan now – I don't think you're ready to move – and I'll top up your medicine so you get a good sleep. Who says I don't look after you, eh?"

Sam doesn't resist. The pain has intensified with the effort of speaking – a drug-aided sleep is welcome.

The blue glow of the TV pulls him back into consciousness and it takes a moment to remember why he's in the spare room. The realisation settles around him like cold tar. He turns his head. The room is empty, but there are noises coming from downstairs. There's a black strip of sky just visible above the top of the wardrobe – it must be after ten. His arm feels heavy when he tries to lift it but he forces himself to slide it across to the bedside locker. There's no phone there – of course there isn't. His hand knocks against something heavy and it falls on the floor, bringing footsteps to the stairs. Sam's stomach clenches as Michael pushes the door open, his eyes searching to see what caused the noise. But it was just a glass of water. Michael cleans it up, telling Sam it's okay – accidents happen.

Sam closes his eyes over tears he can feel welling up.

"Sorry," he says, when he trusts his voice. "And thank you."

"No problem, I'll go down and get you more water."

"Michael?"

His cousin turns back towards him.

"It's not too late to fix this – you just made a mistake. If you give me my phone, I can call an ambulance and say someone broke in – you could just go back to your flat. We don't need to involve anyone else."

"Ah, Sam. You have no idea, do you? There was no mistake. This has been a long time coming."

Sam wants to scream at him but he can't. "*Why?*"

"Why? Why not? You got everything when I got nothing. Circumstances of birth and nothing more." He sweeps his hand around the room. "And now I'm taking some of it back."

"But for what? What do you want with my house?"

"The house? That part's easy. My place is being watched constantly. The Guards raided it a few months back, twice in one week, trying to catch me out the second time. They found nothing, but it was pure chance. And now they're asking questions about something else that happened a few weeks ago – that stockbroker whose ma's a politician."

"Austin Granger?"

"That's him – maybe you knew him, same line of business, yeah? Anyway, I didn't know his ma was a politician when I did it – it's after bringing a lot more heat than normal. So, I needed somewhere to stay – somewhere the Guards know nothing about to keep my gear and my cash. Where's the last place you'd find a skanger like me, eh, Sam? Out in the suburbs, out with the people-carriers and the quiet cul-de-sacs and the nice neighbours. It's kind of like full circle really, isn't it – like going back to that time we used your shed, when we were kids?"

Oh God, what has he done? "Jesus, Michael, you could have just asked me – you didn't have to cripple me. I would have let you stay here."

"Ah Sam, you think that now. But really, if I had come along a few weeks ago and said 'Hope it's okay if I hide out here for a while and, while you're at it, can I just stash some smack and coke and – oh – a few shotguns and a couple of hundred K in cash?' – you and Kate would have been just fine about it? Is that what you're telling me?"

Smack and coke? And shotguns – Jesus Christ!

"I still don't get it – why not just rent somewhere else as well as your own place?"

"But sure why would I rent somewhere when I have the perfect spot here?" Michael seems genuinely baffled.

Horror sweeps over Sam. Has his cousin really maimed him and broken up his marriage because he needed a new bolthole? The insanity of it is terrifying.

"What if I pay for somewhere for you to stay?" he tries. "We could organise that here, and then if I can just get to a hospital, maybe they can do something for me before it's too late?"

Michael smiles and shakes his head, like a parent explaining something to a small child. "No, Sam, it's really just easier this way. And I need you for more than your house. You'll be staying here."

It's suddenly very cold in the room, and Sam doesn't want to hear any more. He closes his eyes, shutting out Michael, shutting out the madness. Praying for sleep to come soon.

Chapter 57

Sam – Thursday, July 28th

The man on the TV says it's Thursday and Sam grabs this piece of information like a life raft. He turns it over in his mind. There's nothing he can do with it right now, but knowing it is better than not knowing it. It's also morning, because there's a morning show on TV. Or maybe it's a repeat of a morning show. But wouldn't they air those in the morning time? His mind is still hazy from the drugs. It always gets worse after the injection, then he sleeps, then he wakes up groggy. But when he sleeps, he can't feel the pain in his legs. Silver linings. His neck is stiff and sore, and he tries to move around on the pillow to get comfortable. Turning his head, he does his regular search on the locker. Water glass – check. Phone – no chance. There's no noise from downstairs – has Michael gone out? He listens, but it's hard to tell with the hum of the TV. He must go out sometimes – to get food and to do whatever he does that isn't being an electrician – maybe now is one of those times. Sam takes a deep breath and tries moving his left leg towards the edge of the bed. The pain rushes through his knee like a hot knife, causing him to cry out. He's not going anywhere. He closes his eyes.

Now the TV is off – Michael has been and gone. Did he give him more drugs? The fogginess in his brain says he did. The light is dimmer now, it must be evening. An unfamiliar pang hits his stomach – hunger. He can't remember the last time he felt hungry. Though if today is Thursday, it's only two days since he was eating and drinking and working like everyone else – it feels like a lifetime ago. On the locker, the water has been topped up and there's a plate of ham-and-cheese sandwiches. Sam picks one up and bites into it tentatively – so far he's had nothing stronger than toast. He waits for the nausea but this time it doesn't come. Progress. Braver now, he finishes the sandwich in two bites and reaches for the next one. This is the first thing that feels good since the attack happened – the bar is truly low. Something catches his eye on the floor beside the bed – a newspaper. Reaching his arm down, careful not to move his legs, his fingertips touch it. He stretches his arm further and manages to pull it up onto the bed. Thursday July 28th is the date – today's paper. He closes his eyes and gives silent thanks. But what will you do with it *really*, asks the little voice inside his head. It doesn't matter, he thinks. It's something. It's better than nothing at all.

On the front page, there's a photo of a little girl smiling out – it's not a professional photo though, it's a snapshot. "**Edie Keogh (2) Still Missing – Mother Appeals for Help**" is the headline. She's from Meadowbrook Drive, according to the report – less than a mile away. Inside there are more pictures and interviews with neighbours. "**Nothing like this has ever happened before – it's a quiet cul-de-sac,**" according to one person. That's what I thought about this place too, thinks Sam. He reads on, determined to get through every word on every page, but his eyes are feeling heavy and as sleep reclaims him, the newspaper falls from his hands and on to the carpet below.

Footsteps on the stairs wake him and when he opens his eyes, Michael is standing over him with both laptops – his, and the old one he gave Michael. An idea flickers. His office will be looking for him. And if he doesn't answer his phone, they might contact Kate. They must have her number as his emergency contact – he's almost certain he filled something out when HR were organising his life cover. He almost smiles.

"Now, don't be getting too excited – I've deleted your work portal and your personal email." Michael pulls up a chair beside the bed and sits down, putting both laptops carefully on the locker. "The only thing still open is your trading account, and I'll be with you the whole time."

"With me for what?"

"Patience." He lifts Sam's laptop off the locker and types something on the keyboard. "Right, I've logged into your trading account already –"

Sam's mouth opens in surprise.

Michael laughs. "Don't look so shocked. You've been logging in every night for two weeks – you're not very careful about shielding your password. Did they teach you nothing about online security at work?"

"I didn't know I couldn't trust my own cousin," Sam says. "We're family. I thought that meant something."

"Aw, look at poor Sam sulking – did you really think it meant something? What about all those years when you were living in the big house on the southside and I was in a shitty flat with my mam? When you were doing your French exchange and I was running messages for the local loan sharks? When your da was at your parent-teacher meeting and mine was in Mountjoy? Did you feel we were family then?"

Michael's face is close to Sam's now. His eyes are wide and

bits of spit fly out of his mouth and onto Sam's cheek. Sam swallows.

"But you always said my mum was good to you – and she was. We did our best to look out for you and include you."

"Really? Sure, your mam felt sorry for me, but it wasn't pity I needed. And your da – he hated me. He hated me every time I walked into your house – he hated me because my old man was in prison, and he hated me for being near his precious son. The look on his face every time he set eyes on me – like he just walked in dogshit." He puts his mouth to Sam's ear now and whispers. "So don't lecture me about family, Sam." He taps Sam on the cheek, then sits back to pick up the laptop. "Right, let's get to work."

A dog barks outside and Sam turns his head to look towards the window.

"Forget what's out there – focus on this," Michael says, leaning across the bed to pull the curtain. "So basically, I have cash, and I need it moved: A lot of cash. It's spread across twenty-four different bank accounts, and I need it cleaned up and back in one account, with no trace to the origins."

Sam stares at him. What does he think this is – a John Grisham film? "Money laundering? Michael, what the fuck do you think I know about money laundering?"

"You know more than I do – you know how to move money, how to invest it, how to buy and sell stock. I can't do that – I don't have the access or the knowledge. Yet. I have cash, and now I want to be able to use it. So clean it up, and put it here –"

He passes Sam a piece of paper with a series of digits on it.

"And where are your bank accounts? Where are those details?" asks Sam, curiosity taking over.

Michael reaches down and picks a plastic bag off the floor. Inside are bundles of bank books – old-style books that predate bank cards and internet banking. The kind of bank book Sam had had when he was in primary school, for saving his pocket-money. How long had Michael been doing this?

"All the accounts are on the internet now – I've written the details for each one at the back of the bank books. They're all separate."

Sam picks up the first book and opens it. Printed in neat block capitals is the name of the bank-account owner – Alan Butler. There are handwritten entries on the first few pages, showing deposits that start back in 1990 and go up to 1997. The last balance is £21,462.15 according to the book. On the final page, there's an eight-digit code, followed by a five-digit PIN, and a new balance of €102,556.15.

Sam looks up at Michael. "Whose money is this? Who is Alan Butler?"

"He's the same person as Barry Cotter, and Colin Doorly, and Donal Egan, and all the rest of them. He's a fella who started out in a tiny flat on Chiswick Street, with a convict for a da and a liar for a ma. He knew he wasn't going to get anywhere without using his head. So he started saving. The banks weren't as strict back then, and ID's were easy to get. Every penny he made from every deal he did went in there. The deals got bigger, the network got wider. People got big into smack in the north inner city and into blow in the suburbs. And everyone wanted more, and I always had more to sell. And now there's over eight million euro and I want to be able to get to it. That's where you come in."

Eight million. His cousin the electrician has just told him that he has eight million euro in drug money and God knows what else, and he wants him to launder it. Sam sifts through the bank books. Each one is different, with various names, account numbers, and cash balances.

"And I need it to be an ongoing channel," Michael

continues. "I want you to move money for me from now on, so that I can centralise it in this account, where it's clean and I have access. And I want you to make more money for me – legit profits, by investing some of what I have. Make my eight million into eighty million."

Sam lets out a bitter laugh. "Is that what this is all about? You broke my legs with a hammer and drove my wife out of the house so that I could help you with money laundering?"

"I told you. I needed your house too, as a base. So it all worked out perfectly – you know your stuff on the money side, and you have a house." He sounds as though he's talking about hiring someone to do odd jobs.

"Why didn't you just ask?"

"Ah here, you say that now but you know you'd have refused. It's illegal – there's no way you'd have done it." He passes the laptop to Sam. "I'll be here, sitting with you while you work. In case you get any ideas about going online or messaging anyone." He picks up the newspaper from the floor. "You get going, and we'll have a tea-break in about an hour."

"Wait." Sam's voice sounds stronger to his own ears, though it's still little more than a hoarse whisper.

Michael looks up from the paper.

"I'm not doing it," Sam says. His first moment of control and it feels good. He folds his arms.

Michael puts down the paper. "Sam, are you under some kind of illusion that you have a choice? Have you forgotten what I did to you?"

"No, but if you attack me again, I'm even less likely to be able to help you. There's nothing in this for me, Michael, and I have nothing left to lose. I don't get the impression you're planning to let me out of here any time soon. So, no. I won't do it."

Michael smiles, then takes out his phone and types something.

"What are you doing?" Sam asks.

"I'm texting your boss."

"Why? What has my boss got to do with anything?"

"Oh – I forgot to tell you, he says hello. And to get better soon after your fall down the stairs. He says not to worry, things will be quiet for the next few weeks anyway, and you won't be missed."

Fuck. Sam closes his eyes. Then he opens them again. "So why are you texting him now?"

"An anonymous tip-off."

"A what?"

"About the photos on your drive at work."

"What photos?"

"The kiddie-porn pics you downloaded online and saved to your work folder."

"Jesus, Michael, what did you do?"

"I didn't do anything, Sam – you did it. Sure how would anyone else have access to your work files? I'm just a dumb electrician from the flats, right?"

Sam wants to throw up. What would happen once his boss gets the message? If he believes it, he'll get IT to check his files and then – what? The Guards? Jesus. They would call the Guards – they'd have to. That's how you always hear about it on the news. Sam covers his face with his hands, trying to think. Then it hits him – if the Guards are called and they come looking for him here, they'll find him locked up and the truth will come out. It won't matter then what's on the computer at work – he'll be safe in hospital and Michael will be in jail. Petrified that Michael will read his thoughts, he keeps his hands over his face.

"So, are we in business, Sam?"

Sam shakes his head. "I can't do it. I can't launder your money." His words come out muffled through his hands. "The prison sentence for that would be much higher than for child porn." He has no idea if that's true or not but maybe Michael doesn't either. There's no sound for a minute or two, and still he's afraid to look.

Finally Michael speaks. "If that's your decision, Sam, that's your decision. You may find you'll wish you'd taken this deal when it was on the table." He stands up and walks to the door. "I'll see you later, and you'll know then what you've done."

Chapter 58

Sam – Thursday, July 28th/Friday, July 29th

The evening light is fading and sleep is beckoning again. Is Michael coming back tonight? Sam looks again at the empty water glass on the locker. For about an hour now, Michael has been stomping about and slamming doors – sulking like Seth and Jamie do when they don't get their way with something. Sam smiles in spite of himself. Michael can say whatever he wants – he's standing firm. Well, lying firm. He drifts into sleep.

He wakes with a start. Shortly after, the back door bangs shut downstairs and he hears the key turn – Michael must be locking up now for the night. Will he bring water up? Maybe he can do without the water – it might be worth it for some peace. But no, there's the familiar sound of steps on stairs.

Sam closes his eyes and tries to slow his breathing. The door is opened and he can feel Michael looking down at him. Then the glass is taken away. Good. Minutes later, Michael is back upstairs, placing the glass back on the locker. It's working.

When it hits, the shock is even greater than the pain – at least at first. Sam opens his eyes and lets out a cry, looking down at his legs. It's difficult to focus – the pain is making him dizzy and sick, but he can see now that Michael has slammed the laptop on his shattered knees. This time he cries. He doesn't care about anything except the pain.

Michael stands over him, smiling down. "I need you awake – there's something I want to show you."

He walks around the bed and Sam flinches, waiting for the second blow. But it doesn't come – Michael heaves the wardrobe away from the window and pushes Sam up so that he's sitting.

The movement brings fresh pain and Sam cries out again.

"Now, look out there – what do you see?"

Sam looks out the window down onto the garden. He doesn't trust his voice so shakes his head – what is he supposed to be looking at?

"Down there," says Michael, pointing towards the end of the garden. "Look at the pond."

Sam does so. At first, the pond looks just as it always does. But there's something in the middle of it – something dark floating in the water. His vision is still blurry – he squints then opens his eyes again, and it comes into focus. It looks like a person – a small child. Floating in the pond. Jesus. It's too dark to make out if the child is face up or face down. He turns to Michael.

"What is that – Michael, what have you done?"

Michael doesn't say anything.

Sam tries to shout but what comes out is nothing more than a croak. "Tell me that's not a child – Michael?"

Michael picks up the newspaper and stabs a finger at the picture on the front page. "See, Sam, this didn't have to happen. If you'd done what I asked, I could have let the drugs wear off her and put her back at her mammy's front door, safe and sound. I only took her in the first place in case you wouldn't do what you were told and, to be honest, I was fairly sure the porn would be enough, and that I'd be putting her back. But you wouldn't listen, and this is your fault."

"Is she – did you . . . Michael, what did you do?"

"Don't worry, I didn't hurt her, I just topped up the morphine and sent her into a deeper sleep, then put her in the pond. She won't have felt a thing."

Sam swallows and tries to focus but dizziness is taking over again – from pain or terror, he can't tell. "Is she lying on her back, Michael?"

"No, Sam, she's face down." Michaels pushes the wardrobe into place to block the window and sits back down on the chair beside the bed. "We need to be really clear about something – you did this. She's been out there for twenty minutes now, face down in the water. Because you wouldn't do things the easy way."

This time Sam does throw up, all over the duvet. Michael pulls it off and takes it out of the room, then comes back with the duvet from Jamie's bed and throws it on. "Now, I think we should be ready to go, right, Sam? Will we get a bit of work done?"

Sam is lying back on the pillow, pale and sweating and shivering. He doesn't speak.

"Because now that we've tested it out, maybe your little neighbour next door would like a midnight swim. I saw her yesterday out with her nanny – tiny little thing." Michael leans down closer to him. "Or maybe I can pay a visit to Galway and have a day out with Seth and Jamie – do they like the pond, Sam?"

Sam's eyes fly open. "Don't you dare say their names. I'll do it – give me the laptop. But don't ever say their names again."

Chapter 59

The Woman – July 2011

It's now or never. The woman takes a deep breath but stops again. Across the room on the other couch, he's deeply engrossed in something on his laptop. The TV is on mute because he can't concentrate when there's noise in the room. She checks her phone – it's on silent. This might be easier if he looks up first. She clears her throat. An irritated frown meets her attempt at a breezy smile.

"Yes?" he asks.

"I was just going to tell you that I have to go to a conference with work next weekend – it's in Cork. You'll be here, won't you?"

He puts down his laptop. "What do you mean a conference at the weekend – nobody goes to conferences at the weekend."

"It's just how they're doing it – teambuilding exercises, talks, and a dinner on the Saturday night."

"And where are you supposed to stay?"

"The Merryman Hotel – it's where the conference is on. Work are paying for everything." Maybe that would swing it – he likes to get things for free.

But no. He gets up and moves over to her couch, sitting down so close beside her that she has to move her legs out of his way. "And who else is going on this trip?"

"Everyone – the whole office." Her voice has a tell-tale quiver now.

"You're trying to tell me you want to go away for a weekend with your boss and all the men in your office, and I'm supposed to be fine with this? Do I look stupid?"

She shakes her head.

"No, really, do I have 'dimwit husband' tattooed across my forehead? Do you think I don't know what goes on at these weekends away?" He stands up now, leaning down over her, eyes bulging.

She should never have asked. It's so obvious now. "I won't go. It's fine – I just thought I'd mention it."

"Oh, so now you're going to sulk, is that it – it's all my fault for not letting you go? You can't wait to get away from here – to go and get drunk and do God knows what with that crowd from your office, and yet I'm the bad guy for not letting you go?" He's shouting now. "You make me sick!" *he roars.*

She sees his hand go up and braces herself, covering her face with her arms. The punch catches her off-guard, hitting her deep in her stomach, winding her.

The woman's eyes fill with tears for the baby he doesn't know is there. And then she wonders if perhaps it's for the best.

Chapter 60

Sam – Tuesday, August 2nd 2016

It's hypnotic, staring at the white stripe of sky above the wardrobe – he doesn't know how long he's been doing it. Michael is engrossed in his phone and hasn't given him the customary rap on the knuckles yet. It will come, but for now he wants to watch the sky. His eyes are sore from looking at the screen for four long days now, and his shoulder hurts – sitting in the bed is not like sitting on his ergonomically designed chair at work. Work. What would they be doing now? He looks at the clock on the screen – 10.14am. The morning meeting would be winding up – they'd be grabbing coffees on their way back to their desks. It seems a world away. He turns his gaze back to the sky but Michael spots him this time and clicks his fingers.

"Back to work, Sam – no daydreaming."

"I need a pen and paper," Sam says.

"For what? Let me guess – you're dreaming about writing a note to the cops and making a paper plane to fly out the window?"

"No, Michael, wonderful as that idea is, it's just how I

work. In the office, I mean. I need to make notes as I go through the trades every day."

Michael pulls a chewed pen out of his pocket and hands it over. "I've no notebook. Is there one somewhere in the house?"

"There's loads downstairs in the big drawer in the kitchen – Kate buys millions of them."

Michael gets up to leave but turns back and takes the laptop with him. "Not that I don't trust you or anything, Sam, but you know . . . can't have you opening Facebook when you're supposed to be working. It's against company policy." He cracks up at his joke. Sam doesn't smile.

The notebook he brings is small and already half-filled with Kate's cramped handwriting: to-do lists and phone numbers and reminders about school meetings. The minutiae of what was once important mocks him, and seeing her familiar handwriting is a fresh blow.

Michael is oblivious. "So I was thinking of going down to Galway – what do you reckon?"

Sam freezes. His voice catches in his throat. "I'm doing what you asked," he whispers. "There's no need to go near them. Please, Michael."

"No, just to visit. To pass on messages, and to make sure Kate stays down there out of our way – you know? Look, I'll text her now. You can help me. It'll be a bit of craic." He pulls Sam's phone out of his pocket and types something, then holds it up.

Kate, I'm so sorry for everything and I really want to see the boys. Do you think I could come down for Seth's birthday?

Sam reaches out to take the phone for a closer look, but Michael pulls it away.

"Ah-ah! Hands off, Sam."

They both wait, then hear the familiar ping. Michael looks

at the screen.

"Right, let's see what she says. **'Sam, I've told you not to contact me. And no, of course you can't come down for Seth's birthday. I don't want to see you.'**" He makes a face. "Aw, I guess you're not forgiven. Right, let's try this." He types something and again shows it to Sam.

Have you told the boys?

Sam winces.

Michael smirks as he waits for the reply. "She says she hasn't. Right – I'll tell her someone needs to bring down that present for Seth. She'll say no to you bringing it . . . who else could I suggest . . . what about yer man Miller, her brother? She'll say no to him too, won't she?"

Sam shrugs.

A reply pings back, and Michael nods. "Yeah, she says 'no way' to sending the brother down – nice." He types again and shows it to Sam before he sends it.

Michael is another option – he said he'd do it if you didn't want me to go down.

The reply is immediate, and Michael grins when he shows it to him.

So does Michael know about your cheating?

"What will we tell her – let's say you did tell me, will we?"

Sam tries to grab the phone but he's too slow.

Michael shows him the message from a distance.

I told him at the weekend. He gave me a bollicking.

When the next reply comes, Michael bursts out laughing, then shows it to Sam.

I always liked Michael. Fair play. Fine, if he wants to bring it down, tell him to come Saturday.

Sam stares at the phone – his whole life just out of reach and in a madman's hand. "Please don't go there, Michael. I'll do whatever you want but don't go near Kate and the boys."

"Relax. I'm not going to do anything. Just making sure she doesn't arrive here unexpectedly. Though she seems to like me – I might see if I'm in with a chance now that you're out of the picture, will I?" He laughs hard at this. "What's the story with the brother by the way?" he asks when he calms down. "He's a feckin' weirdo – he called here yesterday even though Kate and the kids are away. Does he do that a lot?" Sam nods. "I hope he's not going to be trouble," Michael says. "He's the only person around here who might think I don't look exactly like Sam Ford." He pauses. "We were like peas in a pod growing up, weren't we, Sam? Do you remember my mam used to put us in matching jumpers – you were like the second son she never had. I think she nearly preferred you to me."

Sam lies back against the pillow and closes his eyes.

"Do you remember when she brought us to see Santa in the Ilac one year – I was about eight and you were five? The Santa thought we were brothers and Mam didn't say a thing to put him straight. And when yer man said you were very smart for your age, she didn't even say it then – she just beamed. I remember that – the big smile for the son that wasn't hers at all. Poor old Bella. It was fitting really that you were there when she died, wasn't it?"

Sam's eyes open. "Is that what this is about, Michael? Is it because I was there when Bella took those pills?"

Michael shakes his head. "Oh Sam, you just don't get it, do you? It'll be a good story when I've more time. Now, I need to head out and get us some benzos for Saturday – you'll need a good long sleep when I'm in Galway and this stuff won't cut it." He holds up a syringe. "Do you need to go to the toilet before I leave?"

Sam shakes his head.

"Gimme your arm so – you can catch some sleep while I'm out. Jesus, I'm wrecked today, I'd nearly swap places with you." He ties the tourniquet and pushes the liquid into Sam's tired vein, and sleep takes over before Michael has walked out of the room.

Chapter 61

1996

She's snoring lightly when he lets himself into the dark bedroom, but wakes up as soon as the door closes behind him.

"Michael, is that you? You gave me a fright," she whispers, peering through the darkness.

"It is, Ma, sorry to give you a scare." He pulls a chair up beside the bed.

"What are you doing here – I thought you had to go down to Kilkenny for work? Is Sam still here?"

"He is, Ma, he's asleep in my room. I was just in with him." Michael sits back on the chair and folds his arms. "Ma, it's time we had a talk. About my da."

Bella sits up in the bed. Her eyes are wary now. "What do you mean?"

"He's not dead, is he?"

"Of course he's dead. Died in a car crash back when you were a baby – you know that story like the back of your hand."

"I do indeed. Because you've been telling it to me over and over since before I could talk. Did you think nobody would ever tell me the truth?"

She looks down at the blanket on her lap. "I thought I was doing the right thing," she whispers.

"Have you any idea what it was like to go into that school and be told that my da wasn't dead – that he was in the nick? Do you know how much joy those lads got out of being the ones to tell me that? Did you ever see the bruises – the sly digs, the trips in the yard, the punch-ups after school?"

Bella shakes her head and her eyes fill with tears. "I didn't know. Why didn't you tell me?"

"It was too late by then – the damage was done. Anyway, what would you have done? Your track record's not exactly great, is it? Husband in prison, no money, this crappy flat, a shit school, no holidays, nothing. What exactly would you have done to stop me being beaten up in school? Taken me out and sent me to a private school like Sam's? I didn't think so. So don't come at me now saying I should have told you."

Bella pushes herself back in the bed. "I did my best – you were always well-fed and warm and loved. Why are you saying all this now?"

"Because I'm done. I'm done looking after you, and I need this flat. And, as you no doubt know, da's next parole hearing is coming up in a few months. I don't think they'll let him out, but you never know. And I don't want him getting ideas about hooking back up with you and getting his feet under the table. Under *my* table, in my flat. Basically, I need you out of the picture before he's back in it. I have the tenancy application ready to go to the council, so it's time. It's time to go, Ma."

"Go where? Michael, you don't mean it – you can't expect me to leave? What has got into you?" She's still whispering but her voice is shaking now.

"It's time. You don't do anything anyway other than shuffle around here and walk out to the shop every few days and Mass on Sunday. You don't see anyone except me and

Sam. You'll hardly miss it. Now, Sam is asleep in the other room – and I've locked the door. So there's two ways we can do it. You can take the pills you love so much, or we can go with this." He holds up a syringe. "The drug option means burning down the flat too, and Sam with it. It's not my preference – I'd rather keep the flat. So will we go for the pills, Ma?"

Bella's eyes are wide. She pushes herself back further again in the bed and tries to speak. "Michael, what are you talking about? And what have you done to Sam?"

"Oh, precious Sam – he's fine, Ma, he's just asleep, and if all goes well I'll unlock the door when I'm leaving, and he'll find you in the morning. It's much easier this way. You just write a little note, and take the pills. You've been heading that direction for a while now – nobody will be too shocked. All that talk of things moving around at night? You're halfway to La-La-land as it is." He picks up a pill bottle from her locker, and empties the contents into his hand.

Bella is crying now. "Michael, you can't mean it! Have you gone mad?"

"No, Ma, not mad, just moving things along. You get to go to that God you pray to every Sunday, Sam doesn't die in a fire, and I get the flat. Win-win, see?" He picks up the next pill bottle and reads the label. "Jesus, Ma, strong stuff. Do you really take all of these every day? I'm surprised you haven't slipped away already."

She reaches her hands towards him, tears streaming down her face. "Michael, love, you don't mean any of it – come here to me!"

He gently pushes her arms back down. "No, Ma, it's too late now. Let's just get on with this, will we? I think ten of these and ten of the other ones will do it – you won't even feel any pain."

"I won't do it," she says, moving towards the edge of the bed. "I'm going to wake Sam and we're going. You can have the flat."

Michael stands up and holds up the syringe. He puts a hand on her chest and pushes her back down onto the pillow. "No, one way or another, this is it. If I have to inject this into you, I will. But then nobody will believe it was suicide, and I'll have to burn down the flat and everything in it. Including Sam. If you take the pills, nothing happens to him." He leans close to her. "Do you understand?"

Bella is still crying, but silently now. He takes a notebook and pen from her dresser and passes them to her, but her hand is shaking too much, and she can hardly write. She looks up at him, pleading with her eyes. He nods and takes away the notepad. He sits beside her, and passes three of the pills into her hand, then gives her a glass of water. She closes her eyes and swallows the pills. He passes three more, and she does the same. After fifteen tablets, her breathing slows. He nudges her gently awake to take the next batch. Her eyes flutter open, then close again. She starts to lose consciousness, and he takes her hand. He sits there until her breathing stops. He kisses her forehead, then puts one of the two pill bottles into her hand and walks out of the bedroom. He unlocks the other door and checks on Sam – he's still asleep.

Michael closes the front door softly behind him, and as he walks back down towards the lift he whistles quietly to himself.

Chapter 62

Sam - Wednesday, August 3rd 2016

Sam is hunched over the laptop when he hears the familiar ping of his mobile. Michael takes it out of his pocket and starts to smile as he reads. "You dirty dog. All that wailing and crying about Kate thinking you're cheating, and then it turns out you bloody are! So tell me, who's this Nina?"

Nina. Oh God, she's going to get dragged into this too. Sam keeps looking at the laptop. "Hang on, I'm just in the middle of a trade here and need to make sure I get it right."

"Nice try, but you're not getting away that easily. So who is she – some bird at work?" Michael sits back on the chair, grinning at the phone. "Come on, I want details. All that time when I was making it look like you were screwing around on Kate, you never thought to tell me you really were?"

Sam keeps looking at the laptop, furrowing his brow in concentration. How to play this isn't clear, but letting Michael come up with his own answers makes more sense than talking.

"Go on, Sam, give me something. Is she good-looking? Young? Less cranky than Kate, I bet – that's it, isn't it? Nina. Nice name. I think I like Nina. She wants to meet up – what will I reply? Maybe I should meet her . . . "

Sam looks up. "Leave her out of this. I mean it."

Michael shakes his head. "If I don't reply to your messages, people will be calling to see what's wrong – can't have that." He looks at the screen, drumming his fingers on the back of the phone. "Do you ever meet her here – does she know where this house is?"

"No! And don't tell her to come here – Michael, please."

"Relax, I just want to be sure that if I tell her you fell down the stairs and broke your leg, she won't turn up with flowers and a nurse's uniform. She won't, will she?"

Sam shakes his head. "She's never been here and I can't remember ever mentioning the address. I don't think there's any way she could just turn up."

"All right then, we'll go with that. Pity really, I kind of like the idea of meeting Nina." He presses send on the message.

Sam keeps looking at the laptop screen, but he's not seeing anything and his knuckles are white from gripping the sides. He offers a silent prayer to the God he hasn't talked to in twenty-five years. Please let her leave it at that. But God's not listening, and the reply comes within seconds.

Michael reads it out.

Oh my god, r u OK? Do u need anything? Is Kate looking after u?

"Oh, so she knows about Kate?"

Sam nods. This is dangerous ground.

"Jaysus, aren't you the man! A wife and a mistress on the go, and the young one not minding at all that you're married. Does she not want you to leave Kate?"

Sam shrugs. "Sorry, I need to pay attention to this trade – there's a fair chunk of money at stake here."

Michael stretches and lets out a groan, and Sam risks a sideways glance. He's definitely bored with the baby-sitting now. Watching him all day can't be remotely interesting. How long can this possibly go on? Actually he doesn't want to think about that, or how it might end. Glancing towards the window, he wonders again where the little girl is now. Her face is on every news programme, with constant updates on the search. He wants to tell them – to scream at the TV that it's too late. To tell them to stop looking for a live, kidnapped girl; to prepare to find a body. He had begged Michael for two full days to put her somewhere public and let her be found – to let the mother have some peace. But Michael just shook his head each time, then after a while he ignored him completely. The last time he'd brought it up, Michael had slapped him hard across the face and told him Jamie would be next if he didn't stop. So he stopped.

Now Michael is texting on Sam's phone again. To Nina? Or someone else? God knows what he's replying to people. The sheer powerlessness of it swamps Sam again – the phone is so near, but out of his grasp it means nothing.

Michael looks up. "Just replying to your mistress. Don't worry, I'm saying I don't need anything and Kate is here. Will I put kisses? Do you put kisses?" He's sneering again.

Sam shakes his head.

"No kisses it is. And . . . *send.*" He looks around the room then picks up his paper again but he's read it front to back already. He puts it down and yawns.

Sam suppresses a smile. He's trapped here, but actually, Michael is too.

Eventually, boredom wins out, and Michael takes the laptop out of the room. He throws the newspaper onto the bed, saying he's going downstairs for a break. Sam's shoulders ache from sitting up in bed hunched over the keyboard – he tries rolling them back and forward but it doesn't do any good. He leans back against the pillow and picks up the paper.

Edie Keogh is on the front page, but he can't read it. The sound of the back door opening and closing draws his attention to the window. He hears a chair being dragged across the patio and then silence – perhaps the drug-dealing child-killer is taking time out to catch some rays. It would be comical if it wasn't so horrific.

He picks up the pen and notebook from the locker and wonders if he should start a journal. Then he has a better idea.

A beeping sound wakes him – he must have nodded off. Is it his alarm? For a moment, Sam forgets where he is. The spare room is empty of everything but him – where is the noise coming from? A realisation hits – it's his phone. And the noise came from his own bedroom on the other side of the wall. The phone is probably charging on his locker just as it always did. And if Michael doesn't bring it with him when he goes downstairs, maybe he doesn't have it when he goes out of the house either.

Excitement surges up inside Sam. Downstairs, the door opens and closes – Michael is on his way back up. Not today then. But there is hope.

Chapter 63

Sam – Thursday, August 4th 2016

As he becomes aware of being awake, Sam listens as he always does for the sound of the television – tuning into the voices on screen, keeping his eyes closed for as long as possible. It's become a ritual. Work out what show is on, and use that to guess the time of day. It's Teleshopping, so it's early – real TV hasn't started yet. Lying quietly, listening to the television, he forces himself to try moving his right leg – another ritual. And as always, the unbearable pain stops him. He grimaces and opens his eyes. Yes, it's Teleshopping. And he watches as he does every time, because there's nothing else to do.

Sam drifts back to sleep and when he wakes the next time, proper programmes have started. The morning shows and the news are his favourites, because they have the time on screen. It's 8.05am but Michael hasn't come in yet to put him to work. Maybe they're having a duvet day, Sam thinks, and starts to smile at his own joke but changes his mind. He's been in by half seven every other morning so far, cracking the whip – it's odd there's no sound yet. Or maybe he just slept in. In the meantime, Sam's entertainment options are limited – TV stuck on one channel, or yesterday's newspaper. He goes for Option C, closing his eyes to go back to sleep.

When he wakes again, the TV screen says it's 9.32. Lying still, he listens, but there's no sound anywhere in the house, apart from the low hum of the TV. Could Michael be gone out without sedating him? He looks down at the cluster of needle-marks on his arm. Or maybe the sedative wore off more quickly this time? His stomach flutters. Could he do it – would the phone even be there? He hasn't been out of bed without Michael's help since the assault, but then again, he hasn't had the chance to try. How many days has it been now – nine? The bed isn't high. Well, not too high. He'll have to crawl head first – there's no way to put weight on his legs without Michael holding him up. He eases himself over to the edge of the bed and turns onto his front, lowering his hands to the floor. There's a warning twinge of pain in his left knee but nothing unbearable. Yet. The carpet feels good when his elbows touch down. He rests for a moment, then pulls himself forward along the ground so that his left hip is lying on the carpet, while his feet and ankles lie against the bed. Then another break, because the next bit will hurt. Reaching with his hand, he gently lifts his one leg from bed to floor. The pain that shoots through his body shocks him – forcing him to close his eyes and bite down on his arm. He steels himself to go again, lowering his other leg to the floor. Beads of sweat trickle down his forehead as he lies panting on the carpet. Michael could be back any minute – he has to keep going. On his stomach, he starts to pull himself along the floor. His legs groan under the pressure of movement, with every pull forward sending waves of pain, especially in his left knee. On the landing, he lies for a moment to summon the energy to keep going, then starts again, moving towards his own bedroom. He drags himself along the carpet and over the door saddle; the familiar wooden floor is a welcome relief. Another break then; lying still, sweating, breathing hard, pushing away the intensifying pain. Then using every bit of upper body strength left to pull his useless legs across the floor, he makes his way towards the bedside locker. He can picture the phone – the precious, life-saving phone – sitting there, glowing, waiting for him. From the ground, he reaches with one hand to feel for it on top of the locker. Nothing. He pushes himself up a little, to feel further back. Still nothing. Of course – it's on the other side – on Kate's locker. A little voice inside his head says it's not there at all. But it must be there. He heard it yesterday. Was it yesterday? It doesn't matter – it must be there.

He stops again, then begins retracing his journey. By the time he reaches the other side, the pain in his left knee has become almost unbearable. He grits his teeth, sweating, staring at Kate's locker ahead. Only three feet away now, then freedom. Taking a deep breath he launches himself forward, screaming with pain as his left knee gives in completely. But he's made it. He reaches up. Nothing. There's nothing on the floor either, or under the bed. No phone. Of course there's no phone. It could be anywhere – it's probably in Michael's pocket. Crushed and exhausted, he lies on his bedroom floor, his shoulders shaking with heaving sobs.

Downstairs, the front door opens. Sam lifts his head to listen, but his body is completely frozen. Maybe he'll go to the kitchen. But no, the next sound is a foot on the bottom step of the stairs. The ascent is slow, but not slow enough. Knowing it's futile, Sam starts to pull himself back across the room. Using every last bit of strength, he pushes forward and moves about a foot along the floor, then another. It's more than he thought he could do, but nowhere near enough. The footsteps have reached the top of the stairs. With rising panic, he looks at the bedroom door, then puts his head down in his arms, closing his eyes.

The footsteps come into the room, and Michael is standing over him.

"I just needed my phone," Sam tells him, looking up.

"This?" Michael says, taking it out of his pocket.

"Yes. We can't go on like this. Just give me the goddamn phone." It's a pointless request, but really, what does it matter now?

Michael shakes his head and puts the phone back in his pocket. "You don't need it, Sam. You don't exist any more. I'm Sam now, so I need the phone." It's like he's talking to a naughty child. "I trusted you this morning – I had to rush out in a hurry to deal with a problem, and I did hesitate – I did stop to wonder if I needed to knock you out. And I thought, 'No, Sam knows the score'. But I was wrong. And Sam, this is going to hurt me more than it's going to hurt you, but we have to teach you to do as you're told."

Sam sees the raised foot come towards him, then blacks out as his head is smashed to the floor.

Chapter 64

Sam – Thursday, August 4th

Blood-coloured clouds and black haze block Sam's vision when he wakes – are his eyes open or closed? Fear grips him as he tries to work it out. It's okay – they're closed. He attempts to open them, but the thumping in his head gets louder and a wave of nausea stops him. Visions of Michael's boot coming towards his head seep back. How long has he been out? His face is resting on something hard – he reaches out his fingers to feel around. It's the wooden floor of his bedroom – he's still in the same spot. He tries again to open his eyes, breathing against the pain in his head. Sunlight slants through the window and makes long shadows across the floor. Michael must have sedated him after he passed out. Then he hears a voice – Michael is talking to someone downstairs. It's not clear who it is, but it doesn't matter. He tries to shout but retches instead.

Lifting his fist, he bangs it down on the floor, again and again but even as he does the front door closes.

Then come the footsteps.

"So you're awake, Sleeping Beauty? I have your crutches

here. Come on, let's get you back to bed."

Head still thumping, Sam puts an arm around Michael's shoulder and lets him hoist him up. With the crutch in his left hand, they make their way slowly back into the spare room, and he collapses onto the bed. All he wants is sleep, but Michael is in the mood for a chat and pulls up the chair.

"So, do you want to know who I was talking to downstairs?"

Sam tries to shake his head but it hurts too much.

"Here, have a drink of water – that stuff in your veins makes you thirsty." Michael passes him the glass and straightens his pillow. "It was your next-door neighbour. Sylvia is her name – came over to introduce herself. They've been away on holidays and she's sorry she didn't come over sooner. One of those women who wants to be friendly with everyone – you could smell it off her. Sickly sweet and all well-meaning but in a really fake way, you know? She kind of made me want to punch her in the face. Kate never met her, did she?"

Sam takes a sip of water. "No," he whispers, then closes his eyes again as the pain hits. He puts the glass on the locker.

"Yeah, I thought not. Here, take these," Michael says, passing him two tablets. "Anyway, I told her that my wife is down in Galway with the kids, and that I go down a bit at the weekends."

Sam swallows the tablets. They could be anything, but it doesn't matter. In his mind, he punches Michael in the face, again and again. Michael is raw and bleeding, but he doesn't stop. He keeps his eyes closed, and keeps punching, trying not to hear the words.

"I said I'd bring the kids around when they get back," Michael is saying. "They won't be back, but I don't feel I know Sylvia well enough to tell her about my marriage break-up, at least not yet."

Sam clenches his fist but there's no strength in it. He uncurls his fingers.

Michael keeps talking. "She might be a bit of a busybody though – I can't decide yet. She was asking about our little friend in the pond. I'm guessing she was the person ringing the bell in the middle of the night – she's the reason I had to rush out and take the body out of the water."

Sam winces.

"So yeah, I'll have to keep an eye on Sylvia next door."

"Michael," Sam whispers. "There's no way you can keep this up forever. Sooner or later, someone who *does* know me will come looking for me. The woman next door is just one person – there'll be others. This has to end."

Michael sits back in the chair and folds his arms. "Sam, when the time comes to end it, you'll know about it. Don't you worry." He stands up. "Now get some sleep, I need you back at work tomorrow morning."

When the door closes, Sam turns slowly onto his side to sleep, but tonight it evades him. Maybe because he slept all day, or maybe because of the cocktail of drugs in his system, or maybe because of the pain in his eye and his cheekbone and his head. Tentatively, he touches his cheek and winces. He stretches his legs – the pain feels less severe now, although it's probably just because his head is so sore. Through the gap above the wardrobe, he watches the evening sky turn pink and gold. The world on the other side of the window is almost in touching distance but it may as well be a million light years away. He's never getting out of here. He makes a decision. What little power he has now will go into keeping Kate and the boys safe, because unless someone comes to look for him, his own fate is set.

Chapter 65

Sam – Friday, August 5th

The routine is back on. Michael wakes him at half seven with a plate of toast. His neck is stiff and his eye is tender where the boot caught him, but sleep has helped. Michael goes out and returns with two cups of tea, then notices there's no water on the bedside locker and goes to get some. Sam is about to call him to say the glass from last night is on the floor, down the side of the locker, but then he doesn't.

When Michael comes back with the drink and the laptop, Sam clicks into his trading account, and opens Michael's bank account in another tab. He checks the balance, then turns the screen to show Michael.

"See – €6,554,212 – all in a bank account in Luxembourg. All yours, all untraceable from the original accounts, because of the stock you've bought and sold to get there. The other accounts are all empty now."

Michael takes the laptop onto his knee. "It's not as much as it should be though."

"I told you. There's no way to keep the original balance – you knew that from the start. If we wanted to buy and sell and cover our tracks, there had to be a trade-off."

"Hang on," says Michael, putting the laptop on the floor.

He goes off downstairs and he returns with a beer. "Have this to celebrate."

Sam accepts the cold bottle, condensation droplets on the outside making it look all the more inviting on this warm August morning. He takes a long drink and settles back on the pillow to savour the first beer he's had in what feels like years. Beer in the morning is all kinds of wrong, but then everything is all kinds of wrong at the moment. Right now, he wants to push all of it out of his mind – no more thoughts of money laundering or child porn or Edie Keogh. For a few minutes, it's just about enjoying the beer. The always-on TV on the wall is showing the morning news – he closes his ears to that. Closing his eyes too, he's transported somewhere far away. Just this once, no-one else is allowed in. Not Kate, not the kids, not Michael. For this one perfect moment that can be carved out, wrapped up, then set safely aside, as something to hang onto in the darker days that will come.

His dream-world is interrupted by Michael's voice – breaking in like a hammer to glass.

"Now, fun's over. Let's talk about the next stage."

"What next stage?"

"Well, you've lost some of my money, so you need to make it back – and I want more than that. I want you to turn it into eighty million. It's all clean now – do whatever it is you do, and make a killing for me. And I'll tell you what – get me to ten million, and I'll reward you with a photo of Kate and the boys for your room."

"Nobody can turn six million into eighty million or even ten million – it's just not possible."

Michael studies him for a moment. "Fine. Let's aim for the original eight million to begin with so. And you can earn that photo."

"You can keep your photo. I'll work on your investments, but I can't promise anything. Here, give me back the laptop so."

Michael hands over the computer but he isn't ready for work yet. He pulls a key out of his pocket. "Know what this is?"

"No."

"It's the key to next door. Do you want to hear where I got it?"

"Not really."

"You're dying to know. So the old bat who lives two doors up – Rosemary is her name – she and I are great pals now. She's a big fan of Sam Ford – did I tell you that? I fixed her burglar alarm at the weekend and we had a good old chat after. She offered to be a keyholder for me. She was very proud of her status as spare-key minder for all the neighbours – everyone except Tom and Sylvia next door she told me, because they keep it inside their barbecue. She's a bit miffed about that. Anyway, I didn't give her our key – don't worry – we won't have any unexpected old ladies letting themselves in. But it did make taking this very easy." He holds up the key again. "Sitting inside the barbecue, just like she said it would. And I bet your one Sylvia thinks they're very clever keeping it there. I'll get a spare cut and then put this one back before they notice. Smart, eh?"

"Sure, Michael, very smart. But for what? Just to show you can?" Sam asks, watching stock prices on the screen.

"Well, I thought I might pay them a visit. Your one backed down about seeing something in the water but I've a feeling she's not convinced it was her imagination. I might need to do something about that."

Sam stops typing. "Jesus, you can't seriously be thinking of doing something to her – she's just an innocent bystander." But then so was Edie Keogh. He racks his brain for an argument that might appeal to Michael. "Look, if nothing else, it would bring the Guards all over the place and that's the last thing you want, isn't it?"

"Calm down, I'm not going to do anything to her. Not for now anyway. I just want to get to know her a bit better. And make sure she keeps doubting what she saw."

Sam's hands relax on the keyboard. "How do you mean – how can you make sure she keeps doubting?"

There it is – the familiar smug smile – Michael wants to tell him something to show how smart he is. "Easy. You'd be surprised how easy it is. A person starts to sound very paranoid if they're telling everyone things have moved around at night or they're hearing noises – just little things that only they would notice. Everyone else around them starts to think they're stark raving mad. And sometimes they start to think the same themselves."

Sam goes cold. Jesus. It was him all along. All those months, Bella telling everyone someone had been in her house at night. And none of them believed her. They changed doctors, got stronger prescriptions, talked about residential care. And over and over again, they gave thanks that she was in Michael's safe hands – where would they be without Michael they kept asking themselves. Dear God. And for what? He wants to ask but he doesn't want to know. Maybe it just gave Michael the idea – maybe he didn't actually do anything. He looks over at his cousin, and the smile tells him everything.

"It was you, wasn't it?"

Michael nods. "Ma? Course it was. You were all so worried about her, and she thought she was losing it. It was funny to watch all the scurrying and the hand-wringing. All trying to help supposedly, but then again I didn't see anyone asking her to move in with them. Be seen to care, but don't go too far – that was always the Ford family way, wasn't it, Sam?"

Sam closes the laptop. "You made your own mother think she was losing her mind, and you criticise mine for not doing enough? Are you actually serious?"

Michael blinks. "Settle down there, Sam, or I'll have to sedate you."

"So sedate me, I don't give a fuck. It'll give me a break from this fucking trading anyway." He holds out an arm to Michael. "Look, I'll even get the vein for you – see?"

Michael stands up. "I can see you're cranky so we'll take a break. You might want to make sure you're calmer when I see you again. I don't like your attitude." He picks up the laptop and walks out, slamming the door.

Sam sits back in the bed, breathing hard. That probably wasn't a great idea. But it felt good. When Michael is definitely downstairs, he picks up the glass that's on the floor and pushes it down between the mattress and the wall, because it seems like the right thing to do.

Chapter 66

Sam – Saturday, August 6th

"I hate to do this to you, Sam, but I'll be gone for most of the day and I can't take any chances. So this is a bit stronger than the usual stuff. I've checked the dose on the internet and done all the calculations," he holds up the syringe, "so it should be okay."

It's early and Sam is still waking up, trying to take this in. Blinking, he looks at the syringe. What the hell is in it?

"Look, why don't you just leave it? Don't go to Galway. Kate's obviously not coming anywhere near me ever again – your texts have taken care of that. Just stay here, no extra drugs, no visit."

But Michael's not for turning. "I need to check in on her and make sure. I can't have her turning up out of the blue. And I can't manage two invalids in the house – Kate would have to join the kid we put in the pond."

"*We* put in the pond? Tell yourself what you want, Michael, this is all you."

"You had a choice, and you made it – you're responsible for what happened the young one. But you know what – I'll let you choose again this time. I can stay here, and we'll take a chance on Kate turning up unannounced and see how that ends for her. Or I can give you this and go down today – your choice."

Kate probably would show up sooner or later – to collect stuff for the boys or to have it out with him. *Shit.* Michael better have done those calculations right. Sam clenches his teeth and holds out his pockmarked arm for the tourniquet.

"What is it anyway?" he tries to ask Michael after the needle goes in, but the words are too low or maybe he didn't say them at all.

His eyes close, and he's gone.

Someone is shaking his arm, but he just wants to sleep. His stomach hurts and his head is full of cotton wool.

"Stop," he mutters, but the person doesn't hear. The shaking gets rougher. Giving in, he opens his eyes. It all comes flooding back – the trip to Galway, the syringe – he's made it out the other side. And the kids and Kate – are they okay too? He tries to ask but mouth is dry and cracked and his voice is gone again.

"Take this," Michael is saying, and a straw finds its way into his mouth.

His throat hurts when he swallows, but suddenly a desperate thirst overwhelms him. He grabs the bottle and drinks greedily through the straw, then tosses it aside to drink straight from the neck.

"You gave me a fright there – I couldn't wake you at first," Michael says, sitting down.

Sam is shaking. "Really? Would you care?" he croaks.

"Course I would. You're my cousin. And anyway I still need you working on investing my money. You'll have to make up tomorrow for your time off today."

Sam spits out the last of the water. "Sure. Time off."

"So, don't you want to know how it went?"

Sam does – desperately – but he shrugs.

"It went great. Kate is really pissed off with you, especially after I told her you're still seeing Nina. We went for lunch and had wine – very intimate." Michael smirks.

Sam shrugs again.

"And the boys are fine – big hugs for Uncle Michael, and we had great fun with the present you sent down."

Sam keeps his face neutral.

"I reckon I'd have made a good dad actually – they seemed to really like having me around."

Under the duvet, Sam clenches and unclenches both fists but refuses to rise to the bait. "How's Laura?" he asks.

Michael's mouth tightens. Before he can answer, the doorbell rings. Their eyes lock, and Michael gets up, putting his finger to his lips.

Sam tries to pull himself up straight in the bed as soon as Michael is outside the bedroom. He takes some deep breaths, ready to shout. But there are no footsteps on the stairs. Instead, he hears the door of Seth's room opening – Michael checking who's down there. Of course he's not going to answer – Sam slumps down in the bed again.

When Michael comes back in, he's shaking his head. "That fella is going to get himself in trouble if he keeps calling."

"Who?"

"Kate's brother. Why does he keep turning up? If he doesn't back off, I'll have to do something about it."

Oh God, Miller, why do you keep doing this? "Miller's harmless," he tells Michael. "He's just lonely. You don't need to worry about him. Seriously."

"Say what you want, if this keeps up, or if he manages to come at the wrong time, I don't care whose brother he is – I'll take care of it." Michael walks back out of the room and closes the door.

Sam lets out a long breath. Miller better be gone – Jesus, he wouldn't stand a chance if Michael got near him – he's twice the size of him. And Miller has no sense at all – in a million years, he'd never see it coming.

Chapter 67

Kate – June 1984

Kate knew the picnic would be like this. Her mum chattering away to any other mum who looks sideways at her, while she and Miller plod along on their own. The boys from third class are all racing ahead, chasing each other with sticks, and none of them have even glanced at Miller. There's no way he'll join in without being pushed into it. Looking further up the hill, she can see the three girls from her class, arms linked, heads together. They look back and one says something. The other two double over laughing. Idiots.

Kate kicks a stick and it skitters across the dusty path. How much further is this picnic spot? It's so bloody hot too. And of course her mum is keeping all the food and drink till they reach the top, the carrot to get them there. A very uninspiring carrot. Soggy ham-and-tomato sandwiches and a warm bottle of orange are hardly worth all this dust and sweat.

The path twists around a corner and all of a sudden, they're there – the white railing clear against the open sky, and the burst of yellow gorse, unfolding on all sides, creeping down the hill to the rocks and the sea below. In spite of herself, Kate stops to take in the view. Carnross wouldn't be such a bad place if it wasn't for the people. The others have seen it all before, and continue upwards to the grassy peak, setting down rugs and cool-boxes and opening cans of fizzy drinks. Within minutes, the boys are up again and running around, playing some kind of ninja game with big sticks.

Laura nudges Miller. "Go on – join in, love. You'll enjoy it." He doesn't move. "I have a packet of custard creams in here somewhere," she says, pointing at the picnic bag. "I bet if you go off and play with them for ten minutes, I'll have found them by the time you come back."

Miller pushes his glasses up and fixes his eyes on his mother. "Promise?"

"Promise. Now go on."

Kate watches as her brother walks slowly – so slowly – over to the boys in his class. He looks so out of place in his shorts and sandals – all of his classmates are in tracksuit bottoms and football jerseys. His long hair, hanging down over his eyes, contrasts with the buzz-cuts of the others. He's a square peg in a round hole. Or maybe a hexagonal peg, thinks Kate. She keeps watching as he approaches. Two of the boys spot him, and one says something to the group. Kate's heart sinks. But then she sees smiles – they beckon Miller over. She can't hear every word, but it sounds like they're inviting him to join the game.

Kate turns to Laura, who is transfixed by the scene, beaming like she's won the lottery. Just then a toddler runs across their rug, his flustered mother chasing just behind. In his haste, he knocks over a bottle and orange liquid spreads all over the blanket. Laura throws a tea towel on it and waves away the embarrassed mother's apologies. Her name is Barbara, she says, and the little boy is Dónal. His big brother Fergal is in Miller's class. Barbara sits down, bribing Dónal with a packet of Tayto to sit with her. The PTA is the hot topic Laura and Barbara choose, and Kate is bored before Barbara even starts to talk Laura into joining (of course she'll join, Kate wants to say – she's desperate to fit in). She gets up to stretch her legs and walks over to where the ninja game has progressed up the steps of an odd stone structure at the top of the hill. Shielding her eyes from the sun with her hand, she tries to work out what exactly the steps are.

"It's a stepped pyramid – a folly built in 1852," says a voice behind her.

It's Clara – literally the only half-decent person in Carnross.

"What do you mean?"

"Do you know what a folly is?"

Kate shakes her head.

"The owners of the land built it for no reason other than to create work for unemployed peasants. So basically, a pyramid-shaped set of steps that lead nowhere. The views are good from the top – you can see right out over the water."

Kate shakes her head a second time. "Nah, I'm not good with heights – that's way too high for me."

The boys are climbing now, some of them are near the top. Kate feels dizzy just looking at them. Is Miller there too? She can just about make him out, on the second last step from the top. Her stomach lurches. But he'll be fine. Things like this don't faze Miller. And painful though he is, the nerdy little weirdo, she's happy he's finally making friends.

The game recommences on the steps – the boys are poking at one another with sticks and jumping out of the way. Kate's stomach lurches again. How are they not afraid of falling? She looks back at the mothers – they're all busy chatting, but even the few who glance over don't seem worried. Maybe this is how they play in Carnross.

The noise from the steps is louder now and she can make out what they're saying. "What kind of name is Miller anyway? It's so gay. Is that why you wear such ugly clothes? Does your mam get them for free from the tinkers?"

Oh shit! "*Miller – come down – Mum wants you!*" she calls up.

He's on the second step from the top and doesn't seem to hear her. Though you never know with Miller.

"Hey, four-eyes, why don't you go back to where you came from?" It's a different boy talking now. Still Miller says nothing.

Kate waves and calls him again, but he doesn't move. Her heart is pounding. She needs to get him out of there. She eyes up the steps and takes a deep breath. Bloody brothers. She pulls herself up onto the first step as the taunting continues.

"The retard doesn't talk."

Kate looks up. It's a third boy this time. He steps forward, pushing his face right up to Miller's, except he has a good four inches in height on him. He pokes him in the chest.

"You don't talk, do you? Retard!" He pokes him again.

Kate watches as Miller's eyes narrow and he raises his hands. When she thinks back, she knows it can't have taken more than a second but, in the moment, everything is in slow motion. Miller pushes his hands against the boy's chest, and the boy stumbles backwards. He loses his footing and topples off the edge of the second last step from the top. Down he goes, tumbling backwards, head over heels. Kate watches in horror as his head smashes against the corner of the bottom step. Years later, she can still hear the sickening sound of skull hitting stone. He rolls over and lies still, as blood pools in the dust at the bottom of the steps.

Kate is closest to the boy, but she's frozen to the spot. She stares at the blood, and the crumpled shape. People are running towards her. Screaming. Children are crying. One woman turns the boy over and slaps his cheek, again and again. She puts her head on his chest and then her mouth on his mouth. Someone is shouting to call an ambulance, but they're a mile from town. The woman is crying hysterically now, cradling the boy's broken head in her arms. At some point Kate realises it's Barbara. This must be her other son. Oh God, oh God. Where's Miller? She looks up. He's sitting on the top step of the pyramid, swinging his legs, looking down at them all scurrying and screaming below. And she's not sure, but she thinks she can see a ghost of a smile.

Chapter 68

Kate – August 1984

This morning, she doesn't bother to look outside before getting the scrubbing brush and the basin of hot water. She already knows what will be there. The colours change, and the words change, but there's always something. "**Child Killer**" or "**Get Out, Murderers**" or sometimes just an unimaginative "**Die**". Her mother won't let Miller help – she can see why really. He hasn't left the house since the day it happened – not even for the inquest. They taped him and played a video in the court instead, because he's only eight. Accidental death is what they said it was in the end, and sure what else would it be? Her parents had both gone to the courthouse for the inquest but she wasn't allowed to go. Mrs Daly from next door had minded them. Well, she'd put on the TV for them in the sitting room while she sat in the kitchen knitting. When her parents arrived home, Laura had burst into tears, hugging Miller. Kate couldn't tell if this was a good sign or a bad sign – with her mum, you never knew. Her dad just went into his study and shut the door. Then Mrs Daly got up to leave, patting Kate on the shoulder as she let herself out. Laura didn't notice her go

– she was still rocking and sobbing, with Miller sitting motionless in her arms.

Kate got up to turn up the volume on the TV then sat on the couch, hugging her knees to her chest, wondering if it was all over.

Of course it wasn't all over. If anything, it was just beginning. She'd been woken early the following morning by the sound of something smashing against her window. Pulling back the curtain, she found the glass covered in yellow goo. She jerked back as another egg hit the window, then ran in to tell her parents. Her mum jumped up and grabbed her dressing gown, ready to take on the culprits, but her dad pulled Laura back.

"Leave it. You're only fuelling it if you go out there," he said.

"But it was accidental – that's what the inquest said. They've no right to do this."

"Laura, for God's sake, *leave it*! We still have to live here and I have to run my practice here."

Kate backed out of the room at that, but waited just behind the door.

"Is that it, Richard? Is that why you've been so distant with Miller? You're worried about your precious practice and how it will look for the town's most eminent solicitor to be in a spot of bother himself?" She spat the words at him.

Kate had never heard her mother talk like this.

"That's not fair. I'm doing everything I can. This is hard on all of us, but I have to think of the practice too – I can't afford to lose clients over this. My father spent fifty years building it up, and now this – in one afternoon, everything's in jeopardy."

Then silence. Kate stepped forward and peered around the door. Her dad was sitting on the side of the bed and her mum was standing a few feet away from him, with her face in her hands.

Eventually Laura lifted her head again.

"Richard, he's your son. He's in pain. He needs both of us."

"In pain? Don't fool yourself, Laura. He hasn't shown the slightest bit of remorse. There's something not right with him."

The slap was loud and Kate jumped. She watched as her dad rubbed his cheek, then got up from the bed and walked out of the room, paying no attention to Kate as he passed.

When she thought back, while it certainly wasn't the start of the end, it was one of the many nails that kept the coffin shut. Her dad stayed late in the office, then shut himself away in the study when he got home. Sometimes he slept in the room above the office. He barely registered Kate when she was in the room, and completely ignored Miller.

The night it came to a head started out just like any other night. The front door opened and shut around ten, and her dad's keys landed in the bowl on the hall table. The closet creaked as he opened it to hang up his coat, then silence. She pictured him standing in the hall, briefcase in hand, deciding whether to join her mother in the sitting room or go straight up to bed. She waited for the next sound, holding her breath. When it came, it was the familiar sound of the sitting-room door handle. Everything would be okay, she knew it would.

Kate crept out of bed and down the stairs, kneeling on the hall floor with her ear to the sitting-room door.

Her dad's voice was low, but she could hear every word. "Laura, this can't go on. The graffiti, the stone-throwing, the punctured tyres, and now one of my biggest clients has left me. He's a neighbour of Barbara and Colm Quinn, and says his conscience won't let him keep doing business with – and I quote – 'the family responsible for the murder of an innocent child'. He actually wrote that in a letter. As though we are somehow responsible too."

Laura sighed. "But don't you see – we *are* responsible. He's our child – he is us. Nature and nurture. And no matter what, we have to stick by him and stand up for him."

Richard's voice went up a notch. "You act as though it was just a school-yard prank or a silly argument. He pushed a child off a ledge and now the child is dead. And our precious son hasn't given me the slightest hint that he knows it was wrong or feels bad about it!"

"But that's why he needs us. To get him through this."

"I don't think we're qualified for this, Laura. I think he needs professional help. I spoke to a guy I was in college with this morning and he said we'd get a place in St Enda's if he pulls some strings."

Silence.

Richard started again. "It's a residential facility for children with mental health issues."

"I bloody know what it is, Richard," Laura said, her voice low and cold. "And there's no way in hell my son is going there. You can forget that idea. And I'm disgusted that you'd even think of it."

"Jesus, Laura, you give out to me for not helping him but you won't accept professional help when it's on offer!" He was shouting now.

"He needs *us* – not straitjackets and shrinks, for God's sake. He's staying here, and that's it."

"*Then I'm not.*" The door was yanked open, and her dad stormed past her. He grabbed his keys and his coat, left down such a very short time ago, and walked out of the house. He never stayed there another night again.

And now this morning she's cleaning graffiti and keeping her head down, like she does every morning, wondering when and how it will come to an end.

Her mum comes outside, cradling a cup of tea in her hands. Gently she takes the brush from Kate. And as though she's reading her daughter's mind, she tells her it's enough. They're going. They're moving back to Dublin. To somewhere nobody knows them, to start over. Just the three of them. They'll go back to Laura's maiden name, and leave everything Jordan and everything Carnross behind.

For the first time since the picnic at Whitecross Hill, Kate cries – her small body shuddering with horrific pain and shocking, beautiful relief.

Chapter 69

Sam – Saturday, August 20th 2016

Midday. Kate will be here any minute now.

Michael looks at his watch and gets up to turn the key to lock the spare-room door. He puts his finger to his lips. "Remember, if you make a sound, I'll get to her before she gets anywhere near the front door. And by the time I'm finished, her blood won't just be on your hands – it'll be everywhere." Michael grins at his choice of words. "It's your decision to be awake for this, bud – I could have sedated you – still could. It might be easier?"

Sam locks eyes with Michael and shakes his head. "I won't do anything to put her at risk," he says in a whisper. "I promise."

And just like that, there she is. Or at least her sound. The turning of the key, the opening of the door – always the same but somehow different now, knowing it's Kate. Sam trembles at the nearness and the impossibility of it all. Mundane movements – keys hitting table, kettle boiling, fridge opening – she wants to see what he's been eating. Or perhaps what Nina eats. He cringes. Now the back door opening – she's looking out at the garden. Will she step outside? He stays still and waits. The back door closes: she's inside again. Cupboard doors open and shut – is she looking or packing? She'll probably take her favourite mug, and the espresso cups they got in France two years ago. The boys might want the ones with their names on them – will she notice that his is missing, up here on the bedside locker? Probably not. Then footsteps in the hall again, and finally the stairs. He's not breathing now, just waiting. Wanting with every bone in his body to see her, but praying she doesn't come near the door. She goes into their bedroom – she's only six feet away now on the other side of the wall. The sound of wardrobe doors, locker drawers and shoeboxes. Will she look again for signs of the other woman – probably. But maybe Michael didn't leave anything there this time. It's not possible to say which is better any more – that she thinks he's still having an affair or that it's all over. Which one makes her seek him out? That's a bigger question than he can manage after a month of regular sedation and no perspective. She's in Jamie's room now, or maybe Seth's, filling suitcases to take to her mother's rented house. Michael had enjoyed passing that piece of news to him. "That's the nail in the coffin, Sam," he'd said – but Sam didn't care. As long as she's living there, she's not trying to get back in here. The bathroom next; the plop of the medicine cabinet door. It closes again – nothing of interest. Please go downstairs now, he wills her, closing his eyes. Just go – leave this house, and never come back. Send someone – send anyone, but don't you come here and don't bring the boys here. *Please, Kate.* He's nearly sure she can hear him – she's at the top of the stairs. It's working. Then she turns back. Her steps draw closer. She's coming to the spare-room door.

Michael stands up, watching. Sam opens his eyes too now, and both stare at the door. The handle turns down and she pushes, but it doesn't open. She tries again. She puts her shoulder to it, but it doesn't budge.

"Fuck's sake, Sam," she mutters under her breath as she walks away.

And he smiles as he sinks back in the bed. That's my Kate, he thinks. Now go and don't come back.

Chapter 70

Sam – Tuesday, August 23rd 2016

"Do you know where Stanbridge Brown is?" Michael asks, as he sets the morning tea down on the locker.

"It's in the IFSC – why?"

"It's where your one next door works. I saw the name on her swipe card when I was in there, but it didn't have an address."

Sam picks up his tea. "You were in her house?"

"Yeah, I saw it one of the nights last week – she'd left it on the counter."

"But what were you doing in her house?"

Michael looks bemused. "Jesus, you're always shocked about something – you're like an old woman. I told you I had a key and I was going to pay a visit. Just keeping her on her toes with a few surprises when she comes down in the mornings."

"You'll get caught." Hopefully. Sam keeps the last word to himself.

"No chance. I've been doing this for thirty years," he says, on his way out to get the laptop.

Sam stretches his legs. The pain is dull and constant, but nothing like it was at first. He touches his left knee under the duvet and flinches as he does every morning when he feels bone where no bone should be. Shifting in the bed without thinking, he lets out a yell when new pain hits his lower back. Bloody bed sores, and Michael's taken away the cream again – what does he think he's going to do, eat the cream to kill himself?

Michael comes back with the laptop and a bowl of Weetabix. "I thought this might be better than toast," he says. "For fibre – you know, to keep you regular."

"You're so thoughtful."

"Listen, I'm only trying to help," Michael says, passing over the cereal and taking out his phone. "I'll google-map it. The IFSC, you said?"

"Yes, but why do you want to know?"

"I'm going to set up a little surprise for her there. Something at her desk maybe, or if I can't get into the office, something in the car park."

Sam takes a spoonful of Weetabix – actually it's a pleasant change from all the toast. "Would you not leave the poor woman alone – what's the point?"

Michael shrugs. "Why not? She thought it was fine to come over here, sticking her nose into our business. I'm going to show her it's not. And if she doesn't already think she's going mad, she will now. I wonder what the husband thinks – did you ever meet him?"

"No, I told you – your man Noel from across the road was the only one around when we moved in." More's the pity, or someone might have spotted something's up by now. Jesus, all these people going about their daily business with no idea what's going on.

"Noel. Now he's another one – always staring across at the house. What's up with him?"

"I don't know," says Sam, through a mouthful of cereal. "He's a bit neurotic, I'd say, likes things just so, and we got off on the wrong foot when I parked outside his house on the day we moved in."

"So he's met you before?"

Shit. Hadn't he told Michael that already? He thinks quickly. "No, I mean he said it to Kate. I didn't meet him."

"Are you sure? So he doesn't know what you look like?"

Sam nods. "I've never met him – I told you that at the start of the summer – I haven't met anyone. The leafy burbs aren't as friendly as I expected."

"Because it might explain why he's always looking over," Michael says, tapping his fingers slowly on his cup of tea. "Sam, you better be telling me the truth – do I need to worry about our friend Noel?"

"There's no need to worry. He's just keeping an eye on the car, no doubt – making sure we park properly. Look, I'd better get to work – there were some shaky trades last night that I need to check up on."

As Sam opens the laptop, the phone beeps.

Michael takes it out and shakes his head in annoyance. "It's your one Nina again. Still asking if you're okay. Jesus, she's a nag. She must be mad about you, is she?"

Sam doesn't answer.

"Have you any pics of her – anything in your camera roll?"

"No, of course not. I'd hardly take photos of her, would I, for Kate or the kids to see?"

"Relax, I was only asking. Right, what'll I say this time? She's starting to annoy me now."

"Just say I'm still recovering and Kate's still looking after me. That'll keep her away." Sam mentally crosses his fingers as he speaks.

It might keep her away, but you never knew with Nina.

Chapter 71

Sam – Sunday, August 28th

The duvet is too warm but pushing it off means seeing his shattered knees, so it stays put. He can see a glimpse of blue cloudless sky at the top of the window and it's beautiful, but it's harder when it's like this, because he can't pretend it's a choice to be indoors. Back before, a sunny Sunday morning meant football on the green with Seth and Jamie, or a walk on the pier, or brunch outside their favourite coffee shop. When the sky is grey, it's easier. He might just be indoors because he wants to be. But today it feels vexing and abnormal and more wrong than ever. These are the days that make him think the things he doesn't want to think and wonder if he'll ever see the boys again. It can't go on indefinitely. When Michael's had enough or when someone gets too close, he'll cut him loose. Maybe it'll be simple – a bigger dose in the syringe. Or something more dramatic, to satisfy the glint of past wrongs. He's not afraid of dying – not any more. But the idea that he might never see Seth or Jamie or Kate again leaves him frozen. What will they hear in the end – what will they know? And how will it happen? Kate will want to meet him at some point

– that's for sure. And Michael will have to act. A body or a disappearance. And a legacy of what – a child buried somewhere in the garden? Or just an absence, with no trace of anything else at all. And children who think their dad walked away. Michael won't care. He'll do what suits him best, as long as he's made enough money.

Maybe that's it – Sam needs to slow down the investments. Even lose a bit. He can handle the temper if it buys him more time. Not time to sit here with broken knees and bedsores, but the chance of seeing the boys again. Michael has the laptop downstairs but he can start planning. He closes his eyes to block out the sky and work on a new strategy – little losses, and still some gains. It might not work – it probably won't work – but he doesn't have any other cards to play.

When Michael comes up, his footsteps on the stairs are fast and heavy. Sam keeps his eyes closed, and slows his breathing, but when his cousin bursts into the room, his eyes spring open.

"*Fucking bitch!*" Michael says, pulling over the chair. "*Who does she think she is?*" He spits the words through gritted teeth.

"Who?"

"That bitch next door. On her high horse – giving me grief about having an affair. Like it's any of her business – how dare she? I can't bear women like that – always into everyone else's business, and thinking they're better."

"How does she know about it?"

"Fucking Kate. I thought you said they didn't know each other?"

Sam sits up. If Kate's met Sylvia, it could help. How exactly, he's not sure, but his link with the outside world feels stronger. Michael is waiting for an answer. "They don't know each other. Maybe they met since though – when Kate came up and wrote the note or when she came to pick stuff up last week?"

"Well, either way, she has a fucking cheek. 'Cheating is cheating' she said to me, as if it's all my fault. She's going to regret talking to me like I'm some kind of idiot."

Sam stares at him. There's real anger and indignation in his eyes. "But you didn't have an affair, Michael. Why are you so worked up?"

Michael's mouth opens slightly and his arms fall by his side.

"Remember, *I'm* the one who supposedly cheated," says Sam. "So if anything, this just means your plan worked."

"Still, she shouldn't be sticking her nose in. It's none of her business," Michael says, but the white-hot rage is gone.

Sam watches him pull himself together – he can almost see the pieces clicking into place as Michael remembers which parts are true and which parts aren't.

He is not Sam Ford. He has never been Sam Ford.

Chapter 72

Sam – Sunday, September 4th

Like an agitated whirlwind, Michael flies in the door, shattering any pretence of Sunday morning peace.

Sam sits up, pulled out of half-sleep.

"What's wrong?" he asks.

He watches as Michael fills the syringe. His hands are shaking.

"*This is on her!*" Michael says, spitting and fuming. "*That stupid cow next door!*"

"What though? Slow down!"

"No time. She's outside the front talking to the Guards and pointing over here. *Bloody stupid bitch!*"

He finds a vein and sticks in the needle before Sam has a chance to reply, and even as the key turns in the lock sleep is taking over.

When he comes to, Michael's face is hovering over his. He turns his head to throw up, catching Michael's legs and shoes with the spray. Shaking and sweating, he only half notices as Michael jumps back and curses him.

"Too much," he whispers. "You gave me too much again."

"I was in a rush, sorry. I knew the Guards were going to come over and they did. It's not about the kid though – they're looking for your man Noel from across the road. He's missing." Michael is smiling as he says it.

"Did you . . . did you do something to him?"

"I'm saying nothing," Michael says, still smirking.

"Because he knew you weren't me?"

Michael shrugs. "He sounds like he was a tosspot anyway – I doubt anyone will miss him."

"Well, clearly someone does if they've called the Guards. Are you actually serious – did you do something?"

"Like we used to say when we were kids, Sam, that's for me to know and you to find out. Do you remember that? When you'd tell me some word in French and ask me to guess what it was? Like I was some big gobshite who knew nothing. Do you remember?"

Sam doesn't, though it's not impossible either. He decides to ignore it. "So there were Guards here – in the house?"

"Well, at the door, they didn't come in."

Shouting distance. If he'd been awake, he could have shouted, or thrown himself out of the bed onto the floor so they'd ask to search the house. So close. So bloody close. "Why did they call here? Or were they going to all the houses?" he asks eventually.

"They came here because your one told them that Noel called here on Friday night – that's the last time anyone saw him."

"He called here? What did you tell the Guards?"

"That I wasn't here to answer the door – I was out working late at the office. I gave them the number of my PA so they could call to confirm."

"Your PA?"

"Yeah – Jean Duggan's number. She's always had a soft spot for me, and she knows what to say if they call her."

Sam searches his face. Could he really have done something to Noel? Whatever about a small child, surely a grown adult in broad daylight is a different story.

"I'm not worried about the cops," Michael continues, "but your one next door is really pushing me now. She just doesn't know when to back off. I'm going to have take things up a notch."

"If you harm her, you'll just have more police here," Sam says with a sigh. Protecting everyone, including neighbours he's never met, is exhausting.

"I won't hurt her – not yet anyway. But I need to send a message, and I know how I'm going to do it." He picks up the syringe. "Did you know this works really well on dogs too? Though if you get the dose wrong, it can be fatal. Now wouldn't that be terrible, if poor Sylvia found her dog dead tomorrow morning?"

Sam shakes his head, but he doesn't have the energy to argue for the dog's life. Choose your battles, as Kate would say.

Michael gets up to go, and as he walks out Sam hears his phone beep. Maybe it's Kate, telling him she's realised there's something odd about the tone of his texts and she's calling the police. Or his boss, telling him they're sending a doctor to assess him if he doesn't come back to work. Or one of his friends, saying they're worried about him. But of course they're not worried about him – they're just getting on with their own busy lives and busy kids and promising each other they'll meet up soon and definitely before Christmas.

It's not any of them: it's Nina, and Michael comes back in to tell him he's bored texting updates to her and he's cutting her off.

"You're breaking up," he tells Sam. He calls out the text as he types, enjoying every second of it.

I'm sorry, Nina, but it's over – I should never have cheated on Kate – she's been so good to me since my accident. She doesn't know about us, so it's best if we stop now, and never contact each other again.

Michael asks if that will keep stop her. Sam nods slowly, and says yes, he thinks that will do the trick. Even Nina will get the message this time.

Chapter 73

Sam – Thursday, September 8th

These days when Sam wakes up from his drug-induced naps, the smell hits him before anything else – unwashed sheets and rarely washed clothes and badly healing skin. Michael won't let him open the window, so the stench stays inside, worsening by the day. As the haze lifts, he lies still, savouring the peace. There's no sound in the room, no Michael – not yet. These are what count as good times now – when he wakes to a silent room.

The calm doesn't last long – the door bursts open as it always does, and Michael blows in.

"Good evening, Sleeping Beauty, how're things?" he says, sitting down beside the bed. "You might be interested to know I've had visitors – Tom and Sylvia from next door. I'd have called you down to meet them, only you were still out cold from earlier." He laughs at his joke. "So I invited them in for tea and everything and we're great pals now. Me and Tom are thinking about going golfing sometime. I must get my clubs down from the attic."

"*My* clubs," Sam says quietly.

"Ah Sam, I don't think you're going to be needing them any time soon. Do you remember when you used to take me out to the driving range – showing the inner-city eejit how the other half live?"

Sam shakes his head. "It was never like that. You were interested in trying golf, so we went to a driving range. Don't play the poor mouth – there was nothing else to it." He pulls himself up into a sitting position. "Michael, how long do you think this can go on? You're deluding yourself if you think you can make friends with the people next door and go golfing with them and just carry on living here. Sooner or later, someone who knows me is going to turn up."

"Well, you better keep hoping they don't, because that won't end well for anyone. Now, will we have a game of cards?"

But Sam doesn't want to play cards. "Why are you doing this?"

"Why not, Sam? Why should you get everything? It's not my fault my ma was too stupid to spot that my da was trouble. Why should I pay for Bella's mistakes?" Michael raises his hands as though this is a perfectly rational argument. "And you know, till the day she died, she always preferred you. She tried to hide it, but she did about as good a job at that as she did telling me my da was dead."

"Is that what this is all about – Bella? Is it because I was there when she died and didn't stop her? I know it's my fault she's dead but this is too much. You're insane."

"Oh, I know it's not your fault she died. I was there when she died."

Sam frowns. The drug-fog is lingering at the corners of his brain and he can't remember what he did yesterday or the day before, but he's absolutely certain he knows that Michael wasn't there when Bella died.

"What do you mean? It was me – I was there that night. And I know I should have kept a closer eye on her. Believe me, that guilt will never go."

Michael shakes his head. "Nah, Bella wasn't your doing. I told her to take those pills."

"Yes, but they were prescribed for her – that's not your fault either. She just took too many. You didn't know she was going to do it."

Michael smiles. "But I did know it. Because I was there, beside her bed, and I told her to take them. That night, I mean. You were sound asleep, and I locked you in just to be on the safe side. Then I sat beside Ma's bed and told her to say her prayers and to take the extra pills."

Sam goes cold. "Why? Why would you do that, and why would she?"

"Why? Because my da was up for parole, and I wanted to be sure to get the flat. And to be honest, I'd had enough of her. She was a pain at that stage, rattling around the place, needing help with everything. She was good in the end too – she didn't even argue much. She did it for you, Sam, really – I told her she could take the pills, or I'd burn down the flat with both of you in it. She chose you. So I suppose in a way, you're still responsible for her death." He laughs, his mouth wide, his teeth bared.

Sam is transfixed, staring at his mouth. Jesus Christ! Poor Bella. He must have spoken the last words out loud, because Michael is talking again now.

"Poor Bella? She was a waste of space. She never gave a shit about me – she only cared about you, Sam, and in the end that's why she took the pills – because she loved you best."

Sam sits up straighter. "Jesus Christ, Michael! That was all in your head – she was my aunt for fuck's sake, and she was fond of me the way aunts are fond of their nephews, the way

Claire was fond of you! She never *preferred* me to you. My God, this self-pity is incredible – do you even *hear* yourself?"

Michael's mouth is open now but Sam keeps going.

"There are children up and down the country who are not loved enough by their parents, and it has nothing to do with where they're born – there are kids in mansions who crave attention they're not getting and kids in flats like yours and everything in between. There are kids who go to school without hugs and kids who go to school without breakfast and you were neither of those things – not once, not ever. Bella loved you enough for two parents all your life – you never went without."

His voice is getting louder and Michael is clenching and unclenching his fists but Sam's not finished.

"You took something good and turned it into something miserable – and it was all in your head. You fixated on where your dad was instead of looking at what was right in front of you – your mother, making up for all of it every day of her life. You think this was done *to* you and you had no choice – you always had a choice, Michael. You were brought up in a loving home where you wanted for nothing. So fucking what if you weren't in a private school? Most kids aren't. So fucking what if you didn't have foreign holidays? It was the eighties – most children didn't. You spent your life looking at what other people had – what I had – and never took a second to think about what you had yourself. And then you went and killed it all – you took the life of the one person who loved you more than anything."

Sam slumps back in the bed and braces himself for the smack that's coming but Michael drops his fists to his side. For a moment, he says nothing. Sam watches his face – is there a hint of regret there? Maybe, but just as quickly the sneer is back.

"Easy for you to see it that way, Sam, growing up in the big house with everything you wanted, and your parents fawning all over you."

"Enough. Don't you dare speak about my parents." Sam's voice has an iron edge to it, but Michael keeps going.

"Your parents? They were part of the problem. Your da especially. The looks he used to give me. He deserved everything he got in the end."

Sam's fist shoots out before he thinks about it, but he's too weak to make any impact. Michael laughs as he swipes Sam's hand away. "You know what I'll think about till the day I die? Your da's face, just before I hit him with the car. I like to think that at the last second he knew it was me."

Sam slumps back in the pillow, his blood running cold. "No. I'm not buying it. You couldn't have done it."

"Sam, what do you think I do for a living? That was one of the easiest hits ever. He just walked out in the middle of the road, and stood there like a deer, waiting to be run over. It was beautiful. Just beautiful. And then you were all so grateful to me for helping with the funeral." He laughs again. "I almost wanted to tell you at the time, so you'd get the irony. But obviously you might not have found it as funny as I did."

Sam closes his eyes to block out Michael but he can't block the image summoned up by Michael's words. Over and over now, he sees his father standing in the middle of the road, watching as the car speeds towards him, realising too late it will deliberately mow him down. A sob catches in his throat. He turns towards the wall, willing Michael to go away, and for the first time wishing for an end, even if that means never waking up.

Chapter 74

Sam – Friday, September 9th

He knows as soon as he opens his eyes that this is the day. No blurriness, no forgetting, no customary fog. Today is the day it ends. He sits up and slips his hand down behind the mattress. The glass is still there. He stops, but only for a moment, then pulls it out. After six weeks of drifting, everything is crystal clear. He knows what to do. Wrapping the glass in his grimy, yellowed pillowcase, he smacks it hard against the wall, praying it won't wake Michael. The first time, nothing happens. He smacks it again, and this time it breaks. Quickly he empties the pillowcase onto the bed – the glass is in four separate pieces. He tries each one for size then makes his choice. It's no bigger than his palm, and it's not an ideal shape – something long and knife-like would be better. But it's sharp. He shoves the other pieces of glass under the edge of the mattress and puts the pillowcase back on the pillow.

He takes a tissue from the packet on the locker and carefully wraps it around one half of the glass. It's not thick enough – he takes another tissue and does the same. Now he can grip it. It's comforting in his hand. He lifts it in the air and lashes at an imaginary Michael. It's no longer comforting. The thought of slicing through skin turns his stomach – but if he misses it's all over anyway. Analyse it, says the voice in his head. Look at all possible outcomes and weigh up the risks. If he kills Michael, he can take his phone and call for help. If he injures him, he may be able to do the same. If Michael turns the glass back on him, there will be pain and disfigurement and presumably death. He looks at his mangled legs and pockmarked arms and mottled skin and makes a decision. Downstairs, the kitchen door opens. Sam slides the glass under his right thigh and lies back against the pillow. He closes his eyes and waits.

The footsteps on the stairs sound slower today and one part of him is screaming at Michael to turn back. Not because Michael deserves to be saved – Michael doesn't deserve to be saved – but because he might not be able to do it – to raise his hand and strike down as hard as he can, to deliberately slice through skin and flesh. Then he sees John's face again and he stops begging Michael to turn back. Today is the day.

The door opens and Michael walks in. Sam keeps his eyes closed and his hands by his sides. The glass is just millimetres from his fingers and he wants to check it's still there but he doesn't move.

Michael puts the computer on his lap and a cup of tea on the bedside locker. Sam's heart is beating so loudly in his chest he's sure Michael can hear it. Just act normal, says the voice inside his head. You've analysed the situation and decided on a course of action. Stay calm and follow through. He slows his breathing and opens his eyes. Today is the day.

"Right, there's toast here," Michael says, "And I have some good news for you." He's smiling.

Sam doesn't trust his voice, so raises his eyebrows instead.

"My new friends Tom and Sylvia have done you a big favour. You wanted to know where our little friend from the pond was – well, she was in the shed at first – I had to put her there when the bell was ringing that night. Then I put her in a shallow grave beside the pond, ready for the police to find her if you didn't play ball. But since you've done so well on cleaning the money, I've moved her." Michael stops, waiting for a reaction.

Sam feels sick.

"Where?" he manages to croak out eventually.

"Next door," Michael says triumphantly. "Remember I helped dig a grave for the dog and then she didn't use it? Well, I figured, why let all that digging go to waste? So I moved our friend in there last night. You're off the hook for that now, and with a bit of luck, next door will never cop either. Or if your one gets really annoying, I'll send the Guards in to have a look at her house instead. Ha! What do you think?"

Sam swallows, and shakes his head. His eyes are watering now and he doesn't know if it's for Edie Keogh's poor little body or the fear of what he's about to do.

Michael doesn't notice. "Jesus, I thought you'd be more grateful," he says, opening his newspaper. "Right, let's get to work so."

Sam switches on the laptop and logs into his trading account. His breathing feels foreign and awkward, and he risks a sideways glance at his cousin.

Michael catches the look. "What's wrong?"

Sam shakes his head but doesn't trust his voice to answer.

"Are you sick? You're sweating," Michael says, pointing at Sam's forehead.

Sam wipes his brow with his forearm and shakes his head again, then focuses on the screen. Out of the corner of his eye, he can see Michael looking at him for a moment longer, then he goes back to his paper.

Sam taps on the keyboard. He needs Michael to come closer – he's too far away. Slowly he slides his hand down to his leg and feels for the glass. It's still there. Of course it is. He puts his hand back on the keyboard and thinks for another minute. Then he clicks into Michael's biggest fund and switches the display currency to Japanese Yen. Now 545,110 in Euro is showing as 668 million in Yen. He takes a deep breath.

"Michael," he croaks, then clears his throat and tries again. "Michael – look at this!" He points to the screen. "*Six hundred million!*"

Michael drops the paper to the floor and leans across to look. Sam eases his right hand down and touches the glass. Michael's head is on front of the screen and he's babbling something about how he fucking knew Sam could do it, he always knew it. Sam clutches the piece of glass. This is the day. He pulls it out and raises his hand. Michael turns his head. "How is it suddenly six hundred million?" he asks, and his face changes as he sees the glass plunge towards his neck. He jumps back, but not quickly enough. Sam slashes the glass down as hard as he can. He feels it make contact with flesh, slicing through, sharper than he'd hoped. He wants to pull it out and slash again and somewhere deep inside he's shocked at how much he wants to stab over and over but it's too late – Michael is out of reach now, on the floor, crawling backwards until he's lying against the bedroom wall, holding his bleeding shoulder. Alive. Very much alive. And out of reach. His face is contorted with pain and rage and surprise – the last one is the most satisfying of all. Sam sits up straight in the bed, still gripping the glass, willing Michael to come to take it off him so he can try again. His hand is bleeding, the tissue is soaked in red but he can't feel anything. All he wants to do is try again. He waits. He can wait forever now.

Michael pulls himself to his feet, never taking his eyes off Sam. He starts to move towards the bed. Sam clenches the glass tighter, watching Michael's face. The arrogance, the supreme confidence – he doesn't think Sam will do it again. He's so wrong about that. So fundamentally wrong. Sam raises his hand. He's not afraid now – not afraid of what Michael will do, not afraid of cutting. Then Michael turns and picks up the vase from the corner. He lifts it above his head, his eyes wide and flecked with fury. Too late, Sam sees what's coming. He lashes out with the glass but it swipes uselessly through the air, missing Michael's chest by inches, just as the vase comes crashing down on his skull. And again, everything is black.

Chapter 75

Kate – Friday, September 9th 2016

Sylvia leans on the bar and frowns, taking another look at the photo on Kate's phone. "But why would your husband pretend he had a dog called Max, if it was his cousin's dog? It makes no sense." She signals to the barman for two more glasses of wine and hands the phone back.

"But that's the point – you haven't been talking to Sam at all as far as I can see. The person here," she points at her phone, "is Sam. You're saying that's not the guy you've been talking to?"

"But then who is the man I met in your house and why is he pretending to be your husband?"

Kate throws up her hands. "I have no idea. This is all news to me. If he's talking about Max though, I wonder if Michael is staying there, and maybe he thought it would be funny to pretend he's Sam? Or perhaps you assumed he was Sam when you first met him, and he never corrected you? I remember that happened me in my old job once – this new guy started and thought my name was Sophie and I hadn't the heart to tell him it wasn't, and the longer it went on, the harder it was to correct him. So I just left it, and then he moved department and I never needed to tell him at all."

Sylvia is shaking her head before she gets to the end of the story. "No, definitely not. He introduced himself when I called in – I wouldn't have known his name otherwise. Do you have any pictures of Michael?"

Kate scrolls through her camera roll but there's nothing. She thought she had some from Seth's birthday but they're all just of the boys. "Hang on," she says, "I'll find one on Facebook." She clicks in and as though he's read her mind, Michael is the first person in her newsfeed. "There he is in a photo from this evening – he's on his way into that American football game in Belton Stadium. So, is that the person you met?"

Sylvia's mouth opens as she takes the phone for a closer look. "Yes, that's Sam – well, that's the person who told me he was Sam. That's his cousin? Why did he say he was your husband? God, I've seen him in and out all summer, but I've never seen anyone else around at all. If that's Michael, then where is Sam?"

The answer – the only logical answer – is staring Kate in the face. He's staying with his girlfriend. What an asshole. Well, if he's moved out, she's bloody well moving back in – what's the point in Michael living there?

"You know what, I'm going there now to find out what he's up to and to sort this out for once and for all." Slipping off the bar stool, she puts on her coat. "I'm really sorry, Sylvia, I know this is rude. But why am I living in my mother's tiny house in Stillorgan while Sam hands our big family home over to his cousin? I'm not letting him away with that. *No. Fucking. Way.*"

Sylvia puts on her coat too. "You're absolutely right. We can go for drinks again when it's all sorted, and you're back next door where you belong."

Outside, the drizzle has turned to heavy rain, and neither of them has an umbrella – they start to run towards the taxi rank. It's still early – there's a line of yellow lights waiting for them, and they jump into the cab at the top.

Kate gives the address to the driver and turns to Sylvia. "So with all that, I forgot to tell you about Nina."

"Who's Nina?" Sylvia asks, buckling her seat belt and brushing raindrops off her coat.

"Exactly – that's what I was wondering when she knocked on my car window at the school today. Wait till you hear this." Kate takes a deep breath. "So, there I am, minding my own business, when this gorgeous-looking girl turns up and tells me her name is Nina, and she's worried about my husband. Now, this girl is stunning – big brown eyes, skin I'd die for – and when she mentioned Sam, I didn't know what to think. I assumed she's the one – the girlfriend. So I started on at her, saying she had a cheek to turn up and how dare she and all that. I asked her if Sam had sent her, and she said no – that she's worried about him. Can you imagine my reaction?"

"Oh my God, unreal! Did she think you were going to be buddies or something?"

"Well, wait till you hear. So, she tells me she found me because she guessed I'd be picking up the boys from school. Obviously at this point I was livid. And I told her that it was bad enough she was sleeping with my husband, but there's no way she's having anything to do with the boys – ever."

Sylvia nods her agreement. "I'd be exactly the same. You're absolutely in the right."

"But then . . . Okay, wait for it. She bursts out laughing."

"Are you serious? Oh, sorry, you were meant to turn right here," Sylvia says to the taxi driver.

He mutters something and does a U-turn.

"Yes. I didn't know what to think. I mean, she's about twenty, so I thought maybe this is just how girls are today or something. Anyway, I'm about to slap her to get her to stop laughing, and she tells me she's not sleeping with Sam."

"Well, she would say that."

"She says she's his daughter."

"*What?*"

"I know. So basically, back when Sam and I first got together, his ex-girlfriend came home from the States to visit, and he slept with her. He confessed everything to me – the big eejit – and I went mental. We got back together though, and that was that. Except apparently Molly – that's his ex – got pregnant. And Nina was the kid. *Is* the kid."

"Jesus. And he never told you?"

"He didn't know. According to Nina, Molly only got in touch with him earlier this year, because Nina wanted to meet him. Then Molly got sick, and Nina was having a tough time, and apparently he's been helping her get through it all. Or something. To be honest, at that point I wasn't even registering what she was saying. I was just looking at her thinking she's Seth and Jamie's half-sister. I mean, this is huge."

"And Sam never said a thing all these months?"

"Nothing. I don't know why – I wouldn't have minded. I mean the past is the past and I already knew about the one-night stand. But she says he didn't want to tell me until he could find the right moment."

"And is this supposed to be the right moment?" Sylvia asks. She meets the taxi-driver's eyes in the rear-view mirror. Even he's interested now.

"Well, that's just it – she thinks there's something up with Sam. She hasn't seen him since July, then he texted her on Sunday *to break up with her*, which is obviously completely bizarre. She didn't know what to make of the message, and wondered if he's losing it. She replied to ask if everything was okay, but he never got back. And she's never been out to our house so didn't know how to reach him in person."

Sylvia shakes her head slowly. "That's really odd. And how did she find you?"

"Apparently she's seen photos of me and the boys, including one in their uniforms, so she worked out which school it is."

The taxi driver interrupts to ask if he should take the next turn, and Kate confirms he should. Rain is pelting down still, and the windscreen wipers are on full.

"So that's weird – that text she got from him. What's that all about?" Sylvia asks.

"I don't know. I couldn't make any sense of it either – she even showed it to me. And there's more – he told her he'd fallen down the stairs and couldn't see her, because I was taking care of him. Maybe the novelty of having a surprise love-child wore off and he was trying to put distance between them – but that doesn't explain the break-up text." Kate pauses. "And to be honest – it wouldn't be like Sam. He's been a complete dick recently but, if he found out he had a child, I can't see him rejecting her. It's just not him. And 'break-up' is not the term anyone would use to reject their child! It's all very odd."

It's pitch dark now and feels more like winter than early autumn. Kate shivers in her light summer coat – she'll have to pick up some winter clothes while she's at home. And there's the small matter of confronting her husband about the daughter he forgot to mention, and why his cousin is pretending to the neighbours that he's Sam. She shakes her head and wishes she'd had one less glass of wine.

The taxi driver turns the radio volume up as the news headlines come on.

"Gardaí are investigating the discovery of a body of a man in the sea at Dún Laoghaire this morning. The victim has been identified, but Gardaí are not releasing his name until all relatives have been informed. The body, that of a man in his late forties, was spotted by a local woman walking the pier this morning . . ."

Sylvia sits up straighter in the seat. "Oh my God, did you hear that? What if that's Noel?"

"Who?"

"The guy from across the road – he's been AWOL since last week. Rosemary and I were joking earlier that he'd done a runner with another woman. Jesus, I feel awful now for saying that."

"Ah, it probably isn't him," Kate says. "You'd have heard, I'm sure, and the Guards would have been around today if it was."

"But they *were* – Rosemary said two of them called into Georgia this morning. Jesus, the poor woman! God, you just never know what's going on with people."

"Tell me about it," Kate says. "I appear to be married to a complete stranger. I literally have no idea what to expect next."

"Well, if he's pushing his daughter away, cheating on you, and has moved his cousin into your house, maybe he's going through some kind of mid-life crisis?" Sylvia suggests. "I still can't believe the person I've been calling Sam isn't really your husband. Bizarre."

Kate can't believe it either. But even if Sam's gone off the rails, surely Michael will be able to explain what's going on? She sits back in the seat and looks out at the rain, as the taxi takes its final turn towards home.

Chapter 76

Kate – Friday, September 9th

Sylvia is still counting out money for the taxi-driver when Kate puts her key in the front door. Why is she nervous all of a sudden? Something feels odd as she steps into the hallway and it takes her a moment to realise what it is – the house is pitch dark inside. Sam is always telling her to leave the landing and hall lights on when they're out, to make it look like they're home. Flipping light switches as she walks through to the kitchen, she takes a moment to look around. There are two cups on the counter, and what looks like tea in the bottom of both. His girlfriend? Michael? She shrugs. It could be anyone. He's entitled to have callers.

Sylvia comes through to the kitchen and they stand looking at one another for a moment. What now? After the dramatic race to a taxi, it feels anti-climactic.

"I don't think there's anyone home," Kate says. "Maybe I should check upstairs now that I'm here, though?"

Sylvia nods. Kate doesn't move.

"Will I go up with you?" Sylvia asks.

"Yes. Do. I know, ridiculous. It's my own house. But it feels a bit creepy tonight."

Upstairs, Kate puts on the light in her bedroom and looks around. There's no outward sign of any girlfriend – she's being more careful about where she leaves her stuff. Kate opens the wardrobe. Nothing but Sam's suits, all pristine in their dry-cleaning bags. She pulls out a drawer in his locker as Sylvia watches from the doorway. The usual jumble of old receipts, half-eaten packets of sweets and loose coins. She closes it, then moves to the dresser at the far wall and opens the top drawer. Inside, there's a mix of black and grey T-shirts. She lifts one out and holds it up. Putting it down on the bed, she takes out another. None of these are Sam's – unless he's completely changed taste in clothes along with everything else. But no – sports-logo T-shirts were never his thing – he's a polo-shirt guy through and through. So, are these Michael's? And why if he's staying here would he be in the main bedroom instead of the spare room? None of it makes any sense. She takes out her phone and hits the button to call Sam. Enough is enough. But her phone clatters to the floor when the familiar sound of Sam's ringtone blares out from the top of the dresser – it's vibrating and turning like a distressed beetle, balanced on top of the metal dish she uses for her rings. She grabs it and disconnects the call.

"I'm getting jumpy. This house is freaking me out tonight for some reason," she says, putting Sam's phone back on the dresser. "Why doesn't he have his phone with him? Maybe we should just go. I'll call him tomorrow to find out what's going on with Michael." She points at the clothes on the bed. "They're all Michael's – well, they're not Sam's. But if he *is* staying here, why wouldn't he have his stuff in the spare room – odd, isn't it?"

"Should we take a look in the spare room?" Sylvia suggests.

"Okay. It was locked last time I was here though." Kate walks past Sylvia and tries the handle of the spare-room door.

This time it opens. If Michael has been staying here, is it rude to go in? She'll just have a small look. And after all, it's still her house. She pushes the door open and switches on the light and that's when she sees him. He's pale and gaunt and has lost some of his hair, and he's wearing an old T-shirt she's never seen before that's far too big for him. He's lying back against the pillows, with a duvet thrown over his legs. She takes a step closer. His arms lie by his side, on top of a grey, dirty sheet. There's something tied around his left arm – a small belt of some kind. And needle marks all over his skin.

"Sam!" she whispers, taking a step towards him. "Sam! Wake up!" She shakes him, but there's no movement other than a very slight rise and fall of his chest. There's a bottle on the bedside locker with something called midazolam inside according to the label. She holds it up to show Sylvia. "He must be on some kind of drugs – or is he sick?" She turns again to Sam. "Oh my God, I've never seen him like this – *Sam, wake up!*" She grabs him by the shoulders and shakes harder now.

His eyes flicker slightly but stay closed.

"Pass me the bottle – I'll google it," Sylvia says. "Shit, I left my bag on the table downstairs – give me your phone too."

Kate puts her mouth to Sam's ear. "*Sam, wake up* – I don't know what's going on but I think you've taken too much of whatever that is. *Come on, Sam, wake up!*"

"It's a sedative," Sylvia says. "It says here it can cause breathing problems or respiratory arrest or death if used without close medical supervision. Kate, we need to call an ambulance."

"Do it, call." She's slapping his cheeks now, and his eyelids are flickering again but he's still out. "*Sam, for fuck's sake, wake up – what the fuck have you been doing to yourself!"* she shouts, pulling the duvet off him.

She claps her hand over her mouth when she sees his legs. His left knee is twisted and his lower leg is lying at an unnatural angle, not straight down as it should be.

"*Sam, what happened?*" Now she's yelling, and she might be crying, but she doesn't know.

This time his eyes open. They show no recognition – he seems dazed. He stares at her – then suddenly, like a light going on, he sees her.

"Kate." His voice is barely there.

She leans close to him.

"Yes, it's me. Oh Sam, what have you done?"

"Kate," he whispers again, and closes his eyes.

"Did you get an ambulance? Are they coming?" she calls behind her to Sylvia.

"They're coming – I told them it's a possible overdose – they're on the way. Oh my God, what happened to his poor legs?"

Tears are streaming down Kate's face now. "I don't know. I don't know." She turns back to him "Oh Sam. Stay awake, please stay awake. I'm here now."

"Kate," he says, one more time, through barely parted lips, and she hears the sound of a siren in the distance.

Chapter 77

Kate – Friday, September 9th

"Sylvia, can you lock up the house?"

Sylvia nods. Kate's hands are shaking and she can't find her keys in her bag. The paramedic tells her they need to go, and starts to close the ambulance door. "I can't find them – the bloody keys. Look, the house will be fine. I'll call you from the hospital."

Sylvia nods again and the door is closed.

Kate watches her through the ambulance window, growing smaller in the distance as they pull away at speed. The paramedic is checking Sam's blood pressure and asking her something but she doesn't hear.

"Sorry, I said do you have the bottle with you?"

"The bottle?"

"The midazolam. Just so we can see if that's what it is – sometimes drugs end up in wrong bottles or with incorrect labels."

"Shit, sorry, no, I didn't think to take it. My God, will he be all right?"

"The doctors will talk to you once he's in hospital and stable."

Kate takes his hand. "Sam, don't you go doing anything ridiculous like dying on me now. Whatever you've done, we can get past it. You can't leave the boys without a dad – they miss you horribly. I didn't tell you, because I wanted to hurt you, but my God they're missing you. So don't fucking think of dying on me!"

The paramedic touches her arm. Her voice is soft. "The doctors will give you the full picture, but I can tell you his sats are good – please don't worry."

Kate nods, still gripping Sam's hand. Through the rain-splashed window she watches her neighbours' houses zip by – they're all tucked up with wine and TV and early autumn fires, and no idea what's going on outside their walls or inside hers.

Her phone buzzes in her pocket and on autopilot now, she takes it out. A text from Miller. Jesus Christ, he picks his moments.

Hi Kate, how are you? I just want to check if you've seen Sam – I called again and there's still no answer. I know you think I'm just being annoying calling all the time, but I'm a bit worried about him. Can you check in on him?

Oh God. Now she really is going to cry. The one person who spotted that something was up with Sam, and she ignored him completely. And yet he kept trying, no matter how shitty her replies. Her eyes are blurred and her thumbs awkward as she types.

Miller, I'll text u properly later but please don't ever change, love Kate

The ambulance slows to go over the speed bump at the main entrance to the estate, and Sam opens his eyes again. He whispers something but she can't hear.

She bends closer. "Say it again?"

"Michael."

"What about Michael?"

"Guards. Call Guards."

"Has something happened to him too? What is it, Sam?"

He closes his eyes again but he's gripping her hand now. "Michael – did – this."

"Did this? What did he do, Sam?"

"Did – this – to – me."

"Jesus Christ!"

She turns to the paramedic. "Please – would the drug make him confused – hallucinate maybe?"

"If it's midazolam, it can cause memory loss. And, if he's been on it a while and coming off it, it can cause hallucinations. But it looks like he's still on it, so I don't know. If he's telling you to call the Guards, I'd take that on face value and call them."

My God. What on earth would make Michael do this? Trembling, Kate takes out her phone and finds the number for the local Garda station. The story isn't easy to explain. She tells the desk sergeant that her husband appears to have been injured and drugged and that his cousin Michael Boyle may be responsible. Michael is out at the moment but will be home later – possibly to her house at 26 Willow Valley or maybe to his flat in Chiswick Street in the city centre. Even as she says it, it sounds ludicrous.

But they record the details matter of factly. They will try to locate him.

Disconnecting the call, she turns her attention back to Sam. "Sam, can you hear me?"

He opens his eyes and gives her hand a small squeeze.

"Did Michael do this to you?"

The nod is brief but enough.

"My God, why?"

He opens his mouth to answer but can't seem to find the words.

"Okay, don't worry," Kate says. "I've called the Guards and given them his address. I know he's at the game in Belton tonight but there's no point in them trying to find him there. They'll pick him up and find out what's going on. Dear God, how could he do this?"

"Sorry – I couldn't help overhearing," the paramedic says, "but that game was cancelled earlier. There was a suspicious device in the stadium and they had to call in the army, so it never went ahead. Just in case that matters."

Kate picks up her phone again and clicks into Facebook. Michael's photo is still there.

Looking forward to a good game tonight – great atmosphere here at Belton **already**.

"You mean they had to send everyone home during the game?"

"No, it never went ahead at all – word went out on the radio earlier that it was cancelled and people shouldn't turn up. Traffic was chaos then around there, because some people were already on the way and trying to turn back." The paramedic shrugs. "Of course it was nothing in the end – it never is." She pauses for a second. "Not that I mean I wish it was something of course."

Kate stares at her phone, at Michael's smiling face. So the photo isn't from today – it could be from any time. And he could be anywhere right now. Or in the house. Maybe he was there all along.

And Sylvia's there too.

"*Shit.* We need to turn back," she says, searching in her phone for Sylvia's number.

"*What?* We can't turn back – we need to get your husband into hospital."

Shaking her head, she presses Sylvia's number. It rings out. She tries again. Still no answer. Shit.

"I need to get back to her." She looks at Sam again. "Is he going to be okay?"

"The doctors will talk to you – I can tell you he looks stable right now, but not so much that we could risk turning back. We still don't know how much he's been given or that it's definitely midazolam. We should keep going."

"I know. But I need to go back. Can you ask the driver to pull over and let me out?"

"Are you serious?"

"I need to go back to my friend. Once I know she's okay, I'll get her husband to drive me to the hospital – I'll only be a couple of minutes behind you."

"We're a good ten minutes' walk from your house now – it's none of my business but why don't you let the Gardaí handle it?"

"They might not get there in time – and this is all my fault, I brought this on her. I need to go back."

The paramedic looks bewildered but tells the driver to stop.

The ambulance driver pulls in at the side of the road. Kate kisses Sam on the forehead.

"Take care of him," she says to the paramedic, then jumps out into the rain, and starts running back towards Willow Valley.

Chapter 78

Sylvia – Friday, September 9th 2016

The house feels deathly quiet now that the sound of the ambulance siren has faded – only the rain on the skylight in the kitchen makes a noise. Sylvia shivers. Suddenly she has an overwhelming need to be at home with Tom. But first she needs her phone. It's not on the kitchen table, nor any of the counter tops, and her handbag is on the hall table, exactly where she left it, but her phone's not inside. Back in the kitchen, she tries to remember. She definitely left it here – could Kate have taken it in the confusion? Did Kate even come back into the kitchen? It's all a blur of blue lights and sirens and rain. A gust of wind rattles the back door. Could someone else have come into the house? With a deep breath, she reaches out to grab the handle and, pushing it down, she braces herself. But it doesn't move – it's locked. Letting out the breath, she shakes herself. Why would anyone come into the house and take her phone? Maybe she left it upstairs after all.

The lights are out now in the bedroom and the spare room. Kate must have switched them off. In the main bedroom, Sam's phone still sits on the dresser top but there's no sign of

Sylvia's. The spare room door is shut again – she opens it and peers inside. The air smells of hospital and decay – she didn't notice it the first time. Switching on the light, she walks further into the room to look around. She now notices that, oddly, an old wardrobe is blocking the window. There's a glass of water and a bottle of the drug Sam's been taking on the bedside locker, together with a half-empty packet of tissues, a deck of cards, and a chewed biro that's seen better days.

On the floor beside the locker, there's a newspaper, and a cracked vase, lying on its side. In the far corner of the room there's a pair of crutches – a strange place to leave them, so far from the bed. On the carpet beside the crutches she can see reddish-brown blotches – is it blood?

She pulls her coat tight around her. The rain is still pelting down outside. Could she have dropped her phone when she helped Kate to sit Sam up in the bed? Touching the grubby pillow with just the tips of her fingers, she pulls it forward. Still no phone. She probably didn't have it with her in the house at all – no doubt it's in the taxi. As she's turning to leave, something on the wall catches her eye. She leans closer to look, wrinkling her nose at the smell of unwashed bed linen. Behind the pillow, just below the mattress, there's something written on the wall. Without her glasses, it takes a minute to work out what it says, but then her eyes adjust to the tiny, neat letters.

Kate, I hope someday you'll see this and know that none of it was me – there was never any affair, and the photos and the child were his doing. He had my phone, he crippled me, he drugged me – he manufactured all of it. When I'm gone, know that I didn't leave wilfully. It was all Michael. I love you, I love Seth, I love Jamie – and you need to meet Nina – she'll tell you that story. I love you.

Dear God. While she was chatting outside to his cousin,

Sam was here all along. Lying in this bed, unable to get help, while Michael took over his life. How long had he been here? It's at least a month since she first called in and met the person she thought was Sam. And the sobbing she heard through the wall – it must have been him. Had he really been just feet away from her all this time? She steps back from the bed, her mind reeling. The Guards need to deal with this. Where the hell is the bloody phone?

That's when she hears it. A footstep on the stairs. And another. Could Kate be back already? She looks at her watch. No, she wouldn't even be at the hospital yet.

It's him – Michael.

Her mouth has gone dry. Her brain is screaming at her to move but she's frozen to the spot. Another step and then another – so slow, so deliberate – he must be halfway up now. Bending her knees, she drops soundlessly to the floor and, flattening down onto the carpet, slides under the bed. Did he hear her? She lies with her head on her hands, eyes closed, holding her breath. There are no more footsteps. Did he stop? She slides a little further under the bed, waiting without breathing.

The door creaks – he's coming in. Swallowing, she opens her eyes and sees two large boots beside the bed. Nothing moves. Not her breath, not his boots, nothing. The air in the room smells dead. She shuts her eyes, willing the boots to disappear, begging, praying. There's a movement, then nothing. She opens her eyes again and freezes in blind panic. She's looking straight into Michael's face. Blank eyes calmly appraise her, and she understands then that it's no accident – he knew she was here.

A second later, she feels his hands grab her legs, and she's yanked out from under the bed, banging her head on the metal frame on the way. She cries out in pain and fright, and from the floor she stares up at the familiar face of the man next door.

"Sylvia, Sylvia, you just couldn't stick to your side of the wall, could you?"

She wants to scream but her voice won't oblige. The room is bright and spinning, and she only half registers that Michael has picked up a pillow from the bed. Watching from the ground, as he brings it towards her face – it's like a film – like she's not really there, Too late, her reflexes kick in and she brings her hands up to push it off but he is stronger, so much stronger. He presses down on the pillow, and the dead air of the room disappears. The pillow is mashed against her eyes and her nose and her mouth – she fights for breath and fights to force him back – in blind panic, she pushes with everything she has, but he's so much stronger. She's losing strength and losing sense. Everything is slipping away, her arms go limp.

Then with a corner of her brain, she senses the weight lifting and someone roaring. She gulps in a breath and pushes off the pillow. Everything is blurred and too bright but she can see Michael on his knees, turning to look at someone. It's Kate, and she's screaming at Michael to stop. But he doesn't, he turns back to Sylvia and now his face is lit up with rage. She watches in horror as his hands come towards her and grab her by the throat. She pulls on his wrists but he just grips more tightly and starts to squeeze. Kate is still shouting at him to stop, but he's not listening and he doesn't care. Sylvia pulls at his hands, begging with her eyes. Then she sees Kate raise something above her head and watches as it comes crashing down on Michael's shoulder. He lets out a roar and his grip loosens but only for a moment. Kate tries again and this time smashes it down on his head and now he falls, collapsing onto Sylvia. With a cry, she pushes him off. He rolls onto his back and lies still. His eyes are open, and blood pools around his head, creeping towards her across the carpet.

Kate is on her knees now, calling her name.

Sylvia mutters something unintelligible then says "Kate".

"Oh thank fuck, Sylvia. Please tell me you're okay?"

Sylvia nods – right now she can't talk. Her vision clears and she can see that Kate has a golf club in her hand.

"I never swung so hard in all my life. I think he's dead, Sylvia. Jesus Christ, I think I killed him. I smashed it into his head. But he was strangling you, I had to stop him." A sob chokes the last word.

Sylvia closes her eyes again and feels for Kate's hand. "It's okay," she whispers. "You had no choice – they'll know that. Everyone will know that." Her head hurts and her mouth is sore and she's dizzy and sick but she manages to squeeze Kate's hand. "You did good."

Outside, the rain has eased. A car pulls up – there's a squeal of urgency but no siren. A voice calls through the open front door, asking if anyone is home.

In silence they hold hands and wait.

Chapter 79

The Woman – September 2nd 2016

The chops are burnt. Georgia had been staring into space again. Somehow she missed the smell of charred meat and the hiss of a too-hot pan. Bin or serve? Her stomach lurches. Which is likely to cause the most outrage? Or is there time to run to the shop? No, time has run out. The kitchen door opens and Noel shuffles through, still muttering about the man across the road. She can smell the whiskey from the other side of the kitchen. She turns away, shielding her nose, bracing herself.

"What's for tea?" he asks by way of greeting. He pulls out a chair and sits down, wobbling, and knocks a knife to the floor.

She hesitates. Is he drunk enough that he might not notice? Maybe.

"Pork chops and cabbage," she answers, decision made.

"Where's Annabel?"

"She's at a sleepover in Tillie's house – they're working on a project for school so she's staying over."

Noel grunts and opens the paper.

Georgia carefully places two chops on a plate, burnt side down, then spoons mounds of mashed potato and cabbage all over. She puts the plate in front of Noel and goes back to get her own much smaller serving. She sits down and begins eating, watching from beneath lowered lids. Waiting. On a knife-edge. Noel is shovelling potato into his mouth. That disgusting mouth. The stinking breath. The source of so many horrible words. He carries on reading, never looking at her. She eats slowly. Waiting. He picks up his knife and cuts a piece of pork chop, and turns his attention back to the paper as he puts the fork in his mouth. She holds her breath. He chews slowly, engrossed in the paper. The whiskey has done its work. Maybe.

Then his face contorts. He spits out the piece of meat he's been chewing. He turns over the chop, and looks up at Georgia.

"What the fuck is this?"

She doesn't answer. Nothing can fix it now. She's been here before.

"Are you going to answer me?"

Still nothing.

"Can a man not come in after a long day to a proper meal, that isn't burnt to a crisp? Is there nothing you can do right? What is the point of your existence? You find the time to go to work and get your hair done but you can't even cook a simple tea?"

The plate smashes on the floor as he pushes his chair out from the table. She cowers instinctively, but doesn't try to run. The punch catches her on the cheekbone, knocking her off her chair. She curls into a ball on the floor, pain ringing through her face. The kick aimed at the side of her head catches her on the shoulder. He goes again, this time meeting his target. She sees bright lights, then blackness. Peaceful black.

When she came to, it's dark outside. She's cold and stiff. She touches her cheek. It's throbbing but not cut. She pulls herself up off the floor, holding onto the table for support. She can hear snoring upstairs. Whiskey-infused snoring. She walks slowly to the stairs and climbs up, putting her hands on the wall to steady herself in the darkness. In the bathroom, she examines her bruised cheek – make-up will cover it. The side of her head is bleeding a little, just below her hairline. If she wears her hair down, she can hide it. Always hiding. Angry now, she stares at her reflection, dried blood mocking her.

She hears the bedroom door open. She hears him lurch out onto the landing, hesitating at the top of the stairs. Breathing heavily. She quietly pulls the bathroom door open. There he is. Readying himself for his descent, drink and sleep slowing his progress. She steps forward. A floorboard creaks. He turns.

She takes a deep breath.

She reaches out and pushes him hard. He looks at her with surprise, then rage, then fear, all in a fraction of a second as he tumbles backwards down the stairs. His head smashes on the tiled floor at the bottom – the sound reverberating through the house. Trembling, she runs downstairs. A pool of blood is already forming around his head. His eyes are shut. She feels for a pulse. She can't find one, but isn't sure if she's looking in the right place. It almost doesn't matter either way. It has to come to an end now, one way or the other.

She steps over him, and tidies the kitchen – the spilled dinner, the burnt chops. She bends to check again for a pulse. Still nothing. She washes her hands, scrubbing the dried blood from under her nails – is it hers or his? She can't tell. It doesn't matter. She picks up her phone from the table and calls Ben. Ben and Olivia will know what to do – you can always count on family.

THE END

Acknowledgements

To Paula Campbell, Gaye Shortland and all at Poolbeg – thank you for having faith in me, for your openness and support, and for always being at the end of an email!

Thank you to my dad and my sisters Nicola, Elaine, and Deirdre for telling me I could do it, and for your ability to sense deadline panic and jump in to help.

Thanks to my extended family and all my friends who have sent me many, many words of support since I began writing, and particular thanks to my besties – the girls I met in Sion Hill just one day after moving up from Cork – they have been the most fabulous cheerleaders anyone could wish for, and are always on hand to offer support in the form of coffee, wine, and plans to run away to Spain. (Just for the weekend though.)

To the *Irish Parenting* bloggers who helped me get my blogging off the ground when I didn't know a widget from a plugin, and have always been there for virtual coffee, wine and cake. Especially cake. Thank you.

Thanks too to Carmel Harrington and her wonderful Imagine Write Inspire group who encouraged my first forays into fiction – there is no way this book would exist without you all.

Very special thanks to author Margaret Scott – three years ago she told me I should write a book, and last summer she gave me the nudge to submit my manuscript to Poolbeg. In her book *The Fallout*, she quotes Madeleine Albright saying: "There's a special place in hell for women who don't help other women." I would add to that, the world is a better place for people who help others unasked, and I hope I can pay it forward.

To my brave and speedy proofreaders – Damien, Dad, Nicola, Elaine, Deirdre, Tric Kearney (the writer behind the wonderful blog *My Thoughts on a Page*) and Christine Doran (author of the fabulous *Lilac Girl* series) – thank you.

Special thanks to Dr Deirdre Fitzgerald for advising on the medical details, and to Dr Naomi Lavelle for the science – she fact-checks by doing actual experiments instead of just guessing, which is probably why she's a scientist and I make things up.

Thank you so much to the *OfficeMum* readers – for all the words of support over the last four years, for reading and sharing, and for enabling the transition from blog to freelancing to fiction.

To Damien, for listening, for taking the kids out, for putting up with the panic, for cheerleading, and for instinctively understanding when I need cake. And to Elissa, Nia, and Matthew who are not only amazing at coming up with plot twists ("then a ghost appears behind him like in Scooby Doo!") but also fairly handy at taking over running the house for an afternoon, and absolutely brilliant at hugs. Thank you.

And to you, the reader – thank you for reading my first book.